Y01120

Debra Webb is the award-winning *USA TODAY*
bestselling author of more than one hundred novels,
including those in reader-favourite series Faces of Evil,
the Colby Agency and the Shades of Death. With more
than four million books sold in numerous languages and
countries, Debra's love of storytelling goes back to
childhood on a farm in Alabama. Visit Debra at
www.debrawebb.com.

Discover more at millsandboon.co.uk

UNDER THE COWBOY'S PROTECTION

DELORES FOSSEN

IN SELF DEFENCE

DEBRA WEBB

MILLS & BOON

First Published in Great Britain 2019
by Mills & Boon, an imprint of HarperCollins*Publishers*
1 London Bridge Street, London, SE1 9GF

Under The Cowboy's Protection © 2019 Delores Fossen
In Self Defence © 2019 Debra Webb

ISBN: 978-0-263-27400-4

0219

MIX
Paper from
responsible sources
FSC™ C007454

This book is produced from independently certified FSC™
paper to ensure responsible forest management.

For more information visit: www.harpercollins.co.uk/green

Printed and bound in Spain
by CPI, Barcelona

UNDER THE COWBOY'S PROTECTION

DELORES FOSSEN

Chapter One

Sheriff Raleigh Lawton didn't like the looks of this.

The glass on the front door of the house had been shattered, and the chairs on the porch were toppled over. Both could be signs that maybe there'd been some kind of struggle here.

That kicked up his heart rate a huge notch, and he drew his gun, hoping he didn't need to use it. While he was hoping, he added that maybe there was some explanation for the glass and chairs. Maybe the woman who lived in this small one-story house was okay. Raleigh had a double reason for wishing that.

Because the woman, Sonya Burney, was nine months pregnant.

He'd known her all his life, and that's why Raleigh hadn't hesitated to go check on her when the doctor from the OB clinic had called him to say that Sonya had missed her appointment. In a big city, something like that would have gone practically unnoticed, but in a small ranching town like Durango Ridge, it got noticed all right.

The rain spat at him when he stepped from his truck.

It was coming down hard now, with an even heavier downpour in the forecast. He had a raincoat, but he didn't want to take the time to put it on. However, he did keep watch around him as he hurried up the steps and onto the porch.

"Sonya?" he called out and immediately listened for anyone or anything.

Nothing.

He tested the doorknob. Unlocked. And he cursed when he stepped inside. The furniture had been tossed here, too. There was a broken lamp on the floor, and the coffee table was on its side. Raleigh reached for his phone, ready to call one of his deputies for backup, but something caught his eye.

Drops of what appeared to be blood on the floor.

Raleigh had a closer look. Not blood. Judging from the smell, it was paint. And he soon got more proof of that. There was a still-open can in the hall just off the living room, and a discarded brush was next to it. However, it wasn't the can or brush that grabbed his attention. It was what someone had scrawled on the wall.

This is for Sheriff Warren McCall.

Hell.

That felt like a punch to the gut. Because he'd seen a message identical to that one almost a year ago. A message that'd been written in the apartment of a woman who had been murdered. Unlike Sonya, that particular woman had been a stranger to him.

The memories came. Images Raleigh wished that time would have blurred. But they were still crystal clear. The woman. Her limp, lifeless body, and the baby she'd been carrying was missing—it still was.

He prayed that Sonya and the baby wouldn't have similar fates.

Raleigh didn't have any proof of who'd killed that other woman, stolen the child or written that message. But he had always thought the message had been left for him. And Warren, of course.

Warren was his father.

Biologically anyway. Raleigh had never considered the man to be his actual dad. Never would.

He made the call for backup and used his phone to take a quick picture of the message. Actually, it was a threat. Raleigh just hoped that Sonya hadn't gotten caught up in this tangled mess between Warren and him.

"Sonya?" he called out again.

Still nothing, but Raleigh continued to look for her. The house wasn't huge, a combined living and kitchen area, two bedrooms and a bath. He went through each one and didn't see her. But there was another message, and it'd been slopped in red paint on one of the bedroom walls. A repeat of the other one.

The repeat hadn't been necessary. Raleigh had gotten it the first time.

This is for Sheriff Warren McCall.

Warren was retired now, but he'd once indeed been the sheriff of McCall Canyon, a town one county over. He'd also carried on an affair with Raleigh's mom for nearly three and a half decades. Or rather, Warren had *carried on* with her until his secret had come out into the open after someone had tried to kill him. Raleigh's mother had been a suspect in that attack. And Warren's "real" family—his wife, two sons and his daughter—hated Raleigh and her.

Was one of them responsible for this?

Maybe. That was something he would definitely investigate, but first he had to find Sonya.

Since it would take a good twenty minutes for his deputy to get all the way out to Sonya's house, Raleigh kept looking, and he made his way out through the kitchen and to the back porch. The moment he stepped outside, he heard something. At first he thought it was the cool October rain hitting the tin roof.

It wasn't.

There was a woman dressed in jeans and a raincoat. She was facedown, on the end of the porch, and she was moaning. Raleigh ran to her and turned her over, but it wasn't Sonya. However, it was someone he knew.

Deputy Thea Morris.

Seeing her gave his heart rate another jolt. Of course, Thea usually had that effect on him. Not in a good way, either, and it certainly wasn't good now. What the hell was she doing here, and what was wrong with her?

Raleigh didn't see any obvious injuries. Not at first. Then he pushed aside her dark blond hair and saw the two small circular burn marks on her neck. Someone had used a stun gun on her.

"Where's Sonya?" he asked.

Thea opened her eyes, but she was clearly having trouble focusing because she blinked several times. Then she groaned again. She didn't answer him, but he saw the alarm on her face, and she started struggling to sit up. He helped her with that. Too bad it meant putting his arms around her to do that.

And Raleigh immediately got another dose of too-clear memories that he didn't want.

Of Thea being not just in his arms but in his bed. But that was an *old water, old bridge* situation.

"Where's Sonya?" Raleigh repeated. "And what happened to you?" He had other questions, but those were enough of a start, since finding Sonya was his priority right now.

"Sonya," Thea repeated in a mutter. She lifted her hand—not easily because it was practically limp—and she touched her fingers to her head. "Sonya."

"Yeah, that's right. *Sonya.* She's pregnant, and I'm worried about her." *Worried* was an understatement. "What happened to her? What happened to *you*?"

Thea blinked some more, looked up at him, and the concern was obvious in her deep green eyes. "A man. I think he took her."

That got Raleigh's attention, and he fired glances around them, trying to see if he could spot her. But there was still no sign of Sonya.

"The man had a gun," Thea added, and she groaned, trying to get to her feet. She failed and dropped right back down on the porch. She also reached for her own gun, but her shoulder holster was empty. Since she was wearing her badge, Raleigh doubted she'd come here without her gun.

"What man?" Raleigh demanded. "And where did he take her?"

Thea groaned again and shook her head. "I don't know, but he said he was doing this because of Warren."

Raleigh hadn't actually needed that last bit of info to raise the alarm inside him. With the signs of struggle and those stun gun marks on Thea's neck, he decided it wasn't a good idea for them to be out in the open like this. Sonya's place was an old farmhouse with a barn and a storage shed, but the woods were only a short walk away. It would give an attacker plenty of places to hide.

If the man was indeed hiding, that is. If someone had actually taken Sonya, he could be long gone by now.

"We need to get inside." Raleigh hooked his arm around Thea's waist, pulling her to her feet. She wobbled, landing against him. Specifically against his chest. He shoved aside the next dose of memories that came with that close contact.

"You have to go after the man," Thea said. Her voice was as shaky as the rest of her. "You have to get Sonya."

"I will."

His deputy would be here in ten minutes or so, and Raleigh would start searching as soon as he had someone to watch Thea. She wasn't in any shape to defend herself if her attacker returned. At the moment though, he was much more concerned about Sonya. After all, Thea was alive and okay, for the most part anyway, but Sonya could be in the hands of a kidnapper.

Or a killer.

But that didn't make sense. Who would want to hurt her, and what did any of this have to do with Warren? Unless…

A very unsettling thought came to mind.

"Did this happen because Sonya's a surrogate?" Raleigh asked. He helped Thea into a chair at the kitchen table and then went back to the window to see if he could spot any sign of the woman or the person who'd taken her.

"I don't know. Maybe..." Thea's voice trailed off, and that's when Raleigh noticed that Thea's attention had landed on the painted message on the wall. She shuddered, but she didn't turn away. "I don't suppose you put that there?" But she shook her head, waving off her question. "No. You and Sonya were friends."

Raleigh wasn't sure how Thea knew that, but then he wasn't sure of a lot of things right now. "Start talking. I want to know everything that happened." Though it was hard to stand there and listen to anything Thea had to say when his instincts were screaming for him to go after Sonya.

Thea didn't jump right into that explanation; instead, she got to her feet. "We can talk while we look for her. Do you have a backup gun you can lend me?"

Raleigh frowned. Thea didn't look at all steady on her feet, which meant her aim would probably suck, too. Still, she was a cop.

Warren's star deputy, in fact.

Warren had not only trained her and given Thea her start in law enforcement, his father had made it clear that he loved Thea like a daughter. That was convenient, since Thea loved him like a father.

Raleigh wasn't sure how Thea had managed to overlook the fact that Warren was a lying, cheating snake, and he really didn't care. Heck, at the moment he didn't care if Thea was having trouble standing. She had the right idea about looking for Sonya as they talked, so Raleigh gave her his backup gun from his boot holster.

"I got here about a half hour ago," Thea said, glancing at the clock on the microwave. While she held on to the kitchen counter, she made her way to the back door. "Sonya didn't answer my call this morning, so I came over to check on her." She paused. "I've been checking on her a lot lately."

"I didn't know Sonya and you were that close," Raleigh commented. Sonya had only moved to Durango Ridge about ten years ago, so it was possible she'd known Thea before then. Or maybe they'd recently become friends. But after one look in Thea's eyes, he knew that wasn't the case.

Raleigh groaned. "This has to do with Sonya being a surrogate."

Thea nodded and managed to get the back door open. "I haven't given up on finding Hannah Neal's killer."

Neither had Raleigh. And he especially wasn't forgetting her now, because that message on Sonya's wall was identical to the one found at Hannah's apartment a year ago. Hannah had been murdered only a couple of hours after she'd given birth. That same person who'd killed Hannah had almost certainly been the one who had taken the newborn.

"Sonya didn't know Hannah," Thea continued, "but they were both surrogates, and they used the same doctor for the in vitro procedures that got them pregnant."

Raleigh's gut twisted. Because he'd known that. And

he had dismissed it as being something unimportant. Of course, he sure wasn't dismissing it now.

Still, it didn't make sense. Why would someone go after two surrogates to get back at Warren? Especially since Sonya had no personal connection to Warren.

Or did she?

Raleigh didn't have the answer to that, either, but he soon would.

Thea stepped out onto the back porch, and like Raleigh, she looked around. She also caught on to the porch railing to keep herself from falling. Raleigh nearly had her sit down on the step, but babysitting Thea wasn't his job. His job was to find Sonya.

"Tell me about this man who took Sonya," Raleigh demanded. "Was he here when you arrived?"

Thea nodded and followed him into the yard. Not easily, but she made it while still wobbling and using every last inch of the porch railing. "I saw him. He wore a ski mask and was holding her at gunpoint. He was about six-one and about two hundred pounds."

That tightened his stomach even more. Sonya was barely five-three and had a petite build. She wouldn't have stood a chance against a guy that size. Especially if he had a gun.

Thea stopped once she was in the yard, and with the rain pouring down on her, she looked back at him. "Sonya had the baby. Not with her," she added when she must have seen the shock on his face. "But she was no longer pregnant."

That didn't make sense, either. Sonya's doctor was in town. So was the hospital she'd intended to use to deliver. If she'd had the baby there, Raleigh would have certainly heard about it.

"Did she say anything about the baby? About the man?" Raleigh pressed.

"No. He had her gagged and already in the yard when I got here. I moved toward him, but there must have been a second man. Or a second person. He hit me with a stun gun when I came onto the porch. I think they took Sonya that way." She tipped her head to the woods.

Thea was lucky the guy hadn't killed her. Or maybe luck didn't have anything to do with it. Maybe keeping her alive had been part of the plan.

"I would tell you to wait here, but I doubt you will," Raleigh grumbled to her, and he started for those woods.

He didn't get far though, because he heard the sound of a car engine. At first he thought it might be the deputy, but it was a woman who came running out the back door, and Raleigh recognized the tall brunette.

Yvette O'Hara.

The woman who'd hired Sonya to be a surrogate. Like Thea and him, Yvette was wet from the rain. The woman was breathing through her mouth, her eyes were wide and her forehead was bunched up.

"Where's Sonya?" Yvette blurted out.

"We're not sure." Raleigh figured Yvette wasn't going to like that answer. Judging from her huff, she didn't. But it was the best he could do. "Stay here. Deputy Morris and I were about to look for her."

Yvette glanced at Thea. "What's going on? Did something happen to Sonya, to the baby?" She was right to be concerned—especially if she'd noticed the toppled furniture and messages on the walls.

"Stay put," he warned her again.

But Yvette didn't listen. She barreled down the steps, and also like Thea, she had some trouble staying steady. In her case though, it was because she was wearing high heels.

"Sonya's doctor called me," Yvette said, her words running together. "She missed her appointment. She wouldn't have done that if everything was all right."

Probably not. But Raleigh kept that to himself. Yvette already looked to be in alarm-overload mode, and it was best if he didn't add to that. He didn't want her getting hysterical.

"Just stay here," he said. "That way, if Sonya comes back, she won't be here alone."

Yvette finally gave a shaky nod to that and sank down onto the porch steps. Good. It was bad enough that he had Thea to watch, and he didn't want to have to keep an eye on Yvette, too. If those armed thugs were still in the area, it was too dangerous for Yvette to follow them.

Thea didn't stay back though. Despite her unsteady gait, she kept on walking, straight toward the woods, and Raleigh had to run to catch up with her. He'd just managed that when he heard someone call out to him.

"Raleigh?" It was Deputy Dalton Kane. Since Raleigh hadn't heard a siren, it meant Dalton had done a silent approach, and Raleigh was glad he was there. He needed some backup right now.

"Stay with Mrs. O'Hara," Raleigh told him. "The

woman on the porch," he added in case Dalton didn't know who Yvette was. "And get more backup and some CSIs out here. I want the house processed ASAP."

Again, Thea got ahead of him, and Raleigh had to catch up with her. She didn't even pause when she made it to the trees; she just walked right in. Since it was obvious that she wasn't going to be cautious, Raleigh moved in front of her.

"I think the thugs were parked back here somewhere," Thea said. "Shortly after the one hit me with the stun gun, I believe I heard a vehicle leaving."

Raleigh silently groaned. If that was true, then there was no telling where Sonya could be. "Is it possible one of the men had the baby with him?" he asked.

"No." But Thea paused and shook her head. "Maybe. I didn't get even a glimpse of him. After the stun gun hit, I fell on the porch, and I think I passed out."

Perhaps because she'd hit her head. Raleigh could see the bruise forming on her right cheekbone. Of course, if this was a kidnapping, the person could have even drugged Thea to make sure she didn't come after them.

But who would want to kidnap Sonya?

Raleigh drew a blank. Sonya hadn't been romantically involved with anyone. At least he didn't think she had been, but it was possible she'd met someone. It was something Raleigh hoped he could ask her as soon as they found her.

They kept walking, and it didn't take long for Raleigh to spot the clearing just ahead. He'd been born and raised in Durango Ridge, but he hadn't been in this part of the woods. However, like the rest of the area, there were paths and old ranch trails like this one that led to the creek.

"The rain is washing away the tracks," Thea mumbled, and she sped up.

She was right—if there were any tracks to be found, that is. And there were. Despite the rain, Raleigh could still see the grooves in the dirt and gravel surface. A vehicle had been here recently. He took out his phone to get photos of the tracks just in case they were gone before the CSI team could arrive. He'd managed to click a few shots when he heard Thea make a loud gasp.

Raleigh snapped in her direction, following her gaze to see what had captured her attention. There, in the bushes, he saw something that he definitely hadn't wanted to see.

Sonya's lifeless body.

Chapter Two

Thea fought the effects of the adrenaline crash. Or rather she tried. But while she was waiting on Sonya's front porch, she was also fighting off the remnants of that stun gun, along with the sickening dread that another woman was dead.

Oh, God. She was dead.

For a few seconds after she'd seen the body, Thea had tried to hold out hope that it wasn't Sonya. That it was some stranger, but that had been an unrealistic hope to have. After all, she'd seen the gunman taking Sonya. She'd known the woman was in extreme danger.

"Why did the gunman even take Sonya from the house?" Thea mumbled. "If he was just going to kill her, why didn't he do that when he first broke in?"

She hadn't intended for anyone to actually hear those questions. Not with all the chaos going on. But Raleigh obviously heard her, since he looked at her. What he didn't do was attempt an answer, because he was standing in the front doorway while giving instructions to the CSIs, who were now processing Sonya's yard and house.

Because it was a crime scene.

One that wasn't in Thea's jurisdiction.

That's why she just sat there on the front porch, waiting for Raleigh to give her some task to do. *Any* task. Anything that would help them find out who'd done this. That wouldn't stop this crushing feeling in her heart though, and it couldn't bring back Sonya. But maybe Thea could help get justice for the dead woman.

"Please tell me you found the baby," she said when Raleigh finished with the CSIs and started toward her.

He shook his head. "But there's some evidence that Sonya delivered the child here, at her house." Raleigh added a weary sigh to that, and he stopped directly in front of her. "There were some bloody sheets in the washer, and a package of newborn diapers had been opened. So had a case of premade formula bottles. Three of the bottles and four of the diapers were missing."

Well, Sonya had obviously had the baby somewhere, so the delivery could have easily happened here in her home, but that just led Thea to yet another question. Why wouldn't Sonya have gone to the hospital to deliver the child?

However, Thea instantly thought of a bad answer to that.

Maybe the gunman was here when the baby had been born. Those thugs could have stopped her from getting the medical attention she needed.

She looked up at Raleigh, and he was staring at her. His lawman's stare. That meant his comment about the sheets and diapers hadn't been just to catch her up on what they'd found. This was the start of his official interview, since she'd actually seen the man who was likely responsible for murdering Sonya.

Of course, Thea had already told him some details when Raleigh had found her on the back porch, and she had added other bits of info while they'd waited for the CSIs and ME to arrive. Obviously though, he wanted a lot more now.

But Thea didn't have more.

"You should be inside the house with Yvette," Raleigh reminded her. It wasn't the first time he'd mentioned that. "Whoever killed Sonya is still at large, and you could be a target."

"So could you." Best not to mention that the gunmen might want him dead because he was Warren's son.

No.

That would only make matters worse. And as for going inside with Yvette, obviously neither of them wanted to do that, because they both stayed put.

Thea's heart was breaking for Yvette, since the missing baby was her biological child—a daughter, from what Sonya had told her a couple months ago—but Thea didn't have the emotional energy to deal with Yvette just yet. Besides, she didn't even know what to say to the woman. The only thing they could do was hope they found the baby soon, along with finding Sonya's killer.

"I had at least a dozen conversations with Sonya," Thea explained to Raleigh. "I visited her here at her house three times, and not once did she ever hint that she was in any kind of danger."

He made a sound that could have meant anything and kept up the intense stare. He was good at it, too.

Unfortunately, looking at him reminded her of other things that had nothing to do with the murder and missing baby.

Once Raleigh had been attracted to her. Obviously not now though. There wasn't a trace of attraction in his stormy blue eyes or on that handsome face. He was all cowboy cop now.

"And you visited Sonya because of Hannah Neal," he said.

It wasn't a question, but Thea nodded to confirm that. "Hannah was my friend, and it eats away at me that I haven't been able to find her killer."

She caught something in his eyes. A glimmer that she recognized. It ate away at Raleigh, too.

Raleigh hadn't known Hannah, but Hannah's body had been dumped just at the edge of Durango Ridge. That meant it was Raleigh's case, but then, despite his retirement, Sheriff Warren McCall had gotten involved because Hannah had lived in their hometown of McCall Canyon. Plus, Hannah had been murdered in McCall Canyon, too. Murdered, and her killer had left the same obscene message on her wall that he had on Sonya's.

At the time of that investigation, Warren hadn't mentioned a word about Raleigh being his illegitimate son. Neither had Thea, though she had known. She had found out Warren's secret a few months before that, but she hadn't told anyone. And that was the reason she no longer saw the attraction in Raleigh's eyes. He hated her now because she'd kept that from him.

But not nearly as much as she hated herself for doing it.

Thea shook her head to clear it, forcing her mind off Hannah and back onto Sonya. Hannah's case was cold, but what they uncovered here today could maybe help them solve both murders.

"Why exactly did you become friends with Sonya?" Raleigh asked.

It wasn't an easy question. "It didn't start out as friendship. I'd been keeping tabs on the doctor who did the in vitro on Hannah." Actually, she'd kept tabs on anything related to her late friend. "So, when I found out this same doctor, Bryce Sheridan, had done this procedure on another surrogate, I wanted to talk to her. I wanted to see if there were any…irregularities."

Raleigh's eyebrow came up. "You think Dr. Sheridan had something to do with Hannah's murder?"

"No. I mean, I didn't know. I was just trying to find any kind of lead." Thea had to take a deep breath before she could continue. "But after I met and talked to Sonya, I didn't see any obvious red flags. Especially not any red flags about Dr. Sheridan."

That ate away at Thea even more. Because she should have seen something. She should have been able to stop this from happening.

"Both Hannah and Sonya were surrogates," Raleigh said, "and both were connected to you. According to the messages left at the crime scenes, the women were linked to Warren, too."

She couldn't deny that. Thea knew both women and had worked for Warren for three years before he'd retired and turned the reins of the sheriff's office over to his son Egan. It was ironic that all three of Warren's sons had become lawmen, but Thea seriously doubted that Raleigh would ever say that he had followed in his father's footsteps.

"You think I'm the reason these women were killed?" Thea came out and asked him.

Just saying the question aloud robbed her of her breath, and Raleigh didn't even get a chance to answer, because his deputy Dalton came out of the house and onto the porch. He wasn't alone, either. Yvette was with him. The woman was no longer crying, but her eyes were red and swollen, and she had her phone gripped in her hand so hard that her knuckles were white.

"We have to find my daughter, so I hired some private investigators," Yvette immediately said.

"I told her I didn't think that was a good idea," Dalton mumbled.

It wasn't. PIs, even well-meaning ones, could interfere with an investigation to the point of slowing it down, but Thea couldn't fault Yvette for doing this. The woman had to be desperate because her baby could be in the hands of a killer.

"You saw Sonya," Yvette said to Thea. "How was she? Was she weak? Did she say anything about the baby?"

Yvette had already asked these questions several times and in a couple of different ways. So had Raleigh. But Thea didn't mind answering them again. Maybe if she kept going over what she'd seen, she would remember something else. It was a tactic that cops used to try to get more info from witnesses.

"Yes, she looked weak," Thea admitted. "And scared.

The man who took her had his arm around her waist as if holding her up."

Even though that wasn't new information, it caused fresh tears to spring to Yvette's eyes. "What about the second man, the one who had the stun gun. Is it possible he had the baby with him?"

Thea had already considered that and had mentally walked through every moment of the attack. "It's possible. I didn't even see him. In fact, as I said earlier, it could have been a woman."

Yes, she had indeed said that earlier, but this time it caused Raleigh to shift his attention to Yvette. And Yvette noticed the abrupt shift, too.

"Well, it wasn't me," Yvette snapped. "I'd have no reason to take my own child and murder the woman who carried her for nine months."

No obvious reason anyway, but it was odd that the woman had assumed they were thinking the worst about her.

"Do you have anyone with a grudge against you?" Raleigh asked Yvette. "Someone who might want to try to kidnap the baby and hold her for ransom?"

Yvette was shaking her head before he even finished the question. "Of course not. My husband and I manage my late father's successful real estate company. We've never even had a serious complaint from a customer."

No, but that didn't mean someone hadn't kidnapped the baby for ransom. That's the reason Raleigh had told the woman to keep her phone close to her. Yvette had. In fact, she was doing everything a frantic mother would do to find her child. But something was missing here.

Or rather *someone*.

"Where's your husband?" Thea asked. "You called him right after we discovered the body, so shouldn't he have been here by now?"

Since Yvette was still looking a little defensive, Thea expected the woman to blast her for even hinting that Mr. O'Hara wasn't doing all he could to be there to comfort his wife or look for their child. But Yvette's reaction was a little surprising. She glanced away, dodging Thea's gaze.

Now, this was a red flag.

"Nick had some things to tie up at work," Yvette answered after several long moments.

Raleigh made one of those vague sounds of agreement. "Yeah, Sonya mentioned to me that your husband wasn't completely on board with having this baby."

Thea tried not to look too surprised, but she suspected that was a lie. She'd had a lot of conversations with Sonya, and never once had the surrogate brought up anything like that. If Sonya had, it would have been one of those red flags that Thea had been searching so hard to find.

What was equally surprising though was that Yvette didn't even deny it.

"Nick had a troubled childhood," Yvette said, still not looking at either Thea or Raleigh. She stared past them and into the yard. "He was hesitant about us having a baby because of all the money it would cost for a surrogate. And because of all the time I'd have to take off from the business to be a stay-at-home mom. But he finally agreed to it."

Maybe. And maybe Nick hadn't actually agreed the way that Yvette thought. It seemed extreme though to kill a surrogate so that he wouldn't have to be a father, especially since the baby had already been conceived. And born. Still, Thea would look into it, and she was certain Raleigh would, as well.

"Call your husband again," Raleigh told the woman. "I want him to come to the sheriff's office on Main Street in Durango Ridge in thirty minutes. I'll take Thea and you there now in the cruiser, and he can meet us."

Yvette started shaking her head again, and alarm went through her eyes. "He had nothing to do with this, and it'll only upset him if you start interrogating him the way you did me."

Thea had watched that so-called interrogation, and Raleigh had handled the woman with kid gloves. He'd treated her like a distraught mother whose child had been stolen. She doubted Raleigh would show that same consideration to Nick. Because Nick apparently had a motive for this nightmare that'd just happened.

Raleigh checked the time and motioned for Yvette to make the call. The woman hesitated, but she finally went to the other end of the porch to do that. Too bad Yvette didn't put it on speaker, because Thea would have loved to hear Nick's response to Raleigh's order.

While Yvette was still on the phone, Raleigh turned back to Thea. "I'll need you to give me a statement, of course." He hesitated, too. "And you should be in protective custody."

He was right, but it riled her a little that he thought she couldn't take care of herself. After all, she was a cop, and she could point out to him that the thug hadn't murdered her when he or she had the chance. Still, she needed to take some precautions.

Once Yvette had finished her call, Thea stood, ready to go to the cruiser, but she stopped when she heard the approaching vehicle. Raleigh and Dalton must have heard it, too, because they automatically stepped in front of her and Yvette. Thea slid her hand over the gun that she'd borrowed from Raleigh. But it wasn't the threat they were all obviously bracing themselves for.

It was Warren.

He pulled his familiar black truck to a stop behind the trio of cruisers and the other vehicles, and he got out and started for the house.

"What the hell is he doing here?" Raleigh asked, turning his glare back on Thea.

"I didn't call him," Thea said, but it would have been easy enough for Warren to hear about it. After all, most law enforcement agencies in the state had been alerted to the missing baby.

"Raleigh," Warren greeted. He obviously ignored the glare his son now had aimed at him, and he walked right past Raleigh to pull Thea into his arms.

It certainly wasn't the first time that Warren had hugged her. He'd always treated her like family and had practically raised her and her brother, Griff. But it felt awkward now in front of Raleigh—who hadn't gotten that same family treatment from the man.

"Are you okay?" Warren asked her when he pulled back from the hug.

His attention went to the stun gun marks on her neck,

and it looked as if he had to bite back some profanity. When she'd been his deputy, he had always hated whenever she'd gotten hurt or been put in danger, and he still apparently felt that way. Thea appreciated the concern, especially since she'd never gotten any from her own parents, but it made the situation with Raleigh seem even more awkward.

"I'm fine," Thea assured him. She didn't especially want to bring this up, but Warren would soon learn it anyway. "Whoever did this also took the newborn, and he left a message on the wall—"

"Two messages," Raleigh corrected. "There was a second in Sonya's bedroom. They were both written in red paint and used identical wording to what was left at Hannah's place. 'This is for Sheriff Warren McCall.'"

"This man is Sheriff McCall?" Yvette asked. Warren nodded, and she went to him, catching on to his arms. "Who did this? Why would someone take my baby because of you?"

Warren's face tightened. "I don't know."

"But you must have some—" Yvette started, but Raleigh moved her away when her grip tightened on Warren.

"This is the missing baby's mother," Raleigh explained. "Yvette O'Hara."

Warren tipped the brim of his Stetson as a greeting. "I'm really sorry for what happened, but I honestly don't know who took your child." He turned to Raleigh. "Are you sure this is connected to Hannah, or is it a copycat?"

A muscle flickered in Raleigh's jaw. "Too early to

tell. Do you have a reason for being here?" There definitely was nothing friendly about his tone.

Warren sighed. "Yes. I was worried about Thea and thought she might need a ride home because she's so shaken up."

"She will, but only after she's given her statement about the attack." Again, there was no friendliness from Raleigh. "I was about to take her to my office now. No reason that I know of for you to be there for that, but you can wait for her at the café across the street."

Warren would do that if he couldn't get Raleigh to relent and let him stay with her in the sheriff's office. And Raleigh wouldn't back down on this.

They started down the steps, and Thea didn't miss it when she saw Warren wince and slide his fingers over his chest. He quickly moved his hand away, but she knew he'd been touching the scar beneath his shirt. The scar he'd gotten from a gunshot wound six months ago.

The wound itself had healed, but the muscles there had been damaged enough that Warren would always have pain. Something he obviously didn't want to discuss because he shook his head when Thea opened her mouth to ask if he was okay. Maybe it was a guy thing not to want to admit that he was in pain, or maybe he just didn't want to talk about it in front of Raleigh.

"Ride in the cruiser with Raleigh," Warren whispered to her, and he made a lawman's glance around them. "There are a lot of places for a killer to lie in wait on the road that leads into Durango Ridge."

She nodded, but his reminder only gave her another jolt of adrenaline. So did the sound of her phone ringing. Not a reaction she wanted to have as a deputy. Nor was the reaction she had next.

Her stomach went to her knees when she looked at her phone screen.

"Unknown caller," she said.

That stopped Raleigh and Warren, and Yvette eventually stopped, too, when she realized they were no longer moving toward the cruiser.

It could be nothing, maybe even a telemarketer, but Raleigh must have realized it could be something important because he took out his own phone to record the call, and he motioned for her to answer it. She did, and unlike what Yvette had done earlier, Thea put it on speaker.

"I'm guessing you're looking for the kid," a man immediately said. Thea didn't recognize his voice, but it was possible that it was the same man who'd taken Sonya.

Yvette gasped, and Warren motioned for her to stay quiet. Good move because it wouldn't do any good to have Yvette start yelling at this thug.

"Where's the baby?" Thea demanded. Of course, she wanted to ask the snake why he'd murdered Sonya, but right now, the baby had to come first. It was too late to save Sonya, but maybe they could still help the child.

"I'll give her to you. All you have to do is come and get her."

Thea looked at Raleigh to get his take on this. Like her, he was clearly skeptical, but at the moment, this was all they had. Maybe it was a matter of paying a ransom. If so, she figured they could scrape together whatever amount they needed to get the child safely away from a killer.

The conversation must have alerted Dalton because he came down the steps and into the yard with them.

"Where's the baby?" Thea repeated to the man.

"I'll text you the time and the place where you can get her. Oh, and I'll text you the rules, too. Don't forget those or you won't get the kid." He sounded arrogant, and Thea wished she could reach through the phone and make him pay for what he'd done.

She tamped down the anger so she could speak. "How do I know you actually have her? This could be a trap."

"Sweetcakes, if I'd wanted you dead, you already would be. You wouldn't have made it off that back porch of Sonya's house."

Since Thea had already realized that, she knew it was true. But there were plenty of other things that didn't make sense. "How do I know for certain that you have the newborn?" she pressed.

The man didn't answer. Not with words anyway. But Thea heard the sound in the background.

A baby crying.

Chapter Three

Raleigh cursed and snatched the phone from Thea. "Tell me the location of the baby now!" he demanded. But he was talking to the air, because the kidnapper had already ended the call.

"Oh, God." Yvette grabbed the phone, too, and she hit Redial.

No answer.

A hoarse sob tore from Yvette's mouth, and she would have likely fallen to the ground if Warren hadn't caught her. Raleigh didn't thank him for doing that because he didn't want the man anywhere around here. Raleigh had enough distractions with Thea and Yvette, and he didn't need to add his so-called father to the mix.

Raleigh turned to Dalton. "Take Yvette to the station. Call a doctor for her, too. She might need some meds to calm her down."

"The only thing I need is my baby!" Yvette shouted.

The woman tried Redial again, and she was gripping Thea's phone so hard that Raleigh thought she might break it. That wouldn't be good since it was obviously the way the kidnapper had chosen to communicate with them.

"She's a newborn," Yvette went on. "She has to be fed. Someone has to take care of her."

"And the men who have her will do that," Thea said. "They'll want to keep the baby safe and well. Remember, they took formula so she won't be hungry."

True, but that didn't mean a newborn was going to get expert care from the thugs who'd snatched her. That's why they had to find her ASAP.

Dalton gently took Yvette by the arm. "Once we get to the station," he told the woman, "I'll examine the call. I might be able to get a match on his voice, because Raleigh will send me the recording of the conversation."

Raleigh would do that, but he wasn't holding out any hope for a match. Or that the call would be traced for that matter. The kidnapper had almost certainly used a burner cell, a disposable one that couldn't be traced. Still, they'd try.

"What can I do?" Warren asked him.

"You can go home to your wife and family in McCall Canyon until I've got time to interrogate you. After all, it was your name on that wall, and there had to be a reason for it."

That was a knee-jerk reaction. One that Raleigh instantly regretted. Not because he hadn't meant it—he had. But it was the wrong time to vent.

Raleigh took a deep breath to steady himself. "My people have the scene secured," he added to Warren. There was much less emotion in his voice now, which was a good thing. "Give me a couple of hours so I can deal with this kidnapper, and then I can question you."

Warren didn't balk at any part of that, but judging from his tight expression, something was on his mind. "What about Thea?" Warren asked.

Of course. Thea. Warren was worried about the woman he'd practically raised.

"I'll take Thea to the station so we can wait on this thug to call us back," Raleigh answered.

Warren stood there, his hands on his hips while he volleyed glances between them as if he was trying to figure out if that was the wise thing to do. The man didn't budge until Thea nodded.

"I'll be okay," she assured Warren.

"Call me if you need anything," Warren finally said, and he hugged her again. After he pulled away from her, he looked at Raleigh, maybe trying to figure out what to say to him, but he settled for another tip of his hat. This one was a farewell, and he headed to his truck.

Raleigh and Thea were right behind him, and the moment Raleigh had her in the cruiser, he started toward town. It wouldn't be a long drive, only about twenty minutes, but he could use that time to get some things straight.

"The kidnapper said there'd be rules," he reminded her. "That probably means a ransom demand with instructions for the payout so we can get the baby. You won't be involved in that. If I haven't worked out a protective custody arrangement by then, you can wait in my office."

She shook her head. "The kidnapper said I was to come and get her."

"That won't be happening." At least he hoped not anyway. Raleigh didn't want to involve Thea in this any more than she already was.

But obviously Thea wasn't giving up. "I'm the person best suited to make an exchange like that. The kidnapper said if he wanted me dead, he would have killed me on the porch. And he could have done just that."

Raleigh wasn't giving up, either. "Maybe because the person standing next to you was holding a baby, and he didn't want to risk hurting her. That could have been the sole reason he didn't kill you."

She opened her mouth as if she might disagree with that, but she must have realized it could be the truth because Thea huffed and leaned back against the seat.

"I'll get Yvette's husband in for questioning," Raleigh added a moment later. "Right now, he's a person of interest. He could have orchestrated all of this because he doesn't want to be a father."

Though it did seem extreme—unless he hadn't intended for Sonya to die. Maybe the thugs hadn't had orders to kill Sonya or anyone else who showed up. That would explain why they'd had a stun gun with them. It would also explain why the one that Thea had seen was wearing a ski mask. He didn't want his identity known because he hadn't intended to kill any witnesses.

That was the best-case scenario though. It was still possible that the goons wanted Thea dead.

"Warren is a person of interest, too?" she asked.

"Of course." Raleigh would love nothing more than to charge the man with something. Anything.

"And what about your mother?" Thea pressed. "Will you also question her?"

Raleigh's gaze slashed to her, and he nearly had another of those knee-jerk reactions. But he forced himself to see this through her cop's perspective. His mother, Alma, no longer loved Warren. In fact, she might actually hate him.

"Alma thought Warren was going to leave his wife to be with her," Thea continued when he didn't say anything. "That didn't happen, and when he broke off things with her six months ago—"

"Don't finish that," Raleigh warned her. "I know how upset my mother was, and I don't have to hear a recap from you."

Hell, she was still upset. Alma had carried on an affair with a married man, gotten pregnant and had basically lived her life waiting for the emotional scraps that Warren might toss her. Now that the secret was out, she was just seething in anger.

Raleigh hated to admit it, but he was seething, too. Because his mother had lied to him about his father. She'd lied all because she didn't want Warren's secret life exposed. Well, it was sure as hell exposed now.

"Did your mother know Sonya well?" Thea asked. It was a cop's kind of question, because Thea was again trying to link his mom to what was going on.

"Everyone in town knew Sonya," Raleigh snarled. But his mom had known Sonya better than most because Sonya had done some office work at his mother's ranch. "Don't worry. I'll question my mom," Raleigh added. "But there are plenty of other ways for her to get back at Warren. Ways that don't involve kidnapping a newborn baby and killing a surrogate."

It surprised him a little when Thea made a sound of agreement. After all, Warren's wife, Helen, had raised Thea, too, and that meant Thea and the McCalls likely thought of his mother as the villain in all of this.

"There doesn't seem to be a connection between Warren and Sonya," Thea added. "If your mother was going to try to get back at him in some way, she would go after him or someone he cared about."

True. But his mother would only do that if she'd finally gone off the deep end. There were times when Raleigh thought she might be headed there, and he was doing his damnedest to make sure that didn't happen.

"I also want to talk to the doctor who did the in vitro procedures for both Hannah and Sonya," Raleigh continued, and he was about to ask Thea what she knew about the man, but her phone rang.

Unknown Caller.

Raleigh immediately pulled onto the shoulder of the road so he could again use his phone to record the conversation. Once he had it ready, Thea took the call. The first thing Raleigh heard was the baby crying again. It was like taking hard punches to the gut. It sickened him to think of these monsters having that little girl.

"All right, you ready to do this?" the kidnapper asked.

"We are," Raleigh answered, and he waited a moment to see if the guy would ask who he was. He didn't.

Which meant the thug likely knew all the players in this. That wasn't much of a surprise since whoever was behind this had probably done their homework.

"Good. Because I'm gonna make this real easy. Transfer fifty thousand into the account number that I'm about to text to you."

In the grand scheme of things, fifty thousand wasn't much for a ransom demand, which made Raleigh instantly suspicious. Then again, maybe these guys just wanted some quick cash so they could make a getaway. After all, they were killers now, and if arrested, they'd be looking at the death penalty. Fifty would be more than enough to escape.

"If you do it right," the kidnapper went on, "it'll only take a couple of minutes at most for the money to show up. Then you can have the kid."

Raleigh huffed. "How do we know you even have the child? The crying we heard could be any baby. Or a recording. And if you do have her, what stops you from taking the money and running?"

"I figured you'd ask that. Well, I'm sending you a picture of the kid, and since Thea's using her cell for this call, I'll text it to your phone."

The guy didn't ask for Raleigh's number, and several moments later Raleigh's phone did indeed ding with a text message. Two of them, in fact. The first was the routing number for a bank account. Probably an offshore one that would be out of reach of law enforcement.

Raleigh went to the second text. A photo. It was indeed a baby wrapped in a blanket, and seeing her was like another punch. He reminded himself though that the picture could be fake. But this didn't feel like a ruse. Raleigh was certain these snakes had that little girl.

He showed the photo to Thea, and he saw the raw emotions go through her eyes. "Oh, God," she whispered, her voice mostly breath.

She obviously didn't think it was a ruse, either. And that led Raleigh back to his second issue with this ransom arrangement.

"I'll transfer twenty grand," Raleigh told the kidnapper. He could take that from his own personal checking account. "You'll get the rest when I actually see the baby. And Thea will have no part in the drop. It'll be between you and me."

Along with some backup deputies that Raleigh would have in place. The plan was to catch these idiots and make them pay for what they'd done. First though, he had to make sure the baby was safe.

The guy didn't say anything, and the silence went on for what seemed to be an eternity. "All right," the kidnapper finally answered. "Get that money to me in the next five minutes, and then I'll give you the location of the kid."

Before Raleigh could ask for any more time, the kidnapper ended the call. Raleigh didn't bother to hit Redial because it would just eat up precious time.

He had a quick debate with himself as to how to handle this, and the one thing he knew was that he didn't want Thea anywhere near this. That meant getting her to the station.

"Call the emergency dispatcher," Raleigh said as he used his own phone to access his bank account. "Have him connect you to Dalton. Tell him to gather up as many deputies as he can because I might need them. I also need Dalton to get the remaining thirty grand of the ransom money." If nothing went wrong with the first part of this plan, Raleigh wanted to be ready.

"I could do backup," Thea insisted. "I still have your gun, and I'm not woozy anymore from the stun gun."

Raleigh dismissed that with a headshake and motioned for her to make the call. She did, and he continued with his own task.

It took several moments for him to get access to his account, several more for Raleigh to put in the number the kidnapper had given him. The transfer went through without any hitches.

He had more money in investment accounts, but he doubted those would be as easy to tap into. That's why he'd wanted Dalton to come up with the rest. That would involve getting some help from fellow law enforcement, maybe even the DA. Somehow though, they'd come up with that money.

"Dalton said to tell you that he'll get to work right away on all of that," Thea relayed to him the moment she finished her call. She also took his phone and had another look at the photo the kidnapper had sent. "I'm just trying to figure out if there's any resemblance between the baby and Yvette."

"And?" He started driving again so he could get Thea to the station. They were still ten minutes out, so Raleigh sped up. After everything that'd happened, he didn't want to be on this rural stretch of road any longer than necessary.

"I can't tell. You think we should send it to Yvette to see if she recognizes any features? The baby could resemble her husband since it was Yvette's and his fertilized embryo that was implanted in Sonya."

He had another short debate about that and dismissed it. The woman had been so frantic that this might push her over the edge. Raleigh wanted her to stay put with Dalton at least until he could get there.

"Egan would send backup if you need it," Thea reminded him.

She probably hadn't suggested that to rile him. After all, *Egan* was Sheriff Egan McCall of McCall Canyon. Along with being Thea's boss, he was Raleigh's half brother and Warren's son. Raleigh wasn't so stubborn that he would refuse help and therefore put the baby at even greater risk, but he didn't think he would have to rely on McCall help just yet.

Only a short distance ahead, Raleigh spotted a dark blue SUV. It wasn't on the road but had pulled off onto one of the ranch trails. A trail with a lot of trees and wild shrubs. Normally, seeing a vehicle parked there wouldn't have alarmed him. After all, there was pasture land out here for sale, and this could be a potential buyer. But this day was far from normal.

"You recognize the SUV?" Thea asked. She drew her gun, which meant this had put her on edge, too.

"No." And it was parked in such a way that he couldn't see the license plates.

Raleigh considered just speeding up, and once he passed the vehicle, he could get the plates and call them in. But he saw something else. Something on the ground next to the passenger's side door.

"Is that what I think it is?" Thea muttered. "It looks like a baby carrier."

It did. Raleigh had already had a bad feeling about this, and that feeling went up a significant notch when the SUV came flying off the trail and onto the road just ahead of Thea and him. The driver sped away, heading in the direction of town.

Raleigh hit his brakes and slowed so he could have a better look. At first, he thought the carrier was empty, that this was some kind of trick. But then he saw the baby's tiny hand moving away. He heard the cries, too.

His phone dinged with another text. Since Thea still had hold of it, she read it to him. "Change of plans. The kid is all yours. Thanks for the twenty grand."

Raleigh wanted to know what had happened to make them flee like that. He also wanted to go in pursuit, but that would mean leaving the baby out here.

"Call Dalton back," he told Thea. "Let him know what's happening. I want that SUV stopped."

While she did that, Raleigh drew his gun and got out. He fired glances all around them but didn't see anyone. However, the baby's cries seemed to be even more frantic now. She could be hungry or scared.

Still keeping watch, Raleigh went closer, and he prayed this wasn't some elaborate dummy. It wasn't. The baby was real. And there was what appeared to be a note on the blanket that was loosely draped over her.

Raleigh went to her, stooping down, and he touched her cheek, hoping to soothe her. It didn't work. She kept crying, and he was about to pick her up when he saw what was written on the note.

He read the note out loud, so Thea could hear. "'Warren's going to be so sad when he finds out she's dead.'"

Raleigh shook his head, not understanding what it meant. Who was the *she*? Certainly not the baby because she was very much alive. It hit him then. Another she, and this one was definitely connected to Warren. He whipped back around, his attention going to the cruiser.

What he saw caused his heart to go to his knees.

Because there was a guy wearing a ski mask, and he had a gun pointed right at Thea's head.

Chapter Four

Thea was certain that Raleigh was cursing her as he was diving for cover with the baby. She was cursing herself for letting this snake get the drop on her and knocking the gun from her hand. Yes, she was still wobbly from the other attack, but that was no excuse. She was a cop, and she shouldn't have let this happen.

Especially because it could end up getting Raleigh and the baby hurt.

Raleigh was obviously trying to prevent that from happening because he dropped down into the shallow ditch with the baby. It wouldn't be much protection if shots were fired, but it was better than being out in the open. And much better than having the baby in the hands of this thug.

She had no idea who was holding her at gunpoint, but one thing was for certain—if he'd wanted her dead, she already would be. Instead of grabbing her when she stepped from the truck, he could have just put a bullet in her head and then escaped. Raleigh would have had a hard time going after him with a baby in tow.

So, what did the thug want?

Thea prayed that whatever it was, the baby wouldn't be put in any more danger. The newborn had already been through enough.

"Why are you doing this?" Thea managed to ask.

It was hard for her to talk though because he had her in a choke hold, and the barrel of the gun was digging so hard against her skin that she'd probably have a fresh cut to go along with the one she'd gotten when she fell on Sonya's porch after being hit with the stun gun.

Was this the same attacker?

She didn't know, and even if she got a chance to see his face beneath that ski mask, she still probably wouldn't recognize him.

And that only left her with another question. Where was his partner? He had almost certainly been the one to drive away in the SUV—probably after this thug had gotten out and hidden in a ditch to wait for them. But the partner would come back. No doubt soon. That meant Raleigh and she didn't have much time.

"Let her go," Raleigh called out, though he certainly knew that wasn't going to stop this thug. However, he had positioned himself in front of the baby, and he had his gun ready.

Not that he had a shot.

The guy behind her was hunched down just enough that Raleigh wouldn't be able to shoot him. She certainly wouldn't be able to do that, either, not with the backup weapon that Raleigh had given her on the ground. She was only about five feet away from where it had fallen when the guy bashed his own weapon against her hand to send the gun flying. But despite it being that close, there wasn't much of a chance she could get to it without getting shot. Still, she would have to go for it if he tried to hurt the baby. First though, Thea wanted to know what the heck was going on.

"Did you bring the baby here?" she demanded, and she hoped she sounded a lot stronger than she actually felt. Thea was scared. Not for herself but for the baby.

"Nope. It wasn't me. But this is how this is going to work," the guy said in a voice plenty loud enough for Raleigh to hear. "First you're gonna use your phone to transfer the rest of the money. All thirty grand of it. Then, you're gonna bring the kid to me."

Raleigh cursed. "Why the hell would I do that?"

"Because if you don't, I'm gonna shoot this pretty lady here. Warren's going to be so sad if that happens."

It was similar wording to what had been in the note, but Thea didn't take either it or this snake's threat at face value. He could be lying so he could connect Warren to this. Of course, Thea didn't know why he would do that, but it was still a possibility. None of this had felt right from the beginning.

"Did Nick O'Hara hire you to do this?" she snapped. "Is that why you want the baby?"

The thug didn't answer, but she thought maybe he tensed more than he already was. Hard to tell though because he was wired and practically fidgeting. Definitely not someone she wanted with his finger on the trigger.

"Transfer the money now!" he shouted to Raleigh.

Raleigh had his famous glare aimed at the thug, but she also saw him do something with his phone. Even though there hadn't been a lot of time to do it, maybe

Raleigh's deputy had managed to get the money. If not, perhaps she could bargain with her captor to let her call Warren for the funds. That could also buy her some time so she could figure out what to do.

"Once you have me and the money," she said to the guy, "there's no reason for you to have the baby, too. She's a newborn, and she needs to be at the hospital."

"What the kid needs is for the sheriff to cooperate," he snarled. She felt him fumbling around and realized he was checking his phone. No doubt looking to see if the transfer had been made.

Raleigh lifted his head enough for Thea to make eye contact with him, and for a moment she thought he was going to say he hadn't been able to get the money. But the thug made a sound of approval.

"Good job," he told Raleigh. "I knew you'd come through for me."

Thea didn't breathe easier, because she figured what was coming next, and she didn't have to wait long for it.

"Now the kid," the guy said. "Me and Thea are going to walk closer to you to get her. That means you toss out your gun and keep your hands where I can see them."

"So you can kill me? I don't think so. Tell me, why didn't you just take the baby and run?"

"Oh, I will be doing that." He chuckled and started walking with her. "First though, I had to fix a screwup."

Thea wasn't sure if he meant her or not. Maybe his partner and he thought she could ID them. She couldn't. But since a murder charge was on the table, they might not want to risk it. Or it could be something more than that. They could want to use her to get to Warren.

Or make it look as if they were using her for that.

She heard the sound of a car engine, and moments later the blue SUV came into view. It was creeping toward them, the driver probably looking to make sure his partner had what they'd come for—the baby and her. And in a few more seconds, that might happen if she didn't do something.

Raleigh still didn't have a shot, but since he still hadn't tossed out his gun, there was a chance that her captor would shift his position enough for Raleigh to take him out.

"Are you deaf?" the man shouted to Raleigh. "I told you to drop the gun."

There was no way Thea could let that happen, not with the SUV getting closer and closer. Right now the thug holding her was outnumbered, but that wouldn't be true once his partner arrived onto the scene.

She looked at Raleigh again, hoping that he was ready for what she was about to do. If not, it could get them both killed.

Thea dragged in a deep breath, and just as the thug pushed her forward another step, she rammed her elbow into his stomach. In the same motion, she dropped down her weight. She didn't get far though because he still had her in a choke hold.

But she did something about that, too.

Thea twisted her body, ramming him again with her elbow until he loosened his grip enough for her to drop down low enough to give Raleigh a chance at a shot. She prayed it was one he would take.

And he did.

Raleigh already had his gun lifted, and the bullets blasted through the air. One shot, quickly followed by another.

Time seemed to stop. Thea thought maybe her heart had, as well. She could only wait to see what had happened, and several long moments later, the thug's grip on her melted away as he collapsed to the ground. She glanced back at him and saw the blood and his blank, already lifeless eyes. Raleigh's shot had killed him.

"Get down!" Raleigh shouted to her.

Thea scrambled away from the thug, snatching up the gun as she ran, and she dropped down into the ditch. It wasn't a second too soon. Because more shots came. Not from Raleigh this time but from the person who was in the SUV.

The bullets slammed into the surface of the road, just inches from where she was. That told her that she was the target since the shooter didn't try to take out Raleigh even though he also had a gun. But what she still didn't know was why this attack was even happening.

The gunman fired two more shots, both of them slamming into the dirt bank of the ditch just above her head. If he changed the angle just a little or got closer, he'd have a much easier time killing her. However, as bad of a thought as that was, at least this snake wasn't shooting in the direction of the baby.

Thea waited for a lull in the shooting, and she lifted her head enough to take aim at the shooter. He was wearing a ski mask and was leaning out of the driver's-side window. She fired right at him.

So did Raleigh.

She wasn't sure which of their bullets hit the windshield, but one slammed into the glass. It also sent the shooter ducking back into the SUV. Almost immediately, he threw the SUV into Reverse and hit the accelerator.

He was getting away.

Thea definitely didn't want that, because they needed him to get answers. She came out of the ditch, aiming at the tires, and she fired. The SUV was already moving too fast though, and before she could even take a second shot, it was already out of sight.

RALEIGH STOOD IN the doorway of the ER examination room while he waited for his deputy Dalton to come back on the line. If they got lucky, then maybe Dalton would tell him that the driver of that SUV had been caught and was ready for interrogation.

Because Raleigh very much wanted to question him.

Then he'd arrest him for not only murder and kidnapping, but also for the attempted murder of two law enforcement officers, as well.

Thea looked up at him, no doubt checking to see if he knew anything yet, but Raleigh just shook his head. He also kept watch in the hall and ER to make sure a gunman didn't come rushing in to try to finish what he'd started.

There was a lot to distract Raleigh though, and he knew he had to be mindful of that. Thea was holding the baby while Dr. Halvorson, the pediatrician, finished up his exam. An exam that Raleigh hoped would let them know that the baby was all right. It would be somewhat of a miracle if she was, considering the ordeal she'd been through. At least she was too young to know what was going on, but maybe she could still sense the stress.

And there was plenty of that.

Thea's face was etched with worry, and Raleigh was certain his was, too. Because as long as the shooter was at large, then they were probably still in danger. It was too much to hope that the shooter would have fled and had no plans to return.

The doctor pushed his rolling chair away from Thea and the baby, and he stood. Raleigh turned so he could see the doctor but also keep watch.

"She seems to be just fine," Dr. Halvorson said, causing Raleigh to release a breath of relief. "Of course, I'll still run tests to make sure nothing shows up."

The tests would include a blood sample that a nurse had taken from the heel of the baby's foot. The newborn had definitely made a fuss about that, and Raleigh didn't intend to admit that it'd put a knot in his stomach. But when Thea had given her the bottle that the hospital had provided, the little girl had drifted off to sleep.

Thea had had to collect the baby's clothes and diaper. Since the items could have fibers and such on them, they'd been sent to the crime lab, along with the infant carrier. Thankfully, the hospital had had newborn gowns, fresh diapers and a blanket.

"I'm guessing it'll be a problem if we admit her to the hospital?" the doctor asked.

Raleigh had to think about that for a second. "It would, but if she needs to be here, we'll make it work."

The doctor shook his head. "I don't see a reason to

admit her other than for observation. She's a healthy weight—seven pounds, four ounces. No breathing issues or signs of injury."

That was somewhat of a miracle. Too bad Sonya hadn't gotten a miracle of her own.

"Are there any indications that the baby was born from a forced labor?" Raleigh asked the doctor. "Like maybe some kind of drug?"

"I doubt we'd be able to tell that from the newborn, but something like that might be in Sonya's body."

The doctor's voice cracked a little on the last word. That was because he knew Sonya. Most people in Durango Ridge did. And it was hard to lose one of their own. Especially to murder.

"Raleigh, you still there?" Dalton asked when he came back on.

"Yeah." And he stepped out into the hall. He didn't put the call on speaker, because he didn't want anyone who happened to walk by to hear any grisly details. That meant he'd have to fill Thea in on whatever he learned.

"The other deputies didn't catch the guy," Dalton said, sounding as frustrated as Raleigh felt. "The APB is out on the blue SUV, so someone might spot it and call it in."

That could happen, but it was beyond a long shot. There hadn't been any plates on the SUV, so they couldn't try to trace the vehicle. And by now, the driver could have either ditched it or else put on some plates so that it wouldn't draw any attention from law enforcement.

"What about Nick and Yvette O'Hara?" Raleigh asked. "Are they still at the station?"

"She is. I've got her in an interview room, and she's pitching a fit to leave to go to the hospital and see the baby. I told her she shouldn't be out and about, not with the killer at large, but she's insisting."

Raleigh couldn't blame her. All indications were that this was Yvette's daughter, and she was acting the way a distraught mother would. Her husband though was a different story. "See if you can find someone to escort her here." The hospital was only a couple of minutes from the station, so maybe there wouldn't be enough time for a killer to take shots at her. "And get Nick in for questioning ASAP."

Though he figured Dalton already had a list of things that fell into that *as soon as possible* category.

"Will do. We ran the prints on the dead guy, and we got an ID," Dalton went on a moment later. "His name was Marco Slater. Ring any bells?"

Raleigh mentally repeated it a couple of times and came up blank. "No. Should it?"

"According to Slater's record, Warren McCall arrested him for an outstanding warrant on a parole violation. That happened shortly before Warren retired when Slater was driving through McCall Canyon. Warren apparently recognized him from his mug shots."

Now, that was luck. Well, unless Slater had been on parole because of a crime he'd committed in or around Warren's town. Either way, Slater could have a grudge against Warren, and that could be motive for what had gone on today.

"Text me a copy of Slater's record," he instructed

Dalton. "Was there anything on the body to tell us why he went after Thea and the baby?"

"Nothing. The guy wasn't even carrying a wallet, and other than extra ammo and a burner cell, there wasn't anything in his pockets."

So he was probably a hired gun, but maybe the lab would be able to get something from the phone. "Anything new from the ME on Sonya?"

"Not yet, but he said he would call as soon as he had something."

Raleigh needed the info, especially if there was any fiber or trace evidence on the body that could lead them to the driver of that SUV. Or the person who'd put the dead guy up to kidnapping the baby and killing Sonya. The driver could be the boss or just another hired gun.

"How's the kid?" Dalton asked. "And where will you be taking her?"

"She's fine." But Raleigh didn't have an answer for the second question. Since she could still be a target, she would need to be in protective custody. Ditto for Thea and maybe even Yvette. "I'll get back to you on the details," Raleigh added before he ended the call.

He put his phone away and stepped back into the doorway. Of course, Thea's attention went right to him. "The gunman got away."

"For now." He hoped like the devil that would change soon.

"I need to check on another patient," the doctor said. Maybe he sensed that Raleigh needed to talk business with Thea. "Let me know what your plans are for the baby."

He would—as soon as he figured it out.

"You look as if you've had a lot of experience with kids," Raleigh said to Thea while the doctor was clearing out.

"Several of my friends have babies." With the newborn cradled in her arms, she brushed a kiss on the baby's head but kept her attention on Raleigh. Since she was a cop, she obviously knew he'd been discussing the specifics of the case, and there were a couple of the specifics that he wanted to go over with her.

"Marco Slater is the dead guy who tried to kill us. You know him?" he asked.

Raleigh saw the instant recognition in her eyes. "Marco Slater," she repeated. "He had a run-in with Warren years ago. He was supposed to be serving a ten-year sentence."

Well, the guy had apparently gotten an early release. Raleigh would find out more about that when he had Marco's records. "Did Marco hate Warren enough to put together a scheme that involves murder?"

She shook her head. "I remember Marco resisting arrest, and he took a swing at Warren. That's why he ended up with some extra jail time. I don't remember Marco vowing to get revenge though."

Maybe the man hadn't said it, but that didn't mean he hadn't attempted it. It could tie everything up in a neat little package, and Raleigh might not have to investigate anyone else who could have a grudge against Warren.

Like Raleigh's mother.

"There's more," Raleigh went on. "The CSIs are going through Sonya's house, and they found a tape recorder. Apparently, she was recording her calls. Did she happen to mention anything about that?"

"No," Thea answered without hesitation. She paused though. "She did say she'd had a bad relationship a couple of years ago. Maybe the old boyfriend was harassing her or something."

Now it was Raleigh's turn to say, "No. She did have a relationship, and it didn't end especially well, but I know the guy, and he's moved on. He's married, and they've got a baby." Though it was an angle he would check just in case. "I've got one of my deputies skimming through the recording just to see if anything stands out. If not, then I'll go over them more closely tonight."

At least he would do that if he wasn't still dealing with the O'Haras and a kidnapper.

Thea looked up at him again. "I know you're anxious to put some distance between us," she said. "But I'd rather work on this investigation than be tucked away at a safe house, in protective custody."

Yes, he was ready for them not to be under the same roof, but Thea probably believed that was because of the bad blood between them. And there was indeed some of that. But the attraction was stirring again, and Raleigh definitely didn't have time to deal with it. However, he seriously doubted that this would be a situation of out of sight, out of mind. No, now that she'd come back into his life, it wouldn't be easy to forget what they'd once had together.

She kept staring at him, obviously waiting for him to agree or disagree about the safe house. But Raleigh didn't get a chance to say anything, because he heard hurried footsteps.

Someone was running toward them.

Raleigh automatically drew his gun, but the person rushing to the room wasn't armed. It was Yvette, and she was ahead of one of his deputies, Alice Rowe, who was trying to keep up with her. Alice had no doubt escorted the woman there.

"Where is she?" Yvette asked the moment she spotted Raleigh. "Is she all right? I need to see her."

"The baby's fine," Raleigh assured her, and he stepped back so that Yvette could come in.

Yvette didn't take him at his word. No good mother probably would have. She went straight to Thea. Thea glanced at Raleigh, probably to make sure it was okay for her to hand over the baby, and Raleigh nodded. He wouldn't allow Yvette to take the newborn from the room, but he could see no harm in Yvette holding her. Thea eased the baby into Yvette's waiting arms.

Much as Thea had done on the ride to the hospital, Yvette pulled open the blanket and checked the baby. The little girl opened her eyes and looked out for a moment before she went back to sleep.

"Oh, she's perfect," Yvette said, and tears filled her eyes. She ran her fingers over the baby's dark brown hair. "Please tell me those kidnappers didn't hurt her."

"They didn't," Raleigh assured her, and he was about to fill her in on what the doctor had said, but he heard Alice in the hall.

"Stop right there," Alice warned someone.

That sent Raleigh hurrying to see what had caused

his deputy to say that, and he soon spotted the bulky, sandy-haired man trying to push his way past the deputy. "I'm Nick O'Hara," the man snarled. "I know my wife is here because I saw her come into the building. Where is she?"

"That's my husband," Yvette said on a rise of breath. She would have stepped out into the hall if Raleigh hadn't moved in front of her. "Stay put. One of the kidnappers is still at large, and he could come here."

That put a huge amount of concern in Yvette's eyes. She gave a shaky nod and stayed where she was. Raleigh stepped outside, his gaze connecting first with Nick and then with Alice. "Frisk him," he told Alice.

That earned him a glare from Nick, but Raleigh didn't care. Yvette had been checked for weapons when she'd been taken to the sheriff's office, and Raleigh wanted the same to happen to Nick.

"He's clean," Alice relayed when she'd finished patting him down, and she let go of the man so he could come into the room. Nick's glare was still razor-sharp when he looked at Raleigh and Thea. And the look continued when he turned to his wife.

"Nick," Yvette said, smiling. "It's our daughter. She's safe."

The man went closer, peering down at the baby's face, and he shook his head. "That's not our kid." He snapped back toward Raleigh. "I don't know what kind of game you're playing, but it won't work. You can't pass that kid off as mine."

Raleigh glanced at Yvette to see if she had a clue

what her husband was talking about, but she seemed just as confused as Raleigh. Thea, too, because she huffed.

"What are you talking about?" Thea asked.

"This," Nick snarled, and he whipped his phone from his pocket. He lifted it so they could see the picture of a baby on the screen. It was a blonde-haired newborn wrapped in a pink blanket.

Yvette shook her head. "Who is that? Why do you have that picture?"

"Because someone texted it to me about ten minutes ago. Probably the same person who called me from an unknown number a few seconds later and demanded a quarter-of-a-million-dollar ransom."

"A ransom?" Yvette repeated. "Why?"

Nick tipped his head to the baby in her arms. "Because that's not our kid." He took the little girl from his wife and handed her back to Thea. "The kidnappers still have our baby, and we need to find her now."

Chapter Five

Thea had been so sure that Raleigh and she would have answers by the time they left the hospital, but that hadn't happened. And to make matters worse, they had to deal with the possibility that the O'Hara newborn was still out there.

In the hands of kidnappers.

But if that was true, then whose baby was in Thea's arms?

Thea was hoping they'd learn that now that they were at the sheriff's office. Yvette clearly wanted to know the same thing, and for the past hour since they'd left the hospital, she'd kept eyeing the child as if she might snatch her back from Thea. Since Yvette had been giving her that same look from the moment her husband had delivered that bombshell, Thea doubted the woman would try to take the baby and run. Still, she was keeping watch just in case. Yvette definitely looked ready to come unglued.

Thankfully, the baby was staying calm. Now that she'd been fed and changed anyway. Thea had done that as well, figuring that she was perhaps the only person in the building who'd actually had any experience doing it. Plus, she wanted to do it. It felt safer having the baby next to her.

"If the kidnappers really had our daughter, they would have called back by now," Yvette muttered.

That wasn't the first time she'd said something similar, and like the other times, her husband ignored her. Instead, Nick kept his attention on Dalton, who was setting up a recording device in the squad room. A recorder that would be used when and if the kidnappers called back. Before that, Nick had been on the phone, working out arrangements for a loan from Yvette's grandfather. The grandfather had agreed, though the man was apparently too frail to come to Durango Ridge to give his granddaughter some emotional support.

Something that Yvette seemed to definitely need.

Thea knew how she felt. She was still on edge from the attack and Sonya's murder, but she had to tamp down her nerves and focus on the investigation. Just as Raleigh was doing. He had his phone sandwiched between his shoulder and ear as he spoke to someone at the lab. While he was doing that, he was also checking something on his computer.

Thea wanted to help, but Raleigh had already made it crystal clear that she was not to let the baby out of her sight, or arms. He'd been insistent, too, that she stay away from the windows in case their attacker returned. Thea had had no problem with that, but it was the reason that she—and therefore Yvette and Nick—had ended up in Raleigh's office.

Soon though—very soon—they'd need to figure out

if this second ransom demand was some kind of hoax. The baby in the photo Nick had shown them could be anyone's child, and this could be an attempt to milk the O'Hara's out of all that money. If so, it might work, too, since it was obvious that Nick and Yvette were planning on paying the demand.

When Raleigh finished his latest call, he brought his laptop to where Thea was seated, and he sank down in the chair next to her. "I had to have Alice call social services to tell them about the baby," he said, looking down at the newborn. "They're on the way here to take her."

That hit her a lot harder than Thea had expected, though Raleigh was right. There had been no choice about contacting them.

"What?" Yvette questioned. "You can't let them take her. Not until we're sure she's not ours."

"It's the law," Raleigh explained, "now that the baby's identity is in question."

Yvette shook her head and moved as if to take the baby, but her husband stepped in front of her. "This child has parents out there," he said. "Parents who are probably looking for her."

That was true, but there were no other missing baby reports. As a cop, that made Thea think the worst because if there was indeed a second baby, then the kidnappers could have murdered the parents when they took the child.

"But she could stay here with us until we sort it all out," Yvette argued. "And what about her safety? Can they protect her?"

"They know there's potential danger and will bring

in the marshals." Raleigh paused, groaned softly. "It's out of my hands."

Apparently, it had hit Raleigh hard, too. But a police station was no place for a newborn. Especially when they had no idea if she was even a target.

More tears sprang into Yvette's eyes. Obviously, she didn't want this baby out of her sight, but she quit arguing and sank back down into the chair.

"The courier arrived at the lab with the DNA swabs," Raleigh added a moment later. "It'll be a day or two though before we have the DNA results on the baby."

That wasn't a surprise, though Thea wished they could have them sooner. Yvette probably felt the same way. Maybe even Nick, too, since he hadn't protested about giving a sample of his DNA, even though he seemed pretty certain that this little girl wasn't his child.

Once Yvette had her attention back on her husband, Raleigh shifted the laptop so Thea could see the screen, and she immediately saw Marco's records. "He did get an early release," Raleigh pointed out. "He's been out nearly a month now."

Plenty of time to plan the attacks, the kidnapping and even Sonya's murder. But had he done that? Marco certainly had a criminal history. Four arrests for breaking and entering, robbery and even assault. Those were serious enough charges, considering they showed a pattern of illegal behavior, but nothing on the rap sheet jumped out that this man could be a killer.

Of course, maybe Sonya's murder hadn't been planned. Heck, maybe Marco hadn't even had a part in that if it had been premeditated. Everything was in question now because of the second ransom demand.

"Did Marco have the funds to put together something like this?" she asked.

Raleigh lifted his shoulder and set his laptop aside. "If he did, he had it stashed away somewhere, maybe even under an alias. But it wouldn't have taken that much cash—not really. The SUV could have been a rental—Alice is checking on that now. And the driver could have been one of Marco's cronies who was working for a share of the first ransom."

A ransom that he didn't get because the FBI had managed to freeze the account where Raleigh had transferred the money. That was good that he wouldn't be out any cash.

"Dr. Bryce Sheridan is coming in first thing tomorrow morning," Raleigh went on. "I spoke to him briefly, and he claims he only did Sonya and Hannah's in vitro procedures, that he had no contact with either of the women once they were pregnant."

Thea thought about that a moment. "But you're bringing him in anyway?"

"This is a murder investigation. We're in *leave no stone unturned* territory." He paused. "That's why my mother is coming in tomorrow, as well. Sonya worked for her for a while. You didn't know?" he asked, no doubt when he saw the surprise in her eyes.

Thea shook her head. "Sonya didn't mention it."

"It was a few years ago. I'm not sure exactly why Sonya quit or even if she was fired, but those are questions I need to ask my mother."

Apparently, he didn't want to do that unofficially, either, because it could make it seem as if he was giving her preferential treatment.

Nick's phone rang, the sound immediately getting everyone's attention. Raleigh and Yvette stood, and Dalton put his finger on the record button. But Nick shook his head when he glanced at the screen.

"Sorry, it's a business associate," Nick grumbled, and he let the call go to voice mail as he turned toward Raleigh. "Is this normal for the kidnappers to wait so long before calling back?"

Raleigh shrugged. "They could be doing this to put you even more on edge. Their logic could be the more frantic and desperate you are, the more you'll cooperate."

Thea hoped that was what was going on, but this didn't feel right. The O'Haras could pay the ransom only to discover the newborn with them was their child after all.

There were sounds of voices in the squad room, and Raleigh stepped in front of Thea and the baby. Protecting them again. But Thea realized this wasn't a threat when she recognized one of the voices. Her brother, Texas Ranger Griff Morris.

Thea got up and went to the door to look out, and she immediately spotted not only Griff but another familiar face. Rachel McCall Morris. Rachel wasn't only Griff's wife though.

She was also Warren's daughter and Raleigh's half sister.

There was a marshal standing behind her, and Thea

made the connection then. Rachel was a social worker, and she'd come here to take the baby.

"Raleigh," Griff greeted.

They'd met when Thea and Raleigh were dating, but Thea wasn't sure if Raleigh knew Rachel or not. Apparently, he did because he pulled back his shoulders and looked past Griff to stare at her.

The family resemblance was definitely there between the two, and Thea figured if there was anyone in the McCall family who could start mending the rift, it was Rachel. She looked like his kid sister. Plus, she was four months pregnant.

"I volunteered to do this," Rachel said, walking closer. She kept her eyes locked with Raleigh, too.

Even though Rachel and she were close friends, Thea could only guess what was going on in Rachel's mind. Part of her probably resented Raleigh because he was proof of Warren's affair, but then Rachel wasn't exactly on friendly terms with her father after news of that affair had ripped their family apart.

Rachel went to her, tearing her gaze from Raleigh so she could look at the baby. "Are you okay?" Rachel whispered to Thea, and she gave her a gentle hug.

"I've had better days," Thea whispered back.

Griff came to the doorway of the crowded office, and he took in everything with a sweeping glance before his attention settled on her. He didn't hug her, but Thea could see the concern in his eyes. Followed by the relief that she was okay.

"Anything from the kidnappers yet?" Griff asked.

She shook her head and gently transferred the baby

to Rachel's arms. Yvette was right there, watching their every move. And still crying.

"Can't you just wait with her here?" Yvette asked. "We might know something soon."

Soon was being optimistic. Rachel and the rest of them knew that. "We'll take good care of her, I promise. She'll be under guard from Marshal McKinney and a Texas Ranger."

Yvette wiped some tears from her cheek. "Where will you take her?"

Rachel looked at Griff to answer that. "To a safe house. And no, I won't be able to tell you the location," he added before Yvette could ask. "We'll keep Sheriff Lawton informed though, and if anything develops, I'm sure he'll pass it on to you."

It wasn't much of a surprise that Yvette didn't seem pleased about that, either, and Raleigh must have decided it was best not to have the woman around when Rachel and the others actually left with the baby.

"Go ahead and take the O'Haras and the recorder to the break room," Raleigh instructed Dalton. "Have the diner bring them over something to eat, too."

Of course, Yvette protested that, saying she didn't want to leave and that she wasn't hungry, but her husband put his arm around her waist to get her moving. Yvette kissed the little girl, but her husband barely spared the baby a glance before Dalton led them away.

"I'm guessing Nick O'Hara thinks there's no chance that this baby is the one their surrogate delivered?" Griff asked Raleigh.

"It appears that way." Raleigh kept his hard stare

on Nick until he was out of sight. "Either that or he's a jerk. I'm not sure which yet. Yvette admitted that he was having second thoughts about fatherhood."

That caused Griff to mumble some profanity.

Rachel adjusted the baby's blanket while she stepped closer to her brother. She opened her mouth and then closed it as if she'd changed her mind about what to say. "I'm glad Thea and you weren't hurt," Rachel finally said.

Raleigh nodded. Stared at her. Then he huffed. "Thanks for coming."

Even though the conversation was only a handful of words, it seemed to have set some kind of truce in motion. One that Thea was thankful for. It was a start, but she wasn't under any illusions that this would repair what she'd once had with Raleigh. No. Rachel hadn't known about her father's affair until it had come to light after his shooting. But Thea had known. And she'd kept it a secret. That was something Raleigh might never be able to get past.

When Rachel moved to the side, Griff came closer to Thea, giving her a once-over. The kind of look that only a big brother could manage. He respected her wishes to be a cop, but that didn't mean he didn't worry about her.

"You'll make sure she's okay?" Griff said to Raleigh.

Thea huffed and tapped her badge.

Griff huffed and motioned toward the stun gun marks on her neck.

She wanted to remind him that there were times when he'd been hurt, too, in the line of duty, but she didn't want to get into an argument with her hardheaded brother. Instead, she hugged him and gave the baby a goodbye kiss on the cheek.

Rachel turned to go but then stopped and looked at Raleigh again. "Maybe when this is over, we can meet for lunch or something. And yes, I know you don't like or trust us," she added before Raleigh could speak. "But I'm just as upset about what our father did as you are."

"Does that mean we're on the same side?" Raleigh asked, and it had some sarcasm in it. Some of the old wounds, too.

"Yes," Rachel said without hesitation. "And even if we weren't, we're still kin." She smiled and followed Griff out of the room.

"I don't need a family. Or siblings," Raleigh grumbled.

He didn't, but he had them whether he wanted them or not. Besides, one of those siblings might be able to help them with this investigation.

"Egan has the old case files on Hannah's murder," Thea reminded Raleigh. "If Sonya's murder is connected to hers, then it might not hurt to go through everything again." She paused, waiting for him to answer, but when he didn't say anything, she added, "I can ask Egan to send a copy here."

"No." That time Raleigh didn't hesitate. "I'll ask him myself. But you've read everything in Hannah's file. Other than using the same doctor, do they have anything concrete in common?"

Obviously, he was putting aside the nearly identical threats left at Sonya's and Hannah's crime scenes. The threat that mentioned Warren. Thea wanted to put it aside, too, for now anyway, since the latest one could be a ploy to throw them off track.

"No," she answered. "But maybe Dr. Bryce Sheridan is behind this. Maybe there was something illegal going on at the fertility clinic, and he wanted to cover it up?"

Raleigh made a sound of agreement so quickly that he'd obviously already considered that. "But the murders happened a year apart. That's a long time for Dr. Sheridan to wait to cover up something. Unless, of course, he's committed several different crimes." He tipped his head toward the break room. "Right now though, Nick's high up on my list of persons of interest."

She agreed. The man certainly seemed to be anxious to hear from the kidnappers, but it also felt like there was an emotional disconnect. He could be that way though because his marriage was falling apart over his wife's insistence on having a child.

Raleigh dragged in a long breath. "I need to get back to Marco's rap sheet, and then I can make arrangements for a place for you to stay. Unless you want me to take you to the McCall Ranch."

"No." She didn't have to even think about that. "If the gunman that was in the SUV comes after me again, I don't want him to follow me to the ranch. Warren's still recovering from his injuries, and he could get killed trying to protect me."

She wanted to kick herself for putting it that way. It had to be a reminder that Warren had never done anything for Raleigh other than keeping the secret that he was his father. Raleigh had learned the truth about that only after Warren's affair with Raleigh's mother had been exposed.

"You have several people willing to protect you," Raleigh said.

She looked up at him just as he looked down at her. "Yes. But don't listen to what Griff told you. There's no need for you to make sure I'm okay." She added that just in case Raleigh considered himself one of those *several people*.

He continued to stare at her, and that's when Thea realized she was probably standing too close to him. She went to step back, but he took hold of her arm, keeping her in place.

"I think your brother was smart to tell me what he did," Raleigh said. "I believe you're in danger. I believe the driver of that SUV will come after you again. Why, I don't know, but Marco made it pretty clear that you were the target. And even if you're the target only to make us believe it's connected to Warren, that won't stop you from being gunned down."

She knew that, of course, but it sent a chill through her to hear it spelled out like that. Thea hadn't meant for her mouth to tremble and definitely hadn't wanted Raleigh to see it.

"Just because you're a cop, it doesn't mean you shouldn't be scared," he went on. "You should be. And while I understand you not wanting to go to the McCall Ranch so you can keep Warren safe, you'll need to be someplace where you have backup."

Thea clamped her teeth over her bottom lip for just a moment until she could regain her bearing. "I could go back to my office." Egan would make sure she had someone to help protect her, and he would do that even if it stretched his manpower thin. "Then I could come back in the morning when you question your mother and the doctor."

"You'll need a protection detail for the drive back and forth, too."

More manpower. But Raleigh's tone seemed to suggest something else. "You don't want me here for the interviews?"

"No. I do. You know more about Hannah's case than I do, and you know Warren. You might hear something that helps us figure this out." He paused, groaned softly. "If and when we eventually make it out of here tonight, you could stay at my place. It's not far."

"With you?" she blurted out.

The corner of his mouth lifted, but the slight smile didn't last long. "We're former lovers. I can't change that. But I don't want it to get in the way of us doing what needs to be done."

Neither did she, but Thea had to give this some more thought. She'd been to Raleigh's horse ranch and knew his mom wouldn't be there. Alma had her own home and ranch just up the road from his. But still, she'd be under the same roof, and the attraction between them was still there. It was for her anyway.

Thea was so caught up in her own thoughts that the sound of the knock behind her nearly caused her to gasp. She whirled around, but it wasn't the threat that her body had believed it might be. It was Raleigh's deputy Alice, and even though the deputy didn't pose any danger, Thea could tell from her expression that something was wrong.

"Raleigh, you need to hear this." Alice was carrying a laptop that she sat on Raleigh's desk. "I had all of Sonya's recordings of her phone conversations transferred to an audio file that I could share with the lab, and I found something."

That definitely got Thea's and Raleigh's attention.

"It's the last one Sonya recorded," Alice continued. "Unfortunately, they're not date stamped, and she doesn't mention a date or time, so I don't know when the call came in."

Thea and Raleigh both moved closer to the laptop when Alice pressed the play button. It didn't take long for Thea to hear Sonya's voice.

"I swear I didn't know," Sonya said, her voice trembling. "I went in for the in vitro, and I thought that's what I got."

The sense of dread washed over Thea. Because obviously something had gone wrong at the clinic. Or at least Sonya thought something had.

"I'm not sure I can go through with this," Sonya went on. "Now that I know the baby is actually mine, how could I give her up?"

Oh, mercy. Yes, something had indeed gone wrong, and Raleigh was clearly just as stunned as she was.

"Who is she talking to?" Raleigh asked Alice.

But it wasn't necessary for the deputy to answer because the person spoke.

"We had an agreement," the other woman snapped. Thea easily recognized her voice, too.

It was Yvette.

"You're not backing out of our deal," Yvette insisted. "I've paid you plenty of money, thousands, and I'm not going to be punished because the clinic messed up." Unlike Sonya's voice, Yvette's wasn't shaking, but the anger came through loud and clear. "One way or another, Sonya, you will give me that child."

Chapter Six

At least Raleigh didn't have far to go to confront Yvette with what he'd just heard. And he would confront her and demand to know what the heck was going on.

With Thea and Alice right behind him, he went to the break room, where he immediately spotted Dalton and Nick seated at the table. Yvette was pacing, and her gaze zoomed to them when Raleigh stepped into the room.

"Did the kidnapper call you?" she blurted out. She continued to study his expression. "Oh, God. Did something happen to the baby?"

"The baby's fine," Raleigh assured her, "but I'm thinking you might want to have your lawyer come out here."

Yvette pulled back her shoulders. "What are you talking about?"

"This," he said. Raleigh had the laptop in his hands, and he rewound the recording to the last part of the conversation.

One way or another, Sonya, you will give me that child.

Yvette gasped and stormed toward him as if she were

about to take the laptop, but Raleigh handed it to Thea in case he had to restrain Yvette.

"Where did you get that?" Yvette demanded. It was the same angry voice she'd used to threaten Sonya.

Before Raleigh asked her anything, he read Yvette her rights. Obviously, that didn't go over well, and her husband went to her side.

"What's this all about?" Nick asked as he volleyed glances between Yvette and Raleigh.

Raleigh just waited for Yvette to answer.

"Oh, God." Yvette pressed her fingers to her mouth a moment. And she started crying again.

But those tears didn't have the same heart-tugging effect they'd had on him earlier. Judging from Thea's huff, she felt the same way.

"Sonya recorded your whole conversation," Raleigh told the crying woman.

That wasn't exactly the truth. It was only a partial recording. Since Yvette didn't know that though, he was hoping she'd fill in the blanks. Maybe along with confessing that she was the one who'd set up this deadly chain of events.

"What's going on," Nick growled, and this time the demand was aimed at his wife. "What did you do?"

Yvette snapped toward him, her eyes suddenly wide. She started shaking her head. "I didn't kill Sonya if that's what you're suggesting."

"Then what the hell did you do?" Nick asked, taking the question right out of Raleigh's mouth.

Even with all of them staring at her and waiting, Yvette didn't answer right away. Still shaking her head, still crying, she sank down into the chair. "Sonya called me this morning and told me she'd found out something."

She looked up at Raleigh as if pleading with him not to make her explain this, but he motioned for her to keep talking. But Yvette had already given him something critical. The timing of the call. It meant the call could have been the trigger for Yvette to send in kidnappers to get the baby.

Yvette swallowed hard before she continued. "Sonya said she got an anonymous tip that there'd been a serious mix-up when she had the in vitro procedure. The person claimed that my stored eggs were lost prior to fertilization, so the clinic decided to do an artificial insemination on Sonya instead."

Raleigh watched Nick as he processed that. It took him several long moments. "Are you saying the baby is Sonya's?"

Yvette nodded. "And yours. The baby is yours," she quickly repeated. She got to her feet and took hold of his arms when he cursed and tried to move away. "It doesn't matter to me that she's not my biological child. I'll still love her. We can still have the child we've always wanted."

Nick cursed some more and threw off her grip with more force than necessary. "A child *you've* always wanted," he corrected in a snarl. He groaned, squeezed his eyes shut and put his hands on the sides of his head.

The man was clearly shaken by this and was probably seeing the irony. He hadn't especially wanted a child but had apparently fathered one. And Yvette wasn't the biological mother.

It took several more moments for the shock to wear off enough for Nick to whirl back around and face his wife. "What did you do? Did you hire those kidnappers?"

"No!" Yvette certainly didn't hesitate, and she repeated the denial to Thea and Raleigh. "I was upset when I said that to Sonya, but I would have never done anything to hurt the baby or her."

Maybe. But Raleigh still wasn't convinced. "Are there two babies?"

"I don't know. I swear, I don't."

Raleigh had to add another unspoken *maybe* to that. "Who told Sonya about what had gone on at the clinic?"

"I told you already that it was an anonymous tip. Whoever it was sent her results of an amniocentesis to prove it. That's a test of the amniotic fluid around the baby. It can tell if there's something wrong." Yvette swallowed hard again. "And it can also tell the baby's DNA."

Interesting. Raleigh looked at Thea to get her take on this, and she was staring at Yvette. "Why was a test like that done? Was Sonya having medical problems?"

"She'd got an infection early on in the pregnancy, and the fertility clinic had her do the test just to make sure. We never heard back from them, so we assumed all was well."

That didn't mesh with what Dr. Sheridan had told them, that he hadn't had any involvement with Hannah or Sonya after the in vitro procedures. That was almost certainly a lie, one that Raleigh would definitely question him about. But it was possible that someone else in the clinic was responsible for the test and the botched procedure.

"I can't believe you didn't tell me this," Nick said, the anger etched all over his face. "And now Sonya's dead, and we don't know where the hell her baby is. *My baby*," he emphasized.

Yeah, and they didn't know if Yvette was responsible. It was time to move this past the chatting stage and make it a full-fledged interview. Before Raleigh did that though, he wanted to talk to Dr. Sheridan, and as late as it already was, that wasn't going to happen until morning.

"We're holding you for questioning," Raleigh told Yvette. "You aren't leaving the sheriff's office until I have some answers."

"Uh, you want me to put her in a holding cell?" Dalton asked.

If Nick was the least bit concerned about that happening, he didn't show it. In fact, he was looking at his wife with disgust. However, Yvette was definitely concerned.

"But I didn't do anything wrong," she practically shouted.

"You obstructed justice by not telling me the truth in a murder investigation," Raleigh explained. "The murder of a woman you hired as a surrogate. And now I have a recording of you arguing with that very woman just hours before she was killed."

"I didn't kill her." Now it was a shout, and she repeated it to her husband.

Nick huffed again. "You lied to me, too," he said after getting his teeth unclenched. "Hell, you even gave the cops a DNA sample to compare to the baby they found. You did that even though you knew you weren't going to be a match."

She tried to take hold of him again, but he pushed her away. "I thought once you learned the child was yours, that you'd love her. And that we would still be able to raise her. It doesn't matter that she's not a child of my own blood. She would have been *our* child. She still can be."

The anger tightened Nick's face so much that it was obvious he was having trouble reining in his temper. He cursed, groaned and went to stand in the doorway. "I don't even know if there's another baby. Or any real kidnappers." He kept going despite Yvette's continued denials. "Is there somewhere else I can wait for a kidnapper's call? Someplace where my *wife* won't be?"

Well, at least the man was willing to hang around in case there truly was a kidnapper. At this point, Raleigh had no idea if there was one, or if this was part of Yvette's scheme to cover up her crime.

But that didn't make sense.

If Yvette had hired thugs to murder Sonya, then why would there be a second baby? Maybe the thugs had gone rogue and were now trying to milk as much money out of this situation as possible.

"Do you and your wife have joint bank accounts?" Raleigh asked Nick.

Nick nodded. For a moment it seemed as if he was going to ask why, but then his mouth tightened. "You want to examine them to see if she withdrew funds for this nightmare that's going on. Well, you're welcome to do that. I'll get you the account numbers and the passwords. In the morning, I'll call the bank and tell them you can have access to our safe-deposit box. There should be some family jewelry and cash in there."

He figured it was Nick's anger at his wife that was making him so cooperative, but Raleigh was thankful for it. This would save him from getting a court order and a search warrant.

"Take Mr. O'Hara to an interview room," Raleigh instructed Dalton. "Set up the recorder in there in case a kidnapper does call. The night deputies will be in soon so you can turn things over to them."

Dalton nodded, immediately picked up his equipment and started leading Nick out of the break room. Yvette didn't follow, but she did start sobbing again.

"Keep her here and instruct the night deputies to lock her up if she tries to leave," Raleigh added to Alice, and then he turned to Yvette. "Remember that part about you having a right to an attorney. You might need it."

Since that only caused Yvette's sobbing to get worse, Raleigh led Thea back to his office. "You really believe she had Sonya killed?" Thea asked.

"Maybe. And maybe not intentionally." He glanced at Alice's laptop. "I want to go through all the recordings Sonya left. I need to know who gave her that anonymous tip. I'd also like to see if there's something to prove why she started the recordings in the first place."

While he was at it, Raleigh was also hoping he could find a connection between Yvette and Marco. The bank records could possibly help with that. If not, at least he would know if there'd been any recent cash withdrawals that Nick couldn't account for. If there was something like that, then it would be another circumstantial piece of evidence against Yvette.

"How much did Sonya know about Hannah's murder?" Raleigh asked Thea. "Did she know about the message that'd been left at the crime scene?"

There was no need for him to clarify which message because it was no doubt etched in their memories. *This is for Sheriff Warren McCall.*

Thea's forehead bunched up a moment while she gave that some thought. "Probably. When I told Sonya about Hannah and her using the same doctor, Sonya did an internet check to see if there were any other similarities between them."

Then yes, Sonya would have known about the message and could have mentioned it to Yvette. Yvette, in turn, could have had her hired henchmen write that on Sonya's wall to throw suspicion off herself. But there was plenty of suspicion on the woman right now.

Thea tipped her head to the laptop. "If you get me a copy of Sonya's audio recordings, I can go through them, too. I might hear something that I can connect to a conversation I had with her."

Good idea. They could work on that until they found out if Yvette's lawyer was going to show tonight. If he did, then he could start the interview. He still had the kidnapper-ransom issue to deal with, too, if the guy ever called back.

"I'll get you a laptop and the recordings," Raleigh said, heading out of his office.

With a deputy still at Sonya's house and with Dalton and Alice tied up, that only left him with two deputies in the squad room, Miguel Sanchez and Zeb Hooper. Miguel had his phone in his hand, and he was already making his way to Raleigh.

"Sheriff Egan McCall just found an abandoned vehicle on the outskirts of McCall Canyon," Miguel said. "It's a blue SUV matching the description of the one used in your attack."

Good. Because now they could process it for any evidence. Though he doubted it was a coincidence that the vehicle had been found in Warren's town. No. This could be another attempt to connect the murders to him.

Or maybe there really was a connection.

If so, Raleigh needed to find it before Thea and he landed again in the path of a would-be killer.

"There's more," Miguel added a moment later. "There was a dead body in the SUV, and according to his ID, it's someone you know."

Miguel handed him a note with the name, and the moment Raleigh saw it, he cursed.

Hell.

THEA WISHED SHE could turn her mind off for just a couple of seconds. She was exhausted from the spent adrenaline, the late hour and the events of the day, but she couldn't stop the thoughts from coming.

Another body.

And this time, it was Dr. Bryce Sheridan. He'd died from a single gunshot wound to the head that appeared to be self-inflicted.

Appeared.

Egan wasn't convinced it was a suicide though, and therefore neither was Thea. Egan was a good cop, and he had probably seen something with the positioning of the body or the gun that had made him believe this could be a setup.

Until Egan had found the body in the SUV, the doctor had been a person of interest in Sonya's murder. He was also someone that Raleigh and she had counted on to give them answers about Sonya's botched in vitro. But now that he was dead, they would have to wait until morning to get into the fertility clinic so they could access anything they could find.

Maybe before then, Raleigh and she could even manage to get some sleep. But Thea immediately dismissed that notion when she stepped into Raleigh's house. A different set of thoughts hit her then.

Scalding-hot memories of the nights she'd spent here with Raleigh.

Great. Just what she didn't need when she already felt so beaten down from the fatigue. So she had no choice but to stand there and let the memories run their course. Even when the most vivid images and sensations faded though, the thoughts still lingered.

Raleigh had kissed her right in the foyer. That'd been the start of some frantic foreplay that had led them straight to his bed. In those days, their whole relationship had seemed frantic. As if they were starved for each other and couldn't get enough. But that had all come crashing down when Raleigh had found out she'd kept Warren's secret about the affair.

And the secret that he was Warren's son.

When Thea's hand started to hurt, she glanced down and realized she had a too-tight grip on the overnight bag that Griff had packed for her and then sent to Raleigh's office. A bag that hopefully contained the things on the list she'd given him since she'd need a change of clothes and toiletries.

Too bad the bag wouldn't contain something to make her immune to Raleigh.

And speaking of Raleigh, he came in behind her, closing the door and setting the security system. He looked at her, and maybe because he saw something in her eyes, there was suddenly some alarm in his expression. Then he got it.

"Oh," he grumbled. "Yeah."

Thea could practically see the wall he'd just put up between them. A wall that hadn't been there as they'd worked together on the recordings and while waiting for the kidnapper to call back.

A call that hadn't come.

But now that they were back here, at the scene of their affair, then he probably knew it wasn't a good idea for them to be so chummy. With the attraction still simmering between them, even chumminess could lead to sex. Heck, maybe breathing could.

Another couple that definitely wouldn't be getting chummy tonight was Nick and Yvette. Nick had refused to leave the sheriff's office because he wanted to be there in case the kidnapper did call. Since her lawyer wasn't arriving until morning, Yvette was still in the break room, where she'd stay until Raleigh either released her or charged her with obstruction of justice. Maybe even murder for hire, along with other assorted felonies.

Without the evidence that Dr. Sheridan could have possibly given them, Raleigh was in a wait-and-see mode. There was a lot riding on those banking records because even if Yvette was guilty, Thea doubted the woman would just confess to the growing list of crimes.

It was also possible they'd get something from the crime lab. But they, too, had a mountain of stuff to process. Not just any possible evidence they'd gathered from Sonya and the woods where her body had been found, but also the baby's clothes and carrier. And now the SUV might turn up something, too.

Unless...

"What if Dr. Sheridan was the gunman who shot at us from the SUV?" she asked. It was a question that had been going through her head, along with all those other thoughts, and she was certain that Raleigh had considered it, too.

"I'm sure your boss will have the body tested for gunshot residue," he said, and he didn't add as much venom to the word *boss* as he probably could have, considering that her boss, Egan, was also his half brother. "If Sheridan has GSR on him, then we'll know he fired a gun."

True, but it wouldn't necessarily prove he was the

one who'd tried to kill them. Someone could have set up the doctor.

"I can call Egan if you like," she offered.

Raleigh paused as if considering that, but he certainly didn't decline. That's because finding the killer was far more important than their family troubles. "Yeah, if I haven't heard from him by morning."

"If Egan has anything, he'll call," she assured him. "He's a cop through and through like you."

Raleigh opened his mouth, maybe to say he was nothing like Egan, but then he stopped and dragged in a long breath. "I talked to him earlier when you were in the bathroom at the sheriff's office." He paused and gave her a flat look. "He told me to make sure that you were okay."

Thea groaned. Good grief. That was almost identical to what her brother had told Raleigh. "They forget that I'm a cop with just as much training as they have." Well, almost as much.

"No, they remember that. They care about you and are worried because I haven't been able to ID the killer."

She hated that Raleigh was putting all of this on his shoulders. "If I'm the target, then I'm the one responsible for this. I'm the one who dragged you and all of your deputies into the path of a killer."

A possibility that ate away at her as much as Sonya's death. Thea prayed she wasn't the reason for that, too.

The one saving grace in all of this was that the baby was safe. Griff had let them know that when they'd arrived at the safe house, and there'd been no incidents along the way. Now they needed to make sure there wasn't a second baby out there who needed to be rescued from the monsters who'd taken her.

"You should try to get some rest," Raleigh said, pulling her out of her thoughts. "You remember where the guest room is?"

Thea nodded. She remembered though she'd never actually been in it. Whenever she'd stayed over, she'd always been in Raleigh's bed. With both of them naked.

Probably best not to remember that now though.

"I'll need to get back to the office by seven," Raleigh added, already heading in the direction of his bedroom. But he stopped when his phone rang.

Thea didn't groan, but considering the late hour, she figured this was probably bad news. Still, she hoped it was merely an update on the investigation.

"It's Miguel," Raleigh mumbled when he looked at the screen. He hit the answer button and put the call on speaker. It didn't take long for Thea to hear his deputy's voice.

"A detective from San Antonio PD just called," Miguel said. "A woman, Madison Travers, just walked in and confessed to botching the in vitro procedure done on Sonya. And this woman says she believes she knows who tried to kill you."

Chapter Seven

Raleigh wished he'd managed to get a little more sleep. Two hours didn't seem nearly enough, considering the hellish day he was about to face. Still, he was glad he'd managed to get any sleep at all since he'd spent a good deal of the night on the phone with SAPD and his deputies.

Unfortunately, he'd spent some of the night thinking about Thea, too.

He cursed himself for that. He didn't have the time or mental energy to rehash the past, but that's exactly what he'd done anyway.

Having Thea under the same roof with him was a bad reminder of when they'd been lovers. Worse, Raleigh was certain it was the same for her. He hadn't missed the heated looks she'd given him. Also hadn't missed her expression that told him she was just as frustrated as he was about this.

He forced his attention back where it belonged—on the drive to the sheriff's office. No one was following Thea and him, but he needed to make sure it stayed that way. He needed to get to work in one piece so he could question Madison Travers. At least that was one of the things he had to do.

But at the moment the woman was his top priority.

She had not only confessed to the in vitro snafu but also claimed to know who wanted to kill them. Unfortunately, she hadn't wanted to share that info with the San Antonio cops but had insisted instead on talking to Raleigh. He very much wanted to talk to Madison, too, but Raleigh hoped this wasn't some kind of ruse to get at Thea and him again. That's why he hadn't taken Thea to San Antonio to question the woman. Instead, SAPD had waited until morning to bring Madison to Durango Ridge, and she was now waiting for them in an interview room.

Thea was keeping watch as well, even though she was on the phone with Egan to get an update on the Dr. Sheridan murder investigation. She hadn't put the call on speaker, maybe because she hadn't wanted to emphasize to her boss that she was in a cruiser with his illegitimate half brother. But judging from the way her forehead was bunched up, she didn't like what she was hearing from Egan.

"A problem?" Raleigh asked as soon as she'd finished the call.

"No. But it wasn't the answers we wanted."

Hell. As much as he disliked the idea of having his half brother connected to this case, Raleigh had hoped that Egan would be able to clear up some things. Raleigh would take all the help he could get.

"There was gunshot residue on Dr. Sheridan's jacket but not his hands," Thea continued a moment later.

"Egan thinks the pattern indicates that it was transferred from the actual shooter to the doctor."

And that meant someone had tried to make it look as if Sheridan had killed himself in the SUV. If the doctor had actually done that, then the GSR should have been on his hands.

"So he was murdered," Raleigh concluded.

Thea nodded. "Egan said the placement of the gun was wrong, too. Sheridan was left-handed, and the gun was in his right."

So they were dealing with a sloppy killer. Or one that had panicked.

"There's more," she went on. "One of Sheridan's neighbors saw him yesterday afternoon with two men that she didn't recognize. She said she didn't think anything of it at the time, but after she heard about his death, she called SAPD. She didn't see a gun or anything, but she thought the men looked menacing."

"Did she give the cops a description of the men?" he asked.

Another nod just as her phone dinged with a message. "They're having her work with a sketch artist, too, so we might have something we can put out to the media."

That was a long shot, but it was all he had right now.

"There was a picture on Sheridan's phone," Thea went on when he pulled to a stop in front of the sheriff's office. "Egan just texted it to me. It's the same photo that the kidnappers sent Nick."

She showed him the photo on the screen, and it was indeed a match. But what did it mean? Had Sheridan been involved with the second kidnapping? Or had it all been a hoax? Raleigh was thinking hoax since the kidnapper still hadn't called back. Although if Sheridan was the kidnapper, that would explain why Nick had never gotten a call back.

"I'm hoping one of your deputies made lots of coffee," Thea grumbled as they hurried inside.

Raleigh was hoping the same thing, though it was asking a lot of mere caffeine to get rid of the headache he already had. The headache got worse when he immediately saw Nick and Yvette coming toward them. There was a guy in a suit behind Yvette. Her lawyer, no doubt, and he cut ahead of the pair. He didn't stop until he was practically right in Raleigh's face.

"You either need to charge my client or let her go," the man insisted. According to the business card he handed Raleigh, his name was Vernon Cutler. And yeah, he was a lawyer all right.

Raleigh was just ornery enough to say he was charging her, but he looked at Dalton to see if anything had come back on the bank records or the safe-deposit box.

Dalton shook his head. "If Mrs. O'Hara paid off hired guns, she didn't use those bank accounts, and there was nothing missing from the safe-deposit box. Mr. O'Hara gave us a list of the contents, and everything was there."

"What about any activity on Yvette's cell phone?" Raleigh pressed. He'd asked his deputies to check that to see if there were any irregularities.

"She made eight calls to Sonya yesterday. Two before the body was discovered and the rest came after."

"I call Sonya every day," Yvette argued. *"Called,"* she corrected, her voice cracking. "When she didn't answer, I kept trying to reach her because I was worried about her."

Raleigh heard every word of that, but it wasn't those calls that interested him. "Did she have any new contacts over the past week or so?" he pressed.

"No," Dalton answered. "Every call on her phone checked out."

That didn't mean the woman hadn't used a disposable cell phone, or a burner as it was called, but if she had, there was no proof.

"We got the search warrant for the O'Haras' house," Dalton explained. "Miguel's on the way there now to go through it with SAPD."

Good. But a search like that could take hours, and Raleigh doubted they'd find a murder weapon or anything else incriminating that Yvette had just happened to leave lying around.

So basically the only thing Raleigh had against the woman was the recorded argument that she'd had with Sonya. A recording that likely wouldn't be admissible in court since Sonya hadn't informed Yvette that the conversation was being recorded. Of course, the obstruction of justice charge was still on the table, but Raleigh had other more immediate issues.

Madison Travers, for one.

And there was his mother. He saw Alma in his office with her lawyer and longtime friend, Simon Lindley. Neither looked especially happy, and Simon was likely going to pitch a fit that Raleigh was questioning Alma.

"Your client is free to go," Raleigh told Vernon Cutler. "For now," he tacked on to that.

"But I don't want to go," Yvette said. "I want to stay here in case the kidnapper calls."

"You'll have to wait elsewhere," Raleigh told her. "This place is getting pretty crowded."

"Come on," Yvette's lawyer insisted, but he had to practically drag the woman out of the building.

"You should probably try to get some rest, too," Raleigh told Nick. No way though would he force the man to go.

"I managed a nap in the break room. I'd like to stay just in case."

Raleigh nodded and was about to make his way to the coffeepot, but then he saw Thea coming toward him with two cups of coffee in her hand. She was already sipping one and handed the other to him. He thanked her and downed as much of it as he could, even though it was scalding hot. Thea seemed to be doing the same thing.

"Thanks," he said to Thea, and he glanced at his mom. She wasn't glaring. Alma had a sad, how-could-you-do-this-to-me expression on her face. It was very effective at making Raleigh feel like a jerk and a bad son. But since he was a son with a badge, he had no choice about bringing her in.

"I didn't know about the search warrant," Nick said.

Since Nick had been cooperative so far, Raleigh hadn't expected to hear or see any hesitation, but he sure as heck saw it now. "Why? Is that a problem?"

Nick didn't jump to answer that. "No." But that didn't

sound like the truth. And it was something Raleigh would need to dig a little deeper into once he dealt with the other issues. However, he kept his eyes on Nick as he headed back down the hall. The man also took out his phone and made a call.

"You think he doesn't want us to find something in his house?" Thea asked. She'd obviously picked up on the bad vibe, too.

"Maybe." And maybe the guy was just acting punchy because he was exhausted. Something that Raleigh totally understood.

"I'll have Dalton do the interview with my mother," Raleigh explained to Thea, "but I need to speak to her first. You don't have to be part of that unless you're a glutton for punishment."

"Consider me a glutton." She gave him a half smile, but then she quickly got serious again. "I want to hear what anyone has to say about what's gone on. We need to catch Sonya's killer."

Yeah, they did, but he wished he'd had more sleep and more coffee before dealing with this. His mom was only half the problem. She was usually civil, even when Raleigh was calling her into question, but Simon could be a protective SOB. Part of Raleigh was pleased that Simon was so protective, but sometimes that got in the way.

Raleigh was certain it would now, too.

"Why are you doing this?" Simon snapped the moment Raleigh went into his office.

He looked Simon straight in the eyes. "Because a woman was murdered and a baby was kidnapped. A second baby might be missing, as well. I'm sure my mother would want to help with that in any way she could."

"I would." Alma got to her feet, and he saw the concern in her eyes. "Are the babies all right?"

"One of them is. She's with social services. I'm not sure about the other. That's what I'm trying to find out." Along with learning if the still-kidnapped baby even existed.

"I'll help any way I can," his mother said, and then she looked past him and at Thea. They'd met when Thea and he had been dating and while his mom had still been with Warren, and his mother had been friendly to Thea then.

Not so much now though.

Alma didn't glare at Thea or anything, but she quickly turned back to Raleigh, putting her attention solely on him. "You think I know something that could help with this case?" Alma asked.

Simon huffed. "You're a person of interest, Alma. Because Sonya worked for you, and you fired her."

This was the first Raleigh was hearing about the firing, so he stared at his mother, waiting for her to fill him in.

"You really don't think I'd kill Sonya because of what went on two years ago?" His mother patted her chest as if to steady her heart.

Raleigh answered that with a question of his own. "Why'd you fire her?"

"Because she stole some money from Alma, that's why," Simon barked.

"Because she *might* have stolen it," Alma corrected. "Some money went missing. And no, I didn't feel the need to tell you. I handled it myself."

"She didn't tell you because you would have arrested Sonya," Simon interrupted. "Especially if you'd heard the way Sonya talked to your mother. She yelled at her."

Sonya did have a temper, but he hadn't known about her being a possible thief. He hoped that was the extent of the woman's criminal behavior. He definitely didn't want her connected to the mix-up at the fertility clinic, but that was something he could ask Madison Travers.

"Sonya yelled at you?" Thea repeated.

His mother nodded, but Raleigh saw Simon's eyes narrow. "Oh, no. You're not going to pin Sonya's murder on Alma."

Maybe not, but Simon had just provided a motive for his mother to be part of this. It wasn't a strong motive, but it wasn't one he could just overlook, either.

"Did you bring him here?" Simon snapped.

It took Raleigh a moment to realize that Simon was looking over his shoulder. And his attention was on the man who'd just walked into the squad room.

Warren.

Hell.

"I need another cup of coffee for this," Raleigh grumbled, and he turned around to face the man. "It's not a good time," he warned Warren.

Warren acknowledged that with a nod. "I just wanted to check on Thea. And you."

Raleigh hadn't wanted to be included in that, though

Warren's concern did seem genuine. As genuine as his mother's hurt and Simon's anger. Raleigh's anger, too.

"Come on, Alma." Simon took her by the arm. "We're leaving."

Alma didn't put up a fuss about that, but Raleigh had to. "You can take her to the interview room, but you can't leave. Not just yet. I need you to give Dalton your statement about the time Sonya worked for you," he added to his mother.

"She can do that another time, when he's not here," Simon spat out, his venom obviously aimed at Warren.

"I'll go," Warren said.

"No." Alma spoke up. "Simon and I can go to the interview room." She aimed a sharp look at Simon. "Let's just get this done."

Raleigh was glad that his mom had stood up to Simon. It was something she had to do often since Simon always seemed to be trying to control her. Not just in legal situations but in the rest of her life, too.

"Thanks," Raleigh told his mom. He didn't say anything to Simon, but the man glared at Thea, Warren and him on the way out of the office and all the way to the interview room.

"I didn't mean to cause trouble," Warren said. "I was just worried about Thea." He had his hands crammed in his pockets, but he looked as if he wanted to hug her.

"I'm all right," Thea assured him. "I'll be back in McCall Canyon soon, but Raleigh and I need to work this case."

Warren nodded and took out his phone from his pocket. "I've been studying it, too, and I know you probably don't want my help," he added to Raleigh, "but I might have found something."

Warren showed them the photos on his phone. Photos that Raleigh knew well because they were side-by-side shots of the two scrawled warnings that had been left at the scenes of Hannah's and Sonya's murders.

"Egan got the second photo of Sonya's wall from the lab," Warren explained. "He showed it to me since I'm still working to solve Hannah's case."

"*Unofficially* working," Raleigh automatically snapped, but then he waved that off.

He didn't like Warren, but if he'd been a retired cop with an unsolved murder, he would have kept at it, as well. Especially if he'd known the victim the way that Warren had known Hannah. This was personal for Warren, and Raleigh couldn't fault the man for putting his heart into the investigation.

"I have a friend who's a handwriting expert," Warren went on, "and I had him compare the two messages. As you know, it's hard to do a handwriting analysis on something like this, but he believes it's a match, that the same person wrote both messages."

Raleigh had another look at the photos and the warning. *This is for Sheriff Warren McCall.* They certainly looked the same.

"The killer could have used the same hired thug for both," Raleigh pointed out. "It wouldn't have been Marco though since he was in jail a year ago."

Warren made a sound of agreement. "But what if the killer himself wrote these? If this is someone with a grudge this big against me, maybe he or she wanted to do it himself?"

Raleigh nearly snapped at the addition of "she" because it referred to his mother. And while Raleigh couldn't see Alma killing two women, maybe someone close to her had.

Someone like Simon.

"I'll make sure Dalton asks Simon his whereabouts for both murders," Raleigh assured Warren.

"You really think Simon could be a killer?" Thea asked.

Raleigh lifted his shoulder. "I think he loves my mother enough to do pretty much anything. He was questioned about your shooting," he added to Warren. And even though Simon's name had been cleared, at the time he had been at the top of Raleigh's suspect list.

Warren certainly knew that because he'd probably studied every aspect of that investigation. "I... We," he amended, "need to get Hannah's killer so we can try to locate her missing child. The baby would be a year old now, and the biological parents need answers. *I* need answers. Maybe I'll get them if you can find who murdered Sonya."

Raleigh intended to do everything possible to make sure the killer was caught. "Sonya's murder could have been a copycat," he reminded Warren. "If so, then the person who left that message on her wall could have studied the one on Hannah's and made sure the signatures were similar."

"Yes," Warren readily admitted. "And if so, then I've wasted your time. Either way, catch this SOB."

Warren brushed his hand along Thea's arm, and then he headed out, leaving Raleigh with a boatload of feelings that he didn't want. He definitely didn't want to feel anything but disgust for this married man who'd carried on a secret affair with his mother.

Thea shut the door after Warren left. "Are you okay?" she asked. Since that simple question could cover a lot of territory, Raleigh just waited for her to add more. "I know it can't be easy for you to be around Warren."

"It's not." And that was all he intended to say about it.

But it apparently wasn't all that Thea intended to do. She slipped her arm around him and eased him to her. "Yes, I know this isn't smart, but if anyone needs a hug right now, it's you."

The cowboy in him wouldn't admit that, but the hug did feel, well, good. Comforting, even. At least it did for a couple of seconds, and then it turned to something else when that brainless part of him behind the zipper of his jeans reminded him that this was Thea.

And that he still wanted her.

He pulled back, intending to step away, but he made the mistake of looking down at her. Oh, man. It felt as if the air had caught fire. Something was certainly blazing, and he made the mistake even worse by leaning in and brushing his mouth over hers.

That sure didn't help cool the heat any.

And even though he realized that it wasn't helping, he didn't stop. He would have just stood there and kept on kissing her until things went well beyond the comforting-hug stage. Thankfully though, Thea seemed to still have some common sense because she's the one who moved away from him.

"I was right," she said, her voice silky and filled with breath. "That wasn't smart."

Yeah, but it was good. Which, of course, made it bad. Especially bad because he had other things he should be doing. Things that could end up keeping Thea out of the path of a killer.

"I need to talk to Madison Travers," Raleigh grumbled.

He didn't wait around, partly because he didn't want to talk about the kiss that shouldn't have happened and also because he was anxious to see if the woman had any information they could use. Thea followed him, of course, but he wanted her to hear this just in case she picked up on something he might miss. After all, she knew more about the fertility clinic than he did, since she'd been investigating it for a year.

Madison Travers was waiting for them in the interview room, and she immediately got to her feet. She was petite, right at five-feet tall, and she immediately made nervous glances at both Thea and him.

She didn't have a lawyer with her, but there was a uniformed cop at the table. He'd obviously escorted Madison there from SAPD headquarters, and he introduced himself as Dewayne Rodriquez.

"I've read Ms. Travers her rights," Officer Rodriquez said. "And she waived her right to an attorney."

"Because I don't need a lawyer to tell the truth," Madison blurted out. Judging from her red eyes and puffy face, she'd been crying.

Raleigh could have argued that she might indeed need an attorney because if she had done something illegal, then she could be arrested.

"You're Sheriff Lawton?" Madison asked.

He nodded and tipped his head to Thea. "And this is Deputy Morris from the McCall Canyon Sheriff's office. I understand you're responsible for the botched in vitro procedure for Sonya Burney?" Raleigh started. Both Thea and he took a seat at the table, and Madison sat across from them. "I want to hear all about that, but I'm especially interested in who tried to kill us and how you came by that information."

Madison seemed to lose even more color in her already pale face, but then Raleigh had made sure he sounded like a tough lawman. He wasn't going to let the woman skate just because she'd voluntarily gone to the cops. That's because she hadn't come clean for nearly nine months.

"Yes, I'm the one who messed up Sonya's in vitro. I misplaced Mrs. O'Hara's eggs. At least I guess I did because I couldn't find them when we got ready to do the procedure. I told Dr. Bryce Sheridan, and he said he'd take care of it."

"Dr. Sheridan?" Raleigh questioned. "So he knew about this?"

"Of course," Madison answered without hesitating. "He did an insemination instead. That means he just used Mr. O'Hara's semen to inject into Sonya, not the fertilized eggs as originally planned." She paused. "We didn't think it would be successful. Usually it isn't. So we thought we'd have time to find Mrs. O'Hara's eggs before we did the real in vitro in a couple of months."

"Why didn't you just come clean with Sonya and the O'Haras?" Thea asked, taking the question right out of Raleigh's mouth.

Now she hesitated. "I'd already gotten in trouble for improperly storing another sample, and I would have been fired. Bryce was covering for me." Madison started crying again when she said the doctor's name. *Bryce.* "Plus, the clinic is being sued by a former client who's claiming we illegally released medical information about her to her ex-husband. We couldn't have handled another lawsuit. It would have closed us down."

From everything Raleigh was hearing, closing them down wouldn't be a bad thing. Two errors made by Madison and a lawsuit weren't a stellar track record.

"You and Dr. Sheridan were lovers?" Raleigh pressed.

She nodded, wiped away her tears, but kept sobbing. "And now he's dead. Murdered. That's the reason I went to the cops. I thought somebody might try to kill me, too. Those men did this to him, didn't they?"

"Men?" Thea and Raleigh said in unison.

Madison grabbed some tissues from a box on the table, nodding while she blew her nose. "Two of them. They were wearing suits and had badges. They came to the clinic and asked to speak to Bryce. I told them it was his day off, and then they said they wanted to know the names of all his current patients."

Well, that was interesting. "Were the men cops?"

Madison shook her head. "They said they were FBI.

But after they left, I got to thinking that there was something suspicious about them. I mean, they should have known I couldn't just give them the names without a court order."

"The FBI didn't send anyone to the clinic," Officer Rodriquez verified.

So the guys were posing as law enforcement. "When was this?" Raleigh asked Madison.

"About a week ago."

Raleigh figured that was plenty of time for someone who'd planned on attacking Sonya. "Describe the men."

Madison wiped her eyes again while she continued. "I only got a good look at one of them. The other stayed in the waiting room, and he had on a hat and dark glasses. But the other one, the one who talked to me, was bald. Oh, and he had a tattoo on his neck, but he'd tried to cover it up with makeup. I could see the makeup on the collar of his shirt."

Raleigh texted Dalton to bring him a picture of Marco, but he continued with the questions while he waited. "Does the clinic have security cameras?"

"Not inside the building, but we have one in the parking lot."

Raleigh looked at Officer Rodriquez again. "We asked the security company who monitors the camera to provide us with footage," the cop answered. "But they're stalling because they say it could violate patients' rights to release it. We're working on a court order, but it could take a while if they keep fighting it—especially since the murder didn't take place on the grounds or inside the clinic."

Well, hell. That complicated things. "Would it do any good if I talked to them?" Raleigh asked.

Officer Rodriquez lifted his shoulder. "It wouldn't hurt. Their office is in San Antonio. Maybe you could show them a picture of the murdered patient so they can see that the footage is part of an active murder investigation."

Raleigh looked at Thea, and she nodded. "We need that footage."

He couldn't argue with her about that, but he was worried about the risks of being out in the open with Thea. Still, this was the best shot they had right now. Well, unless he could convince SAPD to put more pressure on the security company.

There was a knock at the door, and a moment later Dalton came in with Marco's mug shot. When Raleigh turned the screen in Madison's direction, the woman shook her head.

"Who is he?" Madison demanded, the fear in her voice. "Is he the one who killed Bryce?"

No, he'd been dead by then, but Marco had certainly been willing to murder Thea.

"Is this one of the men who visited you at the clinic?" Raleigh asked.

"No. I've never seen that guy. Why would you think he was there?"

Raleigh was hoping Marco had been there so it would tie everything up, linking Marco to both Sonya's attack and the clinic. He needed to find out if Dr. Sheridan had been murdered because the killers/kidnappers thought he was onto them. If so, they might consider Madison a loose end, too.

And of course, Thea also fell into that same loose-end category.

But Madison had admitted she hadn't gotten a good look at the man with the hat who'd stayed in the waiting room, so maybe that one had been Marco.

"Sonya knew the child she was carrying was hers," Thea said to Madison. "Did you tell her?"

Again, Madison took her time answering. "Yes. I called her yesterday and then sent her results of the amnio to prove it. I just couldn't stay quiet after I got that visit from Nick O'Hara."

Even Officer Rodriquez seemed surprised by that. "When did Nick visit you?" Raleigh pressed.

"Two days ago." Madison's voice cracked. "He had a meeting with Bryce, and I didn't mean to overhear what they said, but Mr. O'Hara was talking pretty loud. He told Bryce that he was leaving his wife, Yvette."

Raleigh had thought that might happen. He certainly hadn't seen a lot of affection between Yvette and Nick. But something about this didn't make sense.

"Why would Nick go to Dr. Sheridan with this?" Raleigh asked.

"He wanted to see the surrogacy agreement. He said he couldn't find his copy but that he thought he remembered there being a way out of the arrangement. Mr. O'Hara didn't want to share custody with his wife. He wanted full custody for himself."

That didn't mesh with what Yvette had told them. She'd claimed that Nick was having second thoughts about the baby, but maybe he was just having second thoughts about having a baby with her.

"After I heard Mr. O'Hara say that," Madison went on, "I knew I had to tell Sonya the truth, so I called her."

"What phone did you use to do that?" Thea immediately asked.

"The one in my office."

Raleigh jumped right on that. "The office where those two men visited you?" He waited for Madison to confirm that with a nod. "Were you with the two men the whole time they were there?"

"No. I went up the hall to see if I could find our other doctor to talk to them, but he was with a patient." Madison's eyes widened. "Do you think they planted a bug or something?"

Yes, he did. Apparently so did Officer Rodriquez because he called someone to ask them to search the clinic for an eavesdropping device.

"Oh, God," Madison blurted out. "If they heard that, then they heard me say I was suspicious of them. They heard everything I said to Sonya."

Raleigh leaned in closer. "What exactly did you say to Sonya?"

The tears started up again. "I told her what I did about the botched procedure, and she was upset. She said that she was going to call you and that you would probably help her go someplace else to have the baby. A place where she could think about what she was going to do. I liked Sonya, and she said she trusted you. That's why I insisted on talking to you."

So, if Sonya was thinking about leaving town, that

might have prompted her killer to spring into action. But it still didn't tell Raleigh who'd murdered her.

Sonya had told Yvette. They had the recording to prove that. But Raleigh wasn't sure if Sonya had had time to phone Nick or not. If she had, the man certainly hadn't mentioned it.

There was another knock at the door. His other deputy Alice this time. She was holding a tablet, and Raleigh could tell from her expression that she had something important to tell him.

"Excuse me for a moment," Raleigh said to Officer Rodriquez and Madison, and both Thea and he went out into the hall with his deputy.

"The lab called," Alice explained, "and they found a fingerprint on the bottom of the carrier seat that the baby was in when you found her." She glanced at the notes on her tablet. "They got a match on the print. A guy name Buck Tanner. He's a career criminal, and that's why his prints were in the system."

Raleigh felt some of the pressure leave his chest. They finally had a name, which meant they could locate this snake and bring him in.

"Is Buck a bald guy with a neck tattoo?" Thea asked.

Alice nodded and pulled up a picture of him. He matched Madison's description of one of her visitors, and Raleigh was about to take the photo in to have her confirm it when Alice stopped him.

"There's more," Alice went on. "I found the name of Buck's lawyer for his last two arrests. It was Simon."

Chapter Eight

Thea knew Raleigh was on edge about this decision to go to Shaw's Security Company in San Antonio to try to get the camera footage from the fertility clinic. She was on edge about it, too, but this was the fastest way they had of finding out who'd visited the clinic with Buck Tanner.

If it was his lawyer, Simon, then Raleigh would be able to make an arrest.

Of course, that alone wouldn't be enough to convict Simon of Sonya's murder. Simon could always claim that he went to the clinic with his client, maybe to discuss something totally unrelated to Sonya. Simon could even dispute what Madison had said. After all, Madison had botched the in vitro procedure and then lied about it. She wasn't exactly a credible witness.

It would have helped if Sonya had recorded her chat with Madison, but if she had done that, it wasn't with the other recordings. In fact, the only conversations that Sonya had taped were with Yvette, and that hadn't started until six weeks into Sonya's pregnancy.

Why?

Maybe Sonya hadn't trusted the woman. But that only brought Thea back to another *why*.

Even though the questions were important, Thea made sure she kept watch around them while Alice drove Raleigh and her to San Antonio. It wasn't a long trip—less than an hour—but they'd taken precautions. They were in the bullet-resistant cruiser, and Alice could give them backup. Raleigh had even considered sending just Alice and Dalton, but he had decided he, as the sheriff, stood a better chance of talking the security company owner into letting him view the footage. Thea agreed.

The visit was a risk, and it also ate up a good chunk of the morning, but Raleigh and she weren't being idle. Thea was reading through the report that the lab had sent them on the evidence that had been processed, and Raleigh was on the phone with his deputy Miguel.

"No, don't ask Simon anything about the visit to the fertility clinic," Raleigh said to Miguel. The call wasn't on speaker, but since Raleigh and she were side by side, Thea could still hear bits and pieces of the conversation. "Just keep looking for Buck Tanner and any financial links between him and Simon. Links that can't be explained as payment for Simon's legal services."

Raleigh and she had already started looking for Buck before they left Durango Ridge, but the man wasn't answering his phone, nor had he been at his house when SAPD had sent an officer out to bring him in for questioning. If Buck was responsible for the murders and the attack, then he had probably gone into hiding.

"Madison's in protective custody," Raleigh relayed

to her as soon as he finished his call with Miguel. "She went willingly because she's convinced she could be a target."

She could be. Ditto for Raleigh and her. And Warren. Since Warren seemed to be at the center of the two dead surrogates, he was perhaps in danger, but unlike Madison, he'd refused any kind of protection. Thea only hoped that Egan and his brother, Court, would keep an eye on him. At least Rachel and the baby were safe, and Thea wanted to make sure it stayed that way.

"What about Nick?" she asked. "Was Miguel able to get in touch with him to ask about the meeting he had with Dr. Sheridan?"

Raleigh shook his head and made a sound of frustration. "He's not answering his phone, either. Someone's on the way to check on him."

Good. Because of all the bad stuff that'd gone on, it was possible that Nick was in danger, too. Besides, it was odd that the man wasn't answering his phone, because he'd seemed so anxious for a call from the kidnapper. Maybe though he'd given up hope about them calling back.

"I don't suppose there have been any reports of missing babies similar to the one in the picture that the kidnappers sent him?" Thea continued.

Another headshake. "But we still don't know how old the picture is. Or where it was taken. It could be a photo of a baby that was taken off the internet."

True. The baby in the photo might not even be missing, much less kidnapped and being held for ransom.

They'd done an image search on the internet to find possible matches, but that hadn't turned up anything, either.

Raleigh tipped his head to the report Thea had been reading. "Anything new in that lab report?"

"Not really new, but Buck's print wasn't from a single finger. It was actually a handprint, and it was in the right position for someone who was maybe holding the baby carrier to keep it steady. In other words, the print wasn't planted."

Not that Thea thought it had been, but it would be nice to rule it out if that's what Buck claimed had happened.

"I also brought these," she said, taking the hard copy photos from the file. They were pictures of Simon, Marco, Nick and even Yvette. "I wanted to see if anyone from the security company recognized them. That way, if they don't let us view the footage, then maybe they'll look at it and compare it to the photos."

Raleigh made another sound of approval, though she was sure he preferred to review the footage himself.

His phone dinged with a text, and he frowned when he read it and showed her the screen. It was from Dalton.

SAPD found an eavesdropping device in Madison's office.

Thea groaned. "That means the visitors—and perhaps the killer, too—knew that Madison had told Sonya about the botched in vitro." She paused, giving that some thought. "You think that was the trigger that caused the kidnapper/killer to go after Sonya?"

He paused, too. "Maybe. And if so, then it points to Yvette as being the killer."

"Yes, it does. Once we're back in Durango Ridge, we need to bring the woman back in for questioning."

Thea saw the sudden change in Raleigh's eyes, and it didn't take her long to figure out why. It was the "we" in that comment. It made it sound as if they were a team. Which they were. But that didn't mean he was comfortable with it.

"About that kiss," he said a moment later. He kept his voice low, probably so that Alice wouldn't hear. "It really shouldn't have happened."

"I won't argue with that." But for some stupid reason, Thea found herself fighting back a smile. There was nothing to smile about, even though the kiss had been pretty amazing. Of course, every kiss she'd ever had with Raleigh fell into that category.

"It's not just because we're working this case," he went on. "It's the baggage."

No need for him to remind her of that. "Because of Warren. Any kiss between us involves him, too."

Raleigh's eyebrow came up. "Trust me. I wasn't thinking about Warren during that."

She lost her fight with the smile, causing Raleigh to add some profanity under his breath. "Neither was I."

Thea would have liked to have promised that there wouldn't be another kiss, but she wasn't in the habit of lying to herself. If Raleigh and she were thrown together, they'd likely kiss again. And perhaps even do more. That was the reason she shouldn't stay at his house another night. The fatigue and adrenaline were already sky-high and that could bring down their already low defenses even more.

Best not to complicate things by having sex with Raleigh. Even if that was something that sounded darn good to her.

She was about to tell him that she would call Court or one of her other fellow deputies to escort her home tonight and stay with her, but Alice took the turn into the parking lot of the security company. That conversation would have to wait.

As Thea had been doing the whole time they'd been on the road, she glanced around, looking for any signs of trouble. It wasn't a large building at all, and there were only two vehicles in the parking lot.

Raleigh had given the owner, Dan Shaw, a heads-up call that they were on the way to see him, and she hoped that one of the two cars belonged to Shaw. Thea didn't want him stalling them by ducking out on this visit.

Alice didn't park in any of the spots. Instead, she pulled directly in front of the door. "You want me to go in with you?" Alice asked Raleigh.

"No. Wait here and make sure no one else comes inside."

Thea hadn't needed a reminder of the possible danger that came with a visit like this, but that caused her heartbeat to kick up a significant notch. She didn't draw her gun, but she kept her hand in position as Raleigh and she got out and hurried inside.

There was a reception desk just a couple of yards

from the door, but there was no one seated at it. In fact, there was no one in the room. Despite that, nothing seemed out of order. There was a cup of coffee and a sandwich still in its plastic wrapper next to an open laptop on the desk.

"Mr. Shaw?" Raleigh called out.

Nothing. But Thea didn't go into alarm mode just yet. There was an office to the right, just off the reception area, and a hall to the left, where there were several other rooms.

Raleigh shouted the man's name again, and when Shaw didn't answer, Raleigh took out his phone and called him. Almost immediately, Thea heard the ringing sound in one of the back rooms off the hall.

Thea looked up at Raleigh and saw that he was just as concerned as she was. Maybe this was just a case of the man trying to hide from them, but it could be something much worse.

Raleigh and Thea drew their guns.

They started toward the hall, but she heard another sound in the room across from the reception desk. Someone was in there, and it sounded as if the person moaned.

Raleigh put his phone away and positioned himself in front of her. "Watch our backs," he told her.

Thea would because, after all, the owner's phone was on the other end of the building. Maybe the owner, too. But it was suspicious that he hadn't come out when Raleigh had called out for him. Suspicious, too, that someone else was nearby in the other room and hadn't said anything.

Raleigh walked closer to the room, keeping his steps slow and cautious, and once he reached the door, he readied his gun.

Then he cursed.

Thea had to lean to the side to see what had caused that reaction, and she soon spotted the woman on the floor. She was on her stomach, her arms and legs flung out in an awkward pose.

And there was blood on her head.

RALEIGH FELT THAT kick of emotion. A mix of dread and adrenaline. There was also some fear, since he figured that Thea and he had just walked into a crime scene.

His gaze slashed to every corner of the room. It was an office with a desk, but there was no one at the desk or beneath it. Only the woman on the floor.

"Is she still alive?" Thea asked, automatically taking out her phone. No doubt to call for an ambulance.

While he continued to keep watch, Raleigh stooped down and put his fingers to the woman's throat. "She's got a pulse." But in addition to what appeared to be blunt-force trauma to the head, she also had two distinctive marks on her neck.

Someone had used a stun gun on her.

Just as they had on Thea when she'd been at Sonya's house.

"Get Alice in here," Raleigh told Thea as she continued to make the call. "I need to check those back rooms where we heard the phone ringing."

And he didn't want to do that unless he had someone to help him protect Thea. Of course, Thea wouldn't appreciate him thinking like that, but she'd already come too close to dying, not once but twice.

Thea nodded and headed for the door but stopped when they heard another sound. Not a moan or a phone ringing this time. Someone was moving around in the room at the end of the hall. There was a sign next to that particular door, and it had Shaw's name on it, which meant that was his office.

"Call Alice and tell her to get in here," Raleigh repeated to Thea. She started to do that, but again the sound interrupted her.

But it was more than an interruption this time.

Shaw's office door flew open, and before Raleigh could even get a glimpse of the person who'd opened it, a shot blasted through the air. The bullet slammed into the wall right next to where Raleigh was standing. Another quarter of an inch, and he'd have been dead.

Raleigh hooked his arm around Thea, dragging her to the floor, but she'd already started in that direction anyway. Good thing, too, because more shots came. Thick, loud blasts that tore apart not just the wall behind them but also the reception desk. Since the desk wasn't much of a barrier at all, Raleigh pulled Thea into the room with the unconscious woman.

The woman moaned as if trying to warn them, but it was too late for that. Thea and he were under fire, and if Raleigh lifted his head to shoot back, he'd be an easy target.

Since the injured woman was too close to the door, Thea dragged her to the side so she wouldn't get hit by a stray bullet, and then Thea hurried back to him. A place he wished she wouldn't be, but he doubted there was any way he could talk her out of it. Plus, he needed the backup.

His phone buzzed, and when Raleigh saw Alice's name on the screen, he handed it to Thea. "Tell her to call SAPD if she hasn't already, but I don't want her coming through that door." She'd be too easy of a target for the shooter.

Thea did as he said, but her attention stayed in the direction of the gunman. So did Raleigh's. Judging from the angle of the shot, it was just one guy, but he could have brought a buddy with him who was holding Shaw. And Raleigh didn't have to guess what the thugs wanted.

They didn't want Thea and him to see the footage from the security camera.

That told Raleigh plenty about this situation—that he would almost certainly recognize the other man who'd gone to the fertility clinic to try to get a list of Dr. Sheridan's patients.

Maybe it was Nick or Simon.

Of course, it could be someone who could be linked to one of those two. And that's why it was important for Raleigh to get his hands on that footage.

"SAPDs on the way," Thea said when she finished her call to Alice.

Good. Because the angle of the shots changed. This thug was moving closer, no doubt trying to get in position to kill them both. That meant it was time for Raleigh to do something about that.

He stayed down, but he levered himself up just

enough to send a bullet in the shooter's direction. Raleigh doubted he'd hit the guy, but it caused the man to growl out some raw curse words, and he kept shooting. However, Raleigh had gotten a decent look at the guy, and he was wearing a ski mask.

Raleigh fired another shot, too, and quickly moved back to cover. Well, as much cover as he had. The bullets were tearing through the wall, and it wouldn't be long before Thea and he couldn't use it for cover.

"Let's shoot at him together," Thea said.

He hated the idea because it would mean her being in the open. For a few seconds anyway. But SAPD or an ambulance wouldn't be able to get in and help until they'd contained the gunman. The woman definitely needed medical attention, and it was possible Shaw did, too.

"Fire now?" Thea asked.

She waited for Raleigh to nod, and together they leaned out, both of them pulling their triggers at the same time. Raleigh braced himself for the guy to shoot back. But he didn't. In fact, there were no gunshots from him, no profanity. Just the sound of someone running.

Hell, now the snake was trying to get away.

Raleigh got up, ready to fire, but the man was already ducking back into the office, and he slammed the door.

"If you want Shaw dead," the man shouted, "then go ahead and try to come back here."

Raleigh didn't want Shaw to die, but he couldn't trust that this goon would just keep him alive. In fact, he might use Shaw as a human shield so he could get out of the building.

The woman on the floor moaned again, a reminder to Raleigh that time wasn't on their side. She could bleed out and die if he didn't do something.

"Stay here with her," he told Thea. Of course, Thea probably didn't mind doing that part, but she knew what this meant.

"You're going out there," she said. Not a question. She knew it had to be done, but he could see the worry all over her face.

Raleigh tried to give her a reassuring nod, but he didn't want to waste another second. With his gun ready, he hurried out of the room, hunkering down behind the reception desk so he could get a better look at the hall. It wasn't long—less that twenty feet—but at any point the thug could open the door and start firing again. If Raleigh couldn't get into one of the other rooms, he'd be a sitting duck.

Even knowing that, he started moving. He ran to the wall right next to the hall and peered around. There was still no sign of the gunman. No sound of him, either. But there was something.

The smell of smoke.

Raleigh got a whiff of it just as it started to seep under and around the sides of the office door. The SOB had set the place on fire.

That gave Raleigh an even greater sense of urgency to do something.

"You might have to get the woman out of here," he called back to Thea, and he prayed that Alice and maybe even SAPD were out there to give her immediate backup.

Raleigh took a deep breath and started running up the hall. The smoke was already getting thicker, and he could smell something burning inside. He put his hand on the door to make sure there'd be no backdraft, but it was still cool to the touch, so he kicked it open.

There were flames all right, and they were already spreading across the wall and ceiling. But that wasn't the only thing that caught Raleigh's attention. It was the back door.

It was wide-open.

And there was no one in the room.

Chapter Nine

Thea sat at Raleigh's desk in the Durango Ridge Sheriff's Office and tried to make sure she didn't show any signs of the raw nerves that were just beneath her skin. She had to be strong. Because Raleigh was already blaming himself enough. If she fell apart, that blame would skyrocket.

No way would he believe this attack wasn't his fault. He was kicking himself for taking her right into the middle of a gunfight. But he'd been in the middle of it, too, and that was one of the main reasons for Thea's raw nerves.

Again, he could have been killed, while trying to protect her.

And now they were in the middle of another round of chaos. One more layer to add to their already complicated investigation. It was more than just a *layer* though to Dan Shaw. He was missing, and his assistant, Sandra Millington, was in the hospital, in critical condition from a cracked skull and blood loss.

Raleigh was pacing in the squad room just outside his office door while he talked to someone in the San

Antonio Fire Department. Apparently, he didn't like what he was hearing, which meant she wouldn't like it, either. Still, Thea tried not to focus on what was likely soon-to-be-revealed bad news and instead continued to read Madison's statement.

There wasn't anything new in the statement. At least Thea didn't think there was. But it was hard to concentrate when she could still hear the sound of those gunshots and see the blood on the injured woman.

Mercy.

She prayed Sandra Millington didn't die. There'd already been too many deaths connected to this investigation. Deaths maybe because of her. She couldn't forget that she'd been Marco's target, and that might mean all of this could be happening because of her or something she'd done.

Her phone rang, and Thea was so on edge that she gasped at the unexpected sound. And Raleigh noticed her reaction, too, because it caused his frown to deepen. But Thea wasn't frowning when she saw the name on the screen. Her heart went to her throat.

Because it was Rachel.

"Is the baby all right?" Thea blurted out as soon as she could hit the answer button.

"She's fine. We're all fine," Rachel quickly reassured her. "I was calling to check on you."

It took Thea a moment to get her voice and her breathing back under control. Despite all the horrible things that had happened, it would be a thousand times worse if the baby had been hurt or kidnapped again.

"I'm okay," Thea lied.

Judging from Rachel's huff, she knew it was a lie. "And is Raleigh *okay*?"

"I think so. Neither of us were hurt."

"No, you were just in a burning building with a gunman shooting at you." Rachel mumbled something Thea didn't catch. "I've always worried about Griff, Egan, Court and you. It's a strange feeling to add Raleigh to that worry list."

Thea didn't have any doubts about that. Didn't doubt, either, that Rachel would soon accept Raleigh as her brother. The question was, would Raleigh accept her as his sister? The bitterness he felt for Warren might get in the way of that.

"I do have another reason for calling," Rachel went on. "Griff's been pressuring the lab to get the DNA results on the baby, and we should have those back later today. Depending on what the test says, we have a decision to make. If the baby is Nick and Sonya's biological child, is there a reason for us not to hand over the baby to Nick?"

Thea groaned. Nick was still a person of interest in the attacks, and they certainly hadn't been able to rule him out. "When you have the results, just call Raleigh and me, and we'll go from there."

They might not be able to keep the child out of Nick's custody, but Thea wanted to delay that until they had some answers.

"Will do. Stay safe," Rachel added before she said goodbye.

Thea put her phone away at the same time that Raleigh finished his call with the fire department. He stepped inside the office and shut the door.

"The fire gutted the security company, destroying all the files and computers," he explained. His forehead was still bunched up, and even though he'd stopped pacing, he looked as if he needed to do something to burn off a lot of restless energy. "It's possible that Dan Shaw had files off-site or in an online storage, but we won't know that until we've talked to him or his assistant."

That tightened the muscles in her stomach and chest. Because they might not get a chance to ask either of them. They'd have to find Dan before they could question him, and as much as Thea hated to admit it, he could be dead. Their attacker could have killed him after he'd used Dan to help him escape.

Thea got up from the desk and went closer to Raleigh. "Any news on Sandra Millington?" she asked.

"She's still unconscious and in the ICU, but the hospital will call if there's any change. There's more," Raleigh said after he paused. "Someone torched the fertility clinic, too. No one was hurt," he quickly added. "But since the fire started in the records' room, whatever evidence was there was likely destroyed."

Mercy. No wonder Raleigh had been scowling and frowning when he'd been on the phone with the fire department. This definitely qualified as bad news. However, it did make her wonder…

"What could have been in those records that the killer didn't want us to find?" she asked. "I mean, Madison's already confessed to the botched in vitro, so what else could have been in there?"

"Maybe something to incriminate Yvette or Nick? Exactly what that might be, I'm not sure, and we might never know."

True, and that led her to the call with Rachel. "Rachel said we should have the baby's DNA results today."

Raleigh cursed, which meant she didn't need to fill him in on the rest. "Nick's still not answering his phone. We don't know if that's because he was the person in the security company shooting, if he's a victim or if he's just lying low. Whichever it is, he's not at his house. We know that because SAPD is there now, carrying out a search order, and the only one around is Yvette."

Thea had known about the search order, but she hadn't realized it was already going on. Good. If there was anything incriminating, maybe the cops would find it so they wouldn't have to turn over the baby to Nick. Thea wanted the man to have his child only after he'd been cleared of any suspicion.

Raleigh looked at her, his gaze sliding from her face to her shirt. At first she thought there might be something sexual in that look, but then he cursed. "You have blood on you. Is it yours?"

She looked down at her sleeve and saw the small rip, along with the blood. Thea had noticed it earlier but had forgotten about it. "It's just a scratch." She'd gotten it when one of the gunman's bullets had shattered part of the door frame and had sent some splinters flying right at her.

It might have only been a scratch, but it seemed to be the final straw for Raleigh. He cursed, groaned and scrubbed his hand over his face. He was obviously about to deepen the guilt trip he was already on.

"That's not a good idea," he said when Thea slid her arm around his waist and pulled him to her.

"I know. A lot of what we do isn't a good idea. But going to the security company was," she added.

He eased back enough to look down at her and frown.

"Sandra's alive because we went there," Thea explained. "If we hadn't gotten to her, she could have been unconscious and trapped in that fire."

Raleigh's frown softened just a little. That was the only part of him soft though. His muscles were so tight that it felt as if she was hugging stone.

"The shooter might not have set the fire if we hadn't shown up," Raleigh pointed out, but he groaned again, maybe dismissing that. Because Thea was betting the gunman would indeed have burned down the place just to make sure they didn't get their hands on any evidence.

Since they had dozens of things to do, Thea was a little surprised when Raleigh stayed put. Surprised, too, at the gentle way he used just his fingertips to push her hair from her face. She figured the gentleness was a real effort for him with all that tension in his body.

She got yet another surprise when he leaned in even closer and kissed her. She felt the stubble on his jaw brush over her face. She took in his scent. And his taste.

The kiss packed a punch. A huge one. Maybe it was her frayed nerves, but she found herself leaning right into that kiss. She moved into the rhythm of it until her pulse was thick and throbbing. Until she remembered why she'd gotten involved with Raleigh in the first place.

When he finally pulled back, Thea didn't have to worry that he would see what a wreck she was from the attack. That's because now he was almost certainly seeing the heat in her eyes. Heat that he'd put there from that sizzling kiss.

Raleigh opened his mouth, maybe to apologize, but he didn't get a chance to say anything. That's because they heard Dalton shout out from the squad room.

"Hey, you can't just go in there," Dalton snarled.

But apparently the person thought the deputy's order didn't apply to him because the door flew open, and Simon was there with Dalton right behind him.

"Sorry about this," Dalton said to Raleigh, and he aimed a cop's glare at Simon. "Some people don't listen."

"*Some people* need to talk to the sheriff," Simon fired back.

But Simon didn't even look at Dalton when he spoke. His attention was on Raleigh and her. Specifically, Simon was noticing the way Thea had her arm around his waist and the fact that their bodies were practically touching. If Simon had come in just seconds earlier, he would have seen more than a touch, but even without that visual, Thea figured the man knew what had gone on.

And he didn't like it.

Maybe because she was close to Warren. However, Simon's anger was directed at Raleigh, too.

"Nice to see you're working so hard to find Sonya's killer," Simon grumbled.

He couldn't have said anything that would have made Raleigh and her move faster to get away from each other. Because it was true. They shouldn't be kissing when they were in the middle of a murder investigation. And Simon was part of that particular investigation.

"Your deputy called and said you wanted to see me," Simon went on. "Well, I'm a busy man. Busier than you are obviously. So what the heck do you want?"

Raleigh took a moment, maybe to rein in his temper, but he used that time to send a withering glare at Simon. "Where were you at the times of Sonya's and Hannah Neal's murders?"

"What?" Simon howled. And he repeated it. "You think I had something to do with that?"

"I won't know until you've answered the question. It's a simple question, and I'd like an answer—now." There was no sign of a temper in Raleigh's tone, but he was all lawman now.

Dalton must have realized that Raleigh had this under control because he walked away, back toward his desk in the squad room.

"I was at home most of the day when Sonya was killed. And no, I doubt anyone can verify that. I didn't realize at the time that I would need an alibi since I'm not a criminal, and I don't have a criminal record."

Raleigh ignored that mini-tirade and kept on. "What about the day Hannah died? And don't say you don't know who she is, because her murder made front-page news around here."

"That was a year ago," Simon snapped. "No way could I remember something like that off the top of my head."

"Then check your calendar and appointment book and get back to me. I'd like an answer ASAP."

She hadn't thought Simon's glare could get worse, but it did. "What the hell is this about?"

"Buck Tanner," Raleigh immediately answered.

Thea watched Simon's expression, and she was certain that Raleigh was doing the same. The man's eyes widened for just a fraction of a second, and then his mouth tightened. "My former client. What about him?"

"Former?" Raleigh challenged. "You were his lawyer of record for his last two arrests, one of them only about six months ago."

"We had a parting of the ways. Now, what's this about?" Simon included her in his volleyed glances, though Thea had no intentions of answering him.

"Buck Tanner's prints were on the kidnapped baby's carrier seat that Thea and I found," Raleigh explained. "I'm guessing you'll insist you don't know anything about that?"

"Of course I don't." But Simon definitely seemed uncomfortable. "Have you talked to him?"

"There's an APB out on him. We'll find him," Raleigh assured him. "Did he have a connection to Sonya? Did he know her?"

"I have no idea." The angry tone was back, but there was still plenty of concern in his eyes. "Are you suggesting that I put him up to something illegal?" Simon didn't wait for an answer. "Because I was his lawyer—that's all."

Raleigh made a *hmm* sound that let Simon know he wasn't exactly buying that. "I'll let you know what Buck says when we find him. And, oh, we're monitoring his phone and bank accounts. Just thought you should know that if you were planning on calling him."

If looks could kill, Simon would have blasted Raleigh and her off the planet. Simon belted out some profanity, turned and stormed out.

"You believe he's innocent?" Thea immediately asked Raleigh.

"I don't know. But something's going on with him."

Thea agreed. Too bad they couldn't find out if that *something* was Simon's plan to get back at Warren. Raleigh must have been thinking the same thing because he took out his phone.

"I'll call my mother and ask her if she ever heard Simon mention Buck," Raleigh explained.

But he didn't get a chance to make the call, because Dalton stepped into the doorway of the office. "SAPD found something when they were searching Yvette and Nick's house. A burner cell that was tucked between the mattresses. They'll send it to the lab to see if they can find out if it was used to make any calls."

"Did Yvette or Nick admit the phone was theirs?" she asked.

Dalton shook his head. "Nick wasn't there, and Yvette left shortly before they found it. You want me to get her in for questioning?"

"Not yet," Raleigh answered. "Wait until we hear back from the lab."

"There's more," Dalton went on. "There was also an envelope underneath a bunch of things in the bottom drawer of the nightstand. The kind of envelope that banks use sometimes when they give you a lot of cash. Someone had marked three thousand dollars on the outside of it, but inside there were only two one-hundred-dollar bills."

Three grand probably wasn't enough to hire two thugs to do your dirty work—like kidnap your surrogate's baby—but maybe it had been some kind of down payment. But the question was, where had Yvette or Nick gotten the money?

Thea looked up at Dalton. "Was there a withdrawal from their bank account in that amount?"

The deputy shook his head. "No cash withdrawal over two-hundred dollars."

It was possible that one of them had made the smaller withdrawals and stashed the money away in those increments, but it would have taken a while for that amount to accumulate. Still, it was doable.

"The lab is going to check for prints on the money," Dalton added.

Good. Then they would know if Nick or Yvette had put it there. Or maybe they both had. This could be their emergency fund, along with the cell phone. Maybe there was no criminal intent whatsoever.

"Let me know what the lab says," Raleigh reminded Dalton. "And make sure someone is keeping a close watch for Buck."

Dalton nodded. "His cell phone isn't in a service area, but if he gets or receives any calls, we'll know about it."

Since Buck was a career criminal, he'd probably ditched the cell. Too bad there wasn't a way for them to legally monitor Simon's phone, but they would need a court order for that. One they wouldn't be able to get because there wasn't enough evidence against him.

Dalton went back to his desk, leaving Raleigh and her standing there in the suddenly awkward silence. "I need to talk to my mom," he finally said. "Not just to ask her about Buck but because Simon will tell her that he saw you in my arms."

Sweet heaven. With everything else going on, Thea hadn't even considered that. But yes, Simon would tell her, and she didn't have to guess how Alma would handle the news because there was no way Raleigh's mom would approve of her son getting involved with her again.

Raleigh took out his phone, but before he could press in Alma's number, he got another call. Her chest tightened when she saw the words *Unknown Caller* on the screen.

"Use your phone to record this," Raleigh insisted, and he waited until she had hit the recording function.

"Sheriff Lawton," a man said when Raleigh answered.

It wasn't a voice she recognized, and apparently neither did Raleigh because he snapped, "Who is this?"

"I'm the man who's going to make your day. You know that missing kid? The one that Hannah Neal was carrying for that couple who hired her to be a surrogate," he added. "Well, I got the kid. And before you ask, she's just fine."

Thea certainly hadn't expected that. Nor was she sure it was true.

"You've got the baby that's been missing?" Raleigh challenged. "You're sure about that, or is this some kind of hoax to extort some ransom money?"

"No hoax, and yeah, I'm sure."

"If that's true, where has the baby been all this time? She's been missing for a year."

"She's been in good hands with a nanny," the man said.

Thea prayed that was true. But that didn't mean the baby would remain in good hands, because this thug probably had demands. Money for sure. But maybe something more—like exchanging the baby for her. That's what Marco had wanted anyway, and this could be Buck, Marco's partner on the other end of the line.

If Buck or this snake did indeed want her, then Thea would try to make that happen. This had nothing to do with her being a cop. There was just no way she could allow the baby to be in the hands of a killer.

"You probably got questions," the man went on, "but you must know that I'm not gonna be real keen on answering them, especially since you're probably taping this and all. But here's the deal. You get the kid, no strings attached."

"Really? No strings?" Raleigh challenged.

"Not a one. If you want the kid, she's right outside the

back door of the diner, the one that leads into the alley. My advice? Get there fast before I change my mind."

And with that, the caller hung up.

"You're not going out there," Raleigh said to Thea before she could even volunteer. "Stay put, and that's not up for negotiation."

Thea understood his concern. They'd nearly been killed just hours earlier, but she hadn't been the only one in the middle of that attack. Raleigh had been, too. Still, she didn't say anything because she knew it wasn't an argument she could win.

Raleigh drew his gun and hurried into the squad room. "Call the diner," he told Alice. "I don't want any of the employees or customers going outside the building, but there could be a baby at their back door."

Alice was in the process of making that call when Thea saw the front entrance of the diner open, and a woman in a waitress uniform started walking toward the sheriff's office.

She was holding an infant car seat, and there was indeed a baby strapped inside it.

Raleigh ran to the door, threw it open, and the moment the waitress reached him, he pulled her inside. "I heard a baby crying," she said, "and when I went to check it out, I found her. There's an envelope taped to the side of the seat, but I didn't touch it. I didn't unhook the straps, either."

That was smart of her, but Thea doubted there'd be any evidence to recover from it. Still, they had something that might link them back to who'd done this.

"Did you see anyone else back there or in the alley?" Raleigh asked the woman.

She shook her head. "Just the baby. Why would someone leave a precious little girl out there like that?"

"I don't know, but I'll find out," Raleigh assured her.

Thea went into the squad room so she could have a better look. The baby was wearing a pink dress and had blond curls. She was fussing and kicking her feet, but she seemed to be unharmed. Thank God.

"I need gloves," Raleigh told Alice, and the deputy ran to the supply cabinet to get him a pair.

Once Raleigh had them on, he took the car seat from the waitress, moving it to one of the desk tops. He clicked a picture of the carrier and baby before he removed the envelope. There was no letter or note inside, just two photos. And the sight of them caused Thea's breath to stall in her throat.

Because the first was a picture of Hannah. Alive. And she was holding a newborn baby. Judging from the looks of it, it was the baby she'd just delivered.

Raleigh moved on to the second photo, and even though Thea had tried to steel herself up for whatever it would be, the steeling didn't work. The sickening feeling of dread washed over her.

In this picture, Hannah was dead. Her lifeless body was sprawled out. And next to her was a man in a ski mask, holding the precious baby in his arms.

Chapter Ten

The nightmare woke Raleigh, and he jackknifed in the bed. The images of an attack had been so real that his body had kicked up a huge amount of adrenaline, preparing itself for a fight. But there was no threat. He was alone in his bed, and his house was quiet.

Quiet but with the smell of coffee in the air.

He threw back the covers and checked the time. It was barely 6:00 a.m., which meant he'd gotten about five hours of sleep. Apparently though, Thea had gotten even less than that, since she was almost certainly the reason for the coffee scent. That meant she was probably up, working, something he should be doing.

Raleigh grabbed a quick shower, threw on some clothes and hurried into the kitchen. Thea was there all right, and there was a half-filled pot of coffee on the kitchen counter. But she was sacked out, her head on the table next to her open laptop and her phone.

The sound of his footsteps must have alerted her though because her eyes flew open, and she reached for her gun. Which wasn't there. Because she was wearing his pj's. Or rather pj's that belonged to him. Her brother hadn't packed her a pair of her own, so she'd had to use a pair of his.

For all of his adult life, Raleigh had only slept in boxers or gone commando, but for some reason his mother always gave him pajamas, slippers and robes as gifts. He'd never used any of them, but they looked darn good on Thea.

"Sorry," she mumbled. She stood and stretched, causing the blue plaid fabric to tighten across her breasts. Plus, she'd missed the two bottom buttons on the top, so he got a nice peep show of her stomach.

Yeah, the pj's looked good on her.

Raleigh felt his body clench, and to stop himself from ogling her, he got his mind on something else. "You couldn't sleep?" he asked, pouring himself a cup of coffee.

"I managed to get in a couple of hours, but I wanted to check on the baby. Well, both babies, actually. Rachel's an early riser because her pregnancy is getting to the uncomfortable stage, so she emailed me some updates. Sonya's baby is fine. And the baby that the waitress found yesterday is with social services and has had her DNA tested."

That was a start, but in addition to keeping both girls safe, they needed to know the identities of their parents. If the older baby was indeed the one that Hannah had carried, then the child would be given to the birth parents, the couple who'd hired Hannah to be their surrogate. It could be wonderful news for them.

Of course, that didn't change the fact that Hannah was dead.

Since Thea had already started her work day, Raleigh did, too. He took his laptop to the table and loaded his email, and he immediately saw one from the lab. According to the test they'd run, there were no prints on the car seat other than those of the waitress. And none on the envelope or the photos. Along with that, there were no fibers or trace evidence. Not good, but the photos would still be analyzed though to see if there was any visual evidence in the background.

Something that Raleigh had already been looking at.

Too bad he'd found nothing. However, he'd had the photos scanned, and he downloaded them from the storage files.

"Griff has been in touch with the San Antonio Fire Department," Thea continued. She got up to pour herself more coffee. "Both fires at the security company and fertility clinic were set with accelerants. Something we'd already suspected."

They had. Ditto for suspecting that Yvette would claim the money in the nightstand drawer was for emergencies, that there was no way she'd ever used the cash to pay a kidnapper. Yvette had also claimed that once there had been three grand in the envelope, but they'd tapped into it for various things.

As for the phone, Yvette insisted she had no idea why it was there. Since they still hadn't been able to get in touch with Nick, Raleigh didn't have anyone to confirm or deny what she'd said. And the phone wasn't going to be of much help because if it had been used to make or receive calls, all of that had been erased, and it had been wiped of any prints.

"I don't suppose you have any news about Buck?" Thea asked, sitting back down beside him again. "*Good news*—like the cops found and arrested him."

She looked at his laptop screen and groaned softly. That's because he had the photo of Hannah dead on the screen. Thea had seen it before, of course, but it never got easier to look at something like that.

"The killer was sick to take her picture," she mumbled and looked away.

Yeah, he was sick, but the ski-mask-wearing thug might have done that in case he ever had to prove that the baby was the one Hannah had delivered. A photo would have come in handy if there'd been a ransom demand. But there hadn't been.

Well, not until two days ago.

Raleigh pulled up the third picture, the one that'd been sent to Nick on his phone, and he positioned it side by side with the photo taken of Hannah when she was still alive. And holding the newborn that she'd almost certainly just delivered.

"They look like the same baby," Thea muttered.

Raleigh agreed, though the lab should be able to determine that. DNA, too. But that wouldn't answer his question of why the kidnapper/killer waited a year to return the little girl.

"At least the baby is healthy," Thea added. "The hospital said she's been well taken care of."

That was something at least, but it wouldn't erase the hell the biological parents had gone through worrying about their missing child.

"Dalton's coordinating all the security cameras for

that block around the diner," Raleigh said after glancing at his next email update.

No one had seen anyone leave the baby, but it was possible one of the cameras had picked up something. But even if they had footage of the person, Raleigh figured the guy was long gone. Something had caused him to give up the child—without collecting a penny—and that meant he was likely going on the run.

But why?

Maybe the guy felt that he was close to being caught. Or if it was Buck, he could have known about the APB and that he would be arrested for murder if he stayed around.

"We need to find the nanny who took care of the baby," Thea said. "If she's alive, that is."

Thea's voice cracked a little on those last words, and she got up again, turning away from him. Since she wasn't looking at anything in particular, Raleigh figured she was dodging his gaze. That's why he stood, too. He took hold of her hand and eased her back around to face him.

There were tears in her eyes.

"Sometimes, it just gets to be too much," she whispered.

He felt the same way. The murders, the kidnappings, the fires and the attacks. And they still didn't know why this was happening. The problem was that it could get a whole lot worse.

Knowing it was a mistake, Raleigh pulled her into his arms and brushed a kiss on the top of her head. He kept it chaste. Well, as much as something like that could be between Thea and him. Which wasn't very chaste at all. He felt the immediate punch from the heat.

And tried to rein it in.

After all, they weren't in his office, where someone could come walking in at any minute. They were in his house, behind closed doors and alone. Plus, there were the memories of when they'd had sex just a few yards away on the sofa in the living room.

Thea looked up at him and frowned. "Should we try to talk ourselves out of this?" The corners of her mouth lifted, and it seemed as if she was going to use that half joke to move away from him.

She didn't.

That's because she kept staring at his mouth, and her body seemed to be issuing this silent invitation for him to kiss her. So that's what he did. Raleigh snapped her to him, and he pushed common sense right out the window when he pressed his mouth to hers.

There it was. More than just a mere kick of attraction. As it always was with Thea, it started out scalding and just got hotter from there. That would have been good if this had been leading to sex. But it couldn't.

Raleigh repeated that.

Though he probably could have repeated it a hundred times and it wouldn't have helped. That's because Thea slipped her arms around his neck and pulled him down even lower so he could deepen the kiss.

The need came, sliding right through him and making him want to take this up a notch. So he did. Without breaking the kiss, Raleigh turned her, backing her against the wall, and he made that need even more urgent when he slid his hand beneath her top.

No bra.

Hell, he was in trouble.

And he kept creating the trouble when he cupped her right breast and flicked his thumb over her nipple. It wasn't hard to find because it was already puckered and tight from arousal. He made that worse, too, by lowering his head and taking it into his mouth.

Thea made a moaning sound. It was all pleasure. She definitely didn't move away from him. In fact, she ran her hands down his back, pulling him closer and closer.

Raleigh lingered there awhile, tasting her, and he took the kisses lower. To her stomach. The waist of the pj's bottoms was loose on her, making it very easy for him to push down the fabric and keep kissing until he reached the top of her panties. A sane man would have stopped there, but he just pushed them down and kept kissing.

Thea cursed, the profanity probably aimed at him. Maybe at herself. But those sounds of pleasure kept urging him on. So did the sight of her when he got her panties low enough. He'd made love to her this way before, but it'd been a long time.

Too long.

And maybe if he kept it to just this, he could convince himself that he hadn't crossed every line that shouldn't be crossed between them. But before Raleigh could take things to the next step, he heard a different sound. One he didn't want to hear. Because his phone was ringing.

Hell. Talk about losing focus.

Thea scrambled away from him and started fixing her clothes. Raleigh did some scrambling, too, and he whipped out his phone to see Dalton's name on the screen. Since it was too early for routine business, he knew this had to be important for his deputy to call him at home.

"What happened?" Raleigh asked when he hit the answer button. And he hoped someone else wasn't dead or had been kidnapped.

"Nick O'Hara just walked in."

Well, at least the man was alive. Since no one had heard from him in twenty-four hours, Raleigh had started to think he was either dead or had fled because he was guilty of something.

"Mr. O'Hara's asking to talk to you," Dalton added a moment later. "I think you should come in because he says he needs to make a confession."

EVEN THOUGH IT was only a short drive from Raleigh's house to the sheriff's office, Thea was on edge for every second of the trip. But at least they might have answers soon. Well, they would if Nick's confession led them to a killer—either himself or someone he'd hired.

"We never did find a connection between Nick and Hannah," Thea reminded Raleigh.

Even though Raleigh's attention seemed to be on keeping watch around them, he made an immediate sound of agreement. "Maybe there isn't one. Sonya's murder could be a copycat killing. One that doesn't have anything to do with Hannah. Or Warren."

She wished that would turn out to be true. It wouldn't bring back either woman, but it might ease the guilt Warren was no doubt feeling since he believed he was the reason for both women dying.

"About what happened right before I got Dalton's call…" Raleigh tossed out there.

Thea certainly hadn't forgotten about it. They were within a heartbeat of having some form of sex. And Raleigh was almost certainly regretting it.

She was about to give him an out. To tell him that being under the same roof had just stirred some old memories. But Raleigh continued before she could say anything.

"If we're together, alone, it'll happen again." He mumbled some profanity to go along with that.

Thea couldn't deny that, and she took a moment to try to figure out how to answer that. "I should stay at my own place tonight. Griff can arrange a protection detail—"

"No," Raleigh interrupted. He looked at her. It was barely a glance, but he managed to put a lot of emotions into such a brief look. She saw the frustration. Even some anger. But she also saw the heat. "I want you in my bed, and your being somewhere else isn't going to change that."

Well, the man certainly knew how to take her breath away. And complicate things. Especially since it was obvious that neither of them should be thinking about sex right now. It was also obvious that it was going to happen whether or not it made a mess out of this situation.

Thankfully, Thea didn't have to say anything else

because Raleigh pulled to a stop in front of the sheriff's office. Later though, there'd need to be a discussion about this. Or perhaps this attraction was past the discussion point.

Maybe she should just go for it. A hot, sweaty round of ex-sex with Raleigh might burn up some of this energy and cool down some of this fire between them. But then she looked at him and decided it was best if she didn't lie to herself. Sex wouldn't cool down anything. It would only remind her of what she'd once had with Raleigh.

And she wanted that again.

"Yeah," he said as if he knew exactly what she was thinking.

He didn't add more. Instead, Raleigh hurried her out of the cruiser and into the squad room, where she immediately spotted Nick. Not alone, either.

Simon was standing next to him.

"My client wants to talk to you," Simon greeted.

"Your client?" Raleigh challenged.

Nick nodded and rubbed his hand over his face. He definitely didn't look like the polished businessman who'd first shown up in Durango Ridge. No. Judging from his rumpled hair and clothes, he'd had a rough time. Thea knew exactly how he felt. But what she didn't understand was why he'd hired Simon.

Simon definitely seemed to be all right with the arrangement though.

The man was practically gloating, maybe because he believed this was some kind of dig against Raleigh and her. However, Thea was far less interested in Nick's choice of attorney than she was in why he felt he needed a lawyer in the first place. Maybe he did intend on confessing to murder.

"This way," Raleigh said, leading Simon and Nick toward an interview room. He motioned for Thea to come, as well.

She braced herself for Simon or even Nick to object to her being there. After all, this wasn't her jurisdiction. But neither man brought it up when she followed them into the room.

Simon and Nick sat at the table, and Raleigh took the seat across from them. "What's this all about?" Raleigh asked.

Despite the fact that Nick had been the one to ask for this meeting, he didn't jump right into an explanation. He groaned. "I was having an affair with Sonya," he finally blurted out.

Along with the shock of hearing that, Thea got a heavy feeling in her stomach. Sonya had never hinted of an affair. Of course, that didn't mean it hadn't happened.

"I'm going to want to hear a lot more about this," Raleigh insisted.

Nick didn't continue though until Simon whispered something in his ear. "The affair started shortly after we met. Right after Sonya got confirmation that she was pregnant."

Raleigh glanced at her, probably to see if she'd had any inkling, but Thea had to shake her head.

"I fell in love with Sonya," Nick went on. "And that's the reason I wasn't too enthusiastic when I thought I'd be raising my and Yvette's child. My marriage was in trouble—and don't blame Sonya for that. I had fallen out of love with my wife before I even met Sonya."

Thea couldn't believe what she was hearing. "Then why the heck did you agree to a surrogate pregnancy?"

Again, Simon whispered something to Nick, and it was Simon who continued. "Mr. O'Hara has come here in good faith, to set the record straight. I won't tolerate either of you judging him for his extramarital involvement."

Raleigh gave both of them a blank stare. "No judging. I'll leave that to a jury."

"A jury?" Nick snapped, jumping to his feet, but Simon pulled him right back in the chair.

"Are you saying you're going to arrest my client?" Simon asked, his tone smug because he knew an affair alone wouldn't be enough of a motive to charge Nick with Sonya's murder.

But maybe there was something else here.

"No arrest. Not yet," Raleigh added. "Right now though, I see a big red flag for *your client*. He's just admitted to an affair with a woman who was murdered. An affair he waited two days to tell us about. And now he admits to a rocky marriage. Is he here to confess to murder or to point the finger at his wife?"

"I didn't kill Sonya," Nick insisted, and he left it at that. Which meant he likely was going to try to pin this on Yvette.

And she might have done it, too.

"Yvette knew about the affair?" Thea asked.

Nick took his time answering. "I never told her, but I believe she found out and killed Sonya."

Raleigh didn't take that at face value. With his raised eyebrows, he looked skeptical. "You got any proof that Yvette did it?"

"She argued with Sonya the morning of the murder," Nick was quick to remind them.

"Yes, because Yvette found out the baby wasn't hers and that Sonya was thinking about keeping the child," Raleigh reminded him right back. "In that case, I think it was justified for Yvette to be upset." He leaned forward, his cop's stare on Nick. "So, how did you react when you found out the baby was yours and Sonya's?"

Nick exchanged glances with Simon before he said anything. "I was, well, shocked."

It was an interesting reaction, considering Nick had just talked about being in love with Sonya. There was something else going on here, and Raleigh picked up on it, too.

"I'm going out on a limb here, but I don't think you had plans to ever divorce Yvette," Raleigh started. "Maybe because she comes from money? I remember her saying you two ran her late father's successful real estate company. So, did you sign a prenup?"

Bingo. Nick didn't have to verbally confirm that for Thea to know it was true, and that led her to a problem that Sonya's pregnancy could have created.

"If Yvette found out Sonya was carrying your baby, she might have thought the child was the result of your affair," Thea suggested. "That would have given her grounds for a divorce. Of course, the affair alone would have also done that, but the baby would be proof that she could use in a court battle. And if she divorced you, you'd be broke and without a job."

That lit an angry fire in Nick's eyes. It didn't have Simon remaining calm, either. "Are you accusing me of setting up Yvette to take the blame for Sonya's murder?" Nick snarled.

"If Deputy Morris isn't accusing you, then I am," Raleigh fired back. "You've got a big motive for wanting Yvette behind bars. Plus, you lied to us. And let's get into the part about you knowing that Sonya's baby was yours, and yet you claimed it wasn't, that Thea and I had gotten the wrong child from Marco."

Nick huffed. "That was an honest mistake. The baby didn't look like Sonya and me, and I thought the other baby did. I didn't know it was a hoax to milk money from me."

Any money would have come from Yvette. If she had fallen for the hoax, that is. She hadn't. Yvette had continued to try to stake her claim to the baby Raleigh and she had rescued. And she'd done that despite the fact that the baby wasn't biologically hers. Maybe because she was desperate to be a mother, but Thea wondered if there was another reason.

Yvette could have somehow planned to use the child to get back at her cheating husband.

"My client has voluntarily explained everything to you," Simon concluded, and he stood. "I'm assuming he's free to go."

"No, he's not." Raleigh motioned for Nick to sit back down. "Tell me about the money that SAPD found in your nightstand drawer. And the phone between the mattresses."

Nick had already opened his mouth to answer until Raleigh added the last part. His mouth tightened, telling them that the man hadn't *explained everything* after all. "The money is for emergencies," Nick said after a long pause. "The phone was the one I used to call Sonya. I couldn't use my regular cell because Yvette would have seen Sonya's number on the bill."

"Now, are you satisfied?" Simon snapped at Raleigh.

"No. I'm more than a little concerned that you're the attorney for two suspects in this murder investigation."

"A suspect?" Nick howled.

Raleigh looked him straight in the eyes. "You heard me. If you're innocent, I'll apologize, but there'll be an asterisk by it because you withheld information about your affair with the victim." Raleigh stood. "Now you're free to go."

Thea and Raleigh walked out, leaving Nick still grumbling about being a suspect. Too bad they didn't have anything to hold the man, but other than circumstantial evidence, there was nothing to tie him to the crime of either Sonya's murder or the kidnapping.

"I'll call the lab and ask them to take another look at that cell phone the cops found between the mattresses," Raleigh said as they went back toward his office. "The calls were all erased, but maybe there's a storage cache they can find. I also need to have another chat with Yvette about the prenup and to find out if she knew anything about the affair."

Yes, because the affair could give Yvette motive for murdering Sonya.

Raleigh reached for his phone, but he stopped when they got to his office. That's because it wasn't empty.

His mother was there.

Thea checked the time to make sure it wasn't later than she thought. It wasn't. It wasn't even seven thirty yet. Pretty early for a visit, which meant something could be wrong.

"Dalton said Simon was here." Alma's voice was a little shaky. Actually, the same applied to her, too. She had a wadded up tissue in her hand, and Thea thought she might have been crying.

Raleigh nodded. "He's with a new client."

"I'll wait out here while you two talk," Thea offered.

But Alma immediately shook her head. "No. Please come in. Both of you. But shut the door. I don't want Simon to know I'm here."

Well, this was interesting, considering that Simon was not only Alma's longtime friend but her lawyer.

"Did something happen?" Raleigh asked once Thea and he were inside the office. He also shut the door.

His mother volleyed some nervous glances at him. "It's about Warren," Alma said after a very long hesitation.

Thea wanted to groan, and she hoped Alma wasn't about to try to accuse Warren of some crime.

"I wrote a letter to Warren," Alma went on when Raleigh and Thea just stared at her. "It was something I didn't want him to read until after my death."

Raleigh's forehead bunched up, and Thea's was certain that hers did, too. "What kind of letter?" Raleigh pressed. He wasn't using the same rough tone he did with Nick, but he was clearly concerned about this.

Alma was concerned, too, because she needed to use that tissue to dab at her eyes. "You're not going to like it, but I told Warren that I loved him. And I still do."

Raleigh mumbled some profanity. "He hurt you."

Alma nodded, blinked back tears. "And I'm sure I hurt his wife. Remember, I knew he was married, and I still kept seeing him."

Thea had to wonder if Sonya had felt the same way about Nick. She hoped it was love anyway and that the love hadn't soured to the point that it would make Nick want to kill her.

When Alma's tears continued, Raleigh went to her and pulled her into his arms. He brushed a kiss on the top of her head. "Why are you telling me this? Did something happen with the letter?"

"Yes, I believe something did."

Thea prayed that Warren's wife hadn't seen it. She was just now back on her feet, recovering from a mental breakdown, and it wouldn't help for her to see something like that.

Alma eased back from Raleigh to face both of them. "I was going to put the letter in the safe in my office, but I got busy doing something else and left it on my desk when I went out to meet with one of the new hands. While I was gone, Ruby said that Simon arrived, and he went into my office."

"Ruby?" Thea asked.

"My housekeeper. She said, when she looked in my

office, that Simon was reading the letter, and that he got very mad and stormed out. Ruby was going to tell me, but then her daughter got sick, and she had to leave. It must have slipped her mind because she didn't tell me about it until this morning."

So Simon had seen, in writing, that Alma still had feelings for Warren. That definitely wouldn't have sit well with him. But maybe it had done something much, much more.

"When did all this happen?" Raleigh asked. "When did Simon read the letter?"

Alma's mouth began to tremble. "The same morning that Sonya was murdered."

Oh, mercy. Maybe that was a coincidence, but it was too strong of a connection to dismiss it.

"I suppose you'll have to ask Simon about it?" Alma said to her son.

"Yes." Obviously giving that some thought, Raleigh stayed quiet a moment. "But not now. Not while you're here." He hugged her. "Just go on home, and I'll take care of it."

But Alma didn't budge. "Are you disappointed with me?" she asked him.

"No. I'm not disappointed," Raleigh assured her. And Thea believed that was the truth.

"Do you think I'm a fool for still having these feelings for Warren?" Alma aimed that second question at Thea.

Thea sighed and repeated Raleigh's "no." Alma wasn't a fool. She was just a woman who couldn't get over her feelings for a man—something Thea could certainly relate to.

Raleigh opened the door and looked out, no doubt checking to make sure Simon wasn't out there. He wasn't, so Raleigh opened the door even wider. "You want me to have one of the deputies drive you home?" he asked her.

His mother shook her head and gave his hand a gentle squeeze. "I'll be fine. I just need some time to myself."

Thea watched the woman walk out, and she felt a strange mix of feelings. Resentment at the part Alma had played in nearly destroying Warren's marriage. But Thea felt empathy, too. She looked at Raleigh to tell him that, but Dalton came toward them.

"The lab just sent over the DNA results on the newborn," Dalton said. He handed Raleigh the report. "And as you can see, it's not what we were expecting."

Chapter Eleven

Raleigh read through the lab report, shook his head and read it again. What the heck was going on?

"The baby isn't Nick's," Thea said as she looked at the DNA results. "She's Sonya and Dr. Sheridan's."

Dalton had been right about them not expecting this. "How did the lab even have Dr. Sheridan's DNA to do the comparison?" Raleigh asked Dalton. And that was just the first of many questions he had.

"He was in the system because he worked in a federal prison for a short time, so when the baby's DNA didn't match Nick's, the lab tech just fed the results through the database. Dr. Sheridan fathered that baby."

It didn't take Raleigh long to figure out how this could have happened. Madison had already told them that Yvette's harvested eggs had been misplaced. Well, maybe Nick's semen had been, too. Dr. Sheridan could have substituted his own to make up for the mistake.

Or he'd been asked to do that by someone.

The only person in this equation who wasn't so eager for that baby to be conceived was Nick. That could mean he was in on this, and if so, he'd have a strong motive to kill the doctor if Sheridan had decided to come clean with Yvette.

"In case Nick's the one behind this, we need to dig into Dr. Sheridan's bank account and see if he was paid off for his part in the botched in vitro," Raleigh told Dalton. "We know there were no large sums of money taken from the O'Haras' bank account, but see if you can figure out another way for Nick to have gotten his hands on some cash about nine months ago."

"I'll get right on that," Dalton said as he went back to his desk.

"You really think Nick killed Sonya?" Thea asked.

"Maybe. If she'd tried to break things off with him, he could have been enraged enough to do something like that. There weren't any recordings of her and Nick's conversations, so we really don't know how things were between them."

She made a sound of agreement. "And then Nick could have killed Dr. Sheridan and burned down the clinic and the security company to cover his tracks." She paused. "Of course, Yvette could have hired someone to do the murders to set up her husband. If she was upset enough about the affair, she might have wanted to get revenge."

True. But it was also possible that the botched in vitro had nothing to do with the murders or the attacks. If so, then this all went back to Simon. And unlike Nick and Yvette, Simon did have a connection to one of the hired guns.

Raleigh's phone rang, and considering everything

that was going on, he halfway expected to see *Unknown Caller* on the screen. But it was a familiar name.

Warren.

Raleigh wasn't especially eager to talk to him, but since this could be about the investigation, he answered it right away.

"I was driving into Durango Ridge to check on Thea," Warren immediately said, "and I saw your mom's car parked on the side of the road."

Raleigh's heart went into overdrive, especially when he heard his mother yelling in the background. "Is she all right?" He couldn't ask that fast enough.

"She's not hurt or anything like that, but she's crying and clearly upset. She tried to drive off, but I took away her keys. I didn't think she should be behind the wheel like that." Warren paused. "And now she's pulled a gun on me."

Raleigh didn't even bother to hold back the profanity. "I'm on the way. Where are you exactly?"

"About a quarter of a mile south of the turn for Alma's ranch."

Raleigh knew the spot. "Tell her not to do anything stupid, that I'll be right there."

He put away his phone and took out the keys for the cruiser parked right out front, but that's when he realized Thea was following him.

"You're not going out there alone," she insisted.

Hell. Now he had to worry about both his mother and Thea. And Warren. He didn't like the man, but he darn sure didn't want his mother to end up in jail for shooting him. Later, he'd kick himself for not having one of the deputies escort Alma home, but for now, he needed to get to her and hopefully defuse a bad situation.

"Come with us," Raleigh told Dalton. He hated to pull Dalton away from the pile of work that was on his desk, but after what happened at the security company, Raleigh didn't want to take any chances.

After Raleigh told Alice what was going on, Dalton, Thea and he hurried outside to the cruiser. Raleigh got behind the wheel, and with Dalton at shotgun, Thea got in the back. Raleigh turned on the flashing lights and siren so he could get down Main Street as fast as possible.

"What do you think happened to your mom?" Thea asked.

He doubted it was anything other than what Alma had already told them. That she was worried about Simon having read the letter. That had already brought his mother to tears before she'd come to the sheriff's office, and those tears had obviously continued after she left.

"I think my mom is worried that Simon murdered Sonya, maybe Hannah, too, and now she's blaming herself." Of course, that didn't explain why she'd pull a gun on a man she still loved, but it could be she'd gotten so hysterical that she didn't know what she was doing. Which made this situation even more dangerous.

Even though it was only a couple of miles, it seemed to take forever for them to get there, and by the time they arrived, Raleigh could feel his pulse drumming in his ears. What he saw sure didn't help with that, either.

Alma's car was indeed there. His mom had pulled off

into a narrow clearing that was in front of a cattle gate and pasture. At least she hadn't stopped on the road. Warren's truck was parked just behind Alma's car, and Dalton pulled to a stop behind it since the road shoulder was too narrow to park ahead of the vehicles.

Warren was there, too. He was standing by the driver's-side door of Alma's car. He had his hands raised in the air. Alma was inside, still behind the wheel, and she did indeed have a gun aimed at Warren. The gun was a Smith & Wesson that he knew his mom kept in her glove compartment.

Raleigh's first instinct was to bolt from the cruiser, but he glanced around first. Something he'd been doing during the whole drive. But he didn't see anyone. Maybe it would stay that way, though this was the road that led into town, so someone would no doubt eventually drive by.

He glanced back at Thea to tell her to stay put, but she was already getting out. And he couldn't blame her. She loved Warren and was probably afraid for his life.

Raleigh and Dalton got out as well, and Raleigh maneuvered himself in front of Thea. He didn't draw his gun, but Dalton did.

"I didn't want Warren to call you," his mom immediately said.

"Then you shouldn't have pulled a gun on him. Put it away, *now*," Raleigh ordered, and he was sure he sounded more like a sheriff than her son. "What the heck is going on here?"

Alma was crying all right, the tears streaming down

her face, and she shook her head. "I just want my keys so I can go home, and he wouldn't give them to me."

But Warren handed them to Raleigh just as Thea went to Warren's side.

"You're not driving home like this," Raleigh told his mother. "And Warren was right to do what he did." And no, hell didn't freeze over because he'd taken his *father's* side on this.

"Alma's not thinking straight. She wouldn't have shot me though," Warren insisted.

Probably not, but it was too big of a risk to take. That's why Raleigh held out his hand for his mother to give him the gun. She didn't jump to do that, but he didn't want to try to wrench it from her hand and end up risking her pulling the trigger by accident. She finally gave it to him and then collapsed with a hoarse sob against the steering wheel.

"This is all my fault," Alma managed to say, though it had to be hard to talk with her having to drag in her breath like that. "Simon did this for me."

Warren didn't seem surprised by that comment, which meant it'd likely been the topic of their conversation before things had taken a very bad turn.

"Simon might not have done anything wrong," Raleigh explained. "Especially nothing that had anything to do with you. We have two other solid suspects in Sonya's murder."

His mother lifted her head, blinked and stared at him. "Are you just saying that to make me feel better?"

"No. I'm saying it because it's true. And even if it

wasn't, you aren't responsible for what Simon does or doesn't do."

She shook her head again. "But the letter…"

Now, Warren did show some surprise. He frowned when he looked at Raleigh. "What letter?"

Since it wasn't his place to answer that, Raleigh just waited for his mom to say something, but she waved it off. "It doesn't matter. I shouldn't have written the letter in the first place."

Alma wiped away her tears and sat up straight. She was probably trying to look strong enough to drive, but Raleigh wasn't buying it.

"Are you going to press charges for her pulling the gun on you?" Raleigh asked Warren.

"No." He fixed his gaze on Alma. "I did wrong by her. By you," he added to Raleigh. "I deserve anything the two of you dish out."

Well, he didn't deserve to be shot, and Raleigh considered it progress that he felt that way. He mumbled a thanks for Warren not pressing those charges, and then he had a quick debate about how to handle this. He couldn't allow his mother to go home alone, and he didn't think handing her off to Dalton was a good idea.

"I need to drive my mother home," Raleigh finally said to Thea. "You can go back to town with Dalton. Or Warren."

Thea seemed to have a debate with herself, too. She volleyed glances at all of them. "Why don't Dalton and I go with you to take Alma home? We could use the cruiser."

Raleigh didn't have to guess why she would suggest

that. It was bullet resistant, and they could be attacked along the way. It was a good idea, but what wasn't good was extending the invitation for Warren to go with them. Warren must have sensed what Raleigh was thinking because he tipped his head to his truck.

"I'll be going," Warren said. "Now that I know Thea's okay, I need to be getting home." He hugged her and headed to his truck.

"I made a fool of myself," Alma mumbled, and the tears started again when Warren drove away.

Despite the crying, Raleigh didn't want to wait around to calm her down again, so he opened her door. "Come on. I'll have someone from the ranch come back and get your car."

His mom didn't argue with him about that, thank God, and he got her moving to the cruiser. However, he didn't get far. Only a few steps. Before Raleigh heard something that he didn't want to hear.

A gunshot.

At first Thea thought the sound was a car backfiring, but she glanced up the road and saw that Warren's truck was already out of sight. And there wasn't another vehicle with a running engine anywhere around.

Raleigh obviously knew what it was though because, in the split second that followed the shot, he hooked his arms around her and his mother, and he pulled them to the ground.

Alma made a sharp gasp of pain, and Thea immediately had a terrifying thought—that the woman had been shot. But Alma had hit her head during the fall.

She'd have a scrape on her cheek, but it was far better than the alternative.

Another shot came, and this one slammed into the ground, much too close to where they were.

Raleigh's gaze was firing all around. He was obviously trying to pinpoint the location of the shooter. Since Dalton was doing the same thing, Thea hooked her arm around Alma's waist and pulled the woman behind the back of her car. It wasn't ideal cover, but at least they weren't out in the open.

But Raleigh and Dalton were.

"Get down!" Thea shouted to them just as two more shots came right at them. The bullets tore into the asphalt and the gravel shoulder of the road.

Raleigh and Dalton stayed low and they scrambled toward the back of the vehicle with Alma and her. Thea had already drawn her gun, but she had no idea where to even return fire.

"You see the shooter?" she asked Raleigh.

"He's somewhere across the road. Call for backup."

Thea did that. She called the sheriff's office and got Alice. The deputy assured her that she'd come right out, but Thea reminded her to approach with caution. She didn't want anyone else killed.

Mercy. This confirmed to Thea she was the target.

Of course, Thea had known that when Marco had taken her at gunpoint, but this reminder hit her like a Mack truck slamming into her. This wasn't just about cops being in the line of fire. Raleigh's mom could be hurt, or worse.

"Raleigh!" Alma shouted. "Don't let those bullets hit you."

Easier said than done. Three more shots came, one right behind the other.

While she positioned her body over Alma's to keep the woman on the ground, Thea lifted her head enough to glance at the direction of the shots. And she groaned. Because there were way too many trees and even some large rocks. The shooter could be behind any one of them.

"I swear, I didn't see a gunman," Alma insisted. "Where did he come from?"

Thea figured he'd parked on a ranch trail just off the pasture and then used the rocks and trees for cover to get into position. Maybe he'd even been following Alma because it would have been easier to get to the older woman than it was Raleigh and her. With Alma's state of mind, she might not have even noticed if a stranger was behind her vehicle.

The next bullet slammed into Alma's car, shattering the window on the rear-passenger's side, and it sent glass flying at Dalton. He moved even farther back, but it wasn't enough. Dalton, and the rest of them, could still be hit.

Thea glanced behind them to try to figure out what to do. Now that Warren's truck was gone, there was an open space between the car and the cruiser. It was plenty big enough for them to be easy targets if they went running out there. But there might be another way around this.

"I can get to the cruiser and pull it up in front of you," Thea suggested.

Raleigh looked back at her, and even though he didn't give her a flat look, it was close. "You're not going there. And if you ignore my order and try it, I will go after you. That means, we'd both get shot."

Thea wanted to believe he was bluffing, but she doubted that he was. No way could she risk something like that. She couldn't lose Raleigh.

Even if he wasn't hers to lose.

"Stay down," Raleigh told her. "And make sure my mom stays put, too."

Thea was trying to do just that, but Alma kept calling out to Raleigh to be careful, and she was squirming so she could look at him, probably to make sure he was okay. Thea couldn't fault the woman for that. Raleigh was her only son, but she needed Alma to cooperate so she could help Raleigh return fire—if they got a chance to do that.

"Raleigh's a good cop," Thea reminded Alma. "Please stay down so I can help him."

Alma looked up at her, their gazes connecting, and even though it seemed to be the last thing the woman wanted to do, she nodded and quit struggling. She practically went limp on the ground.

Thea pivoted, still staying close to Alma but moving to the side so she stood a chance of having a clean shot. She tried again to pinpoint the shooter.

And she did.

Just as Raleigh and Dalton did, too—thanks to the sunlight glinting off the shooter's gun. He was in the center of the pasture, behind one of the big rocks. The rock was the perfect cover, but he had to lean out to shoot at them.

She waited, her heart pounding and her breath so thin that her chest was hurting. But Thea reminded herself that she'd been trained for this, and the stakes were too high for her to fail.

Dalton and Raleigh were obviously waiting, too, and both had their guns pointed in the direction of the shooter. The seconds crawled by, maybe because the guy was reloading, but Thea finally saw him. He moved out from behind the rock, already taking aim at them.

But Dalton, Raleigh and Thea all fired, their shots blending into a loud, thick blast that was deafening. They each fired several more times before she saw a man wearing a ski mask tumble out onto the ground.

They waited with the silence closing in around them. Raleigh was no doubt waiting to make sure the guy was actually dead and that he didn't have a partner waiting in the wings to gun them down when they moved.

She heard the sirens and glanced at the road to see the cruiser flying toward them. Alice, probably. Dalton verified that with a call to his fellow deputy, and Alice pulled to a stop directly in front of them.

Raleigh moved fast to get Alma into the cruiser. "Stay with her," he added to Thea. "I need to see if this guy is alive. If he is, we might finally know who's been trying to kill us."

Chapter Twelve

Raleigh stood at his kitchen counter and tossed back the shot of straight whiskey. It wasn't enough alcohol to cloud his head, but he hoped it would take off the edge. The adrenaline from the attack hadn't zapped nearly enough of this raw energy he was feeling.

Along with the frustration.

Because the shooter, Buck Tanner, was dead.

And that meant he hadn't been able to tell them who'd hired him. Not that he necessarily would have wanted to do that, but Raleigh would have figured out a way to get him to talk.

But now that option was gone, and they were back to square one. Well, with the exception that the two men who'd killed Sonya and kidnapped the baby were dead. That would have felt like some kind of justice if they'd managed to catch the hired thugs' boss, too.

"Did it help?" he heard Thea ask. He glanced over his shoulder to see Thea walking into the living room.

She was in his pj's again.

Obviously, she'd just gotten out of the shower because she was using a towel to dry her wet hair, and she tipped her head to the glass he was still holding.

"The jury's out on that," he said. He lifted the bottle. "You want a shot?"

"No, thanks. I'll probably just grab something to eat and crash. Unless you think we'll need to go back into your office tonight."

He shook his head. With the exception of the DNA on the second baby, they weren't waiting on any lab results, and there were no reports from SAPD on the fires at the security company and fertility clinic.

But there was some bad news he needed to tell Thea.

Since there was no easy way to put this, Raleigh just turned to face her and blurted it out. "Dan Shaw's body turned up about a mile from the security company." The very one the man had owned. "He died from two gunshots to the head."

Thea's breath hitched, and her shoulders dropped. Even though she hadn't personally known him, that didn't matter. Dan Shaw was dead because someone, probably Buck Tanner, had taken him hostage so he could escape.

"I think I'll have that drink now," she said, her voice shaky. She didn't look too steady, either.

Raleigh grabbed another glass from the cabinet, poured her a shot, and when she reached for it, that's when he noticed the bandage on the palm of her hand. She quickly tried to hide it beneath the sleeve of the bulky pj's, but he caught on to her wrist and had a better look.

"It's nothing." She pulled back her hand. "I just cut

it on a rock or something when I fell. I didn't even notice it until we were away from the scene."

Even though Raleigh knew it could have been much worse, it twisted his stomach to know she'd been hurt. He'd seen the blood on her clothes, of course. That's why she'd taken a shower and put her clothes in the washer as soon as they'd gotten to his house, but he'd thought the blood was his mom's—from the scrape she gotten when he'd pushed them to the ground.

"It's nothing," Thea repeated. She had a sip of the whiskey and grimaced, but that bad reaction didn't stop her from finishing off the rest of the shot.

Since looking at that bandage wasn't helping with that raw energy bubbling inside him, he opened the bag of takeout he'd gotten from the diner. Burgers and fries. It smelled good, but Raleigh doubted it would sit well with the knots in his stomach. Still, he wanted Thea to eat, so he put the food on some plates and set them on the table.

Thea glanced at the food and made another face. Not quite a grimace this time, but it was close. But she sat down and picked up one of the fries.

"Did you call your mom while I was in the shower?" she asked.

He nodded. "Like you, she's insisting she's okay. I doubt it's true in either your case or hers."

Thea lifted her shoulder. "My offer still stands. If you want to stay the night with her, I can go to my brother's."

She had indeed made that offer, but Sonya's baby was with Griff, Rachel and a Texas Ranger for extra protection. There'd been no attacks directed at the newborn, and Raleigh wanted to keep it that way. If Thea went there or to the McCall Ranch, the danger might go with her.

Of course, an attack could happen here, too, and that's why Raleigh had closed the gate that led to his house. He'd also alerted the hands who worked with his horses to report anything suspicious to him. Added to that, he'd turned on his security system.

Because the killer was still out there.

Raleigh didn't believe for a second that Marco and Buck had put this together themselves. No. Their boss was probably gathering another team of hired guns, and Raleigh had to be ready for whatever the snake threw at them.

"Alice is staying with my mom," he added. "And the ranch hands there will keep watch."

She nodded, took a tiny bite of the french fry and put it back on the plate. "What will happen to Sonya's baby?" she asked. "Both of her biological parents are dead, and Yvette and Nick don't have a claim on her, thank goodness."

Yeah, that definitely qualified as a *thank goodness*. Both the O'Haras were suspects, and he didn't want them getting anywhere near the baby.

"Social services is contacting Sonya's and Dr. Sheridan's next of kin. Sonya has an aunt who she was close to, and she's already asked about taking the baby."

Thea made a sound of approval but then frowned. Maybe because she'd gotten attached to the little girl when she'd been taking care of her. She tried the fry again, tossed it right back down and got up to go to the window. He'd closed all the blinds and curtains, but she lifted the edge of the blind and looked out.

"We can't live like this," she said. There'd been weariness in her voice earlier, but it had gone up a notch. "We have to know who's behind the attacks." She stayed quiet a moment and then turned back to him. "Why don't we set a trap, using me as bait."

Hell. Raleigh had figured this was coming, and Thea had to know he was going to nix it. He pushed back his plate and went to her. "I'm not going to watch you die so I can catch a killer."

"He or she wouldn't be able to kill me if we did this right. Just hear me out," she added when he opened his mouth to argue. "We could get the word out that I need to go see Warren, that it's some kind of emergency. The killer would probably set up another attack somewhere on the road. But we'd be ready. We could have some of the deputies hiding in the cruiser."

That wouldn't stop her from being killed. Heck, it could get the deputies killed, too.

"This could work," she went on, and he could tell that she wasn't just going to give up on this.

And that's why Raleigh kissed her.

It was playing dirty, but he couldn't listen to Thea talk about sacrificing herself to put an end to this. He kept the kiss short, and he eased back, fully expecting her to yell or even push him away.

She didn't.

Thea stared at him. A long time. And with their gazes locked, she caught on to the front of his shirt, wadding it up in her left hand as she dragged him back to her.

It was Thea who continued the kiss.

FROM THE MOMENT Thea had seen Raleigh in the kitchen, she'd known this kiss was going to happen. There was just too much energy sizzling between them. Too much emotion.

And too much frustration.

Raleigh seemed to try to cure all of that with the kiss. In one quick motion, she was in his arms, and the urgency of his mouth on hers let her know that neither of them were going to stop this. Even if they regretted it. Which they would.

Well, Raleigh would anyway.

Thea wasn't sure she could regret something like this that felt so right. Of course, it'd always felt right when she was with Raleigh. It'd been that way for her even when she'd been with him after learning the truth about Warren's affair. Not telling Raleigh had caused her to lose him, and she'd thought she would never be with him like this again. But she was wrong. It was happening, and it was happening fast.

The kiss became hotter, more intense, and it didn't take minutes but rather mere seconds. Thea just let herself go with it when he pulled her deeper into his arms so that their bodies were touching. It was an incredible sensation with him touching her, but it soon wasn't enough. She needed more.

Thankfully, Raleigh didn't have trouble giving her that.

He popped open the buttons on the loose pajama top she was wearing, and he slipped his hand inside. She hadn't put on a bra after her shower, and without the barrier of any clothes, Raleigh lowered his head and moved the kisses to her breasts.

Yes, this was *more*.

Raleigh kept on giving, too, when he pushed down the bottom of the pj's. She was wearing panties, but he also slid them down her legs, leaving her practically naked. If she hadn't been so desperate for him, that might have bothered her, but Raleigh didn't give her a chance to remember who she was much less the fact that she was undressed, and he wasn't.

He kissed her. In many places. Touched her, too. And Thea let herself be swept up into the sensations that came wave after wave. Every inch of her wanted him more than her next breath, but despite the burning need, Raleigh just kept up with the maddening foreplay.

When she could take no more, Thea did something about his clothes. It was hard to get his buttons undone while still kissing, but she managed it and got a very nice reward. Her hands on his bare chest.

He wasn't overly muscled, but he was toned and tight. Perfect. But then, she thought that "perfect" label applied to many things when it came to Raleigh. Thea kissed his neck and chest.

She would have kept going as he'd done, but he pulled her back up to him, and when their eyes met, Thea recognized the look he gave her. He was giving her an out if she wanted to stop.

She didn't.

So she went straight back to him. This time though, there was no more foreplay—something that her on-fire body was thankful for. Raleigh scooped her up and carried her straight to his room. The moment he had her on the bed, he took a condom from his nightstand drawer.

He moved onto the bed with her, the mattress giving way to their combined weight, and she helped him slide off his boots and jeans. His boxers, too. Everything was frantic now, their movements feverish from the need. He didn't waste a second after he put on the condom.

Raleigh pushed into her.

The pleasure raced through her, leaving her speechless. And breathless. But she could certainly feel, and the feelings soared when he started to move inside her.

The memories came. No way to stop them. They'd been together like this many times, but each of those times had always had the same intensity as the first. This was no different. Except Thea knew that it might be their last. Once Raleigh came to his senses, he might regret this enough that it would never happen again.

A heartbreaking thought.

But it was a thought that quickly went out the window when his thrusts inside her got faster. Harder. Until the need and tension climbed higher and higher.

When Thea couldn't hang on any longer, when she could take no more, she let herself surrender to the pleasure. The climax rippled through her, and the only thing she could do was hold on and let it consume her.

Moments later, as he whispered her name, Raleigh buried his face against her neck, and he finished what they'd started.

Chapter Thirteen

Raleigh closed his eyes and tried to sleep—something that usually happened easily after great sex. And this had indeed been *great*. But the sleep wouldn't come because his mind wasn't nearly as satisfied as the rest of him.

Sex was going to complicate things between Thea and him. Of course, the kissing had already done that, but this would send it through the roof. If the timing had been better, he might have just gone back in for another round of sex and put his worries on the back burner. But the timing only added to the complication.

He got up, but he tried to be as quiet as possible so that he wouldn't wake Thea. However, when he glanced at her, she was wide-awake and staring at the ceiling. Judging from the expression on her face, she was having more than just doubts and regrets.

"Was it that bad?" he joked, and because he was stupid, he brushed one of those complicating kisses on her mouth.

"No." She looked him straight in the eyes. "The frown is because it wasn't bad."

Unfortunately, he understood that. If the old chemistry between them had gone cold, it would have made leaving the bed easier. The kiss she gave him back in return certainly didn't help, either, but Raleigh forced himself to move away from her so he could get dressed.

"I should be keeping watch," he reminded her. "And checking for updates. You should try to get some sleep though."

But Raleigh knew that probably wasn't going to happen, and he was right. Thea immediately got up, and she headed to the guest room. A few minutes later, when she came out, she had dressed. Not in pj's, either, but her jeans and shirt.

"I'll make us a pot of coffee," she said, heading for the kitchen.

Raleigh considered asking Thea if she wanted to talk about what happened, but she was probably just as unsettled about this as he was. Plus, there wasn't time to launch into a conversation because his phone rang.

The call got Thea's attention, and she turned away from the coffee maker to hurry toward him. She was probably expecting it to be bad news, and when Raleigh saw the name on the screen, he considered that, as well. That's because it was Alice calling, and since she was staying with Alma, this could mean his mother was upset again. Maybe this time though, Alma hadn't pulled a gun on the deputy.

When Raleigh answered the call, the first thing he heard was the loud clanging noise. It definitely wasn't something he wanted to hear because he was pretty sure it was the security alarm.

"I think someone broke into the house," Alice immediately said.

The news hit him hard, but Raleigh reminded himself that it could be a glitch in the system. Or maybe his mom had accidentally set it off. Still, it was hard not to feel the fear and panic.

"I've gone into your mom's bedroom with her," Alice added, "and I've locked the door."

"I'm on the way there right now," Raleigh assured her. "Text or call me with what's happening." Though for now he wanted Alice to focus only on keeping his mother safe.

He ended the call and reached for his holster and keys. Thea obviously heard what Alice had said because she, too, grabbed her gun and her phone. Raleigh didn't especially want her coming with him since they'd already been attacked twice while on the road, but he didn't have time to make other arrangements.

He went to the window and looked out. Nothing out of the ordinary, and he hoped it stayed that way.

"Hurry," he told Thea, and the moment he had his own security system disengaged, he got them out the door and into the cruiser that he'd parked right by his porch.

He half expected someone to shoot at them, but thankfully no bullets came their way. So he sped off, while keeping watch to make sure they weren't ambushed. Thea was keeping watch, too, but he handed her his phone. He didn't have to tell her to answer it right away if Alice called back. Thea would. But Raleigh hoped that when Alice did contact them that it would be to say that it was a false alarm.

"Text my deputy Miguel," he instructed. "His number is in my contacts. He'll be at the office, and tell him I want him out at my mom's place."

It might be overkill, but that was better than being short of backup if this turned out to be an attack.

"How many ranch hands does Alma have on the grounds?" Thea asked after she'd fired off a text to Miguel.

"Two right now. She has a lot more who work for her, but they don't live there." Though he might end up calling a couple of them, too.

It was pitch-black, just a sliver of a moon, and there were no lights out on this rural road. No traffic, either, thank goodness, and that's why Raleigh went much faster than he would normally go.

His mom's ranch was only about five miles from his, so it didn't take long to get there. When he took the turn, the house came into view. All looked well, but Thea and he had to drive past some dark pastures. Since Buck Tanner had used a pasture to hide for his attack, that possibility was still fresh in Raleigh's mind.

His phone dinged with a text message. Then almost immediately dinged again. "Miguel's on the way," Thea relayed. "The second text is from Alice. She says no one has tried to break into the room, and she doesn't hear anyone in the house."

That was good, but it might be hard for his deputy to hear much of anything with the alarm still blaring. The only way to turn it off would be for her to go to the keypads at the front and back doors, and Raleigh preferred that she stay put.

Raleigh was about to tell Thea to let Alice know they were nearby, but he caught some movement from the corner of his eye. Thea must have seen it, too, because they both pivoted in that direction and took aim. Raleigh had braced himself for a ski-mask-wearing thug, but it wasn't.

It was Warren.

"Don't shoot," Warren said, leaning out from a tree that was right next to the road.

Raleigh lowered his window and glanced around to see if Warren was alone. He appeared to be.

"What are you doing here?" Thea asked, taking the question right out of Raleigh's mouth.

"I got a call from a criminal informant of mine. He said one of his buddies had been hired to kidnap Alma. That the person who hired the buddy wanted to do that to get back at me."

Raleigh huffed. "And you didn't call me with information like that?"

"I wasn't sure it was accurate. The guy isn't always reliable if he needs money for a fix. He needed money," Warren added.

And despite the tip not being reliable, Warren had come anyway. Later, Raleigh would press him as to why he'd done that and where he'd parked his truck, since it was nowhere in sight, but for now he needed to get to the house.

"My mom's with one of my deputies, but someone broke in. Thea and I are headed there now."

That put some alarm on Warren's face. "I didn't see anyone come onto the grounds, and I was keeping watch."

Later, Raleigh would want to know about that, too. Because if there was indeed an intruder, it was possible he'd been there for a while, before Warren's arrival.

"Let me go with you," Warren offered. "In case you need backup."

Raleigh wasn't sure he wanted that, but he also didn't want to sit around here while his mom was in danger. Nor did he want to leave Warren out here by himself. He unlocked the back door of the cruiser and motioned for Warren to get in. The moment he did that, Raleigh sped toward the house.

He didn't see anyone else along the way, but there was a truck in front of the house that belonged to one of the ranch hands who was supposed to be keeping watch. He pulled the cruiser to a stop next to it. And cursed. Because the driver's-side door was open, but the ranch hand wasn't inside.

Raleigh hated to think the worst, but with all the other attacks, it was the first possibility that came to mind. If someone had wanted to break into the house, they could have eliminated the ranch hands.

Since the driveway was on the side of the house and went all the way to the back, Raleigh kept driving. Kept looking. No one. But even from outside, he could hear the blare of the security system.

He pulled to a stop directly next to the back porch. "Wait here," Raleigh told Warren. "And let us know if anyone tries to come up behind us. Thea and I will go in and check on things." Maybe, just maybe, there'd be nothing wrong.

Raleigh glanced at Thea to make sure she was ready. She was. She had a firm grip on her gun as she opened the cruiser door. Raleigh did the same, but before he could even step out, he heard a hissing sound.

That was the only warning he got before the flames shot up in front of him.

THEA AUTOMATICALLY JUMPED back from the flames and put her hand in front of her face to shield it. But she was on full alert, too, because she knew that this could be some kind of diversion so that gunmen could kill them.

However, it also confirmed that this wasn't just a false alarm.

The threat was real, and that meant not only were they in danger but so were Alma and Alice.

Raleigh ran to her and pulled her back even farther. Like her, he shot glances all around them. So did Warren when he got out of the cruiser.

"The fire isn't touching the house," Raleigh let them know.

At least it wasn't yet. It appeared that someone had poured a line of accelerant and had lit it with perhaps a remote control. But if the breeze blew the flames into the house, it could catch the place on fire.

The fire was creating another problem, too. The smoke. It was thick and dark, and it seemed to come right at them, causing them all to cough. Worse, it was burning her eyes and making it hard to see. Definitely what she didn't want since someone could be out there.

Someone with plans to kill them.

Thea had figured there'd be another attack, but she'd thought it would come down to Raleigh and her against the person responsible for so much chaos. But now Warren was here, and that meant he was in danger, too. Maybe that had been part of the plan all along though.

"Cover me," Raleigh told Thea.

He headed to the far back right corner of the house, where there was some kind of control box. For the automatic sprinkler system, she soon realized. Raleigh hit the button to turn on all the nozzles, and they immediately began to pop up and start spraying water. It meant the three of them were getting wet, but it might keep the flames under control.

"I'll call the fire department," Warren offered, taking out his phone.

Good. And Dalton was on the way, too, but Thea didn't intend to wait. Especially not wait out in the open. With Raleigh ahead of her and Warren right behind, they started up the porch steps.

And they immediately stopped.

"Those are the two ranch hands who were supposed to be keeping watch," Raleigh whispered.

Oh, God. This wasn't good. Because she soon spotted the two men sprawled out on the porch.

"Are they dead?" she asked, afraid to hear the answer.

While Thea and Warren kept watch, Raleigh touched his fingers to one of the men's necks and then the other. "They're alive. It looks as if someone used a stun gun on them. Maybe drugged them, too."

The relief came, but it didn't last because someone had obviously gotten close enough to the hands to incapacitate them. And that someone could now be inside, doing the same, or worse, to Raleigh's mother and his deputy.

"I'll call for an ambulance," Warren volunteered.

Maybe the men wouldn't need medical attention right away, because an ambulance wouldn't be able to get onto the ranch until they were sure there wasn't a shooter nearby.

Raleigh went to the door. "Locked," he said, and he fished through his pocket for the keys.

Maybe the person who'd attacked the hands hadn't gone in through the back, but if he had, he'd clearly locked it behind him. Maybe to slow them down.

Or ambush them when they went in.

Once he had the door unlocked, Raleigh used the barrel of his gun to ease it open a couple of inches. Thea steeled herself up for some kind of attack.

But nothing happened.

Raleigh reached inside to the keypad, hit some buttons and the alarm stopped. Thea immediately tried to listen for any sounds coming from inside, but she heard nothing.

"According to the light on the security panel, the alarm was tripped with this door," Raleigh explained, his voice barely louder than a whisper.

So whoever had broken in had locked the door behind him. There were no obvious signs of forced entry, but someone skilled at picking a lock would be able to get in without leaving any obvious damage. Certainly though, an intruder would have guessed there'd be a security system. But maybe he didn't care, especially since the alarm would have masked his movements in the house.

But there was another possibility.

One that Thea hoped was what had actually happened. That the alarm had scared the guy off, and that he'd gone running. She wanted to confront this monster and stop him—or her—but she didn't want that to happen with Raleigh's mother or Warren around.

"Text Alice and tell her we're here and about to come in," Raleigh told her. "Ask her if they're okay."

Since Thea still had his phone, she did that and got a quick response back from Alice that Thea relayed to Raleigh. "They're fine. No one's tried to get into the room where they are."

Maybe it would stay that way.

Raleigh stepped into the kitchen. He didn't turn on the lights and looked around before he motioned for Warren and her to join him. No smoke inside, thank goodness, but if the sprinkler didn't put out the flames, there soon would be. That meant they'd need to evacuate Alma and Alice. They didn't have a choice about that, but it came with huge risks since it meant they'd be outside, where they could be gunned down.

Raleigh's phone dinged with a message. At first, Thea thought it was Alice again, but it was Dalton this time.

When Thea read the text, her stomach clenched. "Someone put a spike strip on the road after we drove through. Dalton hit it and all the tires on his cruiser are flat. He'll have to wait for Miguel to come and give him a ride out here."

Raleigh mumbled some profanity. Whoever was behind this had wanted to make sure Dalton didn't arrive to help them. And it had worked. But what did this monster have planned for them?

"Tell Dalton not to come on foot," Raleigh instructed. "I don't want someone gunning him down."

Neither did she. Enough people had been hurt or killed.

"After Miguel picks him up," Raleigh went on, "Dalton and he can secure the perimeter of the house and get the two hands into the cruiser."

Thea sent the response to the deputy and then lifted her head to try to detect any trace of accelerant in the house. She didn't want a new fire trapping them inside, but there were no unusual smells. No unusual sounds, either.

Since this was the first time she'd been in Alma's house, she had no idea where the bedroom was, but Raleigh started out of the kitchen. But first he motioned for Warren to keep watch behind them. Thea made sure no one was on the sides of them. Hard to do though because the house was dark.

Raleigh led them through a family room and then a foyer. He tested the knob on the front door. "It's still locked," he whispered to them.

That was good because hopefully it meant no one could get in that way while they were walking up to the second floor. Raleigh went up the first three steps of the curved staircase and looked up, no doubt hoping to get a glimpse of whoever had broken in.

Thea certainly didn't see anything, but she heard something. Not a sound from the second floor or stairs, either. This had come from the living room on the other side of the foyer. Warren and Raleigh must have heard it, too, because they pivoted in that direction.

Just as someone fired a shot right at them.

Chapter Fourteen

"Get down!" Raleigh shouted.

And he prayed Thea and Warren could do that before they got shot.

Warren didn't get down though. He fired in the direction of the shooter.

Even though Raleigh couldn't see the gunman and Warren probably couldn't, either, the shot paid off because their attacker didn't pull the trigger again. Raleigh did hear him scrambling for cover in the living room though. That was good because it gave the three of them a chance to get off the stairs and out of the foyer and into the living room.

It wasn't ideal, but at least there was a partial wall they could use that might prevent them from being gunned down.

From the moment that Thea and he arrived at the ranch, Raleigh had been steeling himself up for an attack. An attack that he had hoped to prevent, but obviously it was too late for that.

But who was behind this?

Raleigh silently cursed that it was something he still

didn't know. And he might not find it out anytime soon. Because the person who'd shot at them could be just another hired gun, someone doing the dirty work for Simon, Nick or Yvette.

Another shot came, and it slammed into the half wall. Since a bullet could easily go through it, Raleigh motioned for Thea and Warren to get to the side of the sofa. That would serve two purposes. Not only would it put some distance between the shooter and them, it would give them a better vantage point to make sure someone didn't sneak up on them by coming through the kitchen. The ranch hands were on the back porch, but even if they had regained consciousness, they still might not be able to stop someone else from getting inside.

His phone dinged just as there was another shot, and this bullet did rip through the drywall and went God knew where in the living room. Raleigh glanced back to make sure Thea and Warren were okay. They were. For now. But he motioned for them to get down.

"Alice texted," Thea whispered. "She heard the shots."

Of course she had. They were deafening, so that meant his mother had heard them, too, and she was probably terrified. Raleigh was feeling some fear of his own because he had to consider that this thug downstairs was just a distraction so his partner could get to Alma.

But if Alma was the target, why hadn't the person just bashed down the bedroom door after he'd broken in?

Why wait?

He couldn't think of a good reason for doing that. So that meant Thea, he or Warren was the target. Or maybe all three. But hopefully his mom would be out of harm's way while he figured out how to safely get to her.

Raleigh scrambled closer to Thea so the gunman wouldn't hear what he wanted her to text Alice. "Tell her that I want Mom and her in the bathtub."

That way, if this clown started shooting at the ceiling, Alice and his mother wouldn't get hit with stray shots.

While Thea sent off the message, Raleigh moved again so he could maybe catch of glimpse of the shooter. He hurried to the other side of the sofa, where he still had some cover, but he was also in a better position to take this guy out.

When the gunman leaned out to fire, Raleigh sent two bullets right at him. He couldn't tell though if he hit him, but at least it stopped the gunfire. Raleigh doubted that would last though.

And it didn't.

It only took a few seconds before the man leaned out again. This time, Raleigh didn't miss. His shot slammed into the guy, and he made a loud groan of pain before he collapsed onto the floor.

While he watched to make sure no one was at the top of the stairs, ready to shoot him, Raleigh went to the thug. The guy had on a ski mask, but Raleigh pulled it off him and checked for a pulse. Nothing.

"He's dead," Raleigh told the others. He made a quick study of the dead man's face, but didn't recognize him.

"You smell that?" Thea asked.

Raleigh was so focused on the shooter that it took him a moment to realize what she meant.

Smoke.

And it didn't seem to be coming from outside.

"Stay put," Warren told Thea.

Before Raleigh could figure out if it was a good idea or not, Warren ran back toward the kitchen. Thea clearly didn't like that any better than Raleigh did, but they needed to know what was going on. And what was going on wasn't good. Raleigh could tell that from Warren's stark expression when he came back into the living room.

"Someone set a fire in the pantry." Warren's words rushed out with his frantic breath. "You have to get Alma and your deputy out of the house. And I need to move those hands off the porch in case the fire spreads back there."

Yes, he did. But that left Raleigh with a huge problem. He didn't want Warren on the porch without backup, especially when the man was trying to move the unconscious hands. But Raleigh didn't think it was a good idea for Thea to be outside, either. Still, that might be better than her being inside a house that was now on fire.

"Go with him," Raleigh told her.

She didn't argue, but he could practically feel the hesitation before she nodded. She tossed him his phone and followed Warren to the back.

Raleigh hated that it had come down to this. Yes, it was her job as a cop, but that didn't make this easier to swallow. He was afraid for Thea. Afraid he might never see her again. And angry with himself for not telling her just how much she meant to him.

He pushed those feelings aside so he could go up the stairs and rescue his mother, but his phone dinged after he'd made it only a few steps. It was another text from Alice.

Someone's breaking into the bedroom.

Hell. For just a few words, they packed a wallop, and Raleigh practically ran up the stairs. Of course, he had to stop when he got to the top because whoever was trying to break into his mother's room would see him the moment he was in the hall.

Unfortunately, there were no lights on in the hall, so it took Raleigh a moment to pick through the darkness and see the shadowy figure outside the bedroom. And it appeared he was trying to get the door unlocked. Raleigh didn't shoot the guy because he couldn't even tell if he was armed.

"I'm Sheriff Lawton," Raleigh called out. "Put your hands in the air."

The man pivoted, and that's when Raleigh caught a glimpse of his gun. A gun he pointed at Raleigh. He didn't give the thug a chance to fire though because Raleigh pulled the trigger first. Two shots slammed into the man's chest, causing him to drop just as fast as his partner had minutes earlier.

Raleigh hurried to him. The guy was dead all right. That felt like a hard rock in his stomach, but he hadn't had another option. He couldn't let the guy shoot him. Nor could he let him break into the bedroom.

"Alice, it's me," Raleigh called out, knocking on the door. While he waited, he sent off a quick text to Thea to let her know he was okay. "There's a fire," he added to Alice, "and both of you need to get out of the house."

Almost immediately, he heard the sound of running footsteps, and a moment later, Alice opened the door. Alma was right behind her, and while his mom did indeed look terrified, he couldn't take the time to console her. The smoke was already making its way up the stairs, and he didn't want them trapped.

Alice hooked her arm around Alma's waist to get her moving, and both women glanced at the dead guy in the hall. Alma looked away, a hoarse sob coming from her throat.

"My house is on fire?" Alma asked. She was clearly alarmed by not just the dead man but also the fact that she might lose everything. Too bad that everything might include her life if there were other hired guns waiting outside.

"The fire department's on the way," Raleigh said.

Later, once he had everyone safe, he would make sure that was true and fill her in on everything else that'd happened. Of course, the fire department was almost certainly nearby, or soon would be, but they were no doubt waiting on word from him to make sure it was safe to come onto the grounds. Right now, it definitely wasn't safe.

"Keep watch behind us," Raleigh told Alice just in

case someone was hiding in another one of the bedrooms off the hall.

With Raleigh ahead of them, he led them to the
stairs, hurrying as much as he could. But he also had
to watch and listen to make certain they weren't about
to be ambushed. He didn't see anyone at the bottom of
the stairs or in the foyer, but that didn't mean someone
wasn't there.

"The cruiser's parked right outside," he told Alice.
"Get Mom inside, and I'll find the others." Including
those two hands who could be hurt.

Opening the door was a risk, but everything he did
at this point would be. Still, the cruiser was the safest
place for his mother.

He eased open the door and looked out. No one. So
Raleigh unlocked the cruiser and then handed the keys
to Alice.

"You're not coming with us?" Alma asked. Her voice
and the rest of her were shaking.

"I'll be there soon," he told her and hoped that was
true. "Move fast," he added to Alice in a whisper. "And
if something goes wrong, drive out of here as quickly
as you can."

Alice nodded, and Raleigh stepped out onto the
porch to give them cover as they ran to the cruiser.
However, Alice and his mom hadn't even gotten in yet
when he heard something that caused his heart to slam
against his chest.

"No!" someone shouted, and Raleigh was pretty
sure that someone was Warren, who was at the back
of the house.

And the shout was followed by another sound Raleigh didn't want to hear.

A gunshot.

THEA TRIED TO keep watch of the backyard as she pulled one of the hands off the porch and away from the fire. It wasn't easy. He was a big guy, and since she couldn't lift him, she had no choice but to drag him down the steps and toward the grassy area behind the house.

Warren was doing the same thing to the second hand, and he was struggling as much as Thea was. She only hoped this wasn't doing more damage to Warren's already injured body, but even if it had, it wouldn't have stopped him.

The sprinklers didn't help the situation, either. They were still going full blast, and while that appeared to be containing the fire in the yard, it was also soaking Warren and her. Plus, the combination of water and smoke in her eyes made it even harder to see.

She'd just made it to the bottom step when she heard the two shots from inside the house. It caused her pulse to skyrocket because they had almost certainly come from the second floor, where Raleigh would be rescuing his mom and Alice.

Thea looked up at the windows but couldn't see anything, and she forced herself not to run inside. However, the second her phone dinged with a text message, she stopped dragging the ranch hand and looked at the screen. It was from Raleigh. We're okay.

The breath of relief rushed out of her, and she prayed it was true, that Raleigh hadn't told her that just to stop her from going inside. She would though. As soon as she'd finished moving the hand, she needed to make sure Raleigh, Alice and his mom had made it out. That meant going inside.

Thea kept dragging the hand. She had to get the man far enough away from the house in case the fire caused it to collapse. He still hadn't regained consciousness, and there was no way he'd be able to move to save himself.

"Over here," Warren told her.

He motioned toward the front of a small barn, where he was heading. It wasn't ideal cover because both ends were wide-open, but it would give them some protection from the sides. As it was now, they were out in the open, where anyone could gun them down.

"Was Raleigh hurt?" Warren asked, and he didn't sound like a lawman but rather a concerned father.

She shook her head. "He said they were all okay."

Thea's arms were aching by the time she reached the barn, but she got the hand in. It was like stepping into a cave since it was so dark. Too dark for her to see any of the corners. Plus, there was a tractor and some other equipment, plenty of places for someone to hide. That's why she took a moment to listen and made sure no one was inside. If someone was, he or she wasn't making a sound.

Since Warren was struggling, she went out to help him drag in the second hand, and she positioned him next to the other one.

"Wait here with them in case the fire comes this way and they need to be moved again," she told Warren. She tried to wipe some of the water off her face. "I need to check on Raleigh to see if he needs any help getting Alma out."

She expected Warren to argue with that because he didn't like her going out there without backup. And he no doubt wanted to argue, but he probably knew it wouldn't do any good. Instead, he huffed.

"Don't go in through the back," he warned her.

She wouldn't. By now, the fire had probably spread into the kitchen. Or maybe even farther into the house. That meant she'd need to go on the side so she could get to the front porch. But hopefully that's where Raleigh would be if he had indeed managed to get his mom and Alice out of the house.

Before she could start running, Warren caught on to her hand and made eye contact with her. It was so dark that it was hard to fully see his expression, but his forehead was bunched up with worry.

"Be careful," he said.

She was about to remind him to do the same thing, but then she saw the change in Warren's body language. His shoulders went back, and he started lifting his gun.

"No!" Warren shouted, his attention on the area behind her.

That was the only warning Thea got before the gunshot blasted through the air.

For a horrifying moment, she thought Warren or she had been shot. But the bullet went into the barn just as Warren grabbed hold of her and yanked her to the floor.

At least that's what he tried to do.

But someone took hold of her from behind, hooking his arm around her throat. In the same motion, he knocked her Glock from her hand and put a gun to her head.

The fear and adrenaline slammed into her, and her body went into fight mode. She rammed her elbow into his stomach, but it didn't work. The man was wearing some kind of body armor, and he didn't loosen his grip. In fact, he tightened it and dug the barrel of the gun into her temple.

Warren cursed and froze, his weapon aimed at an attacker she couldn't see, but he must have realized he didn't have a shot, because Warren scrambled to the side of the tractor. Good. At least he wouldn't be gunned down—which was probably what her attacker had planned to do because he fired another bullet in Warren's direction.

"Let go of her," Warren demanded.

Thea doubted that would work, and it didn't. The man held on. But he didn't start to move as if to escape, and he didn't fire any other shots at Warren. He seemed to be waiting for something. But what did he want and why was he doing this?

"Not much longer now," he growled in her ear. His voice was a raspy whisper. Maybe it was Nick or Simon, but it could be just another hired thug. One that maybe Yvette had sent to attack them.

When she heard someone running toward them, the man shifted her body so that she was facing the opening of the barn. He stayed behind her, using her as a shield.

Just as Raleigh came into view.

He'd obviously run through the sprinklers because

he was wet, and even though he had his gun aimed and ready, he didn't have a clean shot. However, he must have been able to see her attacker's face because Raleigh cursed.

"What the hell do you think you're doing?" Raleigh snapped.

"Finishing this," the man readily answered. He didn't whisper this time though, and Thea had no trouble recognizing his voice.

It was Simon.

A DOZEN THOUGHTS went through Raleigh's head, and none of them were good.

First and foremost though was that Thea was in grave danger. He could lose her right here, right now, to this sick piece of work. Raleigh had to stay alive to try to save her, and that's why he took cover by the side of the barn door.

Thea had to be terrified, but she was clearly trying to rein in her fear. Warren wasn't even attempting the facade. Raleigh could practically feel Warren's rage, and he shook his head, hoping it would keep Warren from launching himself at Simon. Raleigh wanted to try to defuse this, and that wouldn't happen if gunfire broke out.

And it wasn't just Thea and Warren he had to be concerned about. The two hands were on the barn floor, and they could easily be hit with gunfire. Simon basically had five people's lives in his hands.

"I thought you were in love with my mother," Raleigh reminded Simon. He kept watch around them, trying to make sure Simon didn't have another goon who would try to sneak up on them. "You've got a funny way of showing it since you nearly killed her with the fire you had your hired thug set. And now her house is burning down."

No way for Raleigh to save the house. Because it was too risky for him to get the fire department on the grounds. Hopefully Alice had managed to get his mother far from here.

"I *was* in love with Alma," Simon snapped. "Until I read that letter about her still having feelings for Warren. I've waited in the wings for years for her to be through with him, and just when I finally thought it had happened, Alma does something like this."

So that letter was the motive, and Raleigh could fill in the rest. "You killed Sonya and Hannah to get back at Warren, to punish him."

"And it worked. Warren nearly went crazy blaming himself and trying to figure out who killed Hannah." Simon smiled, but it quickly faded. "Except Sonya wasn't supposed to die. The men were supposed to kidnap her, but they overreacted when she escaped and ran."

"They murdered her," Raleigh pointed out. "Since you hired them, you're guilty of murder, too. And endangering the babies. How the hell could you do something like that to them?"

"I didn't endanger them, and I sure as heck didn't hurt them," Simon yelled. He glanced around, too, as if looking for something. Or someone. "Hannah's baby was well cared for, and Thea would have already been dead, but she was too close to Sonya's kid, so Marco couldn't shoot her."

That's why Thea had been spared. All because she was in the wrong place at the wrong time. Another minute before or after, and the baby might not have been close enough to her, and Marco or Buck would have gunned her down. Like Simon was planning to do.

Or not.

Simon obviously had already had a chance to kill her, so why hadn't he? Was he waiting for Warren to come out from cover so he could shoot him first?

Or did Simon plan to kill both Thea and him in front of Warren?

That way, Warren would lose his son and the woman he loved like a daughter. If that was what Simon had in mind, then Raleigh had to stop him. That meant buying himself some time so he could figure out how to safely launch himself at Simon.

"Why involve Sonya, Hannah and Thea in this? Why didn't you just kill me?" Warren growled.

Simon's mouth tightened into a sneer. "Because I loved Alma enough that I didn't want her to grieve. I wanted her over and done with you, and if you'd been murdered, you would have become a martyr to her. That's why I didn't rat you out to your wife and kids. To Raleigh," he added.

Maybe. But Simon might have been worried that Warren would have chosen Alma instead of his wife and family. That definitely wouldn't have worked in Simon's favor to try to win Alma's heart.

"Everything I've done has been for Alma," Simon insisted. "That should prove to you how much I loved her."

No, it only proved that Simon was pathetic. And a killer.

A killer who clearly planned to murder Thea, but he wasn't trying to do that. Why? Simon had Warren right where he wanted him.

A moment later, Raleigh had his answer to that, and it wasn't an answer he liked.

"Finally," Simon snapped.

Raleigh heard the movement behind him, and he turned in that direction. And his heart skipped a couple of beats. Because there was a ski-mask-wearing thug coming toward him, and he wasn't alone.

He had Alma with him.

Hell. This was the reason Simon hadn't already added more murders to his list of crimes. He wanted to kill Alma in front of Warren. Or vice versa. Either way, Simon would almost certainly then try to murder all of them since he couldn't leave this many witnesses alive.

"Where's Alice?" Raleigh asked.

"This jerk used a stun gun on her," Alma answered, her voice cracking. "We didn't see him in time. Before Alice could drive away, he pulled her from the cruiser and left her on the driveway when he took me. Raleigh, I'm so sorry."

He hated that his mom felt the need to apologize for a thug assaulting a deputy and then manhandling her. Hated even more that this was happening. One way or another though, he would stop it. He just had to make sure he didn't get anyone killed in the process.

"Simon," his mother said, her voice quivering even more. She shifted her attention to Thea, then Raleigh and finally Warren. With each shift, her eyes got wider, and he could see the horror on her face when she realized what was happening. "Simon," she repeated.

"Don't look at me like that," Simon growled at her. "You're responsible for this."

"He read the letter," Raleigh told her.

Alma shook her head. "And you felt you had to do this because I still love Warren?" She didn't wait for an answer. "Because Warren doesn't love me. He's back with his wife, and it's over between us."

The glare that Simon gave Alma was scalpel sharp. "It'll never be over between you. Never. But it ends now. Everything ends."

Simon tipped his head to the masked thug, and the man shoved Alma forward, right into Raleigh. Raleigh didn't catch her because it would have meant taking his aim off Simon, but he used his body to help break the fall, and then he maneuvered himself in front of her.

Raleigh braced himself for Simon and his hired gun to start shooting, but the thug took off running. He ran past them and to the back opening of the barn, where Raleigh saw him press something he took from his pocket. Moments later, there was a hissing sound, and the flames shot up in front of the barn.

Alma screamed, and Raleigh prayed it wasn't because the fire had burned her. Even if it had, he couldn't take the time to check because he had to get her out of there. Not in the direction of the fire, either. Raleigh dragged her into the barn.

"If any of you move, Thea will be the first to die," Simon warned them.

Raleigh looked at Simon's face, and that's when he knew. Simon intended for all of them to die.

Warren moved closer to the end of the tractor. No doubt so he'd be in a better position to return fire if he got the chance. Right now, neither Warren nor he had a clean shot, so he had to do something to tip the odds in their favor.

"Get down," Raleigh whispered to his mom, and he hoped she listened. If not, Simon might try to shoot her.

Warren came out from behind the tractor, causing Simon to turn his gun in his direction. Thea took full advantage of no longer having the barrel pressed to her head. She shoved her weight against Simon, causing him to become off-balanced just enough so that when he pulled the trigger, his shot missed.

Simon fired again.

And again.

Thea scrambled away from Simon, making a beeline to her gun that was on the floor. But before she could even reach it, the shot rang out.

It seemed as if time had frozen. Raleigh thought maybe his heart had, too. He knew he hadn't been the one to pull the trigger, but obviously someone had.

This time, it wasn't Simon.

Raleigh saw the shock register on the man's face. Then saw the blood spread across the front of his shirt. Clutching his chest, Simon dropped to his knees, his stare frozen on the person who'd just put a bullet in him.

Alma.

His mother had snatched up Thea's gun. And she hadn't missed. If the shot hadn't killed him, it soon would because he was bleeding out fast.

Despite what had played out in front of him, Raleigh quickly shifted his attention to the thug at the back of the barn. The man had already lifted his gun and was about to fire. But Raleigh fired first. The guy didn't fall on his knees but rather face-first onto the ground.

The adrenaline was still slamming hard through Raleigh, but he checked to make sure everyone was okay. He pulled Thea to her feet. No blood, thank God. It was the same for Warren. But when he looked back at his mother, the adrenaline spun right out of control.

Because his mother had been shot.

Chapter Fifteen

Everyone who mattered was alive. That's what Raleigh kept reminding himself as they sat in the ER waiting room. Thea, his deputies, the drugged ranch hands and yes, even Warren had made it through the hellish nightmare. But at the moment, it didn't feel like a victory.

Because his mother might not make it.

That wasn't easy for him to consider. Especially since the man who'd put the bullet in her had been her friend for as long as Raleigh could remember. At least the *friend* was now dead, and so were all the thugs he'd hired to carry out his sick plan of revenge against Warren and Alma.

Thea was seated next to Raleigh, resting her head against his shoulder. Her hair and clothes were still damp from the soaking they'd gotten with the sprinklers, and she smelled like smoke. No physical injuries, but she had that stark look in her eyes. The one that told Raleigh that what'd happened this night would stay with her forever. It might be something she could never get past. And since he was part of those nightmarish memories, too, Thea might be done with him, as well.

Warren wasn't faring much better. He was sitting across from Thea and him. Again, no injuries, but he had his head in his hands, and every now and then he made a soft groaning sound. He definitely looked as if he needed some rest. And maybe some pain meds since Raleigh knew Warren was still recovering from his own shooting that'd happened a while back.

"If you want to go on home to your wife and kids," Raleigh told him, "I'll call you with any updates."

Raleigh immediately wished he hadn't worded it like that. It sounded bitter. Which he wasn't. Well, not bitter about Warren anyway. It was going to take a while before he didn't feel such things about Simon.

"Helen knows I'm here," Warren said.

Helen was his wife, and Raleigh knew Warren had called both his son Egan and her shortly after they'd arrived at the hospital. Raleigh had only heard bits and pieces of Warren's side of the conversation, but he'd told them that he was fine and there was no reason for them to come and get him. Whether or not they would stay away was anyone's guess.

"Helen is okay with you being here?" Thea asked.

There was plenty of hesitation in her voice. But it was a good question. Raleigh wanted to know the same thing. Warren had put enough strain on his marriage without adding more. Just his being here could be *more* in Helen's eyes.

Warren took his time answering. "Helen's worried about me, but she knows why I need to be here. Because of Thea and you."

There it was again. The confusion swirled with all the other things Raleigh was feeling.

"I know," Warren added a moment later. He no doubt saw the mixed emotions on Raleigh's face. "You don't want me to worry about you, but you're my son, and worry comes with the territory of being a father. And for the record, I worried about you even before my relationship with your mother came to light. I know I wasn't involved in your life, but I loved you," he said in a mumble.

Raleigh wasn't sure he wanted to hear that love thing. But at least it didn't twist at him the way it usually did when he thought about Warren being his father. Maybe that was a start. Thea must have thought so because she managed a very short, very slight smile.

The silence settled among them for several long moments before Warren shook his head again. "I should have figured out it was Simon and should have stopped him before it came down to this."

Raleigh gave a frustrated sigh because he felt the same way.

Thea, however, huffed, and this time when she lifted her head from Raleigh's shoulder, there was no trace of a smile. "I could have missed it in the job description, but a badge or a former badge doesn't give you ESP. Simon hid his true self from a lot of people, and he's the only person to blame for what happened. The. Only. Person," she emphasized.

Raleigh looked at her, their eyes connecting, and he was relieved to see that what she'd said wasn't lip service. That was big of her since he'd come damn close to letting her die tonight.

At least the babies hadn't been around for this particular attack, and now that Simon and his hired guns were dead, they were out of danger. Soon, Hannah's baby would be reunited with her birth parents—something they were eager for. Sonya's daughter might be a little trickier. According to the last call Raleigh had gotten from Miguel, they would still need the DNA results before handing over the child that Hannah had delivered.

Raleigh's phone dinged, indicating he had another text message. He'd gotten a lot of them in the hour that they'd been at the hospital since his mom's ranch was now a crime scene that had to be processed. Or at least it would be once the fire department and medical examiner cleared out and took the bodies to the morgue.

"It's from Miguel," Raleigh told Thea when she glanced at his phone. It wasn't the best of news, but it was what he'd expected. "They managed to put out the fire, but most of Mom's house was destroyed."

"Alma's stronger than she looks. She'll get through this and will rebuild," Warren said, and then his forehead bunched up when he glanced at Raleigh. "Sorry."

Raleigh wasn't sure exactly what the apology was for. Maybe because Warren didn't want to remind him that he knew enough about Alma to make comments like that. But it was the truth. His mom was strong, especially under pressure.

First though, she had to stay alive.

"If it's all right, I'd like to be the one to call Hannah's kin," Warren continued a moment later, and he was talking to Raleigh. "I want to tell them who was responsible for her death. It won't be much comfort to them because it won't bring her back, but at least they'll know."

Raleigh nodded, and it was a reminder that he needed to tell Sonya's relatives, as well.

"So, what will happen with you two?" Warren asked.

The question threw Raleigh, and it caused Thea to pull back her shoulders. She looked at him. Raleigh looked at her. And he realized he didn't have a clue what the answer was. But he knew what he wanted to happen.

He wanted to put the past behind them and be with Thea.

Raleigh wasn't even sure that was possible though.

He didn't get a chance to start figuring it out, either, because he saw Dr. Jacobs, the surgeon, making his way toward them. Thea, Warren and he all stood, and Raleigh could tell they were doing what he was—trying to steel himself up for whatever the news might be.

"Alma made it through surgery just fine," Dr. Jacobs immediately said.

Raleigh hadn't expected the relief to hit him so hard, but it nearly knocked the breath out of him. It did the same to Thea because she practically sagged against him. He looped his arm around her waist in case her legs felt as unsteady as his did.

"The bullet didn't hit anything vital, and I was able to remove it with only a small incision," the doctor went on. "She'll have to stay in the hospital a couple of days, of course, but I expect her to make a full recovery."

"When can I see her?" Raleigh asked.

"You can pop into recovery for just a second or two. She's woozy but awake. Follow me," the doctor instructed. Dr. Jacobs started to move but then stopped and looked at Thea and Warren. "I can only allow immediate family in the recovery room, but if you're close to Alma, you'll be able to see her from the observation window."

Warren shook his head. "I'll just be going. I need to get home." He hugged Thea. "I'm not offering you a ride," he added to her, and even though Warren had whispered it, Raleigh still heard it. "Stay here and work things out with Raleigh."

That sounded like approval for a relationship between Thea and him. Not that Raleigh needed approval from Warren. But it still felt good to get it.

Warren stepped back from Thea and extended his hand to Raleigh. Again, it wasn't much, just a small gesture, but it felt like they were moving in the right direction. Raleigh shook his hand, and judging from the way Warren smiled, it seemed as if Raleigh had handed him the moon. Warren tipped his hat to Dr. Jacobs and headed out while Thea and he followed the doctor down the hall.

"Your mother might not be so happy to see me," Thea muttered, suddenly sounding uncomfortable.

"She's alive. We're alive. That'll make her happy."

Raleigh meant that, too, but he wasn't sure what he'd see when they approached the recovery room. His mother had just been shot. And had killed a man. She might not bounce back from that anytime soon.

Thea stopped at the window while Raleigh went in,

but Alma lifted her hand and motioned for Thea to join him.

"Immediate family only," the doctor reminded Alma.

"Thea's practically family," Alma insisted. "Or she should be."

Coming on the heels of Warren's *So, what will happen with you two* question, this felt like matchmaking. Badly timed matchmaking at that. Thea might still be in shock, and he didn't want to press her with Warren's question or anything else.

Thea walked into the room, her steps slow and cautious. "How are you feeling?" she asked his mother.

His mother managed to eke out a smile, though it was clear she was weak and sleepy from the drugs. "Better now that you two are here." The smile didn't last though, and there were tears in her eyes when she looked at Raleigh. "I had to kill Simon. If I hadn't—"

"None of us would be here," Raleigh interrupted. "You saved our lives. Warren's, too." He debated if he should add more about that, but his mother appeared to be waiting for him to continue. "He stayed here until he found out you were out of the woods, and then he went home."

No need to add that he was going home to his wife. Alma knew that. And she nodded. "Good." And it seemed genuine.

Love had definitely given her a kick in the teeth, but maybe one day she could put aside her feelings for Warren and find someone who didn't make her part of his secrets and lies. Of course, without those secrets and lies, Raleigh wouldn't exist.

"The house is gone, I suppose?" Alma asked.

He hadn't planned to bring it up, but since she had, Raleigh nodded. "I'll do the insurance paperwork to get the rebuild started, and you can stay with me until it's done."

"Thea won't mind if I'm there?" his mother pressed.

"Of course not," Thea jumped to answer. "There's no reason for me to mind." In fact, she said it so fast that it made Raleigh wonder if Thea had plans to avoid his place altogether.

Alma took Thea by the hand and inched her closer to the bed. "You'll always be close to Warren. I would never want to change that. I just want you to know that I'll welcome you, too. I mean, it's as plain as the nose on my face that you're in love with my son."

Thea pulled in her breath, and Raleigh thought some of the color drained from her face. She didn't get a chance to respond though because the doctor tapped his watch. "Your time's up. You can visit Alma in the morning, after we've moved her out of recovery."

Raleigh nodded and then brushed a kiss on his mom's cheek. "Get some rest."

"Tell her you love her," his mom countered, and she quickly closed her eyes, no doubt a ploy so he wouldn't argue with her.

Yeah, she was definitely matchmaking.

Raleigh didn't say anything until they were out of the recovery room and back in the hall that led to the waiting area. "Sorry about what my mom said."

Thea stopped and looked at him. Actually, she glared a little. "I'm not sorry. If she hadn't brought it up, I would have. I'm in love with you." But she immediately continued without giving him a chance to respond. "It's okay if you don't feel the same way. No pressure. But I'm tired of pretending that it's only an attraction between us. For me, it's a whole lot more."

Since it sounded as if she was getting a little angry—and because she wouldn't let him get a word in edgewise—he pulled her to him and kissed her. He made sure it was way too long and way too hot for a hospital hallway. But he'd wanted to make a point. Unfortunately, the point-making got a little clouded when Thea moved right into that kiss.

Thea and he kept it up until he heard someone clear their throat. A nurse, who was smiling at them but had her eyebrow raised. Raleigh knew her. She was Betsy Fay Millard, and she was a close friend of his mother's. Which meant Alma would soon know about this.

And would no doubt approve.

Betsy Fay hitched her thumb to the room next to them. "It's empty if you two need to work something out." She winked at them and strolled away.

Raleigh supposed he should be a little embarrassed about kissing Thea like that in a public place, but embarrassment wasn't a barrier to what he needed to get done. He took Thea into the room and kissed her again, all the while trying to figure out how to tell her the most important thing he'd ever have to tell her.

The second kiss lasted as long as he could make it last until they both needed air. And when they broke away from each other, Thea looked up at him and smiled. That was it. She didn't say anything. Didn't have to. Because he could see in her eyes every drop of the love she felt for him.

Man, it was amazing.

And just like that, everything suddenly felt right, as if all the pieces of his life had lined up the way they should. That made it a whole lot easier for him to say what was on his mind.

"I love you, Thea." Raleigh didn't have to think about it—he meant it with all his heart.

"Took you long enough," she joked. Some tears watered her eyes, but since she was smiling, he thought that was a good thing. She wadded up a handful of his shirt and pulled him back to her.

Raleigh made sure the third kiss was one they would both remember.

* * * * *

IN SELF DEFENCE

DEBRA WEBB

Franklin County, Tennessee, has a large community of Mennonites. During the years we lived in Tennessee we were pleased to call so many of them friends. This book is dedicated to all the folks who embrace and appreciate what makes each of us unique.

Chapter One

Franklin County, Tennessee
Monday, February 25, 9:10 p.m.

The red and blue lights flashed in the night.

Audrey Anderson opened her car door and stepped out onto the gravel road. She grimaced and wished she'd taken time to change her shoes, but time was not an available luxury when the police scanner spit out the code for a shooting that ended in a call to the coroner. Good thing her dedicated editor, Brian Peterson, had his ear to the police radio pretty much 24/7 and immediately texted her.

The sheriff's truck was already on-site, along with two county cruisers and the coroner's van. So far no news vans and no cars that she noticed belonging to other reporters from the tri-county area. Strange, that cocky reporter from the *Tullahoma Telegraph* almost always arrived on the scene before Audrey. Maybe she had a friend in the department.

Then again, Audrey had her own sources, too. She reached back into the car for her bag. So far the closest private source she had was the sheriff himself—which was only because he still felt guilty for cheating on her back in high school.

Audrey was not above using that guilt whenever the need arose.

Tonight seemed like the perfect time to remind the man she'd once thought she would marry that he owed her one or two or a hundred.

She shuddered as the cold night air sent a shiver through her. Late February was marked by all sorts of lovely blooms and promises of spring, but it was all just an illusion. It was still winter and Mother Nature loved letting folks know who was boss. Like tonight—the gorgeous sixty-two-degree sunny day had turned into a bone-chilling evening. Audrey shivered, wishing she'd worn a coat to dinner.

Buncombe Road snaked through a farming community situated about halfway between Huntland and Winchester—every agricultural mile fell under the Franklin County Sheriff's jurisdiction. The houses, mostly farmhouses sitting amid dozens if not hundreds of acres of pastures and fields, were scattered few and far between. But that wasn't the surprising part of the location. *This* particular house and farm belonged to a Mennonite family. Rarely did violence or any other sort of trouble within this quiet, closed community ripple beyond its boundaries. Most issues were handled privately and silently. The Mennonites kept to themselves for the most part and never bothered anyone. A few operated public businesses within the local community, and most interactions were kept strictly within the business domain. There was no real intermingling or socializing within the larger community—not even Winchester, which was the county seat and buzzed with activity.

Whatever happened inside this turn-of-the-nineteenth-century farmhouse tonight was beyond the closed community's ability to settle amid their own ranks.

Though Audrey had lived in Washington, DC, for the past ten years, she had grown up in this part of southern Tennessee. There had never been a murder among the Mennonites that she could recall. In fact, she was reasonably certain there had never been any violence involving one of them, unless the perpetrator was someone who had abandoned the Mennonite life. Even that was nearly unheard of.

Tucking her clutch bag under her arm, Audrey palmed her cell phone and shoved the car door shut with her hip. The four-inch heels she had chosen to wear to the Chamber of Commerce Business Awards Banquet dug into the gravel with each step she made. She sighed. Sacrifices were a part of getting the story. What was the loss of a pair of shoes if there was a nice spike in subscriptions?

For a newspaper, circulation—whether print or online—was everything.

She might be the owner, but she also had the most investigative experience, which meant she had to get out in the field—had to get her hands dirty. How else was she going to turn the *Winchester Gazette* around? She not only had to get the story, she had to uncover the story no one else unearthed. It helped considerably that her family had deep roots in Franklin County, knew God and everyone who lived within a fifty-mile radius of her hometown. More important, the sitting sheriff—his white cowboy hat came into view even as she thought of him—really did owe her.

He owed her big-time, and she intended to see that he never forgot.

She reached for the yellow crime scene tape draped from bare crepe myrtle to crepe myrtle along the front of the yard, raised it and ducked under it. As if he'd sensed the interloper at his crime scene, Sheriff Colton Tanner turned to watch her stride up the driveway, the head-lights from the cluster of vehicles illuminating her path. It wasn't necessary to see his eyes to know his gaze roamed from the top of her blond head down the peach-colored silk blouse and classic broomstick skirt she wore all the way to the sleek matching high heels that would be ru-ined after this outing. As if to confirm her assumption, he shook his head and cut off the deputy who had headed Audrey's way, no doubt to inform her that she needed to stay outside the yellow tape perimeter.

Colt double-timed it down the steps and strode toward her. "Rey, you know you cannot be here."

Rey. From the day she was brought home from the hospital everyone around here had called her Rey. That was the way of things in the South. Your name was ei-ther chopped in half for a nickname or you were called by both your first and middle. No one seemed capable of simply using a person's given name.

"You have a body," Audrey announced, one hand on her cocked hip as she peered up at the man who had shat-tered her naive heart at the ripe old age of seventeen. "I have a newspaper. Alone, neither one is particularly noteworthy. But the story of what actually happened can mean the difference between merely dead and murdered and, in the case of my newspaper, staying in business or going bankrupt. So, like you, Sheriff, I'm here for the story either way."

His gray eyes filled with confusion that quickly morphed into sympathy. Audrey wanted to shake him and tell him she didn't need his pity. She just needed the story. The old saying "if it bleeds, it leads" was far too true. Except right now she would take sympathy or what-ever else it took to get the story. She was just as ruthless as any other reporter.

"Well." He heaved out a breath and braced his hands on his lean hips, matching her stance. "Be that as it may, this is a crime scene, Rey. Police business."

He shrugged those broad shoulders and flared his wide hands. Why oh why had she noticed his lean hips or his long legs or his broad shoulders? Or any of those other utterly masculine assets before recovering control of her wayward thoughts? Dear God, she was hopeless. Or maybe simply desperate. She'd been back in Winchester for over six months and she hadn't had a single date. Hadn't had one for as many months or more before the big move. Quite possibly the only thing wrong with her was nothing more than basic human need.

Whatever the case, she would not be fulfilling that need with this gorgeous cowboy. Not now or ever. They were over. All she needed was information and perhaps a look at the crime scene.

"I'm a reporter," she argued. "I have an obligation to keep the community informed."

"I understand that." He raised a hand before she could interrupt his rebuttal. "But you can't go showing up like this and crossing the perimeter—"

"Please." She reached into her bag and retrieved disposable gloves. "I know my way around a crime scene better than a single one of your deputies. I daresay," she added as she met his weary gaze, "better than you."

Audrey started forward once more. Her destination was the porch. Once she was on the porch she would pull on protective footwear and go right on inside. The door was open. The body was in there and most likely so was the person who pulled the trigger.

"All that research you've done as a big-city crime reporter is not impressing me here," he protested, catching up to her after hesitating five or so seconds—no doubt just so he could watch her walk away. Some things never changed. "This is official police business, Rey. As much as I'd like to do you a favor, you cannot go in there."

She stopped at the bottom of the wooden porch steps. "Are you saying you don't trust me, Colt?"

The pained expression that pinched his handsome face gave her immense pleasure. It really was bad form to enjoy a little payback after all these years, but no one was perfect. When it came to Colt, she knew exactly which buttons to push. Though she'd only been back home for six months, she'd deduced very quickly where she stood with anyone important to her goal of saving the family newspaper. The sheriff was in the top five of that short list. Thankfully, their shared history made him a little easier to handle.

"Rey, you know that's not it. We have official procedures about this sort of thing. I let you in there, evidence could be considered contaminated and my case would be jeopardized."

She sighed as if the idea hadn't once occurred to her. Rules of evidence, something else she knew very, very well. "Then tell me what's going on and I'll be more than happy to get out of your way."

He issued another of those frustrated exhales as he glanced across the yard at the deputy who was supposed to be guarding the perimeter. Audrey suspected the poor guy was in for a dressing-down. Truth was, Colt didn't have even one deputy who would deny her entrance onto any crime scene. Of course, this was the first shooting since she'd taken over the paper.

Not just a shooting; there was a deceased victim. Possibly a homicide.

"Sarah Sauder—she's Melvin Yoder's daughter," Colt said with just enough reluctance to remind her she had forced him to make this confession, "shot and killed a man who broke into her house."

"A robbery attempt?" The idea didn't make a whole lot of sense considering the Mennonites weren't exactly known for keeping valuable items that might be easily pawned or readily sold lying around the house.

Colt shrugged. "We don't know anything yet. Burt's having a look at the body now. You understand that part takes time. It might be a while before the body can be moved, and we're collecting evidence in there." He gestured toward the house as if she might not be following all he'd told her. "Maybe by noon or so tomorrow we'll have some idea what happened here tonight."

Burt Johnston was the county coroner and nearing eighty. Audrey seriously doubted he would take a minute longer than necessary, especially at this hour. Considering his age, getting a call at this time of night wouldn't be something that prompted him to dally. As for the evidence, she had no intention of waiting for forensic reports. Absolutely not. Her goal was to splash this story on the front page of tomorrow morning's edition.

"Why the delay in moving the body?" Usually the police liked getting the body out of the way once the scene was properly photographed and drawn. No need to keep the deceased—the key piece of evidence that deteriorated every second it remained at room temperature or exposed to the elements—amid the fray of fully processing a scene.

"We've got a call into Branch. We want him to have a look at the dead guy—the victim—before we do anything else."

And now they arrived at the meat of the situation. Branch Holloway was a US marshal. Well, well, this wasn't just any dead guy—this was a dead guy with some connection to the Feds. Maybe an escaped prisoner from one of Tennessee's federal prisons. Or a fugitive from the most-wanted list. Her mind ticked off the numerous possibilities that would require the involvement of the Marshals Service.

She asked, "What's the connection to the Sauders?"

Colt removed his hat and plowed his fingers through his hair, the tension in the set of his shoulders warning that he was losing his patience with her. "Sarah says she's never seen him before. She woke up from a dead sleep, heard someone downstairs and did what she had to do to protect her family."

Skeptical, Audrey asked, "Where's her husband?"

"He's on his way home. He was out of town. One of my deputies is inside with Sarah and her kids."

"Did you ID the victim?"

A truck pulled into the yard alongside the sheriff's. Big black crew cab with four-wheel drive. *Branch Holloway.*

Colt touched her arm. "I'm gonna need you to step back outside that yellow tape, Rey."

Now that Branch was here, Colt had to go all cocky and by the book. Colt and Branch had been rivals since high school. Showing up your high school nemesis trumped giving a tip to the girl whose heart you broke any day of the week or, in this case, night.

"Anything else about this incident I can run in tomorrow's edition?" She wasn't leaving without something more—at least not willingly.

"Colt, what's going on?" Branch removed his black Stetson as he approached. He gave her a nod. "Rey."

"Marshal." She returned his nod and smiled as if she'd been waiting all night for him to appear.

When she'd left home headed to college, one of the

few things that had stuck with Audrey was the image of Branch Holloway. Back then he'd been a star quarterback for the Tennessee Volunteers. He'd graduated a couple of years before Colt and her. Like Colt, the man was the quintessential cowboy. She and her best friend Sasha had harbored secret crushes on Branch Holloway. His college football career had made him a real-life celebrity right here in Winchester.

Why couldn't she have fallen in love with this cowboy?

But she hadn't, and however much she'd lusted after Branch, her gaze shifted to Colt. Way back in eighth grade she'd promised to marry Colton Tanner as soon as they both graduated from college. They'd been boyfriend and girlfriend from seventh grade until he cheated on her with her archnemesis near the end of senior year. A blast of fury burned through her even now. She'd wasted all that time only to have her heart shattered. As if she'd telegraphed those thoughts to the man responsible for all her pain, Colt met her glare, and she could see the regret in his gray eyes.

Colt Tanner and Branch Holloway had been the hottest, most popular guys in school. Colt had the coal-black hair and pale gray eyes. Branch was blond with gold eyes. He and Branch were both tall and athletic; still were nearly two decades later. Both had been hometown heroes. Except Colt was a cheater. Damn him.

"Well, I'll let you gentlemen get back to business."

Both tipped their hats at her and bid a good night like true Southern gentlemen.

Audrey turned and marched to the end of the sidewalk and then back down the gravel drive, cringing with each slide of a leather heel between the crushed rocks. She would snap a few photos and hurry back to the paper to update the front page. The Future Farmers of America's upcoming annual pig-catching contest would have to be moved to page two.

By the time she found the perfect angle for a photo of the house and the crime scene tape, Colt and Branch had gone into the house. Audrey took a few more shots with her cell phone and headed to her car.

"Hey there, Miss Anderson."

She hesitated as she reached for the door. Deputy Calvin Stevens grinned at her.

"I guess the full moon brought out the crazies tonight," he said.

"Guess so." She leaned against the door and waited as he came closer. Cal was a big flirt. If he'd been inside the house she might be able to get a little more for her story. She glanced around. How odd that no other reporters had shown up yet. "But it looks like I'm the only one who arrived to watch all the fun," she teased, scanning the road in both directions. "I haven't seen another reporter."

"Sarah Sauder's daddy called the sheriff direct and the sheriff called the coroner. They wanted to keep this quiet." Cal grinned. "I figured the sheriff called you personally."

Well, well. So how did Brian hear about this? Maybe he was the one with the real source in the sheriff's department. "I'll never tell," she said with a wink.

"You probably saw this kind of thing all the time in the big city." Cal gave her a look that said he'd made it his business to learn a whole lot of things about her. "I heard about all those awards you won." The deputy leaned against her car, close enough for her to smell his freshly applied aftershave. Did he keep a bottle in the glove box of his county cruiser?

"I spent a lot of time in the field." The statement

wasn't really an answer to his question, but she suspected he wouldn't notice. He was making conversation with the newest single lady in town. A small-town tradition.

"The sheriff says you trained with cops all over the country."

Only a slight exaggeration, taken directly from the bio on her website. "Wherever the story took me, I immersed myself in the community, including law enforcement."

Cal chuckled. "Is it true you helped to capture a serial rapist?"

"I did." The story had won her the esteemed Courage in Journalism Award. "I was following up on a victim who had survived an attack by the elusive killer when he came back to finish what he'd started."

Audrey had connected with the victim. She'd felt at ease talking to Audrey when she didn't feel comfortable talking to the police. The younger woman had called, said she felt like someone had been watching her for a couple of days. Audrey had urged her to call the police but she refused. What else was there to do but go over to her house and try to help? Still, she had no intention of becoming a victim herself. En route she'd called the detective assigned to the case and let him know what was happening.

By the time she arrived, the rapist was already in the house with the victim. Audrey grabbed her courage with both hands, walked in and distracted him until the cops showed up. Looking back, walking into that house knowing the guy was inside was foolhardy, but she hadn't really had a choice.

"You are one cool lady, Miss Anderson."

"Why thank you, Cal. You should call me Rey. Everybody does."

He shrugged. "All right. *Rey.*"

"It's hard to believe this guy broke into Sarah's house." She made the statement as if she was personal friends with Sarah Sauder and she knew all about the dead guy.

"For sure." Cal glanced at the house, then checked in both directions to ensure no one was nearby. "Especially considering he came all the way from Chicago to do it. Sarah swears she never laid eyes on the guy before. Kind of hard to believe considering he came this far."

Chicago. Interesting. Audrey nodded. "Just totally crazy, isn't it?"

"Oh yes, ma'am. Sheriff Tanner no sooner ran the man's name than some detective from up there called and wanted to know what was going on."

"So this guy has a record?" It was possible someone from Chicago was attempting to horn his way into the local drug trade—not that there was much of a problem in the Winchester area, but most towns had at least some drug issues. Still, why break into a Mennonite woman's house? Unless, being from Chicago, he lost his bearings and broke into the wrong house. To an outsider, the roads around here all looked alike. At night, they all looked alike even to Audrey. Not so surprising, considering she had lived everywhere but here since she left for college.

"Oh yeah. Big-time. That big-city detective said the guy has ties to the mob."

So that was why Colt had called in Branch. Branch's first assignment with the Marshals Service was in Chicago. He likely knew all about Chicagoland crime families. This potential breaking-and-entering had just shifted to something else entirely.

"Do you know his name?"

Cal shook his head. "He's a big guy, though. With red hair. She got him square in the chest with her husband's deer-hunting rifle. One shot. He was probably dead before he hit the floor."

"I'm glad she and the children weren't harmed."

Before Cal could say more, the front door of the house opened and a gurney rolled and rattled its way across the porch.

Maybe she would follow Burt Johnston to the hospital in Winchester. Burt owned and operated the two veterinary clinics in the county. He'd taken care of her beloved collie, Maisey, twenty years ago. Couldn't hurt to ask him for a few details.

He'd tell his coffee-drinking buddies at breakfast in the morning anyway. He might as well tell Audrey now. After all, the newspaper gave him a discount on all his advertising. It was the least he could do.

A murder—even in self-defense—was as scarce as hen's teeth in Franklin County. Especially if it involved a possible mob-connected stranger from out of town and a quiet Mennonite woman who'd lived here her whole life.

Had all the makings of a feature that could be picked up by the Associated Press. This might be Audrey's lucky night.

Chapter Two

Audrey tossed her keys onto the table that sat next to the door. Lifting one foot and then the other, she removed her ruined shoes. She paused for a moment, her toes curling against the cool wood floor. The house was completely dark save for the lamp on the table where her keys lay. It felt so strange coming home to an empty house. Even now, after six months of living in her childhood home as an adult, the hollowness at times startled her.

Her mother had always been so cheerful and vibrant. No matter the season, the house had been filled with the scent and beauty of the flowers from her gardens. Even in the winter she had kept plants blooming in the Victorian-style greenhouse she had built when Audrey was a child. Every single year until the one before last, Mary Jo Anderson had won awards for her lovely gardens. Her gardening had always been her escape, her own special brand of chicken soup for the soul.

Reading had been Audrey's. She imagined it was all those suspense novels that had made her so bold as a reporter. She often told friends she had lived a thousand lives through the books she read. Growing up in a small town, books were her escape.

She picked up her high heels and headed for the staircase. The entire house remained stuck in the Victorian era with few concessions to modern times: a more comfortable sofa in the den and updated appliances in the kitchen. The paint and wallpaper, though well maintained, boasted the same pinks and burgundies from more than a hundred and twenty years ago when the house was built. Her great-great-grandmother who'd actually commissioned the house had insisted on keeping things exactly the way she'd wanted them. Mary Jo, though not exactly a pink-and-burgundy lady, had respectfully left the decorating scheme as the late great Annette Anderson had decreed. Audrey's grandmother and great-grandmother had done the same.

At the top of the stairs, Audrey glanced toward the south end of the second-floor hall. The suite at that end had belonged to her parents. How many nights had she crept quietly through the darkness from her bedroom at the other end to those towering double doors? Her father had always scooped her up and nestled her between him and her mother. A perk of being an only child.

Even after all these years, her heart squeezed at the memory of her father. She imagined that she would always miss him, no matter that he'd been gone for twenty-four years. Weary now, she made her way to her room, the same one she'd slept in growing up, and padded straight to the walk-in closet to put her damaged shoes away. She should probably just throw them out, but the little shoe repair shop on the corner of the square depended on folks like her to stay in business. No one understood the need for supporting local businesses better than Audrey. Though she was far from destitute, the expenses related to her mother's care and turning the newspaper around were quickly draining her savings.

She sighed as she hung up her jacket. Though her mother had changed hardly a thing around the house,

Audrey had altered a couple of things right away. The first being to expand her closet into a decent-sized one. And still she'd had to downsize her wardrobe. Living in the limelight of investigative journalism for all those years had required an extensive wardrobe. Plus, she was reasonably sure she had a slight obsession with clothes, shoes in particular. With her work, it hadn't actually been a problem.

But that life was over.

Audrey closed the door of the closet as well as the one to the past.

No looking back. This was her life now, and it wasn't such a bad one.

She tossed her clutch purse onto a chair and reached for the zipper of her skirt. After leaving the Sauder farm she'd followed Burt to the hospital but had learned nothing. As she left the hospital and headed home, she dictated the story to Brian, her longtime friend and the editor at the *Winchester Gazette*, via her cell. Once she'd sent him the photos she'd snapped, he had laid out the story for tomorrow's front page. It would be tight, but since they were one of the few remaining small-town newspapers that still did their own printing, the job would get done. Newspapers landing on doorsteps and in stands tomorrow morning would showcase what little was known about the shooting. The article was already online.

Sarah Sauder was two or three years younger than Audrey. She remembered seeing her at the family-run bakery as a child and then as the woman behind the cash register since moving back to Winchester. Audrey popped in at least once every week. The Yoder Bakery, though located outside Winchester proper, was considered a local landmark. The peanut butter balls were to die for and her mother loved them. Audrey liked having a special treat for her mother when she visited. She also adored their blueberry scones. She bought those for herself, which was all the more reason not to drop by too often.

But the man who'd taken his last breath on Sarah Sauder's kitchen floor hadn't come to Buncombe Road for peanut butter balls or blueberry scones. And he sure hadn't broken into the century-old farmhouse looking for valuables to snatch. Branch Holloway's presence ruled out any possibility of the man's death being something less than serious trouble.

Wouldn't be drugs or human trafficking. Certainly not gunrunning. At least not involving the Sauders. The man had obviously connected the wrong identity with the house. But that still left the possibility that someone in Franklin County was up to no good and the trouble rippled all the way to the Windy City.

The skirt she'd worn tonight slid down her hips, then she stepped out of it. Frankly, she couldn't think of any criminal activities that rose to that level in which any of the locals, much less the Yoders—in this case the Sauders by marriage—would be involved. Of all people, Audrey was well aware of the reality that what one saw was rarely exactly what lay beneath the skin of others. But these were Mennonites.

She frowned as her fingers hesitated on the buttons of her blouse. She'd forgotten to ask Brian how he'd heard about the shooting. She assumed it was from the police scanner. She would ask him tomorrow.

The buzz of her cell echoed in the room, the sound muffled deep inside the clutch she'd tossed aside. She didn't dare ignore it. There could be breaking news in the shooting…or an issue at the paper.

Since taking over the *Winchester Gazette*, she'd realized how running the family business could consume one's life. As a crime reporter she had given herself completely to the story, but when the story was over there was typically some time before another came her way. Running the *Gazette* was entirely different. It was always there, an endless cycle of need for more content. Another story, another something to fill the pages—advertising. The newspaper had been in the Anderson family for nearly two centuries. How could she be the one to walk away? Her father would have wanted her to take over when his brother, Audrey's uncle Phillip, decided to retire.

She shivered. It wasn't like she'd had a choice. That decision had been taken from her years ago.

She dragged her cell from the clutch. When she had learned the developer who wanted to buy the *Gazette* planned to tear it down, she'd had to take control. The shiver turned into a chill that scurried deep into her bones.

The historic building could not be torn down. Ever.

At least not as long as Audrey was still breathing.

The caller ID read Pine Haven. A new kind of dread spread through Audrey's body. Pine Haven was her mother's residential care facility.

"Audrey Anderson." She held her breath. It had been two days since she'd visited her mom. What kind of daughter allowed forty-eight hours to pass without dropping by or at least calling?

"Ms. Anderson, this is Roberta Thompson at Pine Haven."

The worry in the other woman's voice sent another spear of uncertainty knifing through Audrey.

"Your mother is very agitated tonight. We need to sedate her but she insists on seeing you first. I know it's late but—"

"I'll be right there."

THE DRIVE TO Pine Haven on the other side of town took scarcely fifteen minutes and still it felt like forever. Audrey's heart pounded twice for every second that passed before she was parked and at the front entrance. The night guard waved her through. Evidently her mother had the facility's night shift all out of sorts.

Nurse Roberta Thompson waited for Audrey at the entrance to the Memory Care Unit. Roberta smiled sadly. "I'm so sorry I had to bother you at this hour, but she won't stay in her bed and she's demanding to see you. When a patient is this agitated we nearly always have to use sedation, but your mother's file says you prefer to be called first."

"Absolutely." Audrey held up her hands. "Please. You know I always want you to call. No matter the hour."

Roberta nodded. "Talk to her. You're what she needs right now. Then we'll get her settled for the night."

Mary Jo Anderson was pacing her room when Audrey walked through the door. Her short white hair was mussed, her long flannel gown rumpled as if she'd already tossed and turned all night.

"Mom."

Mary Jo's gaze settled on Audrey's. For a moment she stared, the haze of confusion and distance dulling her blue eyes. She was far away from this place, perhaps not in miles but in time. Audrey knew the look too well. When she came back home to buy the paper and to stay until she sorted out her future, Audrey had been startled by the episodes of total memory loss her mother suffered. Startled and heartbroken. How could she have deteriorated so without Audrey knowing it?

"Audrey." The haze cleared and her mother smiled.

Audrey closed the door and walked over to hug her. "What's going on? Nurse Thompson told me you're upset."

When Audrey drew back, her mother's smile was gone. "They'll find him and then you know what will happen."

The too-familiar apprehension stole back into Audrey's gut. "Let's sit down, Mom, okay? I'm really tired. I'm sure you must be, too."

She ushered her mom to the bed and they sat on the edge.

Mary Jo took in Audrey's jeans and sweater before settling her gaze on her face once more. "You're the prettiest girl I've ever seen in plain old blue jeans, Audrey Rose."

Audrey couldn't help smiling. "You always say that, Mom."

"It's true." Mary Jo sighed, turned away to stare at the wall on the other side of the room as if someone else had spoken to her. "I'm sorry I caused you all this trouble, sweetheart. You should be back in Washington. I've messed up everything."

Audrey put her arms around her mother's shoulders. "You didn't mess up a thing. Remember? I moved back to Winchester six months ago to buy the paper." The surprise in her mother's eyes warned that she'd forgotten. "I took over the *Gazette* for Uncle Phil. He wanted to retire."

She looked away, a classic indication she did not recall. The lines on her face appeared deeper than ever. *Worry.* Even with her memories fading, she still worried. Was that the curse of being a woman? A mother?

Or was it the secret they had been keeping for so long?

Audrey pushed away the thought. That was taken care of for now. No need for either of them to worry.

"We can't hide our secret forever," her mother whispered.

Mary Jo's words brought Audrey's attention back to her. She glanced at the door—couldn't help herself. No one needed to hear this. No doubt anyone who did over-hear would think it was just the disease talking. Still, Audrey would feel better if her mother didn't mention that part of their past. "Mom, you don't need to worry about the secret. No one will ever know. I promise."

Her gaze latched onto Audrey's once more, the urgency there painful to look at. "You can't stop it. Fate or whatever they call it…the Lord. The Bible says so." She heaved a big breath. "They will find us out and it's my fault. All my fault."

She muttered those last three words over and over.

Audrey would need to check with Roberta to see if Mary Jo had any visitors today. Usually something set off this kind of episode. Maybe she'd somehow heard the news about the shooting on Buncombe Road. Audrey didn't see how that was possible. Could have been some other shooting or death. Sometimes startling events sent her mother off on a tangent. On those occasions, Audrey did all she could to soothe her frayed nerves and to guide her toward more comforting memories.

"Mom, do you remember my junior play? You had to make my costume. I was the nurse and you were so upset that I wasn't cast as Juliet."

"The costume was hideous." She shook her head. "You should have been Juliet."

Audrey laughed. "Well, Mrs. Bishop was the director and I guess she wanted her daughter to play the lead role."

Mary Jo chuckled. "I think the only thing worse than that costume was your dress for the senior prom."

"Oh." Audrey shuddered at the thought. The dress was one memory she had worked hard to exile. "It was absolutely awful."

Her mother rambled on about the dress order and the numerous fittings and how the garment still would not fit properly. Audrey had been reduced to tears at least twice until she'd decided enough was enough and had worn her favorite jeans and tee to the damned prom. Half the senior class as well as the school staff had been mortified; the other half couldn't have cared less. Audrey would wager that she was the only girl who had ever dared wear jeans to a prom in Franklin County, maybe in the whole state of Tennessee.

Colt had grinned and told her she was the most beautiful girl in the gymnasium—and maybe the world. The old ache that accompanied memories of her senior year squeezed deep inside Audrey's chest. She had been madly in love with Colt Tanner. They had been planning their future together since eighth grade when he sneaked a kiss on the school bus. That kiss had startled them both. The perfect balance of sweetness and innocence.

She had known the boy and then the man inside out. At least, she'd thought she had. But you never really know a person. Not really. When he'd married someone else—a pregnant-with-his-child someone else—Audrey had realized she could never trust anyone with her heart ever again. If Colt would break it, there was no hope with anyone else.

True to her decision, she never had. In December she would turn thirty-seven. Forty was right down the road. In all probability she would never know how it felt to hold her own child in her arms or to share her life with a man she loved the way her mother had loved her father. Of course her career had been immensely fulfilling— until things had gone so very wrong.

The newspaper would just have to be her baby, she supposed. Certainly the staff was like family. And she still had her mother. Well, most of the time, anyway.

Rather than wallowing in self-pity, Audrey listened as

her mother talked on and on about the distant past—the good days, she called them. The ones before that awful year of darkness that came after her father's heart attack…and the secret that she and her mother would take to their graves.

Some things had to stay buried. There was no other option—not then and not now.

"Then you went off to become the celebrated investigative journalist," Mary Jo said after a long pause, her eyes gleaming with pride. "Your father would have been so proud. He never wanted you stuck here running that damned newspaper. He wanted you to explore the world, to conquer all the glass ceilings."

Except there really was no choice now. Six months ago her mother had called with the news that Phillip was retiring and a developer wanted to buy the paper. Said developer planned to demolish the old building and start fresh—his words. That could not happen. Not in this lifetime. The building had to stay exactly where it was for the foreseeable future.

"To tell you the truth, Mom, I was tired of all the travel and the limelight." Audrey waved off the career that had once been her singular focus. "Let someone else have a turn at being the best." She winked at her mother. "I couldn't hog all the glamour forever."

Mary Jo smiled and patted Audrey on the leg. "You were always such a thoughtful girl. I'll never forget the time you came home and bagged up all your clothes to take to that little girl whose house had burned down. I finally convinced you that we could take her shopping for new clothes. You really made your father and I proud. I know he has watched your career from heaven."

There was another secret Audrey planned to keep. Her mother would never know—nor would anyone else for that matter—that her career had gone to hell in a hand-basket. She'd made a mistake. Ten years at the top of her game and she'd made a totally dumb, foolish mistake. She'd wanted the story so badly, she'd trusted a source without going through all the usual steps to verify that source. She had allowed her friendship with that source to guide her, and she'd rushed to beat everyone else. She'd screwed up.

Big-time.

Bottom line, she had no one to blame but herself. While she had been licking her wounds, her mother had called with news about Phil's retirement. Audrey had done what she had to do. She'd zoomed home and bought out her uncle's portion of the family business. With her savings basically depleted after that, she'd decided to stay on and try turning the paper around. No one knew how to lay out a titillating story better than Audrey. She could have the paper thriving again within a year. No problem. An entire human could be made in less time. Of course she could do it. It was the perfect distraction. If she was busy saving the family legacy, she didn't have to think about the rubble that was once her career.

Or the secret that no one else could ever know.

Her mother laid her head on Audrey's shoulder, exhaustion overtaking her now that the manic episode had passed.

But it was coming home to do what must be done that served up another cold hard reality to Audrey. Her mother was not well. The forgetfulness and absentmindedness were not merely age or the overabundance of civic commitments to which she had obligated herself for the past thirty-five years.

Mary Jo Anderson had dementia. If Audrey had come home more often, she would have realized the lost keys and missed appointments her mother had laughed about on the phone were more than forgetfulness. Far more. But she had been too busy with her illustrious career. She had called her mother every week, sometimes twice, but she hadn't gotten home nearly as often as she should have.

But she was here now. And as her father always said, "when life gives you lemons, you make lemonade."

Tonight's shooting was a perfect example. Nothing promised a bump in circulation like a potential homicide.

Chapter Three

Colt leaned against the cab of his truck and blew out a weary breath. Burt had taken the body. Rather than deliver the outsider to a local funeral home, he was headed to the state medical examiner's office to turn over the body for an autopsy. The department's two-man crime scene unit had gone over the Sauder home with a fine-tooth comb.

The biggest thing missing at the moment was Sarah Sauder's husband. He was supposed to be headed home from a funeral he'd attended up in Hendersonville, but he still hadn't made it back. Seemed to Colt that the man would have moved heaven and earth to get to his wife and children after hearing about the shooting. Sarah and the kids had apparently given up hope of his arrival, since they'd left and gone to her father's house. The lights in the Sauder home were out now and the doors were locked up tight. Colt had suggested Sarah and her kids stay with family until they released the scene. There would need to be another look tomorrow for potential evidence. Not that Colt really expected to find any.

The evening had been a tough one for Sarah. To have strangers walking through her home and touching her belongings was not something to which folks in the Mennonite community were accustomed. They were private people. Kept to themselves and stayed out of trouble. This was not the norm by any means.

US Marshal Branch Holloway paced the road just far enough from Colt's truck to ensure he didn't overhear his cell phone conversation. Branch had an outstanding reputation with the Marshals Service as far as Colt knew, but something had landed him in Franklin County assigned to the federal courthouse last year. Whatever it was, it couldn't have been good. Winchester wasn't exactly a hotbed of criminal activity, and there damned sure wasn't much of anything that rose to the federal level in Franklin County.

Tonight, apparently, was an exception.

Branch had said the victim was some button man for the Chicago mob. Beyond that he'd been pretty tight-lipped. Didn't sit well with Colt. This was his county and by God he needed to know the full details of what had transpired in the Sauder home tonight. He had no intention of relinquishing control over this investigation until he had no other choice. The safety of the residents in this county was his responsibility, not Branch Holloway's.

Branch tucked his phone away and headed toward Colt. Colt pushed away from the truck and set his hands on his hips. "So what did your former boss have to say?"

"I was right. The victim is Tony Marcello." Branch glanced toward the darkened house. "This was no random break-in, Colt. Marcello is the kind of guy who does the dirty work. Collects on loans. Acts as an enforcer or bodyguard. Bottom line, he does whatever he's ordered to do. I can't see a guy like that making this kind of mistake."

Oh hell. "So you're saying the Sauders are involved in some sort of mob business." Colt couldn't see it. Not in a million years.

"Sure looks that way." Branch matched Colt's stance, hands on hips, boots wide apart, as if they were about to see who was the fastest draw. "I've only been back a year so I'm not up to speed on everyone in the area. How well do you know Wesley Sauder?"

"How well do you know any of the Mennonite folks?" Colt tossed back at him. Branch grew up in Winchester. He knew the deal. "They keep to themselves. Yet they're good neighbors, good citizens. Never any trouble—at least if there is any, they take care of it amid their own ranks." He shook his head. "I can't see what you're suggesting by any stretch of the imagination."

"But," Branch said, shrugging, "Wesley was an outsider until what? Ten years ago?"

That much was true. "He moved here about ten years ago, yeah." Colt considered the answers the man's wife had given to the interview questions. "Sarah said he came from Markham, Illinois."

"Markham's not so far from Chicago."

Colt heaved another sigh. "We'll know more when we've run Sauder's prints."

Colt had instructed one of his forensic techs to lift prints from the wooden arms of the rocking chair next to the fireplace. Sarah had glanced at the empty chair when she spoke of her husband. Colt figured the rocker was the chair her husband used.

"There's no Wesley Sauder from Illinois or Tennessee in the database," Branch said. "So if the husband is who he says he is, you won't find anything there."

"Then again, if we get a hit from a database then we'll know he isn't who he says he is." Damn. Branch's contact was able to access the needed information in an instant. Colt didn't have those kinds of resources. As much as he wanted to be grateful for the potential assist in this case, he was mostly ticked off. "Otherwise, the only thing we'll know for sure is that Sauder doesn't have a criminal record and he hasn't needed a background check that required his prints."

"Guess so." Branch was already marking his territory. He wanted this case.

"We could debate what this shooting boils down to all night and we still won't be any closer to the truth than we are right now." Colt wasn't relinquishing a damned thing until he understood exactly what they were dealing with. "We need to do this right, Branch. By the book. No getting ahead of ourselves."

Colt didn't know all the details of why Branch had left Chicago and ended up back in his hometown on a babysitting assignment, but there would be plenty to the story and little if any of it résumé-worthy.

"We'll play it your way for now." Branch glanced once more at the Sauder home. "I'll touch base with you tomorrow."

Colt gave him a nod of agreement and watched him get into his truck and drive away. He sure as hell wished Melvin Yoder wasn't on his deathbed. Tomorrow Colt would check in with the family to see if a short visit with the patriarch of the Mennonite community in Franklin County might be possible. Yoder would know his son-in-law better than anyone. Sauder would never have been able to marry Yoder's daughter if he hadn't approved of the man.

Colt's father and Yoder had been good friends. At least as close as an outsider could be with a member of the closed community. Hopefully that friendship would help now. If the older man's health would tolerate a visit, Colt needed some insight into Wesley Sauder. What the hell kind of man would be a no-show when his family needed him?

There was only one plausible answer: a man who had something to hide.

Colt loaded into his truck, took one last look at the farmhouse. Whatever Sarah Sauder and her husband were hiding, he would find it.

COLT HADN'T MUCH more than pulled into the driveway at his house when another problem cropped up. His son, Key, pulled in right behind him, and it was well beyond his curfew on a school night.

Colt sat stone-still behind the wheel of his truck. He'd already shut off the engine, and the headlights had faded to darkness. His son had no idea he was out here. Probably thought his overbearing, out-of-touch-with-reality daddy was in bed asleep by now. As Colt watched, the eighteen-year-old climbed out of his truck and closed the door quietly. He glanced around the yard and started toward the house.

Staggered toward the house.

Colt swore under his breath. He watched his only child beat a crooked path to his bedroom window, which he subsequently opened and struggled clumsily through, ultimately falling into the house. If Colt was lucky, right on his head. Maybe it would knock some sense into him. The boy was hell-bent on trouble. He'd had everything he ever wanted handed to him on a silver platter—including that brand-new pickup his Granddaddy Wilhelm gave him. The real problem was that between his momma and his granddaddy, the kid was spoiled rotten. Colt was the only one who issued any sort of rules, and shared custody ensured that at least half the time his son had no rules whatsoever.

He was headed down a bad path.

But this was the first time Colt had known him to come home drunk. He glanced in the rearview mirror at the shiny red truck parked behind him. The boy had been driving while intoxicated. Colt had witnessed it with his own eyes. All the other dumb stuff he overlooked was nothing to compare with this. Driving under the influence was not something he could pretend not to notice in order to keep the peace.

"Damn it all to hell."

Colt emerged from his truck, slammed the door and headed for the house he'd inherited from his daddy—the one thing Colt hadn't lost in the divorce. By the time he reached Key's bedroom, his son was lying on the floor where he'd fallen and was snoring up a storm. Shaking his head, Colt closed and locked the window. He picked up the fob to the boy's truck and tucked it into his pocket. No more driving for at least a month. Waking up his son and giving him what for at the moment would be a pointless waste of energy. Arguing with a drunk got both parties nowhere fast.

Morning would be soon enough to tackle this unpleasant task. He considered helping his son into the bed but decided he should sleep it off right where he'd fallen. His cell phone had tumbled from his pocket and lay next to him. Colt made another decision. The kid didn't need his phone for a while, either. A set of wheels and a cell phone were luxuries that not all kids his son's age enjoyed. Why should Key have access to those and more when he couldn't obey the rules?

Disgusted and exhausted, Colt wandered to his bedroom. He placed his hat on the bureau. He needed a shower and a beer. He thought of his son passed out on the floor in the other bedroom. Maybe he'd forgo the beer.

He dropped onto the side of the bed and pulled off first one boot and then the other, tossing the well-worn footwear to the floor. Socks went next. He'd worn cowboy boots his whole life. His daddy bought him his first pair as soon as he could walk. If his dad were still here he would know what to do to steer Key in the right direction.

Sometimes Colt wondered if his ex-wife allowed the boy to run wild just to get back at Colt for the divorce. God knew Colt had never been allowed to behave this way, and he damned sure hadn't intended for his son to end up on this plunge into stupidity. But Karen let the boy do anything he wanted. She'd named him after her daddy, Keyton. Colt had been good with that, since his son would carry the Tanner surname. He'd wanted to be fair. But Karen Wilhelm had never played fair in her life. Key hadn't been a year old the first time Colt caught her cheating. He'd put up with her lies for ten years in an attempt to hold his family together. Then he'd had enough.

He peeled off his shirt and reached for his belt. Key's cell phone blasting a rap tune stopped him. *Mom* appeared on the screen. Colt tapped the screen and answered with the same "yo" his son always used.

"Baby, I just wanted to make sure you got home all right. You were a little drunk."

Outrage coursed through Colt's veins. "You allowed our son to drive when he'd been drinking?"

Silence screamed across the line.

"Why do you have Key's phone?"

The cold fury in her voice was nothing compared to the white-hot rage gushing through Colt at the moment. "Because he dropped it while he was climbing through his bedroom window. At the moment he's passed out on the floor."

"I'm… I'm sure he wasn't drinking that much when

he left here. He must have stopped at a friend's on the way home."

Liar.

"He won't be driving for a good long while. And he won't be available by cell, either."

"My father gave him that truck. You don't have any right to take it."

"You would rather I arrest him for driving under the influence? I can definitely do that, and I don't need your or your daddy's permission to do it."

"You wouldn't dare."

He laughed. "I arrested you, didn't I?"

Of course, her rich daddy had hired the best lawyer in the county to take care of the situation. So far, he'd managed that feat five times. No wonder their son felt no fear of consequences. He'd watched his mother skate out of trouble his whole life. Including ten years of Colt looking the other way while she screwed her way through the county's male population.

"My father will be calling you in the morning."

The call ended.

Colt turned the phone off and shoved it into the pillowcase of the pillow he didn't use. His boy would never think to look there. God knew his momma wasn't coming anywhere near Colt's bed.

He shucked his jeans and boxers and headed for the shower. While he waited for the water to warm he thought of the biggest mistake of his life.

Hurting Rey.

Each time he saw her he was reminded of the enormous mistake he'd made. How the hell had he let her get away? He almost laughed at the idea. He hadn't *let* her do anything. Audrey Rose Anderson did what she damned well pleased, then and now.

She had been his everything since he was a kid. If he was honest with himself, he had been fascinated with her since the first day of kindergarten when she kicked the boy who laughed at him for crying. Cutting the other kid some slack, he had no idea Colt's mother had been dying with cancer. No matter that she'd been so sick, she'd wanted to take her little boy to his first day of school. When she'd left him in the classroom the tears had streamed down his face. Colt had been terrified she would die before he was back at home with her.

After kicking the laughing kid in the shin, Audrey had walked up to Colt and said, "I like your boots. You want to sit at my table?"

They had been friends from that day on. And then he'd fallen in love with her. Head over heels in love. Even now, thinking of her made it hard to breathe.

"You screwed that up, dumbass."

Colt stepped into the shower and drowned the memories beneath the spray of hot water.

There were some transgressions for which there was no forgiveness. Rey reminded him every chance she got.

Chapter Four

"Adding the plea for information was genius." Audrey laid this morning's edition of the *Gazette* on her desk. "Good call, Brian."

Brian Peterson grinned. "I learned from the best."

His enthusiasm was contagious and Audrey felt her own lips pull into a smile, no matter that she was utterly exhausted this morning. As her mom would say, "as tired when she got up as she had been when she went to bed." "My uncle was a good mentor."

"I meant *you*," Brian clarified.

Audrey laughed. "You were helping my uncle run this paper long before I came back to take over."

"I watched your career," Brian argued. "Learned a lot from your approach to a story."

"Flattery will get you everywhere," she pointed out.

"I know." He lifted an eyebrow at her. "I survived kindergarten through senior year with you as one of my best friends. I think I know you pretty well."

"It's a miracle either one of us survived."

Brian was a good friend, had been since they were kids in school. She would never forget freshman year sitting at his side, just the two of them, at a table in the school cafeteria the day another former friend announced to the world that Brian was gay. One of her best memories of that entire year happened on that day. Colt, big football star, had swaggered over to their table and sat down on the other side of Brian. Her chest filled with remembered pride. What had happened to the guy who stood by his friends through thick and thin to make him break the heart of the girl madly in love with him?

"You're thinking about Colt."

Brian's words snapped her back to the here and now. She blinked, rearranged her expression into a frown. "What?"

But her faux look of surprise didn't fool her old friend for a moment. "Uh-huh. That's what I thought."

Rather than have that conversation, she moved on. "Have any calls with useful information come in this morning?"

"A few," he said, "but don't try changing the subject. How long can you hold an eighteen-year-old's drunken mistake against him?"

Okay, so he wasn't going to let it go. Winning the football championship senior year had culminated in a party at a cabin belonging to the family of one of the players. Everyone had gone. Except Audrey. She'd had the flu. The following spring the whole school knew the rest of the story—Karen Wilhelm was obviously pregnant. Karen was only too happy to name Colt as the father. Audrey barely managed to finish out the school year and stumble through graduation. If not for Brian and Sasha, her two best friends, she would have skipped the ceremonial stuff altogether.

"Forever," she said in answer to Brian's question—the one he asked about once a month. "Have any of the calls offered leads we might want to follow up on?" she asked again.

He sighed and shook his head. "Not yet."

"We need to know more about this Wesley Sauder." Audrey walked over to the large chalkboard her father had used. It took up the better part of one wall. Her father had kept all sorts of notes on it, but he'd always kept one small corner free for her to draw and doodle whenever she visited his office. By the time she was in sixth grade she generally walked to the paper rather than go home. She'd done her homework right here in this office.

"You have basically everything we know outlined." Brian joined her at the chalkboard. "Sauder moved here ten years ago from Illinois. The way I heard the story, he came upon Melvin Yoder in a pasture being charged by a bull or something like that. Saved his life. Yoder took him under his wing in the community, and the guy married the older man's daughter. Ten years and four kids later, he's way up the hierarchy in the Mennonite community. Mr. Yoder is very ill, and rumor has it, everyone is looking to Sauder to hold things together moving forward."

Audrey scanned the notes they'd taped to the board. "Sauder is forty-eight, more than a decade older than his wife."

Brian tapped a photo of Sarah he'd dug up from an article done on the Yoder Bakery a couple of years ago. "She is the only daughter Yoder claims and his middle child. At twenty-four and unmarried when the accident happened, she was bordering on old maid status. Giving his daughter as a wife to the man who saved his life killed two birds with one stone, so to speak."

"Seriously?" Audrey couldn't believe anyone still considered an unmarried woman in her midtwenties an old maid.

Brian held up his hands. "Their views are less progressive. We all know you're not an old maid just because you're single and thirtysomething."

Choosing to ignore the subject, she said, "You said the only daughter he claims. Does he have another one? I don't remember another one."

"Bethany. She's several years younger than us. She's thirty-one, maybe. She dropped out of school at sixteen and disappeared. Ran off to Nashville to be a singer."

"What happened to her after that?" Maybe that was why Audrey didn't remember her.

"Fame and riches weren't in the cards for her, I guess. Eventually she came back, but her family shunned her or maybe she shunned them. She works as a waitress at one of the bars on the other side of town. Never married. Just lives her life."

Like you, Audrey.

She thought of the birth announcement she'd noticed in today's paper. Another of her high school classmates was having a child. She and Sasha Lenoir were the only ones left who hadn't married. Even Brian had a husband. Last year they had adopted a little girl. Audrey had shoes. Lots of shoes. And a huge house that felt so very empty. At least Sasha still had her career. She was the best crisis manager in the Northeast. It had been far too long since she and Audrey had spent time together. They needed a girls' weekend. Time to catch up and relax. Time to just be.

"Back in elementary school there was a girl from the class above us who spent a lot of time with Sarah," Brian said.

Audrey dismissed the notions of getaways and looked at Brian in surprise. "Really? Someone from our school?" The Mennonite community had their own school. They didn't socialize with outsiders beyond what was necessary to conduct business.

"Remember the old Yarborough place?"

"The abandoned house that used to be a rental?" The Yarboroughs were long dead when Audrey was a child. Whoever had inherited the place lived in another state but opted to keep the home. One of the local real estate companies had maintained and rented the house until a few years ago. The property was right next to the Yoder place.

Brian nodded, a glint in his eye. "Nikki owns the diner now. She lived in the old Yarborough house all during elementary school. I wouldn't be surprised if she and Sarah have remained friends."

"Nikki Wells?" Audrey vaguely remembered the older girl.

"She's Nikki Slater now. Two kids." Brian sent her a pointed look. "I say this not to remind you that everyone we know is having babies, but because she will show off the pictures, so you might as well be prepared."

"Thanks. I'll head that way. I could use a decent cup of coffee." Audrey smiled as she rounded her desk and reached for her purse. She loved her old friend, but the man did not know the first thing about making coffee.

Brian crossed his arms over his chest. "I make a perfect cup of coffee. Unless you're one of those people who prefer coffee capable of being substituted for asphalt patch."

She flashed him a patient smile. "See you later." Audrey headed for the door.

"One more thing," he called behind her.

She paused at the door. Brian really was her best friend in the world. She adored him despite his inability to understand the purpose of coffee. She needed it strong enough to make her pay attention and packed with enough caffeine to keep her that way. "Yes?"

"Braden House wants to know if you're interested in spearheading another fund-raiser this year. They're still praising you for surpassing their goal last year. No one has ever raised as much money as you did."

Braden House was a refuge for abused women. "I would love to spearhead this year's fund-raiser. It's not until October, right?"

He nodded. "I knew you would. That's why I told them yes yesterday."

Audrey gave him a thumbs-up. "Thanks."

"You are such a do-gooder, Anderson." He rolled his eyes. "You need to funnel some of that energy toward a personal life."

"I am extremely happy with my personal life just as it is—*personal*."

She managed to get the door open this time before he interrupted. "We really need to have someone find out where that water in the basement is coming from," he called after her. "I checked last night and there's a little more than last time. It's not that much water, but it worries me that it's more than just dampness seeping up from the concrete. It's actual water standing on the floor."

Even as her heart pounded harder, Audrey held up a hand and produced a decisive tone. "I'll take care of it. Don't worry. This building is more than two hundred years old. There's probably an underground spring or something. We just need to get all that concrete resealed with that whatever-it's-called stuff that stops water penetration."

"You're the boss."

Audrey laughed at the comment before walking out of her office. In many ways Brian was far more the boss than she was. She didn't mind sharing that title with him.

She descended the stairs and walked directly to the rear exit, grateful the lobby was empty and the receptionist was tied up on the phone. By the time she reached the small employee parking lot just out the back door, her heart rate had settled to some semblance of normal. She would call someone about the basement. There was no denying the issue any longer. Just not today.

She drew in a deep, calming breath of the cool morning air. She was grateful for the matching sweater she'd chosen to go along with her plum-colored trousers. The high temperature would reach into the sixties by noon, but this morning it was well below that mark.

Settling into the driver's seat, she fisted her fingers to rid them of the lingering trembles. For a moment she stared at the building that had been in her family for more than two centuries. She rarely came in through the front lobby. The offices were set up the old-fashioned way, in a ring around the second floor overlooking the expansive lobby. There was a large and a small conference room. Downstairs, the lobby was filled with *Gazette* history. Third graders from the elementary schools toured the exhibit every year. Beyond the lobby, the supply room, the break room and the massive space where the papers were printed consumed the rest of the square footage. The basement had never been used for anything other than storage of unused equipment or ancient files. The maintenance parts of the building, like the heating and cooling systems, were housed there as well.

No reason to be overly concerned about a little water in a basement. It had happened numerous times before.

Not a priority for now.

THE CORNER DINER was on the southeast corner of the square. It was a lunch staple of the downtown square and courthouse crowd. Nikki Wells Slater's family started the diner in the 1940s. At eight forty-five in the morning the breakfast crowd had dwindled.

Audrey sat down at one end of the deserted bar and ordered coffee. Several other business owners smiled as they passed on their way out or paused to say good morning. Audrey sipped her coffee while Nikki took an order at a table. Once she'd delivered it to the order station and turned back to the bar, Audrey smiled.

Nikki wandered over. "You ready for a refill?"

Audrey shook her head. "I'm good. How are you, Nikki?" She had grabbed a quick lunch in the diner on several occasions, but she and Nikki hadn't actually talked beyond a hello or thank you.

"I'm great." She smiled and gestured to the wall next to the order window where photos of her two children, a girl and a boy, formed a cheerful collage. "My kids are happy and healthy and so far my husband is still trying to impress me."

Audrey laughed. "You can't ask for more than that."

"That's the truth." Nikki considered her a moment. "So, how are you, Rey?"

"I'm settling in. Circulation is up in print and in on-line subscriptions. I'm happy."

The other woman's expression shifted to a more serious one. "How's your momma?"

Audrey shrugged. "Some days are better than others, but all in all she's okay. Thank you for asking."

Nikki grabbed a towel and wiped the counter next to Audrey. "That's good. She used to come in here all the time for my momma's lemon pie. She said it was the best pie in the world."

"I've taken it to her a few times since I've been back."

One of these days Audrey might even try a slice herself. "How are your parents?"

Nikki's parents had retired and moved to Florida last year. Even though Winchester was a small town, a lot had changed since Audrey left for college. Thank goodness for Brian. He had spent days when Audrey first moved back to Winchester bringing her up to speed on who had died or moved or married, and anything else he considered relevant. People around here expected you to ask about their kin. Weddings, baby showers and funerals were necessary social events. Miss one and your name was tarnished.

"They miss their grandbabies but they love life on the beach. We go down four or five times a year and spend a week. They come here a couple times a year so it's not so bad. They're happy, that's what matters."

"Are you still friends with Sarah Yoder?"

Nikki studied Audrey for a moment. "She's Sarah Sauder now, but then I'm sure you know that already."

Audrey nodded. "I do. I was at her house last night but I didn't have the opportunity to speak with her. I was hoping you could help me set the story straight for Sarah. No one hates inaccurate news more than me."

Wariness slipped into the other woman's eyes. "How do you mean set the story straight?"

"You know, when things like this happen, there are always folks who want to make the real victim the bad guy. Sarah and I were never friends, but my father and her father were. My father thought very highly of Melvin Yoder. I'm certain he didn't raise a murderer. Sarah did what she had to do to protect her children and herself. I want people to know that before the rumors and gossip muddy the waters."

Audrey said this with as much righteous indignation

as she could muster. And every word was true. Capturing the right story was immensely important to her.

"Of course she did," Nikki muttered. "Anyone who says different is a fool and a liar. Sarah is the gentlest, sweetest person I know. She wouldn't hurt a fly, much less kill a man, unless there was no other choice."

Audrey leaned forward. "That's exactly what I said. But you know those hotline calls come in, and since they're anonymous, people think they can say the most hurtful and ridiculous things." This, too, was true. Though it hadn't happened yet, it would. It always did. "We need to set the record straight."

"I'm sure Sarah told the police someone had been hanging around her place. A stranger sitting out by the road in his black car just watching day in and day out." Nikki's lips formed a grim line. "She said Wesley was out of town and she was nervous. I don't blame her for shooting him after he broke in."

"She probably told her brothers how he was watching her place." The missing brothers were another detail that didn't sit right with Audrey. Where were those three strapping Yoder men when their sister needed help? Not a single one had shown up last night. Something was wrong with that picture, too.

"She couldn't." Nikki leaned across the counter. "Jacob's wife was having a baby. Aaron was at home with their father. Mr. Yoder can't be left alone now. He's very sick and his wife passed away last year."

Audrey nodded her understanding. "What about Benjamin?"

"Benjamin and Sarah aren't on speaking terms." Nikki shook her head. "I guess he's still upset that Wesley—Sarah's husband—sort of took the spot he'd expected to hold as the oldest son."

Good point. "I didn't think of that," Audrey admitted. "I'm sure Benjamin was disappointed at not stepping into his father's shoes."

"The decision created quite the divide. I can't say that I blame Benjamin, but Sarah loves her husband. She supports him over her brother. It's what God intended. Her daddy's decision was his decision, not hers."

"Speaking of brothers." Audrey smiled. "How's your brother? I hear the kids around town love him." Charlie Wells was the sweetest guy. He and Audrey had worked together on the school paper. Why couldn't she have fallen for him?

How come she asked herself that same question about every nice guy she had ever known?

Nikki grinned. "Charlie loves being a doctor. He's the first one in the family to even attend college. I can't believe he took it all the way." She laughed, her fondness for her brother clear in her voice. "Who would've thought that my goofy baby brother would end up a pediatrician?"

"Look at you," Audrey countered. "You're running this place all on your own. The renovations you did last year are amazing. You've done pretty well yourself, Nikki."

She blushed, ducked her head. "Thank you. Coming from a big-city girl like you, that's a real compliment."

Audrey waved her off. "If I can take care of the *Gazette* as well as you have the diner, I'll be happy."

Nikki looked around as if confirming no one was paying attention to their private conversation. "You should talk to Aaron. You didn't hear this from me, but I hear there was some sort of disagreement between Mr. Yoder and Wesley a few months back. By then Mr. Yoder was already bedridden and he'd single-handedly convinced the whole community to look to Sauder for guidance.

Whatever happened, the two men don't speak anymore. Sarah won't talk about it but I get the feeling it's related to something the old man believes about his son-in-law. Some part of his past that he learned from visiting family who came down from Illinois last year."

"Something from Sauder's past?"

Nikki shrugged. "I don't know for sure. Sarah wouldn't talk about it, but something changed between Mr. Yoder and Wesley. Her brothers are upset with him as well. With that rift going on, I doubt she shared her worries with any of them. Now this man shows up breaking into their home and Sarah shoots him. Whatever's going on, it's not right. I'm worried that Sarah's in trouble."

Audrey was ecstatic to learn all these details but why would Nikki spill her guts like this? They had never really been friends, only acquaintances. She'd expected to have to wrangle information from her. And if Nikki really was worried about her friend, why not tell the sheriff? This didn't feel right.

"I'm grateful you've shared your feelings," Audrey confessed. "But to tell the truth, I'm surprised you've been so forthcoming."

Nikki looked around again. "I know you've been gone a long time, Audrey. Maybe you've forgotten that in small towns people take sides. They form opinions based on what they think they know without ever looking at the facts. No offense to Sheriff Tanner and his deputies, but they're not going to look beyond the idea that a stranger showed up in town and broke into a home and ended up dead. End of story. They won't dig around beneath the surface. Why should they? But something's wrong and I think Sarah is scared. She won't even talk to me anymore. Brian told me that no one knows how to dig up the truth better than you. Help my friend, that's all I ask."

So this had been a setup. At least it was the kind Audrey appreciated. "I'll do all I can, you have my word."

"Keep my name out of it if at all possible," Nikki urged. "Sarah is my friend and I don't want to hurt her. I'm just worried and that's the only reason I'm telling you all this."

"Trust me," Audrey assured her. "I have never divulged an anonymous source." Even when she'd wanted to do so after a source let her down. She had taken the fall. Good reporters always did. A good source was priceless. Do them wrong and you lost them and your reputation. In her entire career she never betrayed one and she never lost one. She wasn't about to start now.

The bell over the entrance jingled and Nikki drew away and called, "Morning, Sheriff. Coffee?"

Audrey placed the cash on the counter for her coffee and slid off the stool. The diner was empty save for the cowboy who had just swaggered in. As she watched, Colt lowered onto a stool midway down the counter without so much as glancing her way. He placed his hat on the stool next to him and ran a hand through his black hair. So, this was his way of avoiding any questions she might have.

She never had been put off by anyone's *ignore* mode. With that in mind, she marched down to where Colt sat and leaned against the counter. "Well, good morning to you, too, Sheriff."

He gave her a nod. "Morning, Rey."

"Anything new on the investigation?"

His gaze glued to the menu on the wall—a menu he likely knew by heart already—he moved his head from side to side. "Nothing I can talk about, anyway."

He would have been better served if he'd kept his response to nothing more than the shake of his head. "I take it Branch confirmed the identity of the big guy with the red hair who died on Sarah Sauder's kitchen floor last night?"

He turned to her, his gray eyes narrowed. "Has Branch been talking to you?"

She smiled at the idea that she'd just hit a nerve. Colt had always been jealous of Branch. Then again, what male wouldn't be? Branch was a good-looking *single* man. He'd been a big-shot football star back in high school and college, and he was still a hometown hero. But then, so was Colt.

"Branch understands the value of having a resource in the media on his side." Not exactly a lie, merely an avoidance of the actual question.

"Anthony Marcello is trouble, Rey."

Nikki placed a steaming cup of black coffee in front of Colt. He nodded his thanks and she moved on. The Corner Diner was a popular spot for business lunches and small gatherings. Nikki had worked there since she was a little girl. She had learned when to linger and when to give her patrons the space they needed for private conversations. Still, Audrey imagined she knew more secrets than anyone in town except maybe the stylists in the local salons.

"Maybe so, but he can hardly create any problems now—he's dead." She smiled at the way the lines of frustration gathered around his eyes, and his lips flattened into a grim line. Lips she had kissed about a thousand times.

Do not go there, Audrey.

"The problem is—" Colt shifted on the stool, his knee bumping her thigh and sending a zing of electricity through her "—Marcello has friends. Dangerous friends. You don't need to go chasing down that rabbit hole, Rey.

You need to stay out of this investigation or there will be trouble for you…for all of us."

Chicago. Dangerous. Oh yeah, the dead guy was connected to a crime syndicate. It was the only logical explanation.

"Hmm. I can see you're very concerned for my safety, Sheriff." She cocked her head and stared at him. "But you see, I have a job to do, too, and that's to keep the community informed. Remember? We had this discussion last night. I'm sure they'll want to know what in the world the mob would be doing around here."

Before he could toss a practiced answer back at her, she added, "You know how people talk. The rumors will be worse than the truth."

Chapter Five

Colt wanted to shake the woman. The problem was if he put his hands anywhere on her body he would have an even bigger problem than keeping the citizens of his county safe and calm. The last thing he needed was for anyone to panic.

Before he could muster a proper comeback, she said, "Have a nice day, Sheriff."

He turned on the stool and watched Audrey walk away. The gentle sway of her hips made him sigh. Why the hell couldn't they figure this thing out and stop playing games?

"Here you go, Sheriff."

Reluctantly he twisted around to find that Nikki had prepared his untouched coffee to go. He grabbed the cup and gave her a nod. "Thanks."

She smiled. "You better hurry or she's going to get away."

He didn't bother to mention that Rey had gotten away long ago. Instead, Colt settled his hat into place and headed out the door. Rey was already climbing into her car when he caught up with her. "Look, I didn't mean to be so short with you, Rey."

She stood in the vee created by the open car door.

"I'm not sure what you mean, Sheriff." She slipped on her sunglasses and waited for him to explain.

Damn, she never made things easy. He planted his free hand on his hip to prevent inadvertently touching her. "I had a rough night and I guess I sort of took it out on you."

Her eyebrows went up in surprise. "Did you stay too late at that saloon over in Kelso? Or maybe you did your drinking at home." She tore off the dark eyewear, leaned over the car door and put her face closer to his. "Your eyes do look a little bloodshot."

Before he could stop himself, he leaned down, almost nose to nose. "I was at the crime scene until almost midnight and then I went home. The problem was my son came home about that same time. He was intoxicated. He could have gotten himself or someone else killed driving in that condition. So, yeah, alcohol was involved but I wasn't the one drinking it."

Her breath caught and she drew away. "I'm sorry to hear that." She slid the sleek black glasses back into place but not before he could read the concern in her eyes. "I'm certain you were very upset." Her fingers tightened on the car door. "I'm glad he made it home safely."

"Thanks." He straightened, tried to figure a way to carry on a reasonable conversation with her. But every damned time they said more than a half a dozen words to each other they ended up bickering. "I meant what I said, Rey. If Branch is right about this mob connection, we could be looking at some serious trouble. I don't want you getting yourself in the line of fire."

She smiled but it wasn't the friendly kind. "I know how to handle myself, Sheriff. You don't need to worry about me."

Before she could turn away, his right hand settled on hers, trapping it between the cool metal of the door and his palm. The feel of her skin made his gut clench with need. How many nights had he fought the covers dreaming of her? "I do worry. I worry about everyone I care about."

"I'll keep that in mind."

She tugged her hand free of his and dropped behind the wheel. He closed her door, watched her buckle up, back out of the parking slot and drive away.

Well, at least she hadn't told him to mind his own business. Progress, he supposed. The bell at the top of the courthouse tolled the hour. He might as well head back to the office for his meeting with Branch. The sooner they figured out what Tony Marcello was doing in Winchester, the sooner he could protect the citizens of his county.

BRANCH WAS STUDYING the awards on the office walls as Colt walked through the door. "Sorry to keep you waiting."

Branch extended his hand. Colt gripped it, gave it a shake.

"Not a problem," the marshal assured him. "I was catching up on your career highlights." He jerked his head toward the photos and plaques. "You're doing a good job, Colt. I know your daddy would be proud."

"Thanks. You need coffee or something?"

Branch shook his head. "I'm good." He sat down in one of the two chairs in front of Colt's desk. His trademark Stetson sat in the other.

Colt had always been a Resistol man. He hung his hat on the rack and took a seat behind his desk. "You have any updated information on this Tony Marcello?"

"He was a button man for the Cicero crime family. The Ciceros have been operating illegal activities in Chicago for decades. Marcello has been loosely linked to their operations for the past fifteen or so years. From what we know, he takes care of cleanups mostly. My guess is the family sent him down here to handle some unfinished business."

Colt braced his forearms on his desk. "You think Wesley Sauder is the unfinished business." Damned sure looked that way from where Colt was sitting. He would be the first to say coincidences were hard to ignore when they involved murder.

"I do." Branch nodded. "We need to find Sauder before the next guy they send does. And you can take this to the bank—they will keep sending one of their hired guns until this is finished."

"We can do this together," Colt offered, and then qualified, "but this is my investigation."

Branch held up his hands. "I'm here to assist you in any way you need. I'm happy to leave the investigation in your capable hands, *for now*," he said, adding his own caveat.

Colt stood. "In that case, I guess we should get to it."

Branch pushed to his feet. "I'll keep nudging my resources."

"I've got boots on the ground all over the county," Colt said. "I will find Sauder."

When Branch was gone, Colt went to the conference room where he'd held this morning's briefing. He surveyed the map they'd used to pinpoint the locations where citizens who belonged to the Mennonite church resided. There were four businesses. The Yoder Bakery, a furniture shop, the ironworks and a small construction company. Sauder would be well known to every single one.

He had divided the search areas into grids, but he'd left the businesses out. He planned to handle those himself. His deputies had been given a strict warning not to be pushy or intrusive. These were private people. If they said they hadn't seen Sauder or refused to answer questions, the deputy was to move on and give the name to Colt. He would take care of the more sensitive situations personally.

With a shout to his office assistant that he was heading into the field, Colt picked up his hat and made his way to the door. He might as well start with the bakery. Sarah Sauder would probably be there. Maybe he'd get lucky and her husband would show up, too.

THE BAKERY, like most of the Mennonite businesses, was just outside Winchester's town limits. Members of the community pooled their resources and purchased land whenever a desirable spot came on the market. Then the build would begin. In record time a home would be ready for occupancy or a business would be opening its doors. The Yoder Bakery was the first Mennonite business to appear in the Winchester area. Colt remembered his mother shopping there for certain cheeses. The place smelled the way his mother's kitchen had, always of some freshly baked bread or cake rising in the oven.

She'd been gone nearly thirty years now and he still missed her. Losing his dad two years ago had been even harder. He still had his two brothers but they both lived down in Alabama and he didn't see them nearly often enough.

Basically, it was just him and his son. Key had been mad as hell this morning. Having to ride the bus to school was bad enough but losing his cell phone had been like losing a limb. He'd raised holy hell but Colt had stuck to his guns. No driving and no cell phone for a whole month. The kid would survive, but he wasn't going to like a minute of it. After telling Colt how he needed a life so he would stop hyper-focusing on his, Key had called his mother. Colt had been surprised when she agreed with him. He'd almost marked the calendar hanging on the wall in the kitchen. Then again, he knew better than to trust her. She probably had a plan to undermine his authority. He just didn't know about it yet.

This wasn't the first time his son had accused him of ruining his life. Colt couldn't remember the last time he had gone on a date. Serving as sheriff kept him busy and he hadn't really wanted to…until Rey came back to town.

No use going there right now.

Colt shifted his attention back to the business at hand and parked in the lot at the bakery. Since his truck was the only vehicle in the lot he might have a few minutes before the first customer arrived. He climbed out of the truck, scanning the area. A car was parked next to the building on the end with the side door, but it wasn't Sarah's minivan.

Work started at the bakery at about five in the morning. His stomach was already rumbling in anticipation of the aromas that would be filling the shop. Maybe he'd grab a muffin. He'd been too frustrated with Key to have breakfast this morning. Arguing with his son was the worst way to start the day.

He opened the door and the bell overhead jingled. Every shop in town seemed to have one. The scent of fresh-baked goods filled his senses. A young woman behind the counter looked up. Her brown hair was tucked into her bonnet. She smiled. "Morning, Sheriff."

Colt recognized her then. Ruby Weber. "Good morning, Ruby. Sure smells good in here. You have any of those blueberry muffins ready?"

"Sure do." She put on a pair of plastic gloves and wrapped a muffin for him.

The Mennonite women wore bonnets and modest dresses. Though they kept to themselves, he had yet to meet any member of the community who wasn't polite and helpful when asked a question.

But this time might be different. "Are Mr. and Mrs. Sauder here this morning?"

Ruby placed the muffin on the shelf above the glass case. "Afraid not, Sheriff. I imagine they're too upset to come in this morning after what happened in their home last night."

"Did Sarah let you know she wouldn't be in?" There was always the possibility that the Sauders had packed up and taken off. He'd stationed a deputy near the Yoder farm last night. Sarah and her kids had gone to her father's for the rest of the evening. The deputy hadn't seen them leave, but that didn't mean she and the kids hadn't cut across the farm on foot. Another deputy was watching the Sauder home. No activity there, either.

"She did." Ruby nodded. "She's deeply troubled about what she had to do, Sheriff. I can't imagine living with a man's blood on my hands."

"I need to talk to her, Ruby. We've learned some new information about the man who broke into her home. I'm very concerned for the safety of the Sauder family. If you speak to her again, please tell her that it's very important that she call me." He'd rather not have a meeting at her father's house, considering the man was so ill and didn't need that kind of stress. But if Sarah didn't agree to a meeting soon, he'd have no choice.

"Yes, sir. I'll sure tell her if I hear from her. There's no phone at her daddy's place and cell service is a little hit or miss."

Not much of a guarantee.

A *ding* sounded from somewhere beyond the double

swinging doors behind the counter. Ruby glanced that way. "That's my bread calling. Have a nice day, Sheriff."

"Wait, I haven't paid you for the muffin."

Ruby waved him off. "No charge for you. There's coffee if you want to take a cup with you."

Colt thanked her and watched as she disappeared through those swinging doors. He tore off a bite of muffin and popped it into his mouth. The taste exploded on his tongue. He barely restrained a groan. He'd grab a cup of coffee to go with it. Smelled fresh. There wasn't a thing in the place that didn't smell amazing.

He decided to hang around a minute while he devoured the muffin and guzzled the coffee. Might as well. Maybe Sarah would call or show up. Surely Ruby wasn't going to run the place alone.

His cell vibrated. He popped the last bite of muffin into his mouth and dragged the phone from his hip pocket. One of his deputies confirming that Sauder's minivan was still parked at her father's house.

Colt would just have to take a drive over there and see if she was still there. Maybe he was being overly suspicious. There was always the remote possibility the dead man had picked the wrong house to bust into. *Remote* being the key word in that scenario. Like Branch, Colt wasn't buying the scenario.

There was far more to the story.

He downed the last of the coffee and tossed the cup and napkin into the trash bin. Just before he reached the door, it opened, the bell jingling.

Audrey walked in. "Well, hello again, Sheriff. Looks like we're both craving the same things this morning." She reached out and dusted crumbs from his shirt.

Need, hot and fierce, clutched him. She had no idea

how badly he was craving *her*. He shook off the notion. "She's not here, so don't waste your time."

Rey flashed him a smile and walked around him. "Oh my, the breakfast bars look delish."

His hand was on the door. He told himself to open it and walk out. To go on about his day and to ignore whatever Audrey was up to.

Yeah, right.

Instead, he turned around with every intention of demanding to know if she was following him. The scream that came from the back of the shop snapped his mouth shut and raised the hair on the back of his neck.

Audrey beat him around the counter and through those swinging doors—mostly because she stepped right in front of him and he all but fell on his face trying to keep from mowing her down.

Beyond the swinging doors there was a huge kitchen. To the right was a walk-in cooler; next to it was a matching walk-in freezer. On the left there was the office and beyond that the door to the storeroom stood open; the screams were coming from there.

Audrey reached the door first but Colt was close enough to grab her by the shoulders and set her aside. He barreled through the door.

Ruby stood in the middle of the large storeroom, her face as pale as the white sacks of flour lining the shelf to the right. On the floor, leaning against the row of shelves at the back, was a man wearing black—shirt, pants, jacket—all black. His head drooped forward and the bullet that had torn through his chest had left a gaping hole via which it appeared a good portion of the blood in his body had drained, making a puddle between his spread legs.

Oh, hell.

Chapter Six

Audrey ushered Ruby away from the image of the dead man, Colt spoke quietly into his cell, calling for the necessary backup and, more than likely, the coroner. Once they were through those double doors and in the retail space of the shop, Audrey settled the shaken woman into the only chair behind the counter.

"Stay here, Ruby. I'm going to lock the door and put out the closed sign. Okay?"

She nodded, tears streaming down her face.

Then Audrey remembered she needed keys. "Where do you keep your keys?"

Ruby pointed to the register. Audrey spotted the keys, swiped them off the shelf beneath the register and hurried to the door. Once she'd locked the door, she left the keys in the lock. When the deputies and the coroner arrived someone would need to let them in.

Since she didn't spot any tissues, she grabbed a paper napkin and took it to Ruby.

"I... I should call Sarah."

"The sheriff will prefer that you don't call anyone right now, Ruby. As soon as he gives the okay, we should call your mom." Audrey wanted desperately to go back to where Colt was, but she didn't trust Ruby to stay put. If anyone showed up at the door the rattled woman might very well let them in. "Why don't you wait in the office until Sheriff Tanner is ready to talk to you?"

Ruby stood and allowed Audrey to guide her back through those swinging doors and toward the small office they'd passed before. Once she had Ruby seated at the desk, she grabbed the cordless phone to ensure she didn't use it and patted her on the shoulder. "You stay put. I'll let the sheriff know you're waiting in the office."

Audrey was almost out the door when she had to ask. "Ruby, was the door locked when you arrived this morning?"

The younger woman looked up from the crumpled napkin, her eyes glazed with worry and fear. The haze cleared and she nodded. "Yes. Yes. I had to unlock the door to come in."

"What about the back door?" Something else Audrey had noticed when she and Colt had rushed through those swinging doors. There was a back door.

Ruby scrubbed at her forehead as if digging for the answer. "I don't know. I didn't check. I set right in to my usual routine."

"It's all right. I'm sure Sheriff Tanner will check on that."

Audrey hurried across the massive kitchen to the storeroom. She hesitated at the open door, glanced around to see if Colt was nearby, then walked right up to the body. She was careful to maintain an appropriate distance. She snapped a quick photo of the corpse, then tucked her phone back into her pocket.

If she just had her purse she could put on gloves and check the state of rigor to estimate how long he'd been dead. Blood was coagulated, looked completely dry in some areas.

"What the hell, Rey?"

She cringed at Colt's stern voice. Rather than move, she looked over at him. "He's been here several hours, maybe overnight."

Colt walked over to her, crouched down. "I can see that," he bit out. "Now let's get out of here."

She glared at him. "We're already here. A minute won't change the fact that we both walked into the primary scene."

When he opened his mouth to argue with her, she went on, "You have gloves on." She nodded to the latex he'd pulled over his hands. "Check his fingers and then his arms."

Jaw clenched, eyes shooting daggers at her, he reached for the dead man's fingers. They moved easily. "Loose." Then he tried moving the arm, bending the elbow. "Still rigid."

"He's been dead overnight. Twelve or more hours." She'd seen enough bodies and interviewed enough medical examiners to have a reasonably good handle on how things worked the first twenty-four or so hours after death.

Another of those glares arrowed in her direction. "Let's go, Rey."

This time she didn't argue. She had what she needed to know. This guy had probably died around the same time or a little before the one in Sarah Sauder's kitchen. Considering this bakery belonged to Sarah's family as well, finding yet another gunshot victim turned the case in a whole different direction.

When they were outside the storeroom, she mentioned, "Ruby said the front door was locked when she came in. But she didn't check the back." Audrey glanced in the direction of the rear exit.

"Were you questioning her? Damn it, Rey." His long-fingered hands bracketed his waist. "You need to wait out front. Sit your butt on that bench and just wait until I tell you to move."

Like that was going to happen. "Please. Arrest me or throw me out, but do not tell me what to do, Colt Tanner."

"Fine. Audrey Anderson, you are under arrest for interfering with an investigation."

He removed a pair of cuffs from the hip pocket of his jeans. Her jaw dropped in disbelief. "You cannot arrest me, Colt Tanner. I walked into this establishment like any other customer. I cannot be held responsible for what happened after that."

"Give me any more grief and I'll add resisting arrest." Fury radiated from him like heat from a roaring fire.

He was serious.

She held out her hands and he snapped the cuffs on her wrists, all the while reciting her rights as if she were an actual criminal. It wasn't the first time she'd been hauled away from a crime scene in iron bracelets. It was just the first time Colt Tanner had dared to defy her.

How the hell had that happened?

Long fingers wrapped around her upper arm and he guided her through the bakery's swinging doors and to the bench beyond the counter. "Now sit. And don't say one word."

When he'd disappeared into the back once more, Audrey reached into her pocket for her cell, iron bracelets clinking. Colt was going to regret this. She punched the contact for Brian and pressed the phone to her ear.

"Where are you? I've put off the staff meeting."

"I'm at Yoder Bakery," she whispered. If Colt heard her on the phone he would take it from her. "There's another body."

"Oh my God. Who?"

"Don't know. I took a photo. I'm sending it to you."

"Colt will have a—"

"We're not printing it. The photo is for ID purposes only. Strictly between you and me."

"Why are you whispering?" Brian whispered back.

"Colt arrested me for interfering in an investigation. Looks like the guy has been dead since around the same time as what's-his-name who Sarah Sauder shot." What the hell was the guy's name? "Marcello. Tony Marcello."

"Wait, wait, wait. Colt arrested you. Are you serious?"

Audrey glanced toward the doors, blew out a breath of exasperation. "As a heart attack."

"I'll be right there." Brian was no longer whispering. He was damned near shouting.

"No," Audrey ordered as loudly as she dared. "Focus on ID'ing the dead guy. I'm okay. I have to go."

Brian was still speaking when she ended the call. Keeping an eye on the doors, she tapped the photo and sent it to Brian via text. The dead man was dressed the same as the other one, black pants and shirt, but his black jacket was a hoodie. He looked a good deal younger than the other guy as well. Was he shot before or after Marcello? Maybe this guy explained why Wesley Sauder never came home.

Audrey tucked her phone away. The sound of engines outside had her turning around on the bench. Two deputy cruisers and the coroner's van skidded to stops in the parking lot. Burt must have been on his way to the clinic. He was never this quick on the draw. She glanced at the door. Might as well let them in.

She pushed to her feet and went to the glass door and twisted the key. The door was yanked open, setting the bell above it into a stunted tune. Audrey stepped back to prevent being trampled by four men in tan and brown uniforms. The last of the four nodded and said, "Morning, Ms. Anderson."

James Carter's son. The Carter family had run the local hardware store for five generations. The one just off the downtown square, Mr. Carter would remind her, not the big-box place on the boulevard.

"Morning," she replied.

It was Burt who stopped and stared at her shackled state. "What in the world?"

"Colt's mad at me," she confessed.

Burt's eyes widened behind his glasses. "Did you shoot someone, Rey?"

"No." She glanced toward the back of the bakery. "But I might before this is over."

"Burt!"

They both turned at the sound of Colt's voice.

"What's the holdup?"

"Gotta go!" Burt shuffled away, skirting the counter and hurrying toward the door where Colt waited.

The sheriff didn't so much as glance at Audrey before disappearing once more.

The sound of tires squealing drew her attention back to the big window where handmade posters boasted today's specials, including peanut butter balls—buy four, get two free. Her mouth watered despite the circumstances. The van that squealed to a stop belonged to the *Tulla-homa Telegraph*. Audrey locked the door and hurried behind the racks of baked goods. When she felt confident no one outside could see her, she relaxed. Annalise Guthrie was the dauntless reporter who liked trumping Audrey's stories.

"Not today, honey," Audrey muttered.

Her cell vibrated. She dragged it from her pocket and checked the screen. Brian. "Hey. What'd you find?"

"Casey Pranno. Guess where he's from—"

"He works with Marcello?"

"You know it. I spoke to Wanda Mulberry over at the post office not five minutes ago when I dropped off the mail. If any new marshals have shown up she would know, since Branch's office is in the same building. No new faces yet, but she did say Branch had just torn out of there. She saw him bust out the front entrance and hustle out to his truck. He'll probably be there any second."

No sooner had Brian said the words, than two deputies hurried through the swinging doors and to the front entrance. After unlocking it they pushed out. Audrey didn't have to sneak a look to know they would be setting the perimeter and shooing the other reporter outside the set boundary.

"Put together a background piece on Marcello and Pranno. If we have nothing else, we'll run that on tomorrow's front page, but hold the presses as long as possible."

The tinkle of the bell warned that someone was coming in. "Gotta go."

Audrey slid her phone back into her pocket and craned her neck to see who stepped beyond the racks blocking her view of the door.

Branch glanced left, then right, spotted Audrey and automatically removed his hat. "Rey, you hiding over there?"

She moved a few steps closer but not close enough to be spotted via telescopic lenses peering in through the glass front of the shop. If Annalise was out there, there would be others. She waved her hands. "Colt arrested me for interfering with his investigation."

Branch shook his head and walked over to where she stood. "Has he lost his mind?" He reached into his pocket, withdrew a key and released her. "You must have really ticked him off."

She rubbed her wrists. "I might have."

But he deserved it. She could tick him off every day for the rest of his life and it would never be repayment enough for what he had done to her. All the details she kept to herself. Branch had been in college by the time she and Colt broke up, but he'd likely heard the rumors.

Branch grinned. "You always were a feisty one."

He had no idea. The image of that cold, damp basement beneath the newspaper flitted through her head. "I'll take that as a compliment."

"Come on." He jerked his head toward the counter. "We'll see what Sheriff Tanner has to say when I tell him I'm taking custody of his prisoner."

Audrey couldn't help herself—she smiled. "One of these days you two are going to have to put your gridiron days behind you."

"I doubt that's going to happen before one or both of us is laid out for visitation over at DuPont Funeral Home."

Like the family newspaper, DuPont Funeral Home was one of the oldest establishments in Winchester. Though Branch meant that remark as a joke, Audrey couldn't laugh. DuPont had taken care of her father after he died. She had no desire to see anyone else she cared about inside that old Victorian house–turned–funeral home.

The thought of the spooky old place made her shudder.

"You cold, Rey?" he asked as he ushered her through the swinging doors.

"I'm good. Thank you."

She heard the muffled sound of that bell over the entrance door again and two more uniforms crowded into the bakery kitchen. These two she recognized from last night. The evidence techs.

"I should probably stay over here," she said to Branch when he started for the storeroom door.

He gave her a nod and moved on. Audrey was perfectly content to watch. If she leaned forward ever so slightly she could see Colt in the office with Ruby. She could imagine the poor woman was terrified.

Pies prepared for sliding into the ovens lined the stainless counter of one table. Audrey stepped back to ensure she was not in view of the office door and snapped a photo of the pies. The dusting of flour on the shiny steel provided a perfect backdrop to the pies. It wasn't the sort of grisly photo she generally took at a crime scene, but this was a Southern small town. Readers would eat this up.

Having been caught in situations like this before, she sent the photo to her email, then deleted both it and the one of the dead man from her phone. Colt would want to check her phone. While she was at it, she deleted the calls to and from Brian. Feeling cocky, she leaned against the wall next to the sink a few feet from the swinging doors. On the wall above the sink was another handmade sign. This one ordered employees to wash their hands before waiting on customers and then again when returning to the kitchen.

She wondered if Wesley Sauder had come to the bakery and found himself face-to-face with the man lying on the floor in the storeroom, while his wife was being visited by the man she'd shot in her kitchen.

If Sauder was dead, his wife would likely say so.

He was in hiding, Audrey would bet. Somehow he had crossed the mob and they were after him. It wasn't necessary to be a cop to know that whoever sent these guys wouldn't stop until he achieved his goal. If anyone in local law enforcement had any doubts, they should be fully convinced now.

Colt came out of the office. His gaze landed on her and his lips tightened. She noticed when she examined his face for tells. He was still angry.

He strode over to her. "What the hell are you doing back here?"

She held up her hands. "Branch uncuffed me and brought me back here. He told me to wait in this spot and I've been doing exactly that." Before Colt could open his mouth and unleash the storm of fury whirling in his eyes, she added, "There are reporters out front. He didn't want any of them to see me."

He certainly couldn't deny the validity of the excuse. Instead, he grabbed her by the arm. "Come with me."

She blinked. Before she could demand what he meant, he executed an about-face and strode to the door marked Employees Only. She followed. Once inside the cramped bathroom, he shut the door.

"Are you trying to get on my last nerve?"

Maybe the bad night he'd had was making his temper flare so easily. The Colt she knew was generally far more patient than this.

"I am not. I was here for a scone. To my knowledge that isn't against the law." He didn't have to know she'd stopped in hopes of seeing Sarah. "When Ruby screamed, we both ran to where she was." She shrugged. "And you arrested me. I'm a victim of circumstance."

He plowed a hand though his hair, reminding her of all the times she used to do that.

Stop.

"I'm sorry I took my frustration out on you." He heaved a big breath. "But you shouldn't have gone into that storeroom. You went too far, Rey."

"His name is Casey Pranno. He was an associate of Mr. Marcello's—the other dead guy."

Colt closed his eyes for a second, shook his head. "Please tell me you did not take a picture of that man's body and send it to anyone."

Okay, so she had no choice but to tell him. "Only to Brian. We're not printing it. I've already deleted it from my phone."

"You swear to me, Rey. Swear right now that you will not print that photo."

If he hadn't sounded and looked so damned desperate she might have made him beg a little more. "I swear, Colt. You know me better than that. I would never disrespect your office." She shrugged again. "Not unless you made me by leaving me out and blocking my efforts to do *my* job."

"Okay." Another big breath deflated his lungs. "You can go now if you like."

"You mean I'm not under arrest?"

He glanced at the ceiling.

"I didn't tell Branch what I just told you."

Looking down at her, he held her gaze for a moment that lapsed into two. And in that extra second she felt the heat and desire for him that she had not felt since that first time he kissed her in eighth grade.

"Thank you."

She nodded, uncertain of her voice.

"You can go out the back to avoid the reporters."

"Won't do any good." She'd only just realized this part. "My car is out front."

Her vanity plate read PAPRGRL. Everyone knew who drove that car.

"All right. You can stay back here but stick to that

sink over there like it's your long-lost best friend. Do not move from that spot."

"I won't."

He reached for the door, the move putting his face so very close to hers.

"As long as you give me an exclusive sound bite," she added.

He turned, looked directly at her, practically nose to nose. "I'll give you whatever you want, Rey. I always have."

And then he was gone.

She leaned against the wall, had to wait until her heart stopped pounding before she moved.

She was not, *was not* going to get tangled up with Colt Tanner again.

Never, ever, ever.

Chapter Seven

Colt pulled loose the posted warning that proclaimed the Sauder house to be a crime scene and folded it in half. He used the key that belonged to Sarah to unlock the front door of her home. Both the Sauder home and the bakery were now crime scenes. He walked into the house and turned on the overhead light. It was late afternoon with plenty of daylight left, but the windows were darkened with curtains and sheers.

Though this wasn't the first time in his career he'd had murder scenes to investigate two days in a row, it was the first time both scenes had belonged to the same family. He moved around the living room. A sofa sat on one side of the room; a couple of rockers flanked the fireplace. Not much else in the way of furnishings or decor. There was an old rotary phone on one of the side tables. The few Mennonites who had phones were the ones who were business owners. Most didn't care for the bothersome devices. A walk through the four bedrooms revealed the same: beds with plain linens, a chest with drawers—most of which were empty—and a few modest garments hanging in the tiny closets.

Each room in the house had been searched and scrutinized for evidence not once, but twice. There was nothing here that seemed connected to the dead man or Chicago and certainly not to organized crime. The one bathroom in the house revealed even less. Homemade soap and shampoo, towels hanging over the rim of the tub. There was a straight razor, a comb and a brush. Beyond the place on the wood floor where the small pool of blood had left its stain, the kitchen offered only the necessities. Pots and pans, the dishes and glassware in the cabinets. A well-stocked pantry. One drawer held a couple of table-cloths. Another was packed with hand towels and oven mitts. None of the fingerprints taken from the home were found in any databases. Made sense, since the dead guy had been wearing gloves.

Colt checked the back door. The victim had entered the home through that door. The lock was a piece of cake for even an amateur burglar. A guy like Marcello likely unlocked the door with his eyes closed and one hand behind his back. Colt had suggested Sarah have a dead bolt installed. If her husband wasn't handy with a drill and a screwdriver, Colt felt confident one of her brothers could handle the job.

After locking up and taking a walk around the yard, he loaded in his truck and headed for the Yoder place. He would talk to her again, see if she'd suddenly remembered anything she was too upset to recall last night. Colt didn't see any reason not to release her house. His evidence technicians had searched the house thoroughly, including checking for loose floorboards and hidden nooks in the walls, the crawl space and the attic. There was nothing useful to the investigation in the Sauder home. Whatever secrets they were keeping, they'd left nothing for anyone to find.

Melvin Yoder's farm was barely two miles down the road. The house sat on a rise overlooking pastures in front. Cows grazed, barely noticing as Colt turned onto the long drive. Behind the house, fields already prepared for crops extended for as far as the eye could see. Beyond all that were the woods. Yoder owned hundreds of acres. His name was well known throughout the county. He had a reputation for honesty and kindness. Would he have taken in a man with connections to organized crime?

Not knowingly, Colt was certain. He'd heard rumors of a falling-out between Yoder and Sauder, but so far no one had confirmed as much. Maybe this afternoon he'd learn the whole story. After talking to Sarah, he needed to stop by the bakery and check on the progress his evidence techs were making. Then he'd need to follow up with Branch. He wasn't about to let Branch get too far ahead of him or leave him out of the loop in this investigation.

He thought about how Branch had removed Audrey's handcuffs this morning. Colt had always suspected that Branch liked her. He really didn't have any right to be jealous or to begrudge the other man a shot at a relationship with Audrey. But the thought tore him apart inside.

Colt parked behind the minivan that belonged to Sarah Sauder. He got out of his truck and shut the door. The chickens pecking at insects around the yard raised their heads and eyed him speculatively. The dog stretched out on the front porch didn't bother lifting its head, but its tail swept back and forth across the worn wood. Colt remembered the dog as a pup from his first weeks in the department as a brand-new eager deputy. He and his father had stopped by to offer their condolences when Mrs. Yoder passed away. Pepper had to be fifteen or sixteen years old now. No wonder she didn't bother getting up.

Before he took his first step toward the house, his cell vibrated in his hip pocket. He tugged it out, hoping like hell it wasn't another murder. *Key* flashed on the screen. Colt sighed and paused to take the call from his son. "What's up?"

"How am I supposed to get home from school?"

It wasn't quite three yet, but the dismissal bell would be ringing any minute. "Take the bus."

"No way."

The shock in the two words reverberated loud and clear across the airwaves. Key hadn't ridden the school bus since he was in third grade and it was the thing to do with all his friends. After that, his mother or Colt had taken him to school and picked him up until he was sixteen and started driving himself. At almost eighteen, the bus was so not cool.

Too bad.

"Like I told you this morning, take the bus or walk."

Colt had given him strict orders about transportation. No going anywhere in a vehicle with his friends. No rides to and from school from his mom or Colt. He rode the bus or he walked. End of story.

The call ended.

Colt shook his head. Part of him felt like a heel for being so hard on the kid, but the cop in him knew better than to ignore the warning signs of trouble. If he got away with drinking and driving now, it would only get worse later. The idea that his son could have killed himself or someone else last night terrified Colt.

Damn his ex for allowing the boy to run wild. Damn him for letting her do it. Watching his son stagger across the yard had been a serious wake-up call.

The chill in the morning air was long gone. The afternoon sun was beating down as if it were summer already instead of the final days of winter. But then that was life in the South.

He climbed the steps and crossed the porch. A pot of

tulips not quite ready to bloom sat next to the door. Melvin's wife had been dead for years now. Sarah probably kept her mother's flowers going. Melvin Yoder didn't seem like the type to plant or weed flowers. Then again, when a man loved a woman so much, he might do most anything to keep the things that meant something to her going.

Colt would never tell a soul, but he kept all the things he'd given Rey and the things she'd given him in the closet of his room, including the locket he gave her when they were thirteen. After they broke up, she'd packed up every single gift he'd ever given her and shipped them back. Her momma could have dropped it off if Rey didn't want to, but he'd figured she wanted to make a statement by using a delivery service. There was something final about getting that box delivered by a stranger.

He'd opened the box a hundred times over the years.

"Kind of pathetic, Colt," he muttered as he raised his fist and rapped on the wood frame of the screen door.

It was quiet beyond the door. He'd been in Melvin's house before, when he was a teenager. No television. There had been a radio but it hadn't been turned on at the time. Colt had come with his daddy to tell the family that their younger daughter, Bethany, was in the hospital after a drug overdose.

Bethany had survived but her relationship with her family hadn't. She'd ended up taking off for Nashville to try making it as a country music singer. Truth was, she was pretty good. But Music City had been hard on her. Eventually she'd shown up back in Winchester waitressing at one bar or another.

No one in her family had spoken to her since the day she left town, fifteen years ago. She was thirty-one now, just a couple of years younger than Sarah. Living in Winchester and totally ostracized from her family had to be tough.

The door opened and Aaron Yoder stood on the other side of the screen door. Colt sure hated to do this at Melvin's house but the second murder and Sarah's avoidance pretty much left him out of options.

"Afternoon, Sheriff," he said. "You here to see Sarah?"

Colt nodded. "I figured she was home." He jerked his head toward the driveway and her parked van. "Is Wesley here?"

Aaron's jaw tightened—just a little, but Colt noticed. "No, sir. He's not here. You want to come in and talk to Sarah? She just got the children down for a nap."

Colt grimaced. "I don't want to disturb the kids. She could sit on the porch with me a few minutes if she doesn't mind."

"No need. The children are in the back bedroom." Aaron reached to open the screen door; Colt stepped back. "Come on in."

"Thanks." Colt crossed the threshold, removed his hat and glanced around. "How's your daddy?"

"Not too good," Aaron admitted as he closed the door. "He sleeps a lot now. They say that's normal at this stage."

Cancer was an ugly disease. "I hope all this business at Sarah's house and at the bakery hasn't been too hard on him."

"He doesn't want to talk about it, so I let it go."

"Sheriff."

Aaron's posture stiffened at the sound of his sister's voice. Definite tension.

"I'm sorry to have to bother you again, Sarah. But I need to ask you a few more questions in light of what we found at the bakery this morning."

She nodded once. "Come into the sitting room, Sheriff. You want some water? I have lemonade, too."

"No, thank you, ma'am."

"I need to check on Poppa," Aaron said before disappearing down the hall.

When Sarah had settled on the couch, Colt sat down in one of the chairs flanking a table. "Sarah, I really do need to speak with your husband. Can you tell me how to find him?"

She turned her hands up. "With all that's happened, he's going door to door reassuring everyone that we've nothing to fear."

"Sarah, does your husband know either of the men who were killed on your property?"

She moved her head side to side. "He surely does not. We believe the one who broke into our home killed the other man in the bakery and then came to our house. There has to be some kind of mistake. We don't know these men or why they've come all this way to do whatever it is they intended to do."

"You know your husband lived near Chicago and both these men are from Chicago. They worked together, so I'm not inclined to believe they just drove down to Tennessee to kill each other."

A shrug lifted her cotton-clad shoulders. "I sure don't know what to tell you, Sheriff. We're as confused as you are."

"Sarah." He leaned forward, braced his forearms on his knees, his hat in his hands. "Whatever these men are after, the people who sent them won't stop just because the first round of their soldiers has been taken care of. There will be others. If you or your husband knows of some reason they want to hurt your family, you need to share that information with me. It could mean the difference between life and death."

She shook her head again. "Good gracious, Sheriff. Why would they want to hurt us? We're just common people. Serve the Lord. We sure don't have anything valuable but our children and our souls."

"Sarah, is it true that Wesley and your father had a falling-out a few months ago?"

She made a face. "Where on earth did you hear a thing like that? My poppa thinks the world of Wesley. You should know that, Sheriff. You were raised here. You know how much Wesley helped Poppa. My brothers were all so young and couldn't do the things that needed to be done. We would have had an awfully hard time without Wesley."

"Is there any reason for you to believe that your father or one of your brothers knows these men?"

"Lord have mercy, no. My brothers and I might not always get along but they would never be involved in trouble. We don't break the law."

"I wish I could make you understand how important it is that I speak with Wesley." An idea occurred to Colt. "We're worried that these two hit men may have your husband confused with someone else. I can't help him if he doesn't talk to me. This is a very serious situation, Sarah. It's not going to just go away."

"Sheriff, I'm afraid you're barking up the wrong tree. Wesley and I are the victims here. Someone came into our home and our bakery. Two men are dead. It's an awful thing, but it has nothing to do with us."

Colt wished he could believe her story. "You and your whole family are in danger because of this, Sarah. I need to speak to Wesley."

"I'll try to find him," she promised. "I'll tell him how badly you need to talk to him. Maybe he can make time."

Colt stood. "I sure appreciate your cooperation, Sarah. Please give your daddy my regards."

She nodded and looked away as if the mention of her father pained her somehow. Well, he was dying. One estranged daughter in the family was more than enough. Obviously, Sarah didn't want her relationship with her father to end that way.

Sarah followed Colt to the door. "Did you find anything in the bakery that will tell you what happened, Sheriff?"

The way she phrased the question, as if she already knew the answer and just wanted to see if he did, made him want to fire a dozen more questions at her.

"Not yet, but we're working on it. We're hoping the victims' cell phones will give us some answers." He stood on the porch, settled his hat into place. "Be sure to tell Wesley I need to talk to him as soon as possible."

"I'll let him know," she called after Colt.

He had a feeling he wouldn't have an opportunity to talk to Wesley Sauder until he hunted him down and handcuffed him to a chair.

The metal bracelets hanging on his belt made him think of snapping them onto Rey's wrists. Somehow he needed to get it through her head that this investigation could turn into a very dangerous situation. He wanted to protect her.

Before he called it a day, he would be following up with her. Whether she wanted his protection or not, he needed to keep close tabs on her or she would be eyeball-deep in the trouble he suspected was about to descend on his county.

Who was he kidding? She already was.

Chapter Eight

Happy Kids Daycare Center was established nine years ago by Happy Jennings. According to Audrey's mother—before dementia stole so many of her memories—Happy graduated from high school and went to nursing school in Tullahoma at Motlow College. She tried the nursing field working at the hospital and then a local doctor's office. But Happy was never *happy* working with the sick and the injured—never mind the dying. So she started a day care center and it was a big hit. All the mothers who had made fun of Happy all through school, primarily laughing at her name, were thrilled to have someone watching over their offspring all day who was also a registered nurse.

Now, nine years later, Happy was the administrator over a dozen employees. Happy Kids had won numerous awards from the Chamber of Commerce as well as the city of Winchester. Who was laughing now?

Happy Kids was a bright yellow building that had once been a church right off the square in downtown Winchester. The fenced yard was dotted with colorful swings and slides and sandboxes. Audrey opened the gate and made her way to the entrance. Tulips and daffodils filled the window boxes and the pots on either side of the door. At this hour, half past five, most folks had picked up their little ones. According to the sign on the front door, the center closed at six.

Beyond the door, a reception area was empty. Like the exterior, the walls were a bright yellow with clouds on the ceiling and multicolored linoleum tiles on the floor. A door across the room opened and a young woman, all smiles but looking a bit harried, entered the lobby.

"Hello. May I help you?"

An employee. Great. "Hi, I'd like to see Happy if she's available."

"Her office is right down that hall." The woman pointed to a narrow hall on the far west side of the room.

Audrey thanked her and headed that way. Once she was in the hall, she understood why Happy's office was this way. Large windows overlooking the shared interior play area were on one side while windows to the outside play area were on the other. Ingenious. A handful of children were running around the inside play area, laughing and trying to be the one who got the bright red ball next. Around the perimeter of the play area were doors and more large windows; beyond each window was what appeared to be an individual classroom. Happy's office, the entire wall facing the hall made of glass, had the perfect view into the play area and classrooms.

Ideal setup.

Happy spotted Audrey before she could rap on the glass door. She motioned for her to come on in. With a pointed look at Audrey's flat abdomen, she asked, "Are you here to preregister?" Happy gestured to a blue chair in front of her desk. "We do have extensive waiting lists. Most mothers sign their kids up before they're born. You're smart to come in now."

It wasn't until she said the last that Audrey realized

Happy thought she was pregnant. "Oh no." She waved her hands back and forth. "No babies in my future."

Whether it was her words echoing in the room or the other woman's pained expression, Audrey suddenly felt hollow. She drew in a sharp breath and forced the ridiculous reaction aside. She didn't have a significant other at the moment; how could she be having a baby anyway? Audrey felt reasonably confident raising a child was far easier with a partner.

"Oh!" Happy laughed her trademark cackle and shook her head. "I'm sorry. It's just that most people who drop in…" She shook her head again. "Anyway, how are you? You look fantastic! Being back home agrees with you, Rey."

Audrey relaxed, though the uneasy feeling lingered despite her efforts to dismiss it. "I'm glad to be home. Close to Mom. Taking care of the paper."

Happy's expression shifted to one of concern. "How is your mother?"

"She has her good days and her bad ones." There was always that question.

Everyone who'd grown up in Winchester knew the Andersons. The name was synonymous with news. Audrey didn't need to ask to know her mother likely spent the past decade or so raving about her world-traveling daughter always in the headlines of some big paper. Mary Jo Anderson made it sound as if Audrey was some big celebrity whose life was filled with awards, exotic locations and excitement. The awards came, that was true. And there had been plenty of excitement and great locations. But there had also been loneliness and the ever-nagging sense of regret.

What if she'd stayed home; could she have helped her

mother more? Would she be married now with children to bring to Happy's day care center?

Would she and Colt have worked things out?

Shock radiated through Audrey and she blinked, that last thought startling her more deeply than anything had recently—even finding a dead man in the storeroom of her favorite bakery.

"Don't we all," Happy mused. "But the bad days often remind us how lucky we are on the good days." She sighed. "So, to what do I owe the pleasure of your visit, Rey? You know you have always been one of my favorite people. The nicest girl in school."

Audrey smiled. "If I recall, there was a time when you and Aaron Yoder were an item of sorts."

Happy's expression shifted to something slightly less than happy. "You're looking into the murders. I heard about the other dead man they found at the bakery."

"I am." Audrey shook her head. "I just can't see Sarah shooting one man, much less two."

"I guess any of us could if he broke into our house or place of business and threatened us or our children."

That much was true. "There are some who believe Sarah might be covering for one of her brothers. Maybe Aaron." This part was pure conjecture. Audrey had overheard one of the deputies make a comment to that effect.

Happy's face changed again. Shock claimed her expression, and the slightest hint of anger glinted in her eyes. "That is the most ridiculous thing I have ever heard." Outrage weighted her tone. "Aaron would never shoot anyone unless they shot at him first. Were those dead guys armed? Did they fire their weapons first? Where in the world did you hear such a thing?"

"No indication either of them fired first." Unless the bullets had lodged inside someone—like Wesley Sauder or one of the brothers. There were no bullets or casings found at the scene. This she knew for a certainty. No word yet on whether either of the victims' weapons had been fired. If the lab had confirmed as much, Colt was holding back that information.

Happy shook her head adamantly. "I am telling you right now, Rey, he couldn't do this. Aaron is the most tenderhearted man on this planet. He would never hurt anyone unless he had no choice."

"Are you and Aaron still friends?" As the other woman's expression closed, Audrey hastened to add, "I'm not here to cause Aaron any trouble. I want to help him. This is what I do, Happy. I have traveled the world, like my mom said. I've done all sorts of stories, but I'm most known for the ones that bring the truth to light. This is not my first murder investigation."

Happy shrugged. "Your momma always said you were a hero to a lot of people in a lot of stories."

Okay, that might be stretching things a bit, but mothers had a tendency to brag. "I do what I can. If there's anything you can do to help me help Aaron, I'm sure he will appreciate it in the long run."

"Aaron hasn't mentioned anything like this," she countered, unknowingly admitting to exactly what Audrey wanted to hear.

"Is there a problem between him and Sarah or between Sarah and their father?"

Happy stared at her desk for a moment, likely weighing how far she wanted to go with what she knew or suspected. No matter that she and Aaron could never have a life together; she still cared about him. That was the Happy Audrey knew. Loyal to the bone.

"Whatever you tell me will remain in confidence," Audrey assured her. "I'll use the information to help find the truth, but I'm not going to report what you tell me. You have my word."

"Sarah and her daddy had a big argument about two months ago. Melvin learned some disturbing information about Wesley, Sarah's husband. He was very upset about all of it."

"Do you know what sort of information he discovered?" Audrey was practically on the edge of her seat. There had to be a connection between Wesley Sauder and one or both of the dead guys. One so-called button man might make a mistake and show up at the wrong place, but two different men making the same mistake? Not likely.

"He wouldn't say." She shrugged. "Maybe his daddy didn't give him all the details. Either way he wouldn't talk about what the problem was. He only said that Wesley Sauder was not the man they had all thought he was. You know, that could mean anything. I did see bruises on Sarah's arms once. She claimed she fell and hurt herself, but I didn't believe her. But I've never seen anything but good out of Wesley. Goodness sakes, he was always doing for others. Spearheading every build in their community, helping the businesses to thrive. His work even crossed over to our community. None of this makes sense."

"Do you know Wesley beyond what you've heard from others about him?"

She shook her head. "Not really. I mean, I know him when I see him, but he's not the sort who associates with you unless it somehow benefits his cause. Aaron told me he didn't waste his time on people who don't matter. But if you talk to anyone else, they'll tell you what a good man he is, how he helps everyone."

It sounded as if Aaron was definitely not a fan of his brother-in-law. And Happy was torn between her loyalty to Aaron and the reputation Wesley Sauder had garnered for himself.

"What makes Aaron so unsure of Wesley?"

"You know, he has never really said a whole lot about him. But he did remind me that Wesley just happened to come along at the same time that old bull charged Melvin and injured him so badly. Aaron said he never could understand what made the bull charge. He never had before. At the time, they were all so grateful Wesley was able to get Melvin out of the pasture and to the hospital that no one asked any questions. Looking back, I have to agree with Aaron—it seems awfully convenient that he came along on that deserted road at exactly the right time."

"Why would Mr. Yoder put so much support behind Wesley in the community rather than one of his own sons?" This part truly puzzled Audrey.

"In part, I suppose, because he was older," Happy offered. "Aaron and his brothers were all so young back then. By the time they were old enough, Wesley was the person everyone looked up to. It was too late to change what was done."

"Would Aaron or any of his brothers protect Wesley? Help him hide from the police or a threat of some sort? Like those two men who showed up and broke in?"

Happy shook her head slowly from side to side. "No way. They dislike him intensely. Wesley would never go to one of them."

Well, well, there it was. "Does Aaron have any idea where his brother-in-law might hide out?"

"If they knew, I'm pretty sure one of them would find a way to get word to Colt." Happy looked beyond Audrey at the wall of windows across the narrow hall. "The trouble is, it could be anyone in the Mennonite community—besides them—hiding Wesley. They all love him. He's like the messiah or some celebrity."

"Is there any possibility that Aaron or one of his brothers handled the situation?" Audrey pressed the other woman with her gaze. "If Wesley was causing problems for the family, this situation would be the perfect time to get rid of him and allow the world to think another one of those guys from Chicago took care of him."

Happy was shaking her head again. "They would never do that. Never. You have to believe me on that one, Rey. They're not like that. The Yoder boys—men— are good, kind souls. They couldn't kill anyone. I'm not even sure they could or would kill someone to protect themselves. More likely they'd just injure the attacker real bad."

"Not even if their daddy told them to take care of Wesley?"

She laughed then, but there was no humor in the sound. "Melvin Yoder would never go against God that way. He would sooner sacrifice himself than someone else. If there was ever a man born without a mean bone in his body, it was Melvin Yoder."

This was getting Audrey nowhere. She needed to know where to look. "Is there someone in the Mennonite community who would be more likely to hide Wesley? Maybe someone Aaron mentioned as being a particularly close friend of his brother-in-law's?"

Happy considered the question for a moment. "Ezra Zimmerman. He and Wesley are tight, according to Aaron."

Finally, there was a piece of information she needed. "Thanks, Happy. I appreciate your candor."

Audrey stood; the other woman did the same. "So you know, Colt asked me pretty much the same questions."

"He did?"

Happy nodded. "Couple of hours ago."

"Did you tell him what you told me?"

"No. I was actually going to drop by the newspaper after I closed the center to talk to you. No offense to Colt, but he's following the law. If I was going to help Aaron and his family, I wanted someone who was going to follow their heart. I know you'll do that, Rey."

Audrey smiled. "I owe you one, Happy."

"A nice half-page ad about our upcoming registration might be nice."

"You've got it. I'll have Brian contact you."

Audrey left the Happy Kids Daycare Center and drove straight to Ezra Zimmerman's dairy farm. The wife and two children were home, but not Ezra. His wife had no idea when he would be home, and she had not seen or spoken to Wesley Sauder. She thought her husband might be home later that night.

Since it would be dark soon, Audrey decided to drive back to the paper. She would check in with Brian and let him know her plan. She was staking out the Zimmerman place for the night. She'd need binoculars, water and snacks. Toilet paper for trips into the woods across the road.

Most important, she needed to borrow Brian's black car. Her silver one wasn't so good for hiding.

"I THINK I should do this with you," Brian insisted as she slid behind the wheel of his compact black two-door sports car.

"One of us has to put the paper to bed, and that's you." She started the engine. "I have my cell, a charger, water and snacks." And the toilet paper. All of which was in the minuscule back seat. Was a human really supposed to ride back there?

He heaved a disgusted sigh. "Fine, but if anything happens to you, just know that I'll feel guilty for the rest of my life. How can you do that to a friend?"

Audrey laughed. "But you can say I told you so."

"Just be careful. I don't want you to end up like those two interlopers."

"I will be very careful. Don't forget about that ad space for Happy's center. I promised her you would take care of it personally."

"I'll take care of it. You just take care of you."

She gave him a thumbs-up, and when she would have shifted into Drive and pulled away, Colt's truck parked next to her.

She looked from the big black truck to the man standing outside the window of her driver's-side door. "Tell me you did not call him."

Brian held up his hands. "I swear I did not call him."

Colt opened the passenger-side door and dropped into the passenger seat of Brian's car. He pulled off his hat and placed it in the back seat on top of her supplies. "Ready?"

She glowered first at him, then at her trusted friend and employee. She powered up her window and shifted into Drive. "What're you doing here, Colt?"

As she rolled away from the newspaper parking lot, he tugged on his seat belt and made himself comfortable by powering the seat back as far as possible, which was not very far. She was surprised his long legs fit into the vehicle, much less the rest of his lean, hard body.

Dear God, stop with the physical details already!

"Keeping you out of trouble, Rey," he said in answer to her question.

She glanced at him as she pointed the car toward their destination. "I'm not in trouble, Colt."

"Not for a lack of trying," he grumbled.

"Did Brian call you?" She couldn't believe he had lied to her—straight to her face.

"He did not."

"Happy, then?" Why hadn't Happy just told Colt about Ezra in the first place? Damn her.

"I said Brian didn't call me. I didn't say he didn't tell me."

Fury tightened Audrey's lips. "He sent you a text."

"Three," Colt confirmed. "One: 'you gotta get over here, Colt.'"

She was going to have a very long, very unpleasant conversation with Brian.

"Two: 'she is planning a stakeout tonight.'"

Audrey put her anger on pause. "What about the third one?"

"'I'm worried she might need backup.'"

A grin spread across her face. "So he didn't tell you where I was going?"

FIVE HOURS LATER there hadn't been any movement at the Zimmerman place. Ezra's truck had been parked in the driveway when they arrived and it still was. The lights had gone out about ten. Colt was happy she was prepared for the stakeout. She had chips and her favorite chocolate bars, which happened to be his favorite as well. They'd binged on the junk food the way they had back in high school, but they washed it down with water rather than colas.

Still, she would be sorry tomorrow.

"This wife is his second one?" Audrey asked. Her mother had mentioned Mrs. Zimmerman dying a few years back. If memory served, the Zimmermans didn't have children. But there had been a really young woman, maybe midtwenties, and two children when Audrey knocked on the door. The woman had said she was Ezra's wife.

"Yep. His first wife died a while back, maybe five or six years ago. They had been married since they were teenagers. He married again about three years ago and had two kids."

"Living alone gets to you sometimes. It's probably really difficult after spending your whole adult life with someone and then finding yourself alone."

The words echoed in the confined space and Audrey flinched in the darkness. That was one admission she would have preferred to keep to herself. She certainly hadn't intended to say it aloud to Colt. "Mom said that to me a couple of times," she amended, her words tumbling over one another. "You know, before I came back home."

He was silent for a while. Surprisingly, sitting in the dark with him was easy. She didn't feel the usual tension that accompanied being within a dozen yards of him. Maybe it was not being able to see his face or those gray eyes of his. No, she decided. It was because he couldn't see her. Couldn't spot the way her pulse quickened whenever he was close or the way her lips burned, requiring that she moisten them repeatedly, for the taste of his.

She sighed. Would she never get past this ridiculous physical attraction that should have vanished eons ago?

"I know what she means," he said, his deep voice low and somehow soothing in the darkness. "I've been single for going on eight years and the loneliness creeps up on me sometimes."

"What do you mean?" She stared at him, wished she could see his eyes just now. "You have your son. How can you be lonely?" God knew, he'd probably had his pick of the single ladies in the county. Maybe even a few who weren't single. Anger stirred deep in her chest.

"Shared custody, remember?" He leaned his head back against the seat. "He came to my house on Friday, stayed until today. Now he's at her house until this Friday. It's a really crappy way to raise a kid. I hate it more than you can imagine."

Audrey didn't want to hear about his issues with *her*. Before she realized what she was doing, she'd crossed her arms over her chest and stared straight ahead. Couldn't help herself. Talking about the other woman—no matter that it was eighteen years later—made her angry still. Hurt, still. Maybe that hurt was the kind one never recovered from.

"I know I've said this a thousand times." His voice was soft now, gentle. "But I'm sorry for what I did. I love my son and I can't regret him, but I would give anything on this earth if I hadn't hurt you."

She moistened her dry lips for the hundredth time, worked hard to keep the anger and resentment out of her voice. "That was a long time ago, Colt."

"No amount of time will change how much I regret being so stupid."

Audrey had to bite her tongue to prevent saying she was glad to hear it. "We've all made mistakes."

He exhaled a big breath. "Some of us just make bigger ones than others."

"You think Sauder is in there?" She had to change the subject before she said something she would regret.

"I don't know, but if he is, I want to be here when he comes out."

Audrey didn't say anything else after that and neither did Colt. She considered powering down the window to let in some air. His aftershave was nicely understated, barely there in fact, but the soft scent of lemons and leather was driving her mad.

Maybe she should just close her eyes and pretend she was somewhere else.

Somewhere far away from Colt Tanner and the past that appeared determined to linger in the present.

Chapter Nine

Wednesday, February 27, 6:15 a.m.

Audrey woke to the gentle sound of rain, the lingering taste of chocolate in her mouth and the scent of Colt Tanner warming her senses. Would she never stop dreaming of the man?

"Morning."

She froze.

Car. Stakeout. Zimmerman place.

Her head was lying on his shoulder.

Audrey jerked upright. Banged her head on the seat back. "Good morning." She grabbed her bottle of water and busied herself with guzzling the remainder. Then she leaned forward and peered at the old farmhouse on the opposite side of the road. "Anything moving over there this morning?"

It was raining. Not hard, just drizzling, but enough to prevent opening a window.

"Couple of cows and a few chickens moving about."

She shot him a sour look. He grinned. "You know what I mean."

"No one has gone in or out the front door. No movement around the house, aside from what I've already told you about." That lopsided grin appeared again.

She glanced away, couldn't bear to look at him or see that grin. Not like this. "Should we knock on the door and ask him if he's seen his buddy Sauder?"

"How about pulling into the driveway? Then we'll go from there."

Audrey started the car, anticipation of something other than the man seated far too close to her zinging through her veins. She wanted the story on Sauder. This was big and it was happening right in her backyard. She parked behind Zimmerman's truck and shut off the engine.

"So let's see who's home." She reached for the door.

"*We* aren't going to see who's home, but I am." He opened the passenger-side door. "Stay put, Rey. I mean it."

"Whatever you say, Sheriff." She propped her arms on the steering wheel and stared straight ahead. It was easier to lie to him when she wasn't looking at him.

"Do not get out of this car," he reiterated before closing the door.

Mad as hell, she watched him climb the steps and cross the porch. Even more maddening was the idea that he still looked great after sleeping all night in a compact car. His shirt wasn't even wrinkled, but it was getting all wet in the rain, plastering to his body.

"You are so bad, Rey," she muttered as she glanced at her reflection in the rearview mirror. She groaned. Mascara was smudged beneath her eyes. Her hair was mussed.

From the corner of her eye she saw movement. A figure—a man—was running across the field beyond the house. She glanced at the front door. Zimmerman was talking to Colt.

Audrey bolted from the car and lunged across the yard, rain slapping her in the face. "He's running!"

Before she reached the fence, Colt darted ahead of her, flying over the fence with only one hand braced on the top rail to launch his body. The fleeing man was disappearing in the distance. She couldn't be certain it was Sauder, but who else would be running? Seemed like a very good question to ask the homeowner.

Audrey turned around and headed back to the house. Mr. Zimmerman stood on the porch watching the show. "Is that Wesley Sauder?"

Zimmerman shrugged. "Could be."

Which meant yes. "Mr. Zimmerman, you do realize…"

Before she could finish her statement, the man had turned and walked back into his house, closing the door behind him.

So much for neighborliness.

Audrey crossed the yard, then dropped back into the car and backed out of the driveway. She might as well drive in the direction Colt had disappeared. Whether he caught the guy or not he would need his cell phone, which was lying on the console, and he certainly would need a ride.

About a mile beyond the Zimmerman driveway, Colt waited on the side of the road. The thick woods behind him were likely the reason he'd lost the running man. He was soaked to the bone, every inch of fabric clinging to his muscular body. Another groan emanated from her. She needed to take care of those basic needs or she was going to screw up royally.

Colt climbed into the passenger seat. "Lost him in the woods."

"I asked Zimmerman if that was Sauder and all he said was, 'Could be.' Then he went into the house and closed the door. I don't think he's going to be amenable to answering questions."

"At least we know Sauder is staying close."

They drove back to the Zimmerman house and Colt knocked on the door. No answer.

When Colt dropped back into the passenger seat, Audrey asked, "You really think that was him?" She headed back into town, doing everything within her power not to look at the way his wet clothes had molded to every square inch of him.

"I'm reasonably sure it was him all right. I got a pretty good look at him twice. I can't believe he outran me."

"I can't imagine it's easy to run in cowboy boots." She glanced down his long damp legs at the footwear in question.

"I guess I'm used to doing whatever I do in boots."

A vision of Colt kissing her senseless before pulling her into his truck filled her head. She blinked the memories away. Yes, he rarely pulled off his boots. But then they'd always taken the fastest route possible to what they wanted. She pushed away the thought. Reminded herself that she shouldn't be going there, particularly with him so close…so wet…and so…

Stop. Stop. Stop.

"If you'll drop me off at the paper, I'll get my truck and run to the house for a shower."

She cleared her throat, focused on the practical. "I need to do the same."

The silence that thickened between them for the rest of the drive had her reliving the time they had gotten caught in the rain, ending up soaked to the bones just as they were now. Only that time they had made love. Hard as she tried she could not make the images go away.

What in the world was she doing?

By THAT AFTERNOON she and Brian had laid out a good, meaty article about organized crime and its reach for Thursday's edition of the *Gazette*. Somehow she had to find a way to get Sarah to talk to her. Maybe she should pay a visit to Nikki Slater again. If her husband was in trouble, would Sarah share her concerns with her best friend? Seemed the logical thing to do. Unless she was afraid of putting her friend in the crosshairs. Both Colt and Branch had warned that more of the men looking for Sauder—if that's what they were doing, and it appeared to be—would be coming. If Sauder had something they wanted or knew something he shouldn't, they wouldn't stop coming until they had handled the situation.

But what could this seemingly community-and-family-oriented Mennonite man know about organized crime? He'd been living in Winchester for more than ten years.

Maybe it wasn't what he knew now, but something he had known before?

Audrey still had a few contacts in Chicago. She might as well reach out and rattle that cage, see what shook loose. Judd Seymour was the top crime beat reporter in the Windy City. Audrey called, got his voice mail and left him a message.

Brian poked his head into her office. "You have a minute?"

She smiled. "Always." She cringed as he sat down. "Oh, I forgot to put gas in your car and Colt got the passenger seat wet and the floorboard muddy. I'll pay for the cleaning."

Now that she thought about it, she'd been almost as wet and muddy as Colt. If she hadn't been so distracted by him in his wet clothes and the fact that Sauder had given them the slip, she might have taken better care of Brian's car.

Brian laughed. "Not to worry. I topped the tank off at lunch and dropped the car off for detailing at the car wash. You'll find a charge on the newspaper's account for all of the above."

"Good." She folded her arms over her chest and eyed her friend and partner in most crimes. "So, you set me up last evening."

Brian blushed. "Possibly. For the most part I was worried about you. I like having you here. I don't want to lose you."

"Mm-hmm."

"I really was," he argued. "Ezra Zimmerman lives in a pretty remote area. Besides, if you and Colt can figure out the most likely places Sauder would hide, what makes you think the bad guys looking for him aren't able to do the same thing?"

Audrey laughed. "Okay, okay. All is forgiven."

He narrowed his gaze. "So, how did it go? I mean, you did spend the entire night in a rather cramped space with *him*."

"It was…fine." She nodded. "For the first time in eighteen years we didn't bite each other's heads off."

"Sounds like progress."

Before she could set him straight, her cell shuddered against her desk. "Excuse me." She grabbed her phone.

Brian stood. "Back to the grind."

She gave him a salute and answered the call. "Audrey Anderson."

"Audrey, how are you?"

Judd Seymour.

"Judd, hey, thanks for returning my call." After her exit from the *Post*, she was surprised he even bothered. Unless, of course, he'd heard about the shootings. She was more than happy to juggle a little quid pro quo.

"Anytime, Audrey. You will always be my favorite Southern lady."

Oh yeah. He wanted information. "Good to hear, Judd. What can you tell me about the organized crime in your fair city?"

"It just so happens that I've been doing a little research on the Cicero family."

"Perfect. The Cicero family is the one I'm primarily interested in."

"They've been around for a very long time, Audrey. Five generations."

"Yeah, I read that online. I also read that the current head of the family has a trial coming up. The Feds have been putting the evidence together for years, trying to get this guy on a docket. You think the trial has anything to do with what's going on in my little town?" Didn't seem possible, but stranger things had happened.

"As far-fetched as it sounds, I think that's a strong likelihood."

"I need more than your conclusions, Judd. What makes you believe this is the case?"

"I did a little digging," he went on. "Twenty-odd years ago, Winchester showed up in an investigation on the old man, Louis Cicero. Nothing came of it, but I thought it was strange that Winchester, Tennessee, a speck on the map, would be mentioned in the pile of documents related to all the crimes the cops and the Feds can't seem to prove against the family. To tell you the truth, I don't think they'll ever get this trial started. They have some circumstantial evidence, but they just don't have anything solid enough and no witnesses."

A rush of cold poured through her. "Was there a person's name mentioned in connection with Winchester?"

The sound of papers shifting went on for a few seconds. "No name, just that there was a snippet of discussion picked up on the wiretaps. Winchester was mentioned several times. It reads like the old man thought there was trouble of some sort down there. But no names. Criminals tend to use code words, you know. Sometimes the Feds figure them out, sometimes they don't. They've always needed someone on the inside of the organization, but no one who dares talk about the Cicero family ever lives long enough to do it in front of a camera or a judge."

"You said twenty-odd years ago. Exactly when was this?" A choking sensation made it difficult for Audrey to breathe.

"Let's see. The notes show that the first mention was just before Christmas more than twenty-four years ago. The final mention was March 15 the following year."

"What was said about March 15?" Her voice sounded stilted, felt raw. March 15, twenty-four years ago, her father had his heart attack and died…and the thing in the basement happened.

More shuffling of pages. "Here we go. The transcript says, 'We've lost interest in Winchester.'"

"Whatever they thought would happen or was happening fell apart, I guess," she suggested. Or died. Her heart was beating so fast she could hardly breathe.

"Based on what I'm reading, I'd say there was something or someone in Winchester they wanted but it didn't work out."

"Thank you, Judd." She forced a laugh. "I'm not sure what any of that means, but now I know the connection."

"Two of the Cicero family's people have managed to get themselves dead in your town, Audrey. What's going on down there?"

"I wish I knew, Judd. I really do." She shared what she could. Basically what the paper had printed so far. She owed it to Colt to keep quiet about what happened at the Zimmerman place this morning.

"Keep me posted, will you?"

"Sure thing. I hope you'll do the same."

"I will. Good to hear from you, Audrey."

When the call ended, Audrey pulled up her contacts and tapped another number. Since her mother's memories were lost, there was only one other person she could ask about twenty-four years ago.

PHILLIP ANDERSON WAS only too happy to drop by the newspaper after his racquetball game. He played every Wednesday afternoon. He was dressed in sweats when he arrived. Audrey took his wet umbrella and propped it in the corner. It had been raining off and on all day. The same was forecast for tonight. It was that time of year. She rounded up a bottle of water for Phil and closed the door to her office.

Phillip frowned. "Has something happened to Mary Jo?"

"Oh, sorry. No. Mom's okay." She shrugged. "No change."

He nodded and took a long swallow of water. Phillip was five years younger than his only sibling, his brother—her father, who had died twenty-four years ago next month. He was sixty-two; her father would be sixty-seven if he were still alive.

"When Dad was still alive, did he or the newspaper ever have any trouble with organized crime?"

Phillip coughed, almost choked. "What?"

"Was there any trouble that you were aware of between Dad and a representative of organized crime from, say, Chicago?"

Phillip sat his bottle of water aside and sat up a little straighter. "What's this about, Rey?"

"During the four or five months before Dad died, there was something going on with one of the organized crime elements in Chicago and there were comments about Winchester. My source believes there was something here they wanted."

"If something like that was going on," he said, "we sure as hell didn't know about it, because it would have been on the front page if we had. You know your father was one to push the envelope. He wouldn't have sat on something like that."

She did know that. But she also knew her father had died suddenly and that a stranger had been in his office at the time. "Do you remember anyone from out of town who visited the office during that time?"

More frown lines formed on his face. Phillip and her father had looked very much alike as younger men. She imagined this was what her dad would look like now. Lots of laugh lines with that deep, booming voice that resonated through a crowd. Everyone had liked her dad.

Her heart hurt at the idea that he'd died so young. Only a few years older than she was now.

"I can't say that I do, but you know Porter was always searching for ways to expand and to increase circulation. He had more visitors than a head of state. I was like Brian, more focused on editorial and production. Your father was the businessman. The face of the *Gazette*."

Hearing her uncle talk about her dad had memories of him echoing inside her. The sound of his voice, the breadth of his strong shoulders and the smile that always told her everything was all right. As much as she missed him, she could only imagine how much her mother did. He had been her everything. After he died, she threw herself into raising Audrey and taking care of things around their big old house. And of course there were her civic duties. Mary Jo Anderson lived to support community fund-raisers. But there was always a sadness about her.

Still was.

"You're not thinking your father had some affiliation with criminal activity?"

His indignant tone said all that needed to be said on the matter.

"Of course not," she assured him. "On the contrary, I'm worried he may have known something that garnered the wrong attention, which is why I asked about visitors during that time frame."

Phillip nodded. "I'll study on it. If I think of anything or anyone, I'll be sure to let you know."

"Thank you, Phillip."

"We still on for dinner on Sunday?"

He and her mother had shared Sunday dinner for as long as she could remember. When she was a child, her father was there, too, of course. As was Phillip's wife. But she was gone now, too.

How long would it be before no one was left except Audrey?

But right now she still had her mom and uncle. "I look forward to it."

Audrey walked him out. He bragged about how he'd beaten the mayor again this afternoon. Two weeks in a row now. When he'd gone, she wandered back into the building. She had the sudden, nearly overwhelming urge to visit her mom. Talking about her dad always made her yearn to hug her mom.

Frantic voices and crying whispered through her mind. The two of them shared a bond that no one else could ever be a part of. Not even Phillip. There were some things that had to stay in the past. No matter what happened.

Audrey paused at the bottom of the stairs. Instead of going back up to her office, she went around behind the staircase and opened the door to the basement. She never went down there. Never.

But there came a time when a person had to face her fears. Face the part of her past that haunted her. Considering what Judd Seymour had told her and what was happening with Wesley Sauder, today was that day for Audrey. She couldn't keep pretending that what was down there had nothing to do with what was happening. Because somehow it did. No matter that twenty-four years had passed, there was a connection, perhaps a thin one but a connection nonetheless.

She opened the door and flipped the light switch. Fluorescent lights blinked and buzzed until the artificial glare filled the darkness. She took the three steps across the landing and began the descent down the iron staircase that reminded her of the fire escape on the outside of the building. Both of the interior staircases, this one as well as the one leading to the second floor, were made of iron and offered a very urban, industrial feel. The interior of the first and second floors had been redone in the fifties and then again in the nineties. Before long Audrey would need to put her stamp on things. For now, she couldn't imagine changing a thing.

If only she could make this part go away.

There was nothing particularly eerie about the basement. The walls were brick, as was the rest of the building. Shelves lined the walls. On the shelves were boxes and plastic containers filled with ancient memorabilia as well as all the things that two hundred years of living collected. There was a musty smell in the air. The dampness Brian told her about, she acknowledged. Somehow water was seeping from beneath the concrete. Portions of the floor looked wet. Brian was right in that the issue needed to be addressed at some point. She just had to figure out a way to do it without anyone learning her and her mother's secret.

The basement floor had once been brick, but plumbing renovations when she was twelve had required that a large portion be dug up. Once the work was complete, her mother had ordered concrete poured over the entire floor. To level it and make it more stable, she'd insisted.

They had thought that would be the end of it.

Audrey walked to the center of the room and stared at the floor. "Who were you and what the hell did you want?"

Chapter Ten

With most of his deputies searching the county for Wesley Sauder and that crucial forty-eight-hour mark in the investigation rapidly approaching, Colt was just about at his wit's end with Sarah. He stopped by her daddy's place again, but Aaron told him she'd gone back home since her house had been released. Sarah's kids had gathered around their uncle and stared expectantly at Colt as if he had the answer to what was going on in their suddenly upside-down lives.

More than a little frustrated, he had then gone to the Sauder home and gotten no answer after knocking repeatedly. Pulling into the bakery parking lot he now understood why. Sarah's minivan was there. The open sign on the door was flashing. His evidence techs were loading into their van—the one that had cost the county an arm and a leg. The rain had let up for a bit. Nothing like conducting a search in the rain.

The driver, Deputy Roland England, powered his window down as Colt approached. "I was just about to call you, Sheriff."

"Did you finish your second sweep?" His rule was that every crime scene received at least two sweeps by his evidence techs. Almost every time, something new was found the second time around.

"We collected a good deal of trace evidence, but who knows if it's anything relevant. By the way, we were packing up when Branch dropped by. He said he'd need to see whatever we found since the Marshals were taking over the case. He was supposed to call you about it."

He had called and Colt hadn't answered. He shook his head, set his hands on his hips. "Is Sarah in there?"

"She just got here." England glanced at his new partner, Jonathan Gates. "We heard Branch talking on the phone. Sounds like they're pretty sure Wesley is some kind of federal fugitive."

Damn it. So they had info they weren't sharing. Irritation coiled in Colt's gut. He glanced around, didn't see Branch's truck. "Is he still in there?"

"After that call he had to leave, said he'd be right back."

His absence gave Colt a little time, maybe not much, but something. He nodded to his deputies. "All right then. Let me know what the lab says as soon as you can."

"Yes, sir."

As the van rolled out of the parking lot, Colt strode to the door of the bakery. The curtain in the window moved. Probably Sarah. He hoped she would be more cooperative today. This might be her last opportunity to talk to him.

The bell jingled as he opened the door. Sarah glanced up from behind the counter as if she hadn't known he was outside and pushed a smile into place. The expression didn't reach her eyes. Frankly, she didn't have a thing to be smiling about. Her husband and her father were at odds. And now her husband was hiding from serious trouble. Not to mention her husband's past had caused her to have to kill at least one man. And another man had been shot and killed in her place of business. In Colt's opinion, she had her hands full.

He glanced around, didn't see any sign of a coworker. "Afternoon, Sarah."

She gave a nod. "Sheriff. I just pulled fresh muffins out of the oven."

He might not have much time, so he should get right to the point. "Sarah." He removed his hat and stood face-to-face with her, only the counter separating them. "I know you're worried and scared, and you have every right to be."

"Sheriff, I've already told you and Marshal Holloway all I know. Wesley left home to attend a funeral and I haven't seen him since."

"He was at Ezra Zimmerman's place last night. I'm guessing another friend in the community is hiding him today."

She looked away, busied herself with placing a row of freshly baked muffins from the pan into the glass display case.

"I don't know enough about whatever life he's running from to say whether your husband was a bad man or not—"

"He's a good man," she snapped. "Everyone knows that. Wesley has never caused any trouble here. He has a long-standing reputation of helping folks. You know that, Sheriff. So does everyone else around here."

Until now, Colt didn't mention, and the man suddenly appeared hell-bent on making up for lost time and then some. "I know that, Sarah. I'm not accusing Wesley of anything bad. But the Marshals aren't looking at this the way I am. I'm looking at Wesley as the husband and father—the farmer and the pillar of the community— I know him to be. But I'm the only member of law enforcement who's doing that. No offense to Branch, but he doesn't know Wesley. This is strictly about the case for him. Unless you tell me how to find Wesley first, I can't help him."

Her watery eyes lifted to meet his. "You promise you'll protect him?"

"You have my word that I will protect him or die trying."

"He's a good man, Sheriff. He's not that person anymore…the one those horrible men are hunting. He had no idea they were coming for him when they showed up here. The one you found in the stockroom surprised him. He had a gun. Wesley had no choice; he had to defend himself. At the same time that other man was breaking into our home. He was going to use me and the kids to make Wesley do what he wanted. We both did what we had to do."

"Do you know why they're after Wesley?"

She shook her head. "He said the less I knew the safer I was. I haven't seen him since that night, Sheriff. I swear. He's hiding and I don't blame him. They want him dead. He knows things they don't want to come out. That's all I know. They'll do anything to stop him. Wesley begged me to take the children and hide, but I can't do that. We need this business to be operating if we're to survive. My kids are safe with my brother."

"I'll have a deputy watching after you, Sarah. But tell me, where would Wesley go?" Even as he asked the question he heard a vehicle arrive. He glanced over his shoulder, spotted Branch's truck parked next to his. "Tell me where to look. I will find him and I will protect him through this."

"Try James Ed Wenger. He and Wesley are friends."

The bell jingled, announcing Branch's arrival.

"I'll take one of those fresh muffins," Colt said. "If the coffee's fresh, I'll have some of that, too."

"Hey, Colt." Branch joined him at the counter as Sarah busied herself filling his order. "I left you a voice mail. We need to talk."

"I was just about to call you back." Colt gave him a nod. "My evidence techs were still here when I arrived. I understand you have an update for me."

Branch hitched his head toward the door. "Let's talk outside."

Colt tapped the counter. "Be right back, Sarah."

The door jingled and they waited for a woman, a child on each hip, to come in before exiting. Branch walked over to his truck and opened the driver's-side door. Colt waited near the hood. He understood jurisdiction and all that legal stuff, but this was his county. He had been elected to serve and protect the people within its boundaries. As much as he appreciated help from the TBI fellows, the FBI and the Marshals occasionally, he didn't appreciate having an investigation taken over by anyone else.

Branch placed a manila file on the hood and opened it. "This is Thomas Bateman." He tapped the photo that was obviously a younger Wesley Sauder.

"All right." Colt moved a little closer so he could see the next photo or page in Branch's show-and-tell.

"This—" he tapped another photo, this one of an older man "—is Louis Cicero. He's the current boss of the Cicero family. His father was the patriarch before him and so on. They're one of the oldest organized crime families in the country. Various members of the family have been prosecuted for all manner of illegal activities over the years, but we've never been able to make the big charges stick and we sure as hell have never been able to nail one of the top guys." He flipped back to the photo of Bateman, aka Wesley Sauder. "But this guy could nail Louis Cicero. Cicero has one son—Louis Jr. They call him L.J. He and Bateman were best friends. Bateman worked with *the* accountant who took care of Cicero business. Bateman was being groomed to take over one day when he cut and run. Rumor is, he took a serious piece of evidence with him."

"How the hell did he end up a Mennonite?" Talk about going undercover. Then again, with the mob after him, he had to be desperate for a deep cover.

Branch shrugged. "We can't be sure how that happened. I assume he happened upon this Wesley Sauder—who died around that same time—and decided to claim his identity. It happens all the time. An accountant would certainly know how to make that happen. He was able to vanish just like that." Branch snapped his fingers. "He'd probably been planning his escape for a while. He was sitting pretty and making big money when he jumped ship."

"So he was part of this mob family?" Damn. Colt felt bad for Sarah. She would be devastated.

"In a white-collar way," Branch explained. "We have no reason to believe he ever killed anyone. But he was involved, yes."

"So what prompted his change of heart? He had to know they would come looking for him."

"He was in love with Louis's daughter, Sophia, but her father wanted her to marry a man in another crime family, an effort to mesh the two families. When her father wouldn't be dissuaded, Sophia realized her only way out was to go to the FBI and try to help take her father down. Bateman agreed to do this with her. She ended up dead and he disappeared."

A new tension trickled through Colt. "Did he have anything to do with her death?"

"Chicago PD investigated and concluded that she was killed by a crazed crackhead. She was a victim of circumstance—in the wrong place at the wrong time, according to their report. Said crackhead ended up dead in his cell. Hanged himself with his pants."

"Bateman lost it and decided he had to get away?" Didn't make a whole lot of sense for a guy sitting pretty, as Branch put it, in a mob family. Bateman hadn't gotten where he was at the time by being stupid. He lost the woman he loved, but why throw everything else away? Even Colt knew that a man just didn't leave an organized crime family once he was in—particularly as deep as Bateman had been.

"Sophia was young and idealistic," Branch explained. "Her father's intentions for her made it easy for her to decide to go after him. She wanted out of the family business and she was willing to sell Daddy out to make it happen. Despite the seemingly cut-and-dry circumstances of her death, the FBI believes her father discovered what she was up to and ordered her executed."

God Almighty. "Do you think her own father had her killed?"

Branch nodded. "I do. So does everyone else who worked the federal side of the investigation. At any rate, she and Bateman hadn't turned over what the agent needed to move on Cicero. At the time, the thinking was that after she was murdered Bateman took the evidence as a sort of insurance for his future."

"Does Sarah know about this Sophia Cicero?" Colt could just imagine how she would feel knowing her husband had lived this sort of life before showing up here. But to know he did so because he'd loved another woman would be a hard pill to swallow. Worse, Sarah had to feel as if their marriage and their children were nothing more than a cover for him to stay hidden from the reach of his former life. Yet she wanted to protect him. She loved him despite it all, that was clear.

"If she does, she's not talking." Branch shook his head. "We need her to cooperate."

Colt scrubbed a hand over his jaw. "Bateman is a possible witness in a major federal case. I guess I can see why you need to assume control of the investigation."

"It's not personal, Colt," Branch assured him. "We have an opportunity here and we have to be extremely careful. Cicero has murdered dozens of people, not to mention he's thought to be supplying drugs and guns at an unparalleled level and pace. We need to stop him and his organization once and for all. Bateman—Sauder—can make that happen."

Colt nodded. "I'll do everything in my power to help."

Branch clapped him on the back. "We appreciate it. Your deputies need to be on their toes. Cicero will keep sending his people until he finds Bateman. You can count on that. They won't think twice about killing anyone who gets in their way."

Colt got it. No one was safe until Bateman was found.

Sarah met him at the bakery door with his bag of goodies. Her eyes told him all he needed to know. She was counting on him to protect her husband…to protect her future.

With his coffee ensconced in the cup holder and his muffin in hand, Colt headed for the office. His first step was to get the word out to his deputies that he needed everyone focused 24/7 on finding Sauder until this was done. Next, he intended to talk to Audrey about letting folks in the community know they had to take the necessary precautions. A press conference couldn't be put off any longer.

AFTER BRIEFING HIS deputies and arranging a press conference for five that evening, Colt dropped by the paper. He wanted to give Rey a heads-up. He'd promised her an exclusive and he intended to deliver on that promise. She would want to be at the press conference. He'd told his assistant he would notify the *Gazette* personally.

As soon as he walked into the lobby he spotted Rey in her office. He removed his hat and stood for a moment staring up at her beyond the glass wall. Each of the offices had a glass wall that looked out over the lobby. She was arranging something on the small conference table in her office. Maybe the layout for tomorrow's paper.

He liked watching her. The way she moved, so purposeful yet so graceful, the way her blond hair fell around her shoulders. Most of all he loved to hear her talk. Loved her laugh. Mostly, he loved everything about her. She was the most beautiful woman he had ever laid eyes on. No matter the hurt that stood between them and the years that had passed; he still considered her his.

Not smart, Colt.

"Good afternoon, Sheriff. May I help you?"

He drew his gaze from Rey to the receptionist. "Morning, Tanya. I was just going up to see Rey."

"Sure. I'll let her know you're on the way up."

He crossed the room and climbed the iron staircase. Rey's father had been into transparency before it became a popular buzzword. The offices had their glass walls, and so did the printing room and the big conference room. The local schoolkids loved touring the building and seeing the way the news business worked. Visitors and clients could see the inner workings firsthand by just walking into the lobby. No matter that Rey had traveled the world and had such an exciting career; he had always believed this was where she belonged.

She waited for him at her office door. "I'm hoping your visit is about news on the case. I have a big hole in tomorrow's front page."

"I have plenty to share, you just can't print all of it yet."

She gave a nod. "Come in. Let's hear what you've got."

Colt spent the next twenty minutes explaining everything Branch had told him. Rey listened, nodded occasionally, but didn't ask any questions. He was beginning to think Branch had already spoken to her when she finally reacted.

"You want to warn the community to be on the lookout for any suspicious strangers."

This wasn't a question. She understood that he had a responsibility to do just that. "To the best of my ability. I can't mention the Cicero family, I can only tell them to report any suspicious activity or strangers who approach them asking questions about any other residents."

"Wow." She leaned back in her chair. "You live in a small town to avoid this kind of thing and then it comes to you."

"Someone usually brings it," he pointed out.

She nodded but she seemed preoccupied. She had appeared to be distracted the whole time he was bringing her up to speed. Something wasn't right. "You okay, Rey? I mean, you seem particularly unsettled by all this."

"Do you remember when we were kids, your father ever talking about anything like this? You know, organized crime in Franklin County?"

He thought about her question for a moment, then shook his head. "There's been the occasional locally organized crime. A drug lab. We even had a team of counterfeiters once. But nothing like this, that crossed state lines."

"I just remember overhearing some things my dad said when I was about twelve. I've checked the files, there weren't any particular stories about organized crime going on at the time, certainly nothing beyond our state lines. But there was something. I just haven't found it yet. A contact of mine in Chicago said there were mentions of Winchester in some of the wiretaps the Feds had done on one or the other crime families in Chicago."

That was news to Colt. "Branch didn't mention anything, but I'll ask him."

She nodded. "I appreciate it. So, I'll put together what I can for tomorrow's paper and urge the folks to be on the lookout."

Colt took that as his cue and stood. "I'll be on my way." He settled his hat into place. "Just so you know, I enjoyed having your company during last night's stakeout."

She blushed and that made him smile. "As I recall, you hijacked *my* stakeout."

He grinned. "I guess I did."

He was at her door when he worked up the nerve to ask the other question on his mind. He turned back to her. "Maybe we can talk about the case some more over dinner?"

She smiled. "Maybe."

He gave her a nod and went on his way. It wasn't a yes, but it wasn't the usual hell no, either.

They were making progress.

Chapter Eleven

Franklin County Veterinary Clinic

Audrey waved to Burt Johnston's receptionist as she passed through the lobby. Burt had told her to come on back at quarter to four. The yapping of dogs accompanied her trek toward the offices. This was the largest clinic in the county. Burt took care of everything from birds to horses. He didn't really do much of the hands-on work himself anymore. There were four veterinarians and several assistants. He mostly oversaw the operation and focused on being the county coroner.

She waved to one of the techs she'd gone to high school with before knocking on Burt's closed door. The other woman was busy examining a black Lab. Audrey hadn't had a dog or a cat since she was a kid. Now that she was back home maybe she should think about getting one.

The big old house was a lot lonelier than she remembered. Of course she'd never lived there alone before. A dog would be nice.

"Audrey, if that's you, come on in. If it's anyone else, go away."

She laughed as she opened the door. "It's me."

He dropped his feet from his desk to the floor and sat

up straight. "Close the door behind you." He closed the romance novel he was reading and tucked it into a drawer.

Audrey did as he asked and moved a cat from the chair in front of his desk. The animal curled around her ankle and purred. "Good kitty." She lowered into the chair and stroked the furry beast now stretching and rolling on the floor. She did all this so Burt wouldn't see her grinning about his secret attraction to romance novels. Her mother had told her when she was a kid that Burt loved to read the same books she did. She made Audrey promise not to tell and she never had.

He finished off his cola and sat the can on his desk. "You want chocolate?" He held the bag of chocolate candy up for her to see.

"No thanks."

He stuffed another piece into his mouth before hiding the bag in the file cabinet behind his desk. "Ever since the heart attack I have to hide everything I enjoy."

"Mrs. Johnston wants to take care of you." A wiry tail switched back and forth as the cat waited for more attention. Audrey scratched at her belly.

"There are some things a man needs and, for me, those things are my chocolate, my books and the occasional nip of bourbon." He shrugged. "The way I see it, what she doesn't know won't hurt her."

Audrey understood now. "Your staff would tell her about the chocolate if they knew." She nodded toward the file cabinet.

"Spies," he griped. "Every one of them."

She bit back the smile. "I'm certain they mean well."

He grunted. "So how can I help you today, Audrey? You want to know something about those two bodies?"

"Actually, I wanted to talk to you about my dad."

His bushy eyebrows knit together as his face furrowed

into a frown. "That was a while ago, Rey. He had a heart attack. There wasn't any need for an autopsy. His personal physician confirmed a diagnosis of coronary artery disease. He was young for the disease to have been so advanced, but that's the way it is sometimes. He'd been taking medicine, but sometimes it's just too little, too late. Your momma witnessed the heart attack so there wasn't any question about cause of death. What specifically about his death is on your mind?"

"Did you examine his body closely? The way you would one when foul play is suspected?" She doubted he did but she needed to know.

"Now that I did. In those days I was still learning a lot. Much of taking care of animals is the same as taking care of humans, but there are still considerable differences. Every new body was an opportunity to familiarize myself with procedure. To tell you the truth, every body tells a different story. Edward DuPont taught me a lot. He says you can read a body the same way you can a book. His daughter says the same thing. She spoke of it in that book she wrote, *The Language of Death*."

Rowan DuPont was older than Audrey but she remembered her. She'd had a twin sister who drowned. Not long after her mother had hanged herself. Tragic. The DuPonts always seemed a little strange. Maybe it was because they lived and worked in the family funeral home.

Audrey shifted her thoughts back to her father. "Did you note any signs of a struggle? Bruises or scratches?"

Burt opened his mouth, but then snapped it shut. "Give me a minute. Do you have time for me to pull the file?"

Audrey moistened her lips and nodded. "Absolutely."

He turned his back to her and started riffling through the drawers of the file cabinets lining the wall behind his desk. "The clinic's files are in the file room. These files are related to my work as coroner."

"How long have you been serving as coroner?" She couldn't remember but she knew he was in the position when her father died. Seeing his face and hearing his re-assuring words had stuck with her all these years. There wasn't a lot about that night she remembered, but Burt was one part she did recall.

"Here we go." He shoved the drawer closed and turned to settle back into his chair.

Audrey reminded herself to breathe.

Burt placed the manila folder on his desk. It looked so innocuous. Like hundreds of others in this building and back at her office at the newspaper. But this one was very different. Inside that folder were the final reports related to her father's last moments of life and his death.

Burt glanced up at her. "You're welcome to look at the file yourself, if you'd like."

She held up a hand and shook her head. She wasn't sure she could bear to see the photos. "You can give it to me in layman's terms."

"All right. So there was a small scratch on the side of his neck. Nothing significant. He could have done it shaving that morning or even scratching himself." Burt made humming sounds as he perused the file. The sort that suggested he was questioning what he was reading or was confused by it somehow.

Her nerves were jangling by the time he looked up over his glasses. "There was a bruise on his right shoul-der. One on his lower back. And another on his left shin. My notes show that your mother said he'd taken a tumble down the stairs the night before."

"Oh." Audrey nodded. "I remember now." This was

a lie, but she understood that if her mother had told that story, it needed to be told.

Burt studied her for a long moment. "Is there something you're worried about related to your father's death?"

The words were on her tongue. But she couldn't share her true concerns with him or anyone else. "No. No. It's something one of my contacts said to me about this Sauder case."

Burt closed the file and cocked his head. "I am now thoroughly confused."

"He has evidence that during the same time frame, when my dad died, there was some organized crime activity related to the same group involved in the Sauder case going on in Winchester. He couldn't say what the connection was, just that it involved Winchester at that particular time. Colt said he doesn't recall anything happening at that time but he's going to check his files."

Burt tapped his forefinger against his chin. "There was a little something-something going on at the newspaper. Mary Jo should remember. As I recall Porter said there was a push coming from up north to buy up a bunch of newspapers around here, in Alabama and Georgia. You know, Southern small-town papers. I don't recall the reasoning, but Phil said Porter was fired up about it. That was perhaps a month before he passed."

Audrey's heart pounded a little harder with each word he uttered. "Did my father mention anyone calling him or visiting him in relationship to this push to buy?"

"No, not that I remember. You should ask Phil. I'm certain he would know. He and your father were partners after all."

But Phillip had said he knew nothing—that her dad knew nothing—about any issues related to organized crime. Had he been left out of the loop? Or had he lied to her? She couldn't exactly call him a liar. What she needed was some sort of evidence.

"Thanks, Burt, for looking into this for me." She stood and reached across his desk, offering her hand.

He pushed to his feet, gave her hand a shake. "You let me know if there's anything else I can assist you with. I'm always happy to try to help solve a good mystery."

All of these pieces of information definitely met the criteria for a mystery.

As Audrey left the clinic she couldn't stop obsessing on the idea that Phillip had lied to her. Her mom's story about the fall down the stairs was the only explanation she could have given to cover for the bruises.

How else was she going to explain what really happened without confessing to murder?

PINE HAVEN REALLY was a lovely place if one had to be imprisoned. In reality it was a prison of sorts. Or maybe the minds of the residents were the real prisons. Her mother was physically fit, but her mind had let her down. Now she had to live like *this*.

Audrey regretted the thought instantly. Facilities like Pine Haven were a godsend in situations like her mom's. Yet it felt wrong to keep her here. She had loved that big old rambling house. She would have stayed there until the day she died if not for her inability to remember what she'd done two minutes ago. Like walking out of the house and leaving the burner turned on under an empty teakettle. Or the faucet running in the tub. Or the door unlocked. The car running in the garage. All those things had happened and Audrey had been left with no choice.

She found her mom on the terrace staring out over the beautifully landscaped grounds. Audrey sat down in the chair beside her. "It's a lovely day."

"It surely is," her mom said, not taking her eyes from whatever was in those trees that held her spellbound. Buds were opening, and soon the leaves would unfurl and fill the branches. The grass would need to be cut. Shrubs were already sprouting errant twigs. Tulips, daffodils, crocuses and hyacinths filled the mounds around trees and the urns strategically stationed around the terrace. Her mom loved flowers. The beauty of this place was one of the reasons Audrey had chosen it over several others. Plus it was close to home.

"I went to see Burt Johnston today."

Mary Jo turned to face her. "How is Burt?"

"He's well. His usual jovial self. Reading his romance novels and sneaking chocolate."

Mary Jo laughed. "He always did love those romance novels. And Iris? Is she keeping his sugar down? He gave her such fits about his diet. Poor woman has the patience of Job."

Audrey didn't bother reminding her mom that Iris would never be able to keep Burt Johnston on the straight and narrow where his chocolate was concerned. She wouldn't remember it five minutes from now. "He said Dad had bruises in several places on his body when he died."

Mary Jo nodded, her eyes still tracking Audrey's. "I told Burt he'd fallen down the stairs, but that wasn't true. You know it wasn't true." She looked back to the trees. "I don't even remember all the lies I had to tell in the days after he died. I could only do whatever necessary to keep you safe. To ensure no one ever knew what really happened."

Audrey's heart ached. "Did he fight with that man?"

Mary Jo's face pinched with confusion. "What man?"

"The man who tried to hurt Dad. Did he fight with him?"

"Oh my, I don't know." She shook her head. "You know we don't talk about that man. It's best never to speak of him again."

If only that were possible. "Mom, did Uncle Phillip know about the man?"

She looked properly horrified. "Why, heavens no." Then her face scrunched up again. "At least I don't think so. He wasn't there. You know, he was always gone some-where when your father needed him most. Probably tak-ing some girl out. He was a rascal back then, your uncle Phillip."

"You're certain Dad didn't tell him about the trouble from the man?"

"No, no, your father died. He couldn't tell anyone."

Audrey sighed. This was pointless. "I mean before he died. Did he tell Uncle Phillip before he died about the trouble with the man?"

She stared at Audrey for a long moment before ask-ing, "What man?"

Audrey sat in silence with her mom for a long while. Then she hugged her and gave her a kiss goodbye. She doubted the secrets her mother kept from those days could ever be exhumed. Maybe she was right and Phil-lip knew nothing about whatever the man wanted and whoever had sent him.

But Audrey knew something. She knew in all likeli-hood that the man who had sent two killers—so far—to find Wesley Sauder was the same man who sent the one who tried to kill her dad.

She drove across town, turned into the parking lot of the newspaper and sat for a while staring at the building. She had a few minutes before the press conference Colt had scheduled. She couldn't remember very much about that night all those years ago. Her mind had blocked the

most painful parts. She remembered her mother screaming. Audrey had been in her uncle Phillip's office. So
Phillip hadn't been there. She couldn't have been playing
in his office if he had been there. She remembered going
round and round in the chair behind his desk. There was
that strange pop, and then her mother was screaming.

Audrey remembered seeing the man on the floor...
and all the blood.

Voices echoed in her head. Her mom's. Her dad's. The
other man wasn't talking. He was down...on the floor.

Jack...her dad had called him Jack.

Audrey dug in her bag for her cell phone. She called
Judd Seymour. "Hey, Judd, you have a minute?"

"I do but only one. I'm on my way to a meeting."

She could hear the city sounds in the background.
Horns blowing. Cab drivers shouting. Those were the
sounds that had once followed her to sleep at night and
greeted her each morning. She did not miss the big city.

The admission startled her. It was the first time she'd
felt that way, or at least the first time she'd recognized
she felt that way since returning to Winchester. Was her
new life here growing on her? Wasn't coming back home
supposed to be temporary?

No time for that kind of soul-searching.

"During that time frame we talked about—twenty-
four years ago—do you remember a guy connected to
the organized crime family named Jack? You know, the
family from the wiretaps?"

"Jack Torrino? Is that who you're referring to?"

The name didn't ring any bells for Audrey. "I can't be
certain. I only have the name Jack."

"Torrino is the only Jack I'm familiar with from that
era. He would have been affiliated with the same family
we discussed before. Why do you ask?"

"I think maybe he was in Winchester in March of that year."

"Well, if that's the case, you've just solved a quarter-century-old mystery, because twenty-four years ago Jack Torrino disappeared. No one has a clue what happened to him or where he ended up."

"Thanks, Judd."

The call ended and Audrey sat very still. She knew exactly where Jack Torrino was.

Chapter Twelve

Colt climbed back into his truck and sat there for a long moment. The press conference had gone off without a hitch. Branch as well as Chief of Police Billy Brannigan had been on either side of him. Colt had warned the citizens of Franklin County to be on the lookout for any suspicious activities and to report any such activities or strangers to the hotlines his department had set up. Since the press conference he had interviewed several of Sauder's closest friends and not one owned up to having seen him. Sarah had told him he would have a difficult time getting any of them to speak against her husband. They all knew what Colt wanted: to find Sauder. Somehow they all managed to avoid giving him any information without actually lying. Even Wenger had played him off.

He was getting nowhere way too fast.

Colt started his truck and drove to the only other place he could think of where he might learn something. It was a long shot, but it was the only shot he had at this point. Wesley Sauder or Thomas Bateman, whoever he considered himself to be these days, was going to get himself dead otherwise.

The Cow Palace didn't open until nine but most of the staff would be there prepping for the coming night. Colt had frequented the place with a fake ID like most of his friends during his senior year. His own wild behavior that year was what scared him the most about his son. Colt knew the trouble he'd gotten into; he didn't want Key to go there. Colt had been a pretty good kid, but he'd had his moments. Any one of those moments could have turned out far worse and he could have lost his life.

It was bad enough that he'd lost Audrey.

His son wasn't speaking to him at the moment. Not a big surprise. He'd given Colt the silent treatment whenever he was angry since the divorce. Not that he could fault the boy. He'd learned the tactic from his mother. Colt was far from perfect and he'd made his share of mistakes with their son, but Karen was a user. He hoped like hell he could prevent Key from following that path. A man was only as good as his word. Failing to live up to it, just once, could turn out to be the biggest mistake of his life.

Colt thought of Rey. If he hadn't broken his word to her...

Too late to go there now. He had broken his word. The only good thing to come of that misstep was his son. Somehow he had to make sure he didn't screw up the most important thing in his life—being a father.

And one way or another he would find a way to win Rey's trust again. He didn't want to spend the next eighteen years without her in his life—completely.

THE COW PALACE sat between Winchester and Decherd. The building had once been a livestock market where horses and cattle—mostly the latter—were brought for sale to the highest bidder. His daddy had brought him to the auctions a few times when he was a kid. By the time he was fifteen, the market had moved to a different, larger location between Winchester and Fayetteville. The old building, which looked like a large barn, had sat empty for a couple of years. Then some enterprising group had come up with the bright idea to turn it into a saloon. The Cow Palace had been born.

Folks came from all over to attend the celebrity events held in the now-famous venue. The building had been expanded three times. After the divorce Colt had frequented the place for a time and then he'd realized he wasn't going to find what he was looking for there. He'd been divorced nearly eight years now and he hadn't found the right one yet.

Maybe that was a sign that he'd let the only right one for him get away when he was too young and dumb to realize the magnitude of his mistake.

He parked and strode across the parking lot. There was no changing the past. But maybe he could divert the course of Sarah Sauder's husband's future. Because if he didn't find him soon, his kids were going to grow up without a father. Branch Holloway had lived away far too long. Folks didn't know him the way they did Colt. If he couldn't get any answers, Branch damned sure wouldn't be able to get any.

The front entrance was locked, so Colt went around to the back. Three guys, stockers, bartenders or kitchen help, stood around in a huddle smoking. They looked up and called out greetings.

"Afternoon," he said. "Is Beth working?" He knew she was because he had dropped by the trailer park where she lived. She hadn't been home and her neighbor had said she was at work.

"She's getting tables ready." One of the men jerked his head toward the employee entrance. "Go on in, Sheriff. Ray Stokes, the manager, is in there, too."

Colt gave the man a nod of thanks. Stokes wasn't exactly a friend. Evidently the man who'd warned him that

Stokes was inside knew as much. Back in his early deputy days Colt had hauled Stokes in for drunk-and-disorderly charges on several occasions. Stokes had settled down eventually and taken over managing this place when it changed owners. The current owner lived up around Nashville and likely didn't know Stokes was a knuckle-head and plain old pain in the ass.

The walk through the stockroom and the kitchen took all of twenty seconds and already Stokes was waiting at the end of the bar. Evidently his man outside had called or sent him a text warning that Colt was on his way inside.

"Evening, Sheriff." Stokes stood, feet wide apart, arms at his side, braced for whatever was coming.

Colt set his hands on his hips and eyed the man speculatively. "You expecting trouble, Ace?" Back in the day Stokes went by the nickname Ace because no matter how deep into trouble he managed to dig himself, he always seemed to have an ace up his sleeve to salvage the situation.

"When I hear the law is sniffing around before I even open, it can be a little troubling. Do we have a problem, Colt?"

Colt shook his head. "Not to my knowledge. I just dropped by to talk to Beth." He gestured to the lady pulling down stools and stationing them around the tables.

Stokes glanced at Beth and then narrowed his gaze at Colt. "Long as you don't slow down her work, I got no problem with you talking to her. I do need her on shift tonight, so if you're planning to haul her in, I'd ask that you come back after midnight."

"I don't have a beef with Beth, either. Just need to ask her some questions."

"Leave him alone, Ray," Beth called out to her boss. "Come on over here, Colt, so I can keep working."

Stokes shot Colt one last glare before moving back behind the bar that snaked around two sides of the enormous space. The ceiling soared upward at least thirty or so feet. What was once an arena for showing off livestock was now a massive dance floor with a center stage. Tables surrounded the dance floor, filling the rest of the space all the way to the outer walls. There were two emergency exits, a main entrance and the rear one Colt had walked through. Lights and speakers hung in the enormous open space overhead.

"Let me guess," she said as he approached, "you're here to ask me about Sarah's husband."

Colt grabbed a stool from where it sat seat-down on top of the table, settled it onto its legs and tucked it in. "You've been keeping up with the news."

"It's not every day that my big sister shoots a man dead." She moved on to the next table. Colt followed.

"I guess she did what she had to do." He reached for another stool. "What can you tell me about her husband?"

Beth laughed. "You're forgetting I was exiled from the family long before Sarah married Wesley."

"No, ma'am," Colt countered, "I haven't forgotten. I just figured sisters have a bond, you know? Maybe the two of you talk from time to time with or without your daddy's approval."

Most kids broke the rules occasionally, particularly once they were grown up. Parents' wishes weren't always followed to the letter. God knows he didn't always do what his daddy told him to or he would never have gotten off onto the wrong path in the first place. He sure wished he could make Key see that as much as he resented Colt's guidance, age and experience made a man wise. He should defer to wisdom.

Kids never wanted to go there. Some things they had to learn themselves.

"We talk," Beth admitted.

She continued pulling down stools, placing them just so and then moving on. Colt did the same. He waited as patiently as possible for her to continue. Not exactly the easiest thing to do with the minutes ticking like bombs in his head.

"When she met Wesley, I was still in Nashville. She was so excited. He was way older than her and so charming." Beth hesitated, her expression distant, remembering. "She said he'd lived in the big city most of his life and that he was the most thoughtful man she had ever met."

"Did her opinion of him change over time?" Colt couldn't help wondering if the man was able to repress his criminal side so thoroughly. But then he'd been an accountant, not a killer.

"No. She has never complained about him even once. He has been the perfect husband and father. Kind, generous with his time and affection. Faithful."

Colt focused on the stools as she went on. His guilt prevented him from making eye contact for a half a minute or so. He'd failed on that last one. And even eighteen years later he felt the shame of it.

"Poppa was taken with him as well. He saw Wesley as the kind of strong leader the community would need in coming years."

"But something went wrong." Colt followed her to the next table. "Mr. Yoder learned Wesley's secret."

Beth nodded. "A family from Markham—the town Wesley claimed as his home—paid a visit to Winchester for the funeral of a distant relative. Wesley couldn't possibly have known that anyone in Markham knew anyone in Winchester, much less was distantly related. The folks who visited were quite shocked to learn that the Wesley Sauder they'd buried a decade before was alive and well in Winchester."

Branch had told him most of that part. He likely didn't know about the family who had visited Winchester and outed Wesley. "So Sarah's husband had assumed a dead man's identity." Happened a lot. Generally not so literally. More often just online for credit or tax purposes. But like Branch said, this guy had needed a whole new life. And being an accountant he knew the ins and outs of making his new identity legit.

"How is it that Mr. Yoder kept this news to himself, since it obviously happened a couple of months ago? Rumor is, he and Wesley had their falling-out right after Christmas."

"My poppa is a thorough man. He wanted to see for himself if what this family said was true so he sent my oldest brother, Ben, to Markham to get the whole story. This was just last month. When Ben returned with the confirmation of what they'd been told, Poppa was ready to call a meeting and throw Wesley under the bus, but something stopped him."

She moved through the arrangement of four more barstools without speaking. Colt nudged, "What do you think stopped him?"

Beth paused and met Colt's gaze. "I can't tell you that part, Sheriff."

He had a feeling the part she didn't want to talk about involved her brother. "Beth, the only thing I want to do in all this is protect the community. Two men are dead. Both of them probably deserved what they got, but we might not be so lucky next time. Next time an innocent person could die. Sarah or one of her children. Whatever you're holding back, I promise you if you give me the whole story I'll do everything in my power to protect you and whoever it is you're protecting if possible."

She reached for another stool. "Benjamin did more than take a picture of the grave and visit the congregation where he found a photo of the deceased Wesley Sauder. He had a picture of Sarah's Wesley with him. He went around asking people if they knew him. 'Course he didn't find anyone who admitted to knowing Sarah's husband. But Sarah and I think it was him showing that picture around that brought all this down on Wesley."

Unfortunately, Sarah and Beth were most likely right. Ben probably showed the photo to the wrong person on the street and word got back to the head of the Cicero family that the missing accountant was in Winchester posing as the Mennonite Wesley Sauder.

"Was Ben or Mr. Yoder contacted by anyone?" Though they had no phone at home, there was a phone at the bakery. The bakery was listed under the Yoder name.

"Sarah said she received several strange calls. The caller would ask for someone named Bateman. She told them they had the wrong number. But when she told Wesley the other day, he went crazy. Told her he had to get out of town. He warned her to keep the shotgun close whenever she was at home and to take it to the bakery with her. This was last week. Then he disappeared. Just took off, claiming he needed to see after the family of some friend who had died. Sarah was seriously upset."

Colt paused. "When did Wesley get back?"

Beth released a big breath. "Not until yesterday."

Which meant he wasn't in Winchester on Monday night. Wesley Sauder—aka Thomas Bateman—couldn't have killed the man in the storeroom at the bakery. Oh hell. "Beth, what happened at the bakery?"

She stared directly at him then. "Sarah called me. She

was alone at the bakery. They're closed on Sundays, you know. She was cleaning, stocking. The kids were there, too. She wanted to talk. She was scared. She thought someone had been following her."

Holy hell.

"She was right, someone was following her. He walked around the building. She saw him through a window so she hid the children behind some boxes in the walk-in cooler. The next thing she knew the man was inside. She'd forgotten to lock the back entrance. He was demanding to know where Wesley was. She kept telling him she didn't know but he wouldn't listen. He backed her into the storeroom." Tears slid down her cheeks. "He was going to kill her, Colt."

"But you got there just in the nick of time."

She nodded. "I brought my .38 with me, just in case. I never expected to have to use it." Her lips trembled. "When I told him to stop, he turned around and the only reason I'm not dead is because I shot first."

The words rang in the air for an endless beat. "It was self-defense, Beth. If you hadn't shot him, you and Sarah and the kids would be dead."

She nodded, swiped at her cheeks. "I guess you have to arrest me now."

Colt shook his head. "No. I'm not going to arrest you for defending yourself. But I will need a statement, and I'll need one from Sarah confirming what you've told me."

"Okay. I'll finish up here first, if that's okay."

"Sure. I'll help you." They moved to the next table. "I'll also need the gun you used."

"It's buried in the flower bed in front of my trailer."

"When we leave I'll call my evidence tech and have him go by and pick it up if I have your permission."

"Do what you have to do," she agreed. "I'm trusting you, Colt. I screwed up my life once, but this time I did the right thing. Don't punish me for doing the right thing."

The fear and resignation in her voice tugged at his protective instincts. He could only imagine how terrified she had been when he walked in a little while ago. "I'll see to it that no one punishes you for this, Beth. I just wish you'd come to me."

She nodded. "I know. It was a dumb decision to try to cover up what I'd done. I guess after everything else I've screwed up, I couldn't deal with my family thinking I was a killer, too."

"You're not a killer, Beth." Colt touched her arm when she reached for another stool. "You're a hero. You saved your sister's life and the lives of her children. Your daddy will be proud when he hears about that."

More tears spilled down her cheeks. "Maybe."

"Tell me how I'm going to find Wesley before his old friends do. I know he's close, hiding out within the Mennonite community, but none of his friends will tell me anything."

"They're protecting him," Beth confirmed. "They know him as Wesley Sauder, the good man who saved my poppa's life. He's been especially helpful to their community. They're not going to easily accept that he's not who he's claimed to be all this time."

"So they're not going to talk to me."

"Probably not." She smiled across the table at Colt. "But one of their wives might. Go see Jenny Hoover. Tell her I sent you." A frown lined her brow. "But you'll need to take a woman with you. I'd say I would go, but if anyone sees me that could get her into trouble." Her expression brightened. "Take Audrey Anderson. Everyone knows her. Jenny will talk to Audrey."

Sounded easy enough.

All Colt had to do first was get Beth out of here without having to kick Ray Stokes's ass.

Chapter Thirteen

Audrey left the office once the paper was put to bed. She needed to visit her mom again. It likely wouldn't do any good, but she had to try. She had a name now, though she wasn't sure that would help in any way. She had tried all afternoon to piece together the shattered memories. But too many fragments were missing.

Basically she had been a child when it happened. Time had done its job, putting distance between her and the trauma. Her mind had buried so much of that night that her recall was no more reliable than her mom's. But she had to try to remember. What happened when she was twelve years old had some bearing, however remote, on what was happening now. She was certain of it.

There was a connection.

What if Wesley Sauder or Thomas Bateman, whatever name he went by, hadn't come to Winchester by chance? Would he know why Jack Torrino had shown up in her father's office all those years ago?

Had Sauder passed the newspaper offices every day for the past ten years knowing the Anderson secret? Audrey had to talk to him before he was hauled away by Branch or killed by another mob thug.

She needed the truth.

But what if the truth was not what she believed it to

be? What if her father had somehow been involved in organized crime?

"No way." She would not believe such a thing. Surely her mom or Uncle Phil would have known something was going on if that were the case.

Or perhaps her mom had urged her to forget that night because there was something more unseemly going on?

Her fingers tightened on the steering wheel. She had no idea where she was going. Out of town, along the back roads. Wesley Sauder was hiding somewhere and she intended to find him. She needed answers. The not knowing was driving her mad. The rain had stayed away so far, but it was supposed to start up again later tonight. He had to be lying low somewhere.

As if she'd telegraphed the thought to local law enforcement, blue lights appeared in her rearview mirror. She frowned. The truck was Colt's. Why would he be blue-lighting her? She glanced at the dash. She wasn't speeding.

Cursing her bad luck, she pulled to the curb and put the car in Park. Then she waited. If he asked to see her license she was going to punch him.

He swaggered up to her window. She watched each step in her side mirror, her pulse reacting. Why didn't her libido just die? Experiencing all the sudden urges for Colt was making her crazy. She did not want to repeat the same mistake she'd made as a kid. She'd given him too much of her life already.

When he braced his hands on the roof of the car and peered down at her, she powered down the window. "Was I speeding, Sheriff?"

"No, ma'am." He moved down to the window then, propping his crossed arms there. "Why aren't you answering your cell?"

Her cell hadn't rung? She poked a hand into her bag and retrieved her phone. Three missed calls. "I didn't hear it ring." She checked the sound—it was off. "Oh." She switched the setting from mute. "Sorry, I was in a meeting. I just forgot to turn on the ringer when I left the paper."

The truth was she was so distracted and frustrated she hadn't even thought about her phone.

"I need you to take a ride with me, if you will."

Her heart stumbled. Did he already know about Torrino? How the hell had he figured it out? Judd would never tell anyone about her questions and even if he did, there was no way to take her questions and follow them back to anything related to her parents or the newspaper, much less that damned basement.

"Why?" Her voice was a little too high-pitched.

"I want to interview Jenny Hoover. Sarah's younger sister Beth thinks Jenny's husband might know where Sauder is. He won't tell me, but Beth thinks Jenny will talk. To *you*."

Audrey vaguely remembered Jenny Hoover; she had been Jenny Kauffman back when they were kids. If talking to Jenny would help Audrey find Sauder, she was more than happy to do so. But she and Colt had to get one thing straight first. "On one condition."

"I let you have the exclusive," he said with a shrug. "You got it. I've already promised you the exclusive."

She shook her head. "I need to ask Sauder a couple of questions before you turn him over to Branch."

Colt drew back the slightest bit. "Do you mean privately or in my presence?"

She chewed her lip. "Privately."

"I don't know about that, Rey. There are all kinds of rules about witnesses and—"

"Two minutes, that's all I'll need."

Big exhale. "All right. As long as it's within my power to allow, you will have two minutes. Can we leave my truck at your house? I don't want to spook Jenny by showing up in my vehicle, particularly at this hour."

He was right. It was half past eight. "Of course."

"Great." He smiled. "I knew I could count on you, Rey."

He might not feel that way when he learned the secret she and her mother had been hiding for more than two decades. Reminding herself to breathe, Audrey drove to her house. Colt parked his truck and hustled over to climb into her passenger seat.

"What if Jenny's husband is home?"

"Beth says Wednesday nights are meeting night for the men. They'll be at the church until after ten."

"I imagine Sauder is too smart to be there with them."

"If he's not, then I don't know how he was ever an accountant for a crime family."

Audrey laughed, couldn't help herself. "You have a point."

En route to the Hoover home they drove past the Mennonite church, and there was quite the crowd of vehicles there. Some sort of meeting was certainly taking place tonight. The Hoover farm was on Walnut Grove Road. Like the Yoder place, this one had been in the family for several generations. Since the first Mennonites came to the area, actually.

Colt followed Audrey across the yard and up the steps onto the porch. He took a position to one side of the door as she pulled open the screen door and knocked on the wood one beyond it. The lacy curtains in the window had moved twice. Jenny or one of her children already knew they had company. It was quiet inside. Audrey knocked again. Hearing the sound of footsteps inside, she allowed the screen door to close. Another day was all but gone and still no sign of Sauder. It seemed impossible that a fugitive could stay hidden like this in such a small town with every cop in the various law enforcement agencies looking for him.

The door opened and Jenny peered through the screen door. "You're Audrey Anderson."

Audrey smiled. "In the flesh."

Jenny glanced at Colt and her awed expression slipped. "Sheriff."

"I realize it's really late but if you have time," Audrey said quickly, not wanting to lose this chance because the woman got hung up on the idea that Colt was now standing next to her, "I would love to talk to you for a few minutes. Beth Yoder sent me."

Jenny's attention rested on Audrey once more and that fangirl expression was back. "All right." She stepped back, opening the door wider. "Would you like a cup of tea?"

Audrey gave her the brightest smile she could muster. "Tea would be lovely."

"The kitchen is this way," she said, ushering Audrey across the room.

Audrey heard the front door close and then the steady fall of Colt's steps as he followed them into the large but simple kitchen.

"How are your girls?" Audrey asked as Jenny put the teakettle on the stove and lit the burner under it. "I saw their artwork on the wall at the bakery. They're both very talented."

Jenny blushed as she settled white cups into saucers. "They're doing well. Ana is getting married this summer and Ruth is traveling to Virginia to spend the summer with her grandmother. It's going to be an exciting summer for them, but certainly a long one for me without my girls."

Audrey kept her opinions to herself about how two such talented young ladies should be heading off to college. She had no right to judge and certainly no grounds upon which to suggest how anyone should raise her children.

"I would love to do an article about the wedding, if you and your husband would permit me."

The other woman's eyes danced with obvious delight. "I'll ask him. He'll be home later in an hour or so."

"I think it would be a lovely local life piece."

The kettle whistled and Jenny prepared the tea. When they had settled around the kitchen table, Jenny said, "I guess you came to ask me about Sarah's husband."

Audrey nodded. "We're really worried about him. More of those bad guys could show up at any moment—they may already be here—and we need to find him before they do. If you can help, you would be doing Sarah and her children a great favor. The truth is, they're in danger, too. I can't emphasize enough how important it is that Sheriff Tanner find Wesley and help him. I really believe he's the only one who can give Wesley a fair shake in this mess."

Jenny nodded. "I told Allan we should talk to Sheriff Tanner." She glanced at him, her first concession to his presence since they gathered at the table. "But he wouldn't listen."

"Men always think they know best." Audrey shook her head. "I'll never understand that mentality."

Jenny sighed. "It's a burden at times."

"Do you know where Wesley is staying?" Audrey asked. "You have my word that Sheriff Tanner will protect him. Whatever you tell us will go no further than this room."

"Mine as well," Colt offered. "Wesley Sauder is my responsibility to protect. But I can't do my job if I don't know where he is."

"The last I heard Allen say, he was staying at the Zimmerman place." She looked from Audrey to Colt and back. "But he's moved and no one is talking. I honestly don't know where he is."

As disappointing as it was, Audrey believed her. "If you had to guess, where would you start your search for Wesley?"

The other woman looked Audrey straight in the eye and said, "At his house."

Audrey was surprised by her answer, then the rationale behind it dawned on her. No one would be watching his house. They were all too busy looking everywhere else. "Thank you, Jenny. You've been a tremendous help."

They finished their tea in record time and Colt thanked Jenny as she walked them to the door. She nodded but said nothing else to him. To Audrey she said, "I love your newspaper, Ms. Anderson. A lot of us live vicariously through you and the introspections column you do about all the places you've visited and the things you've done."

Now that was a compliment. She'd only started that column because Brian insisted. She supposed he'd been right to encourage her in that direction. "Thank you, Jenny. It really was nice to see you again."

At the car Colt held the door for her, then shut it once she was behind the wheel. He rounded the hood and slid into the passenger seat. "There's just one problem with her theory," he said as he pulled the seat belt across his lap.

"What's that?" Audrey snapped her seat belt into place

and started the engine. She looked at him and waited for an answer.

"I've had a deputy watching the Sauder home since Sarah went back there."

Audrey guided the car down the drive and onto the dark road. "What if he was already back in the house before you assigned surveillance? What if..." She braked and looked at him across the dim glow of the dash. "What if he never left the house?"

"I saw him running from the Zimmerman house." Colt countered.

"Did you, or did you see someone who looked like him?"

His brow furrowed in concentration. "God Almighty, you could be right." Colt shook his head. "I kept asking myself how any man could leave his wife and children alone to save his own life. Maybe he didn't."

Audrey drove as fast as she dared on the twisty back roads between the Hoover place and the Sauder home. Colt had a death grip on the armrest of the door but he didn't caution her to slow down even once.

The dark house looming at the end of the driveway was a huge disappointment. Colt got out and knocked anyway, but no one was home. Without a warrant he couldn't go in, not since the house had been released and was no longer considered an official crime scene.

Warrant or no, Colt walked around the house, checking the barn and the smokehouse. Both were open. Audrey followed along behind him, mostly because she had no desire to sit in the car in the dark all alone. He walked out to the road and spoke to the deputy in the cruiser watching over the house. Audrey stared at the dark windows. She couldn't help wondering again if Wesley Sauder knew anything about the man who'd given her father trouble all those years ago.

"Sarah and the kids haven't been back over here tonight," Colt said as he joined her at her car. "If you don't mind, take me back to my truck and I'll pay the Yoders a visit. See if Sarah and her kids are over there."

"I can take you there." She was certainly in no hurry to get home to an empty house. When she put it that way it sounded so sad. For the past six months she'd lived alone in that old house without thinking too much about being lonely. Suddenly that was all she could think about.

"If you're sure you don't mind."

"I don't mind. Really. It's no problem. Besides, it's already so late we should do this the most efficient way possible."

"Good point."

They rode in silence. Audrey couldn't stop obsessing about the man, Jack Torrino, who had disappeared. What if Sauder couldn't shed any light on why he had come to Winchester? Where did she go from there with her questions?

There was always hypnosis therapy to see if anything could be excavated from her head. Did she really want to risk allowing a doctor, despite being bound by confidentiality, to hear what really happened that night? Would it be better just to leave the past in the past?

She just didn't know anymore.

The stop at the Yoder home proved futile as well. The children were there, tucked in for the night, but Sarah Sauder wasn't at her father's house. Aaron insisted he had not seen her since she left to return home when her house was released.

"Where to now?" Audrey asked Colt once they were back in her car.

"Let's call it a night. I need to think on this some more and regroup in the morning."

"You're the boss."

"I'm sorry about asking you to dinner tonight and then dragging you into all this instead."

She flashed him a smile. "It's okay. We can have dinner another time."

An entire minute passed with him staring at her profile. She didn't have to turn toward him and it didn't matter that it was dark in the vehicle save for the dash lights. She could feel him watching her.

"What?" she finally demanded.

"Do you mean that?"

She started to ask what he was talking about and then she realized what she had said. "Of course I meant it. We all have to eat sometime. No reason friends can't have dinner."

"Okay."

That one word—four letters—whispered through the darkness like a caress. How could she feel all these confusing emotions at a time like this? Or maybe they were just her mind's way of trying to escape what was happening. But there was no escaping. This case was about to explode and the big secret she and her mother had been keeping all these years was going to be amid the rubble.

Audrey drove through the darkness, her mind drifting back to the things she did not want to think about but had no choice. She had lived with this secret for twenty-three years, eleven months and about two weeks—why couldn't she just let it go? Hope and pray that this investigation would somehow skirt right on past her family and the newspaper?

She would never be that lucky.

"Rey?"

She turned to Colt, blinked. "Yeah?"

"We've been sitting at this stop sign for two whole minutes."

"Oh. I'm sorry." She shook her head, checked both directions, then prepared to pull across the intersection. "I was a million miles away."

"I figured."

More of that silence settled around them as she drove to her house. She'd pulled into the driveway and parked next to Colt's truck before he spoke again. "Thanks for chauffeuring me around and helping with Jenny Hoover."

"I wish we'd found him." She climbed out of the car. When he'd done the same she locked it with her key fob. "Maybe tomorrow."

The porch light was on but it didn't quite reach this part of the driveway. She walked beside him to his truck. The moon was bright enough for her to see his face and the weariness there. This was his county and he was worried about the safety of all the residents. As worried about her own problems as she was, she could only imagine the burden he carried.

"Maybe tomorrow," he agreed.

"Good night, Colt."

When she would have turned away, he touched her arm. "I'm glad we've spent some time together the past couple of days, despite the circumstances. It's been nice."

As much as she wanted to make some flippant remark and walk away, she couldn't do it. Not now. He needed her support and he was right. "It has been nice. I don't want to go back to avoiding each other. I want to be friends." There, she'd said it. What was more, she meant it.

He smiled and her heart swelled so big she couldn't breathe.

"I will take being friends, Rey, but I have to be completely honest with you. I will always dream of more."

Maybe if he'd said he wanted more or needed more she might have been able to simply turn around and go into the house. But he said dream…he would always dream of more.

She went up on her tiptoes and kissed him on the jaw. "Night."

His arms went around her waist before she could move away and he pulled her to him. His lips landed on hers and he kissed her so softly, so sweetly that she thought she might cry. Instead, she melted against him and he deepened the kiss.

When she could endure the tenderness no longer without dragging him inside and to her bed, she drew back. "Drive safely."

"I will. G'night."

She hurried up the steps and to the door. He watched until she'd unlocked it and gone inside, then he drove away. She observed from the window until his taillights disappeared into the darkness.

That was the moment when she understood she could never again pretend there was nothing left between them. There would always be something wonderful, something special between them. All they had to do was find a way to work it into who they were today.

Her cell rang, drawing her back to the here and now. She dragged it from her bag and tapped the screen without even checking to see who had called. "Anderson."

"Rey, you have to come to the office."

Brian. "What's wrong?" He sounded frantic, upset... worried.

"The basement has flooded. The water is knee-deep and rising. I was able to get a contractor over here and he's trying to get the water stopped. But he has to dig up..."

Audrey didn't hear the rest of what he said. She was running back to her car. She had to get to the newspaper. *Now.*

She had to stop the digging...

Before it was too late.

Chapter Fourteen

Colt had no sooner left Rey's place than his cell vibrated against his belt. He tugged it from its holder. Didn't recognize the number.

"Colt Tanner."

"Sheriff, this is Wesley Sauder."

Colt slowed for the turn onto his street. He tempered his tone and chose his words carefully. "Mr. Sauder, I'm glad you called. I want to help you, but we need to talk as soon as possible."

"I don't have time for talking right now, Sheriff. They've got Sarah."

Worry twisted in Colt's gut. "Tell me where you are and I'll come right now."

"I'm at our home. Hurry, Sheriff. I can only talk to you. I can't trust anyone else. Especially not any of the Feds. Just you, please."

"On my way, Sauder." Doing a one-eighty, Colt punched the accelerator and headed for Buncombe Road. "Is it safe for you to stay in the house?"

"I'm in a hidden safe room. I'll stay in here until you get here."

No wonder they hadn't been able to find the man. Colt should have thought of that sooner. A man like that, who never knew when his past was going to catch up to him, would take certain precautions. There was likely a hidden space between closets or rooms. Rey had been right. Sauder was likely at home all along. Considering that revelation, Colt wondered if Wesley was the one who shot Marcello instead of Sarah?

"Damn it, Sauder," he muttered. Hopefully the kids would be safe at the Yoder place, but Sarah could end up dead.

Colt gunned the engine for all it was worth. The sooner he was there, the sooner he could properly assess the situation. His first instinct was to call Branch, but he hesitated. Sauder wanted him to come alone. Could be a setup, but he didn't see the point. If the mob thugs had Sauder, they would take him out or take him back to Chicago; the end result would be the same either way. They wouldn't waste time on Colt—some small-town sheriff who knew nothing about them or their organization was no threat.

The promise he'd made to Rey would have to wait. Whatever was happening with Sauder right now, it was too dangerous to involve her. There was already one too many potential victims for his liking. He sure as hell wasn't bringing anyone else into this dangerous situation. His best bet was to get the lay of the land and go from there.

Before he could stop himself he thought of the way Rey had kissed him and then the way he had kissed her back. As much as he wanted to he couldn't analyze that kiss right now or the fact that she'd kissed him first. How very much he wanted to do more than kiss her would have to wait. He'd hurt her badly. It would take time to regain her trust all the way. He had waited a very long time already to have a second chance, but patience was required if they were going to continue moving forward.

He refused to allow anything outside a life-and-death situation—like this one—to get in the way.

When this was over, he and Rey would see where this first step took them.

The drive to the Sauder home took a full ten minutes despite his best efforts. Colt pulled into the drive and skidded to a stop. He walked straight over to Deputy Avans, who was tonight's surveillance detail.

"You can take a break, Deputy. I'll be here for a half hour or so."

"You sure, Sheriff?" He looked from Colt to the house and back.

Colt slapped the roof of the car. "I'm sure. Go. Come back in half an hour."

"Yes, sir."

Avans was concerned. He didn't want to go, but he did as he was ordered. When he was out of sight, Colt crossed the road and walked straight to the front door of the house. The door opened and Sauder stayed behind it in the darkness. As soon as Colt was across the threshold, the door closed, leaving the room in total darkness.

"This way, Sheriff."

Colt blinked as his eyes adjusted to the darkness. He followed Sauder into the center hallway, away from rooms with windows. A lit candle sat on a narrow table. He turned to Colt, his face pinched in fear.

"They told me if I turned myself over to them, they would release Sarah. I'll do whatever I have to do, no question about that, but I don't trust them to stick to their word."

"Are the kids safe where they are?"

"Yes. Benjamin and Aaron are watching for trouble. I've warned them not to allow anyone to get close to the house. I've also alerted several neighbors who are keeping an eye out around the Yoder farm."

"I have most of the story, Wesley," Colt said, keeping the conversation friendly, just two neighbors talking. "You were friends with Louis Cicero's son. You went to college together and later you were hired by his father. But it was your friend's sister that changed everything."

He nodded. "I was in love with Sophia. We wanted to get married but her father had decided she would marry the son of someone who would provide good business alliances. It's the way of things in that world. Alliances are often made with marriages. Sophia went behind his back—mine, too—and started talking to the FBI. She told me she was going to find a way out for us. I had no idea what she had in mind or I would have stopped her. Not that I wanted to protect her father—certainly not— but I understood the move was suicide. By the time she told me what she'd done it was too late. I could join her or end up on the wrong side of the sting. Of course I joined her."

"You believe Louis Cicero killed her."

"I know he killed her. Her brother told me. He was devastated. But what could he do? The man is his father and he knew his future depended on which side he chose. He chose his father's. Family is everything and she betrayed them. I pretended to go along with their thinking. No one knew Sophia and I were in love or that we had gone to the FBI together. First chance I got, I took a little insurance and I disappeared."

"You assumed someone else's identity and burrowed into a community where you would be protected as long as you were accepted." This was the one part that bugged the hell out of Colt. He remembered Melvin Yoder's accident. The possibility that this guy could have somehow masterminded the accident wasn't lost on him considering all that he knew now. "You took advantage of an awfully convenient situation to get your foot in the door."

Sauder frowned. "Are you talking about what happened to Melvin all those years ago?"

"It was a mighty big coincidence."

"You should ask Ezra," Sauder offered. "He was supposed to be there with Melvin that day but he forgot. When Melvin got into trouble with that bull, he didn't have the help he needed. It was sheer luck I came along when I did." He gave a somber nod. "Melvin and I never told anyone Ezra let him down. He made a mistake. It was best to let it go."

Colt was glad to hear it. He hadn't wanted to believe Sauder had fooled everyone so thoroughly.

"I'm a criminal, that's true," Sauder went on. "I worked for a man operating one of the largest organized crime families in the country. I did what he told me to do. But it was all on paper. The tools of my trade were a calculator and a computer. I'm not a killer, Sheriff. I'm just a man who was a fool when he was younger and I've spent the past ten-plus years doing everything within my power to make up for it."

Colt's father had often spoken of the good work Wesley Sauder had done for the community, and not just the Mennonite community.

"Why didn't you take the evidence to the Feds and ruin Cicero?" Colt countered. "He murdered the woman you loved. How could you disappear and start over without avenging her death?" The question had to be asked. Sauder might be a good man now but he'd obviously been a coward then.

Sauder dropped his gaze for a moment before meeting

Colt's. "How do you think the old man found out what Sophia had done?"

The question stunned Colt for a moment. "Are you suggesting someone in the FBI's Chicago office told him?"

"I'm not suggesting anything," he argued. "I'm telling you that's what happened."

"Do you know who it was?"

"I do. He's a big shot in the DC office now."

"Can you prove that allegation?"

"I can and I will. Just help me get my wife back."

Colt nodded. "Do you know how many we're up against?"

"Doesn't matter. I'm ready to turn myself over to them and take whatever they have planned for me. If I'd thought for a second they would stick by their word, I would have done it already. All I need you to do is make sure Sarah gets away safely. Nothing else matters to me."

"You know they'll kill you."

"I'm sure they'll torture me first. They'll want to make an example of me before they're done. As long as Sarah and the children are okay, they can do whatever they like to me."

He was either telling the truth or he was the best damn liar Colt had ever encountered. "Well, all right then. There's just one problem. As much as I'd like to play the hero, I know my limitations, Wesley, and I think you know your own. We're going to need the right kind of backup."

He nodded reluctantly. "I guess you're right." He covered his face with his hands. "I just don't want them to hurt her."

"We're going to do everything possible to make sure that doesn't happen."

Colt called Deputy Avans and had him come into the house. He used the excuse that the back door lock was broken. He met him in the living area. No need for the deputy to see Sauder and get excited. He was fairly new in the department.

"I'm concerned about who may have come into the house without our knowledge," he told the young man. "I want you to track down Branch Holloway and tell him to meet me here. Tell him to hurry. He and I need to talk."

"Yes, sir."

When Avans was gone, Colt locked the door and returned to the hall where Sauder was pacing.

"Now, let's go over exactly what happened. Sarah wasn't at her father's house when I went by there tonight. The kids were there but Aaron claimed he hadn't seen her since she came back home after we released this house."

Sauder nodded. "We didn't want to risk the kids getting pulled into this, so she left them with her father and brothers. She was going to see them and then come straight back. I didn't want her to go, but she said she had to see her babies. She never made it to Melvin's house."

"I've had this house under surveillance. Sarah hasn't been here, either."

He shrugged. "We have an underground tunnel from the barn into the safe room between the two bedroom closets. We've been staying in the tunnel most of the time except when Sarah went to the bakery or to visit the kids. We wanted anyone who was watching to believe that I was gone. Tonight we decided to get the evidence I've had hidden for all these years. We were going to offer it to them if they would just leave us alone. But our plan was too late."

"So the man or men who have Sarah know you're close."

Sauder nodded. "He wants me to bring the evidence

to him. He'll let Sarah go and I go back to Chicago with him. That's the deal he offered and I accepted. I just need you to ensure he holds up his end of the bargain."

"Are you certain it's just one man?"

He nodded. "There were three when they first showed up on Monday evening. This one is Saul the Saw. He's one of the most experienced and most ruthless hit men in the family, but he hasn't done the dirty work himself in a long time. I'm sure the old man sent him just to be sure the job got done. With the other two out, Saul has no choice but to finish this personally. He never fails, Sheriff. Never. There's no way he's going back to Chicago without me. He would kill himself first."

Suited Colt just fine. He would be more than happy for Saul the Saw to end up in the county morgue or for him to spend the rest of his days in Nashville's federal prison.

"Well then, let's go rescue your wife, Sauder."

Chapter Fifteen

Audrey was ready to scream by the time the officer finally strolled up to her window and handed her the speeding ticket. How was she supposed to get to the newspaper and stop the travesty playing out there parked at the curb waiting for this officer to do his duty?

When he leaned down once more she clamped her jaw shut to keep from spewing those very words at him.

"The court date is at the bottom," he informed her. "You be sure to pay your ticket before that date or make the scheduled appearance."

Audrey continued to hold back the rant she wanted to make. She would be calling Chief of Police Billy Brannigan about how long it took one of his officers to write a damned ticket. She'd almost lost her mind waiting on the man.

"I'll be sure to do that, Officer."

"You slow down, Ms. Anderson. You're lucky I was feeling generous and just gave you a speeding ticket. You can't be driving sixty in a thirty-mile-an-hour zone."

"I'm so sorry. As I said there's an emergency at the paper." She could literally see the newspaper building from where she was sitting. If she'd only made it another block before he noticed her, she wouldn't be patiently sitting here forcing a smile she in no way felt. She silently urged him to walk away...to get back in his cruiser and be gone before she imploded.

"Have a nice night, ma'am." He tipped his head and sauntered on back to his cruiser.

"You, too, Officer."

Probably all of his speeding stops had excuses. But hers was real. She swallowed hard as she shifted into Drive and rolled forward. As much as she wanted to stomp the accelerator and fly the final few hundred yards, she was well aware the officer would be watching. So she drove the speed limit, made the turn onto the street adjacent to the newspaper and then the final turn, a left, into the rear parking lot.

Her heart sank as she spotted the plumbing contractor's truck. She parked, scrambled out of her car and rushed into the building through the rear entrance, which was already unlocked. The door was blocked with a rubber shim to keep it from closing and locking out anyone who needed access.

If she was too late... God, she did not even want to think that way.

She reached the door to the basement and it swung open before she could grab the knob.

At the sight of her, Brian grabbed his chest. "You scared the hell out of me."

"What's going on down there?" Suddenly she didn't want to go down those stairs. Flashes of memories from that night zoomed through her mind like lightning strikes. Her mother crying. Her father dead on the floor in his office...and the other man. Oh God, the other man had been dead, too. Shot in the chest. Blood everywhere. Scrubbing the wood floor in her father's office.

She put a hand to her stomach to stop the roiling there. Oh God.

"The water just kept getting deeper and deeper." Brian shuddered. "I moved everything up to the higher shelves while the contractor was trying to figure out how to get the water turned off. Apparently our main shutoff failed and they had to find the nearest shutoff the city installed for the block. Do you know how complicated that was? This building—this whole block—is so old no one knew where to look." His eyes rounded and he spread his arms wide. "The blueprints had been modified so many times it was impossible to make sense of them."

Audrey held up her hands. "Just tell me they got the water shut off."

He nodded. "Finally. Now the fire department is on the way here. They're going to pump the water out of the basement and then we'll go from there."

Her heart slid back into her chest and started to beat once more. "I thought you said something about digging."

"Not yet," he said. "Not until the water is pumped out. He's called for jackhammers to break up the concrete."

The back door burst open and two firemen in full turnout gear hustled into the building dragging an endless line of hose behind them.

"Over here," Brian called.

Before Audrey could say anything else or intercede, her lifelong friend showed the firemen down the basement stairwell with their hose that snaked back out the door and to a truck, she supposed, that had pumping capabilities.

This was a mess. It could not happen. No one could dig up the basement under any circumstances. Removing the water she understood; that had to be done. But the rest couldn't happen.

She took a breath. Reached for calm, couldn't find it. She had to stop whatever was planned after the water was pumped out. Maybe she should shut the paper down. With sudden, acute clarity she abruptly understood that was the only answer. She should have done exactly that when she first came home. But the idea of ending her father's legacy out of fear seemed wrong. Besides, she'd used the excuse that she wanted to carry on the family legacy to halt Phillip's deal with the developer.

Now she was in a corner and there was no way out.

Oh God. She didn't want to think what this would do to her mom.

Brian reappeared and she wanted to shake him, to order him to stop this and to let her go home and think. She needed to figure out how to repair the situation before anything else happened. Turn it around somehow.

Audrey summoned her voice, struggled to keep it even. "When the water is removed, let's call it a night and tackle this problem tomorrow. Let the basement dry out." Sounded completely reasonable to her.

"Are you kidding?" Brian looked at her as if she'd lost her mind.

"No," she snapped. "I am too stressed right now to deal with this, Bri. I need… I need to think. To figure all this out."

As if he'd only then realized she was extremely upset, Brian put his hands on her arms and said, "Audrey, I know you've got some sort of issue with the basement, but this has to be taken care of tonight. We don't have a choice in the matter."

"Why?" she demanded, her worry instantly morphing into irritation. This was her building; if she wanted to stop the planned repairs, she should be able to make that happen. The notion sounded childish even to her but she couldn't feel any other way at the moment.

"No one beyond this building along the entire block

has water now. The city shut it off to prevent the swimming pool forming in the basement from rising to this level. Until the repairs are made here—in this building—the water for the entire block has to stay off."

The reality of what he was saying finally bored its way through the haze of confusion and desperation swaddling her brain. There was no stopping this. All she could do now was hope they wouldn't have to dig in a certain spot.

Except she wasn't a fool. The last time that floor had been opened up it was to work on the underground plumbing, and that was exactly where they would need to dig this time. Defeat tugged at her, made remaining vertical almost impossible. She couldn't stop this.

Not this time.

The pump in the truck outside started to hum and churn. Audrey hugged herself, unable to move. She should go to her office. Call Colt. Call her uncle Phillip. He would need to know what was about to happen. Should she sign the deed to the newspaper back over to him tonight? There was no way to know how long it would take to sort out the legal mess. Would they charge her and her mom? Her mom wasn't mentally fit for trial but she would have been all those years ago.

Did that make a difference?

Audrey just didn't know. Was the fact that she had been a child at the time an asset to her case? Doubtful. Besides, any district attorney worth his salt would want to know why she chose not to tell the truth after becoming an adult. There was no excuse for the decisions she and her mom had made.

When the pump finished drawing out the water, the firemen hustled up from the basement, coiling the hose as they moved. Brian thanked them for their help. Audrey should have said something but she couldn't. She just couldn't. What they were doing would change everything. Would reveal this terrible thing.

More men in work boots carrying large tools and dragging more hoses, these considerably smaller in circumference, rushed in and filed down the stairs. Outside a compressor fired up, the sound wafting into the lobby and reminding her that this was really happening.

Her throat was sand dry. The sound of the jackhammers made her flinch. She tried to settle her trembling body but that wasn't happening this side of the grave. She should just go down there and see what they found. Maybe she'd get lucky and a sinkhole had swallowed up the remains of Jack Torrino.

"I should make coffee," Brian said, dragging her from the disturbing thoughts. "You look ready to collapse."

"I'm okay," she lied.

"The one thing you are not is okay," he argued. "What's going on, Rey? What is it about this basement that freaks you out so badly?"

She shook her head. "I'm okay. We should go down and see what's happening."

"If you're up to it."

"I need to be down there."

Once they were through the door, her hand settled on the iron railing and she steadied herself for what was to come. Slowly, she descended into the massive basement that spread out nearly the entire footprint of the building. As Brian had said, he'd moved all the stored boxes to the higher shelves. She should thank him for taking care of this while she was out searching for Sauder.

How had she ever allowed this to go on so long? When she bought the paper she should have spoken to Colt and told him the whole story. But she'd kept that awful secret, and now the whole world was about to know the ugly truth.

By the time they reached the final step the noise was deafening. The jackhammers were like machine guns firing in automatic mode. What was worse, they were digging exactly where she had known they would. Dozens of knots tightened in her belly.

"Rey, you're shaking."

Brian touched her arm and Audrey faced him. "Brian, there's something you should know."

He leaned closer. "What did you say?"

She put her face to his ear. "Let's go back upstairs where we can talk."

Audrey couldn't get up the stairs fast enough. She suddenly felt cold. She hugged herself and tried to find the best way to tell her friend what she had been keeping secret for better than half her life. He had a right to know. He had been with this paper since finishing grad school. It was wrong to leave him in the dark when all hell was about to break loose.

"What's going on, Audrey?" He searched her face, his eyes filled with worry. "I've never seen you so upset. Not since you learned about your mother's dementia."

"Bri, you remember when my father died. It was a real shock. He seemed as healthy as a horse and then he was dead."

"I do." He sighed. "It was a difficult time for you and your mother."

Audrey smiled, her first of the night. "You were there for me. The best friend anyone could ever want."

He grinned. "Colt was, too, as I recall."

"He was." She thought of that kiss tonight. What in the world had she been thinking? That she was tired of being lonely and holding grudges and pretending she didn't care about him anymore. "I'm not sure I could have gotten through that time without the two of you."

"That's what friends are for." Brian frowned. "I really should make coffee. I think we're going to be here for a while and you look terrible."

He was right. She could wait five more minutes. She'd waited more than twenty years already. "Coffee sounds great."

Down the hall beyond the door to the basement was a break room. Audrey watched her friend's efficient movements as he filled the carafe and then poured the water into the reservoir. A few scoops of Colombian dark roast in a filter, and then he pressed the brew button. Instantly the aroma of smooth, dark coffee filled the air.

He poured two cups, added sugar to his own and then carried the coffee to a table. "Sit. Talk to me."

For a minute, Audrey sipped the warm brew, grateful all over again for his suggestion. She took a deep breath and began. "That night when Mom found Dad, that wasn't the only thing that happened."

She fell silent again. Grasping for the proper words to say to explain what happened. How in the world could she hope to explain murder?

"I'll need a little more than that, Rey. What else happened that night?"

"Mom and I were worried about Dad. It was well past dinnertime and he hadn't come home. He wasn't answering the phone in his office and Uncle Phillip was out for the evening. Since there was no one else to call to check on him, we drove over here. The building was dark—or it looked that way from the outside."

She savored another sip of coffee before going on. "Mother and I parked and found the back door unlocked, which was very unusual. Since Dad was alone at the paper he would never have left the door unlocked. When we got into the lobby we looked up, seeing his office light. We could see that he was arguing with another man."

Brian lowered his cup to the table as if it suddenly felt too heavy. "What man?"

Audrey shrugged. "I have no idea. Just a man."

"Did your mother go up to the office?" His face warned that the possibility of where this was going had disturbed him.

Audrey nodded. "We hurried up the stairs. She ushered me into Uncle Phil's office and told me to stay put until she returned for me. Then she rushed out. She told me later that when she got to his office, my dad and the other man were struggling. There was a gun on the floor. Mom said she shouted at them to stop. Pleaded with them, but they didn't stop. It was obvious to her that it was the other man who wasn't going to stop. And then—"

"Peterson!"

Brian's name echoed down the hall. He jumped. Put a hand to his chest. "Don't move. I'll be right back."

Audrey felt her body collapse into itself as he hurried from the room. She closed her eyes and tried to slow the spinning in her head.

Vibration in her pocket snapped her eyes open. She dragged her cell from her pocket and checked the screen. She hoped there wasn't a problem with her mom. Could be Colt. She frowned, didn't recognize the number. Then the area code sank in. Chicago. Could be Judd.

She hit accept. "Audrey Anderson."

"Can you repeat your name?"

Audrey frowned, drew the phone back and checked the screen again. Then she said, "Audrey Anderson."

"Ms. Anderson, this is Detective Robert Dickson of the Chicago Police Department."

Frowning, Audrey wandered into the hall, moving toward the door to the basement. The racket had stopped. She could only assume they had finished breaking up the concrete. Had they started to move the debris yet?

"How can I help you, Detective Dickson?"

"You have an acquaintance in Chicago named Judd Seymour?"

"I do. He's a friend and business associate." Her pulse rate accelerated; something dark and terrifying moved inside her. "What's this about, Detective?"

"Ma'am, when was the last time you saw Mr. Seymour?"

Oh God. Something had happened to him. "I haven't seen him in a year or so, but we spoke just this morning."

"Can you tell me the nature of your call?"

Nerves jangling, Audrey held her ground. "I'm afraid I'm going to need to know what's going on before I say more, Detective."

"Ma'am, Judd Seymour is dead. He was murdered in his home office. He spoke to you and then he made a couple of calls to numbers we haven't been able to trace. So I'm going to need you to be as cooperative as possible starting right now."

Judd was murdered only hours after talking to her about this Torrino guy? Had he contacted the wrong source and that source tipped off someone who didn't want Judd or anyone else digging into the past?

Audrey explained to the detective that she'd called Judd about an old case that might be related to a new one happening in Winchester. She had to be careful because she didn't know how much Colt would want her to share. When she'd answered everything she could answer, the detective reminded her that he would likely need to speak to her again. She assured him she would be happy to co-operate in whatever way necessary.

When the call ended, she called Colt. She got his voice mail. "Hey, it's me. I... I'm at the paper." She turned and walked toward the basement. Whatever was going on down there now it was entirely too quiet. "I need to talk to you. There's something I have—"

The grating sound of a car alarm echoed from the parking lot. Audrey paused, turned back to the rear exit and moved in that direction. The headlights of her car flashed in time with the obnoxious sound.

Her car's alarm was the one going off.

"Damn it. Call me when you can. I need you, Colt."

She ended the call, walked out the door and toward the car. She pulled the fob from her pocket and shut off the alarm. When she was within a few steps of reaching it she noticed the passenger-side window was shattered.

"What the hell?"

A hand snaked around and clamped down on her mouth, yanked her backward against an unyielding chest. Cold, hard steel jammed into her temple. "Scream and you're dead."

Chapter Sixteen

Colt was now officially on Branch's bad side. The marshal was damned ticked off. First because Colt hadn't called him the minute he heard from Sauder, and second because he refused to allow Branch to take charge. As angry as he was, in light of the situation, Branch had put his irritation and frustration aside until this was done.

Saving Sarah Sauder's life had to take priority.

Six of Colt's most trusted deputies had fanned out in the woods behind the Zimmerman property; two more were hidden behind farm equipment between the house and the barn. Colt had made his way through the darkness to the smokehouse only a few yards from the end of the house nearest the back door. He was close enough to kick a rock and hit the back of Ezra Zimmerman's house. Branch was in the hayloft with a sharpshooter set up, night-vision scope included, ready to take out the bad guy if things went south.

Now that they were in place, it was time for Wesley Sauder to move. Branch had refused to proceed under the radar like this without rigging up a tracking bracelet on Sauder. Colt didn't actually blame him. The FBI and the Marshals Service had looked for Thomas Bateman for a long time. They had him figured for dead. Now that they knew he was still breathing, he wasn't getting away again.

The deal was—assuming everyone survived this operation—Bateman, aka Sauder, would testify against Louis Cicero in exchange for immunity. He and his family would go into witness protection for the rest of their lives. It stunk for Sarah because she had family, but it was the best deal they were going to get.

The old pickup belonging to Sauder rolled into the driveway. Renewed tension poured through Colt. He hoped like hell Sarah made it alive and uninjured through this mess. It would be good if Sauder did as well, but Sarah was his first priority. Branch could focus on his fugitive.

All Sauder had to do was go inside and tell the guy, this Saul the Saw, that if he wanted the evidence he'd stolen when he disappeared, he had to let Sarah go. Then the two of them would pick up the evidence and do whatever Saul had been ordered to do.

It was risky as hell. But they'd had little time and they couldn't see into the house—the window curtains were all pulled tight—so their options had been limited. Sauder had refused to wear a wire and to be honest Colt didn't consider doing so a very good idea. The first thing this bastard would do was frisk him for a wire. There had been no time for a camera or a microphone to be snaked through a hole into the house as would ordinarily be the case. Firing a flash-bang into the house would likely get Sarah killed since she wouldn't know what to do to protect herself. There were too many variables to play this any other way but the one currently in motion.

Sauder climbed out of the truck and walked up to the front porch. As soon as Colt heard the door open and then close, he moved through the darkness to Sauder's truck.

Thank God for all the cloud cover tonight. He'd had no time to change into darker clothes. He'd had to make do with the jeans and blue shirt he was wearing.

Seconds of nothing but the quiet of the night ticked by. He could smell the coming rain in the air. Hopefully this would all be over before that happened.

Shouting echoed beyond the closed door and windows. Saul the Saw was not happy.

Moments later, the back door opened and voices echoed in the night. Sauder's pleading tone and the growling sound of the other man warned that the two would be coming around the end of the house.

Colt hadn't spotted a vehicle. However the man had gotten here, the vehicle was not anywhere close to the house.

Colt braced as the sound of their footsteps told him they were heading for the truck. He was crouched at the tailgate. As long as they didn't come to the back of the vehicle, he was good.

"You drive," he heard Saul the Saw order.

A high-pitched shriek cut through Colt like a knife. They hadn't left Sarah in the house. She was with them. He wasn't completely surprised. Old Saul the Saw would have considered the idea that Sauder was leading him to a trap.

Still, there had been a chance in his excitement over winning that he might have fallen for the first option.

The driver's-side door opened. The truck shifted and then the door closed. Sauder was in the truck.

"Open the door and get in," Saul ordered.

Sarah whimpered and then the passenger door squeaked. The truck shifted again and she cried out.

She was in the truck.

Colt lunged upward and rushed along the passenger

side of the truck. He grabbed the so-called Saw by the hair of the head and jerked him backward. His weapon discharged into the air.

Colt shoved the barrel of his own weapon into the bastard's skull. "Drop it or you're a dead man."

The weapon thudded on the ground.

Wesley Sauder and his wife emerged from the truck, alive and unharmed.

It was over.

As soon as Branch took custody of Saul the Saw from Chicago, Colt breathed a little easier. He pulled out his cell to call Rey and saw he already had a voice mail from her. He walked away from the scene and pressed Play. Her voice whispered in the darkness. She sounded worried or upset. The sound of a car alarm echoing in the background made his heart jump. Then she went on and the fear in her voice twisted inside him.

"Damn it. Call me when you can. I need you, Colt."

He grabbed the nearest deputy and told him to take over for him; he had to get to Rey. Something was wrong, bad wrong.

Thursday, February 28, midnight

IT WAS MIDNIGHT when Colt rolled into the parking lot of the newspaper office. There were official vehicles everywhere. Two city cruisers. Chief of Police Billy Brannigan's truck. The damned coroner's van. Colt's heart rocketed into his throat. What the hell had happened here? He'd tried to call Rey back a dozen times but she hadn't answered. Worry gnawing in his gut, he bolted from his truck and rushed toward the rear entrance.

A Winchester PD uniformed officer was guarding the door. He stepped aside without Colt having to say a word. Good thing; he was in no mood for any territorial nonsense. Inside the newspaper building there were two more uniforms loitering around the lobby. The door to the basement was open and the coroner's assistant, Lucky Ledbetter, was talking on his phone.

As Colt approached the door, Ledbetter ended the call and tucked his phone away. "Hey, Sheriff, I guess you got the news."

Colt shook his head. "I've been at another crime scene. What's going on here?"

"Water main for the building ruptured. The city had to shut off the water to the whole block. Couple of guys from the fire department came over to pump the water out and then Smith Grider started digging up the basement floor to get to the damaged pipes to make the repairs." Ledbetter scratched his head. "It's the craziest thing. They found bones—human bones."

Dread coiled through Colt. "I guess I'll go down and have a look."

"Some creepy stuff for sure, Sheriff."

Colt descended the stairs and took in the scene in the basement. Grider had cracked open the concrete and opened up the ground beneath to expose the water lines. The entire hole was maybe six by ten feet. Burt Johnston stood in the middle of the muddy mess, fishing waders on and holding a human skull in his hands. More bones bobbed in the knee-deep water.

Hells bells. Someone had been buried in this basement? On instinct, he mentally ticked off any longtime missing persons. There wasn't a soul he could think of in his lifetime who had gone missing and remained unaccounted for.

"Colt, you have any idea where Audrey is?"

He looked up at the sound of Chief Brannigan's voice.

"Isn't she here?" She had said she was at the paper when she called. Dread gnawed at Colt.

Brannigan shook his head. "She wasn't here when I arrived. She's not answering her phone, either, so Brian went to her house to see if she'd gone home. He said he'd check with the nursing home to make sure nothing had come up with her momma."

Worry twisted a little tighter inside Colt. "What's going on with this?" He hitched his head toward Burt and the bones floating around his waders.

"Don't know. Grider called me as soon as he spotted the skull. Burt is trying to gather up all the pieces." Brannigan assessed Colt for a moment. "You've known Audrey and her family your whole life. Any clue how this could have happened?"

Colt shook his head. "I can't think of anyone who went missing and hasn't turned up. Not in the last thirty-odd years anyway." Colt turned to the coroner. "Burt, you got any ideas on how long these remains have been down here?"

Burt placed the skull on the trace sheet he'd laid out next to the hole. A number of other bones—a rib cage, humerus, femur. Damn.

"Well—" the coroner set his gloved hands on his hips "—considering I recall when Porter Anderson had these pipes replaced the last time—that's when the concrete was poured, by the way." He gestured to the rubble that was concrete and stone. "This floor was originally brick and stone. When the pipes were replaced the last time, concrete was poured over the whole thing to level it up." He frowned. "That was right around the same time Porter died. But these aren't his bones. He was buried over in Franklin Memorial Gardens with the rest of his kin."

"So," Brannigan spoke up, "you're saying the bones have been here maybe twenty-four or twenty-five years?"

Burt nodded. "As close as these bones were to the pipes, they couldn't have been here before the last repair job." Burt nodded toward Grider. "Smith says his daddy did the previous work and he helped him. Twenty-four years ago next month."

Grider nodded. "We had most of this main portion of the floor dug up. If the bones had been there then we would have seen them. Someone had to put them here right before we poured the concrete. Probably buried them in the dirt around the repaired pipes the night before we poured. Wasn't no other chance to do something like this, as I recall."

Yet that didn't make a lick of sense. Colt asked, "Has the concrete been opened since you and your daddy poured it?"

"No, sir," Grider said with a shake of his head. "This floor was as smooth tonight as the day my daddy floated and troweled it. Besides, if anyone had cracked it open lately it would probably have been me."

Colt and Brannigan exchanged a look. Brannigan doled out the next question. "Did your daddy have anyone working for him who might have had something to do with this?"

"The same four people, including me, have been working for Daddy the past thirty-five years." He shook his head. "Someone had to do this after our crew had gone home for the day. Like I said, probably the night before we poured the concrete."

That didn't leave many options. Colt said, "How about calling whoever can pull out the file and find out the exact date the concrete was poured?"

Grider reached into his pocket. "I'll call my wife and have her pull the file."

"Thanks." Colt turned back to Brannigan. "We should send someone over to pick up Phillip Anderson and bring him over here."

"Got someone knocking on his door at this very moment," Brannigan assured him.

Hurried footfalls on the stairs had Colt and the chief of police turning in that direction. Colt hoped it was Rey. No such luck. Brian. The man looked worried. Colt's gut clenched.

"Audrey isn't at home and the nursing home hasn't seen her tonight. Her mother is sleeping." Brian looked from one to the other. "I was in such a hurry I didn't notice before, but the passenger-side window in her car is shattered."

Fear put a choke hold on Colt. The memory of the car alarm going off in the background of her voice mail slammed into him. "She was outside when she called me."

The words were no sooner out of his mouth than the three of them were rushing back up the stairs. Outside, Colt was the first one to reach Audrey's car. It was empty. Air finally made it past the lump in his throat.

"Something's wrong." Brian shook his head. "She wouldn't leave in the middle of all this." He turned toward the building. "She was worried sick about the whole mess."

Colt's cell vibrated against his side. He snatched it off his belt and stared at the screen. *Rey.* Thank God. "Rey, where are you?"

"Hello, Sheriff Tanner."

Colt looked from Brian to Brannigan. "Who is this?" he demanded.

"That's not important, Sheriff. The only thing you

need to be concerned with are two facts. You have something that belongs to me, and I have something that belongs to you."

"Where is she?" The fear and worry had morphed into something black and menacing. If this bastard hurt Rey...

"You bring Bateman and his evidence to me and I'll give you the woman. Does that work for you?"

"Name the time and place." Colt wasn't taking any chances with Rey's life. Sauder/Bateman was sitting in his lockup at this very moment while Branch interrogated Saul the Saw. He could have him out of there before Branch knew he'd walked through the door. But he knew better than to attempt this on his own.

Emotion was already driving him.

He needed help. And truth be told, there wasn't another lawman he trusted more than Branch.

"I'll call you back in one hour. Be ready to trade, Sheriff, or she dies."

The call ended.

With both Brian and Brannigan demanding answers, Colt put in a call to Branch. When the other man answered, he said, "We need to talk."

Chapter Seventeen

By the time the man told Audrey to pull over, they were just outside Winchester in the historic part of Belvidere at an old gas station that had been closed since she was in college. During the drive she had also concluded that the man was Louis Cicero's son, L.J. He was about the same age as Sauder—Bateman, she reminded herself. He was a little more polished than the two dead guys had been. No need to see the labels to recognize a leather jacket that cost more than the average person made in several months' work. The shoes fell into the same category, hand-tooled leather, probably couture, and the jeans and shirt wouldn't be found in any big-box department stores.

"Get out of the car. Make any sudden moves and I'll put a bullet in your head."

"Whatever you say." She opened the door and climbed out.

He did the same, came around the hood to join her on the driver's side. "This way." He ushered her toward the gas station.

At the entrance—a plate glass door that was now boarded up, as was the rest of the glass front—he pulled the plywood away from the door and opened it. Inside was black. He dragged the plywood back into place, then used the flashlight app on his phone to move about. He shuffled her into what had once been an office, she presumed, since there was an old metal desk. On the desk was a portable lamp—the sort that looked like a camp light and ran on a battery.

He turned on the light, then used his gun to point to a plastic milk crate in the corner. "Sit."

Audrey did as she was told. He'd already called Colt so help would come. The real question in her mind was how did this guy think he was going to walk away from this? He had no backup as far as she could tell. There was the one weapon in his hand. It was an automatic, a nine-millimeter or a .40-caliber. She hadn't managed a close enough look to say for sure. Either way, he had maybe a dozen or so rounds. Unless he was a dead shot and had several extra clips in one of those high-end pockets, he was screwed.

Not exactly a good position for him or for her.

She should be afraid; she was aware of this as well. But what was the point? Frankly, she had bigger problems. They'd probably found the bones by now. Everything was upside-down. Her mom couldn't remember what happened. Neither Audrey nor her mom was even sure who the dead guy—or what was left of him—was. Maybe the Jack Torrino guy.

Her captor sat on the edge of the desk and checked the time on his Rolex.

"I guess you and your friends were supposed to take care of this for your father. Their failure makes you look bad, huh?"

He assessed her for a long moment. "In my line of work," he said, "you learn to always take out a little insurance to slant the odds in your favor. You are my insurance, Audrey. It took me a couple of days to determine the best insurance policy to go with, but I'm putting my money on you. The good sheriff has a thing for you. He'll do whatever I tell him."

She ignored his attempt to make her afraid. Better men had tried. She opted not to bother telling him that the thing she and Colt had shared burned out a long time ago and had only recently flickered back to life. He might very well be putting all his eggs in the wrong basket.

Instead, she decided a distraction was what she needed. "Did your father send a Jack Torrino to Winchester about twenty-four years ago?"

He puffed out a laugh. "I haven't heard that name in a hell of a long time." He peered at her. "What the hell do you know about Torrino?"

"You tell me what he was doing in Winchester and I'll tell you where you can find him." Sounded fair enough to her.

He frowned. He wasn't a bad-looking guy. Handsome, actually, in a brooding, self-centered sort of way. "Now why the hell would I care where Torrino is? If he ain't dead, he will be if I find him."

"Like I said," Audrey tossed back, shrugging, "I can tell you exactly where he is. I just want to know why he came to Winchester all those years ago."

"My old man got a wild hair to buy up newspapers. Especially small-town newspapers. He was buying them all over the country. I doubt even he knew exactly what the point was. To look respectable, I suppose. He's always been a little eccentric. Anyway, Torrino was his point man. He did the negotiating with those who didn't feel inclined to sell."

Audrey's heart rate spiked. Like her father. "So he came to provide a little influence in the negotiations on the *Gazette*."

"If he was here, that's most likely why he came."

"Well, that explains a lot." All these years she had wondered what really happened that night and who the stranger was who had been buried in the basement—the dead man she had helped her mom drag down two flights of stairs and bury in the dirt around the plumbing pipes while her father lay dead from a heart attack on his desk.

"So, where is he, assuming you actually know?"

"They just pulled his bones out of a muddy hole in the basement of my newspaper. The one he probably tried to strong-arm my father into selling."

Another of those surprised chuckles erupted out of his mouth. "Your old man killed him?"

"Something like that."

"Couldn't have been you—you would have been just a kid."

She shook her head. "No. I didn't help kill him. I just helped bury him."

He grunted. "Maybe I picked the wrong girl to kidnap. The sheriff might not care if he gets you back."

She shrugged. "You could be right."

He aimed his weapon at her head. "In that case, you're of no value to me."

The air stalled in Audrey's lungs but she didn't flinch, didn't even blink. She would not allow this scumbag to see her fear.

"Except—" he lowered his weapon "—I saw the way he kissed you outside your house. A man kisses a woman like that, he cares. He'll come and he'll bring whatever he has to in order to get you back."

"If I'm lucky." She leaned against the wall and crossed her arms over her chest. "But you know he won't make it easy for you to get away. If I were you I'd cut my losses and head back to Chicago. Two of your guys are dead already. A third is probably in custody if he isn't dead, too.

I'm sure your father would be very upset if you ended up that way."

"If I go back empty-handed, he'll kill me himself."

Audrey thought of the story she'd heard about his sister. "The way he did Sophia?"

Fury lit in his dark gaze. "Don't piss me off, lady. Unlike my father, I take no pleasure in watching another human suffer. But I'll do what I have to. My sister made her own choices and she paid the price. I'm not responsible for what happened to her."

Audrey thought about that for a moment. "What about your friend Thomas Bateman? You plan to watch him suffer, don't you? And you will be responsible."

"Thomas made his own choice long ago. I'm just here to clean up the mess he made. What happens to him next is not up to me."

"But you know your father will kill him, maybe after torturing him. Thomas has children. He has a wife. They count on him."

"He knew what he was doing when he went to the Feds about my family."

"So you do like to watch others suffer."

He stood, moved closer to her, forcing her to tilt her head back as far as possible to maintain eye contact. "Are you trying to annoy me?"

"No. Just stating the facts. I'm a reporter, that's what I do."

He backed up a step, settled onto the desk once more. "Yeah. I looked you up on the internet. You were a hotshot reporter until that jerkoff lied about what he'd really seen in that shack in the woods."

And therein lay the rub. A man had murdered his whole family before turning the gun on himself. Her informant had claimed to be the man's best friend. He alleged he'd been in the room when the murders happened. He'd run, too afraid to face the police after what he'd witnessed. But he'd lied. He hadn't watched a damned thing.

It was a rookie mistake to go with his account even with an impossible deadline.

"Sometimes you screw up. You make a mistake." She held his gaze a moment. "But this is a massive screwup, L.J. You will not walk away from this."

The man was closer to fifty than forty. He couldn't be this shortsighted.

"Let me show you a few things." He grabbed her by the arm and pulled her around behind the desk. "Look under the desk."

She leaned down. There was something under the desk but it was too dark to be certain of what the object was. But every instinct she possessed warned it was an explosive.

"I can't see anything. It's too dark."

He crouched down next to her and turned on the flashlight app again. "See that?"

Her heart stumbled in her chest, then sank to her knees, nearly dragging her down with it. "I see it."

He grabbed her arm and hauled her back to the crate, then pushed her down onto it. He checked his watch again. "In ten minutes I'll call and tell your sheriff where to bring Sauder and the evidence. Once he brings him inside, the whole place goes up in smoke. I'll be waiting just up the road, on that hill, so I can watch the fireworks. One push of the right button and boom! The evidence and Bateman will be history."

"You get to go back home with proof that Daddy can trust you to step into his shoes when he retires."

"You really are starting to annoy me, Ms. Anderson. How about you shut up now?"

She pinched her lips together and watched him check his Rolex again. He was anxious. Maybe even a little nervous.

A dozen ways to attempt disabling him ran through her brain. She could charge him the next time he checked his watch. She could wait until he made the phone call to Colt and charge him while he was distracted with the call. He was so full of himself that he hadn't bothered to restrain her. She could use that to her advantage. All she had to do was stay alert. React quickly and make whatever she did count.

"Here we go." He stood.

Audrey's heart lunged into her throat.

"Nice meeting you, Audrey Anderson. Too bad it was only for a short time. Hope you've been good, otherwise I'll probably be seeing you in hell one day."

He leveled the weapon at her and the air evacuated her lungs. He backed toward the door. When he stood squarely in the doorway, he flipped a metal latch on the door. *A hasp.* When the door was closed the hasp would fit over the eye loop; the insertion of a padlock would secure the door.

He was going to lock her in.

She pushed to her feet before she realized her brain had given the order to stand.

He shook his head, waved the gun at her. "Sit down and stay calm. You'll have about twenty minutes to contemplate all the things you should have said and done before you die."

One hand dipped into a jacket pocket and pulled out a padlock. He closed the door. She heard the hasp slide onto the eye loop and then the padlock snap shut. Then she heard him talking.

She pressed against the door to hear what he said.

He provided the location and a deadline. Twenty minutes. Colt was to show up for the trade in twenty minutes or she died. He was to bring Bateman and his evidence to this gas station. He would leave Bateman and the evidence inside and walk out with Audrey. As long as they drove away without any trouble all would be good.

Except she and Colt wouldn't be walking out of here any more than Bateman would. They would all be blown to smithereens.

She started to scream his name. As loud as she could, she screamed for him to stay away. When she could no longer hear Cicero talking she understood that he had walked out of the gas station. Now he would go to his lookout position—probably the church at the top of the hill where he'd have a bird's-eye view—and watch. When Colt arrived…

She couldn't let that happen.

He'd told Colt to be here in twenty minutes. She had to do something to make sure he never set foot in or near this building.

She had to get out.

Pushing with all her strength, she tried to force open the door. Wouldn't budge. No windows. The walls were some sort of wood panels, so there was no kicking her way through.

With no other options, she looked up.

The ceiling was a grid of old dropped ceiling tiles. All she had to do was get up there and she would find a way out of the building via the attic space.

But first she had to get up there. She grabbed the crate she'd been sitting on and stacked it on the desk. Then she climbed up onto the desk and then onto the crate. She could reach the tiles. Stretching, she pushed one out of the way. The grid didn't exactly look particularly sturdy.

She needed to be closer to the wall rather than in the center of the room. It made sense that the metal grid would be anchored along the walls. She stepped off the crate and then jumped off the desk.

Holding her breath and praying the explosives wouldn't somehow ignite, she pushed the desk against the wall. She climbed back on top and scooted the crate against the wall and stepped onto it. This time when she moved a tile, she spotted the place where the grid framework mounted to the wall. She reached for it and slowly but surely pulled herself into the attic. It took three attempts and her arms felt like limp noodles by the time she made it, but she was in the attic.

Damn, she should have thought to bring the light. She stared down at the thing. No way was she going back down after it. Pulling herself up here a second time might not be possible. Besides, time was running out. She had no choice but to feel her way around. On one end she could see light filtering in through the attic vent of the building. There wasn't much of a moon tonight. Had to be the streetlamp on that end. She headed in that direction. It was the end opposite the church so the bastard wouldn't be able to see her from his vantage point. Of course she couldn't be sure he would park at the church, but it would give him the best vantage point so she was going with that scenario.

She cut her hand on something metal. She winced. Maybe an electrical box of some sort. Maybe something stored up here. She tried to think when she'd last had a tetanus vaccine. A tetanus shot would be the least of her worries if she didn't make it out of here.

Finally, she reached the end of the building. She sat for a moment to slow the pounding in her chest. Then she took another precious minute to get her bearings. There was no reason for Cicero to be watching this end of the building. He would be watching the road coming from Winchester and the parking lot out front.

With a deep breath, she started pushing on the vent, hoping like hell the nails or screws or whatever was holding it attached to the wood siding were either rusted or broken. She just needed them to give way.

The vent pitched forward. Audrey grabbed on to the edge of the wood siding before she plummeted to the ground the way the vent had. Giving herself another few seconds to steady herself, she calculated the distance to the ground. At least ten to twelve feet. If she lowered her body feetfirst out through the hole, holding on to the bottom of the two-by-four framed opening, her feet would be dangling approximately five or six feet off the ground. She could manage that drop, hopefully without breaking anything.

"Big breath."

She drew in, let it go.

Slowly, she edged out of the hole, allowing her lower body to slip out first. Seconds later she was hanging by her hands. She hoped there was nothing—like a protruding nail—sticking out of the siding or it could rip open her skin, put out an eye.

"Just let go, Rey."

Holding her breath, she relaxed her fingers and her body dropped.

She landed on her feet first and then on her back. The impact vibrated her bones, made her teeth clack together.

Her head was okay. Neck, she stretched it this way and that; her shoulders, arms, back and legs were okay. No pain, just that freshly jarred sensation. She rolled over onto all fours. If she stood and moved, he might spot her.

So she crawled around to the back side of the building. She didn't have her cell so she couldn't call Colt.

If she ran out into the street to try to stop him when he arrived, Cicero would likely shoot at her or at Colt.

"Think, Audrey," she muttered.

If she could make it to the nearest house before Colt arrived, she could borrow a phone. But there couldn't possibly be much time left. He would likely be here any minute. She couldn't take the risk.

There was only one option. She had to find a hiding place and wait until he drove up. Then she'd have to call out to him to drive away.

That could work…if he would listen to her.

Colt Tanner was as hardheaded as she was. Talking him into driving away and leaving her would be like convincing a leopard to change its spots.

Not going to happen.

She needed a better plan.

Colt would be coming from Winchester. There was only one way into this old part of Belvidere from that direction. He would pass the church before reaching the gas station. She could make her way through the woods, slip around behind the church and onto the other side of the rise. She could catch Colt before he topped the hill and stop him there.

Even as the idea occurred to her she saw headlights coming over the hill beyond the church.

"Damn it." Too late.

She flattened on the broken asphalt and low crawled toward the front corner of the building. Sure enough, it was Colt's truck. He slowed and made the turn into the parking lot.

Her heart thundering, she held perfectly still while he climbed out of the truck and skirted the hood to the passenger side. He opened the door, and a handcuffed Bateman was ushered out of the seat.

"Don't turn around, Colt," she called out in a stage whisper. She prayed he would hear and understand her words. For all she knew the bastard on the hill had binoculars.

Colt stilled. Both hands on Bateman.

"L.J. Cicero is watching. I don't know how many weapons he has but there's a bomb inside the gas station. I was able to get out. When you and Sauder—Bateman go in, he's going to detonate the bomb."

For a few seconds no one moved or said a word.

"Can you run?" Colt asked.

Audrey didn't like the question, but in light of their precarious situation, she answered. "Yes."

"When I count to three I want you and Bateman to run. Run into the darkness. Run fast. I'll call out to you, telling you to stop. Ignore me and just keep running."

"What about you?" Audrey's heart was in her throat. She did not want him hurt.

"I'll be right behind you."

Audrey started to argue but Colt said, "One. Two."

She scrambled to her feet.

"Three."

Bateman ran toward the old general store down the road.

Audrey headed into the woods between the gas station and the old store.

When she was deep enough in the woods she glanced back to see if Colt was behind her the way he'd promised.

Nothing but darkness.

She opened her mouth to shout his name and an explosion knocked her onto her butt.

The sound vibrated the air. The ground shook.

For half a minute she couldn't hear...couldn't breathe.

Finally, she scrambled to her feet. Steadied herself against a tree. Her ears felt as if they were stuffed with cotton. She recognized the feeling. Acoustic trauma.

Where was Colt?

Pop, pop, pop echoed in the distance. The sound was muffled and seemed far away, but she recognized it. *Gunfire.* She started running back the way she'd come. The old gas station was mostly a pile of rubble. Part of the far wall where she'd hidden was still standing.

She ran faster, toward the church. Halfway up the hill Bateman caught up with her. His hands were no longer cuffed. They reached the church parking lot together. Dozens of vehicles descended upon the area at the same time. Blue lights strobed in the darkness.

Where was Colt?

"Colt?"

Cops were everywhere. She spotted Branch. Saw Chief Brannigan.

Where was Colt? Fear tightened in her chest as the sound of all those gunshots fired in her mind. What if he'd been shot? She stared back down the hill at the dust rising from the rubble beneath that lone streetlight.

"Rey!"

The sound of his voice burst through every defense she had built these eighteen long years. She ran to him. Threw her arms around him and held him so tight she was certain he couldn't breathe.

His arms were just as tight around her. "You okay?"

"I am now." She drew back, inspected him in the flashing lights. "Are you hurt?"

"No, ma'am, but I can't say as much for the guy on the ground over there."

Relief rushed through her. She hugged him again. They were okay. They were both okay.

She stilled.

But there was still the matter of the bones.

Chapter Eighteen

Two weeks later

March came in like a lion, as the old saying went. Audrey's life felt as if it had been buffeted again and again by the strong winds heralding spring. The district attorney, Marion Steele, had come to the conclusion that Mary Jo Anderson had shot and killed Jack Torrino in self-defense. The disposing of his body was, however, a different matter altogether. Taking into consideration her dementia, he opted not to pursue the matter, concluding that it would be a waste of the court's time and would not serve any reasonable purpose. In the end, no charges had been levied against Audrey's mom. DA Steele had further decided that she, being a child at the time of the event, was a victim of circumstance and not responsible for the actions that occurred that night. Her uncle Phillip had been cleared. He'd had no idea about the man buried in the basement.

Jack Torrino's remains had been identified and released to his next of kin. Audrey's attorney had spoken to the family and no civil suit was expected. Thankfully, the man whose body had been buried in the basement hadn't left a wife or children behind. Audrey had often wondered if there was a wife or kids who had spent all those years searching for him…missing him, but she had never dared to pursue the idea. Torrino's sister had allayed her worries when she told the attorney that Jack had abandoned his family, her and his brother, when he joined the Cicero crime family.

Audrey stood on the second-story landing of the newspaper and looked out over the lobby, where children from the elementary school were listening to Brian talk about the history of the *Winchester Gazette*. She smiled. This truly was where she belonged now. She had needed time to find herself and to come to terms with the past. She had done both in the last few weeks. She smiled, happy, really happy for the first time in a very long time.

The intercom in her office buzzed and Audrey wandered back to her desk. "Ms. Anderson, there's a call for you on line one."

"Thanks, Tanya."

She picked up the receiver. "Audrey Anderson." Another smile tugged at her lips as she sat down behind the desk that had belonged to her father.

"Audrey! Wow, you are on fire, lady."

Ronald Wisner, her old boss at the *Post*. "Hey, Ron. Thanks for picking up my article on Jack Torrino and the Cicero family." She'd been brutally honest in the article about her and her mother's part in how Torrino met his end. It was time—past time—that secret was fully unearthed.

"How could I not? Louis Jr. spilled his guts and you got the exclusive? How often does that happen?"

"I was in the right place at the right time," Audrey said. She looked around the office. The words were truer than she'd realized when she came home six months ago. This was the right place. The timing was spot-on, as well. She was smarter, stronger. Seeing the world and ferreting out the big stories were enormous accomplishments. But everything led her back home. To put to rest the past… and to be close to her mom.

Now she could relax and just be.

"Well, I wanted to congratulate you and remind you that you always have a place here if you decide to return to DC."

Audrey appreciated the offer. She'd had about a dozen already in the past week. But that was the way of things. One big story could make or break a career. "Thanks, Ron. I'll keep that in mind. For now, I'm very happy right here at home."

Home. She liked the sound of that.

"I hear every publishing house in New York has reached out to get your story. What're they calling it? *Old Bones*?"

"If I decide to do the story, you'll be the first to hear about it."

"An interview would be nice."

After another assurance he would hear from her before anyone else, the call ended. Audrey glanced around at the dozen or so flower arrangements that had been delivered from former colleagues and one very special person. She touched the petals of a pink tulip amid the huge bunch in the glass vase that sat in the center of her desk. The tulips were from Colt. The card reminded her that he owed her a dinner.

She'd meant to call and thank him yesterday when the flowers arrived, but she'd been on her way out the door. Audrey had taken her mom for a ride to see how the trees had budded and bloomed. They'd had a perfect day. Mary Jo hadn't gotten confused or forgotten who Audrey was even once. She'd been her old self. They had spoken about Torrino and how that was over. There was no longer anyone buried in the basement. Audrey had explained how the DA had concluded Mary Jo's actions were in self-defense. The most important part was that her mom had understood. She had nodded and said she was glad that awful nightmare was finally over.

Audrey walked back out onto the landing to watch the children below in the lobby. The tiniest catch of yearning tugged at her. "Let's not get ahead of ourselves, Rey," she chastised.

As if fate wanted to remind her that a child had changed her life forever, Key Tanner came into view. He crouched down next to one of the kids and appeared to explain what the little girl was seeing on the other side of the glass wall. Something about the printing presses. A week ago one of Key's friends had been badly injured in an accident where the teenage driver had been drinking. Everyone had survived and would be okay, but the accident had been a serious wake-up call for Colt's son. He'd apologized to his father and started volunteering for all the projects possible at school to occupy his time rather than partying every available minute.

Audrey was grateful to see the change. Colt wanted his son to be safe and happy. What parent wouldn't?

As he stood, Key glanced up. He spotted Audrey and waved. His smile was so like his father's. Truth be told, he was the spitting image of his father at that age. Audrey waved back.

As many times as Colt had apologized for what happened all those years ago, she understood that he could never regret that beautiful young man currently ushering third graders around the lobby. She didn't want him to regret his son. Really, what was the point of regretting anything about the decisions they had made in high school, good or bad?

This wasn't high school anymore. It was time to put that part of the past to bed once and for all. One never knew when everything could change. Sarah Sauder likely never expected to be whisked away to some unknown place with a new name and no possibility of ever seeing her father and brothers again. Her life would never be the same, but at least they would all be safe.

Audrey's father's heart had given out on him during the strain of that tragic night twenty-four years ago. Today her mom resided in a memory care unit because her mind was failing her…her brain refused to work logically and accurately. Audrey didn't want to waste a moment more of her life.

A door at the main entrance opened and Colt walked in. He paused just inside and removed his hat, the way a true gentleman would. A smile stretched across her face and her heart thumped a few extra beats. Hat against his chest, Colt looked up, his gaze captured hers, and he smiled.

Inside, Audrey melted. She held on to the railing to prevent running to him. As she watched, he strode across the lobby, pausing only long enough to give his son a nod before climbing the stairs.

Each step closer made breathing a little more difficult. It was foolish, she knew. She was thirty-six years old. He was her first lover, but certainly not her only lover. And yet right now she felt as giddy as a virgin anticipating her first kiss.

"Morning, Rey."

Her pulse reacted to the deep, smooth sound of his voice. She steadied herself. "Morning, Colt." She stared down at the students scurrying around below. "Your son is doing a terrific job with the kids."

"I wish I could take all the credit, but I heard someone visited his school and talked about the growing incidence of tragic accidents among reckless teenagers."

"I might have given some pretty gruesome details in that talk to the senior class."

"I'm glad you did. I could spout the same statistics all day long and he wouldn't listen to me. Coming from you, he paid attention. The whole class was impressed."

Audrey waved off the idea. "That's only because I was on *Good Morning America* day before yesterday."

He grinned. "That might have had something to do with it."

GMA had asked her to do a spot related to the Cicero case. She'd flown up to New York one day and flown back the next. She'd been exhausted when she made it home that night, but she'd had to be up bright and early the next morning for her Career Day chat with the senior class at Winchester High School. The trip hadn't exactly been glamorous, but new online and paper subscriptions for the *Gazette* were up 200 percent. Brian was ecstatic. And the senior class had been duly impressed.

Colt frowned. "I guess you heard the news about Mr. DuPont."

Audrey's shoulders slumped. "I did. How awful for Rowan. And what a loss for the community. Brian's putting together a huge spread in memory of him."

Edward DuPont, the owner of DuPont Funeral Home, had been murdered in his daughter's home up in Nashville, ninety miles north of Winchester. It was a terrible tragedy.

"Billy told me Rowan's coming home to stay. She's taking over the funeral home."

"Really? I hadn't heard that part." Rowan DuPont's family had operated that funeral home for several generations, the same as the Andersons had with the newspaper.

The paper and the funeral home were started by founders of Winchester. Though she and Rowan had never been close, they clearly had a great deal in common. Winchester was a small town; everyone knew everyone else. Rowan had left for college and made a life for herself in Nashville as Audrey had entered high school. Rowan was a celebrated author and she'd worked with Metro Nashville PD for years as an adviser. Like Audrey, she knew her way around a crime scene.

"My daddy said Rowan and her sister learned how to prep a body for viewing and burial before they were old enough to drive," Colt noted. "I guess it makes sense that she'd want to take over for him now."

"I can understand how she might." Audrey had basically followed in her father's footsteps—even if a little belatedly.

The DuPonts had some very dark tragedies in their history, too. Raven, Rowan's twin sister, had drowned when she was twelve and her mother had committed suicide a few months later. Audrey's friend Sasha Lenoir had a haunted history as well. Sasha's father murdered her mother and then killed himself when Sasha was just a kid. How was it the three of them, Audrey, Sasha and Rowan, could all have such darkness in their pasts and have grown up in the same small town?

Life was strange.

"I was hoping you might be able to take off a little early and go to a late lunch," Colt said, drawing her from the dark thoughts.

She eyed him, feigning suspicion. "How do you know I haven't already had lunch?"

He shrugged. "I might have a source in the paper."

Brian. Audrey laughed. "So he told you I'd been too busy for lunch today, did he?"

"He might have mentioned it."

She shook her head. "Lunch sounds great. Let me get my phone and purse."

Colt followed her into her office. "You know, I was thinking, spring break is coming up next month and the seniors are taking a class trip. I've got a whole slew of vacation days built up and with Key gone..." He shrugged. "Maybe we could get away for a few days."

Colt looked more nervous than she'd seen him since he was fifteen and asked her mom for Audrey's hand in marriage. He'd explained his entire life plan for the two of them to her mom that day.

"Now that's a tempting offer, Sheriff." She moved around to the front of her desk and stared up into his eyes. "If you're sure that's what you want to do."

It was in that moment, staring into his gorgeous gray eyes, that she realized she had just recalled the memory of him informing her mom of his intentions and hadn't even thought about what happened later, when they were seniors. Maybe the past was finally, completely behind her.

And the future was looking brighter all the time.

"I've never been more sure of anything in my life." He tossed his hat onto her desk and took her face in his hands. "I have loved you since I was five years old, Rey, and I want to spend the rest of my life showing you just how much."

Her lips trembled and she wanted to kick herself for being so emotional as a tear slid down her cheek. But she decided she didn't care. "I'm glad to hear it, because I would hate to be in love with you all by myself."

He kissed her and he stopped all too quickly, but the sweetness and the sincerity in that brief kiss were all the assurance she needed to know that they were in this together.

Loud clapping echoed in the lobby.

They jumped apart, remembering the crowd downstairs. Colt's son was clapping. As they watched, Brian joined him. Then the students and their teachers.

Key gave his father a thumbs-up and Audrey relaxed. If they had his son's blessing, they had nothing else in the world to worry about.

"Let's go to lunch." Colt grabbed his hat. "We'll finish this in my truck someplace where we won't be interrupted." He offered her his hand.

Audrey put her hand in his, ready to follow him toward the rest of their lives.

* * * * *

COMING SOON!

We really hope you enjoyed reading this book. If you're looking for more romance, be sure to head to the shops when new books are available on

Thursday 7th February

To see which titles are coming soon, please visit

millsandboon.co.uk/nextmonth

LET'S TALK

Romance

For exclusive extracts, competitions
and special offers, find us online:

 facebook.com/millsandboon

@MillsandBoon

@MillsandBoonUK

Get in touch on 01413 063232

For all the latest titles coming soon, visit

millsandboon.co.uk/nextmonth

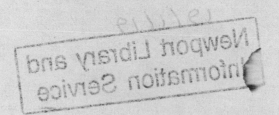